# Moron

Moron

# Moron

# A Story of The
# All Volunteer Army

by:

Danny G.I. Pummill

Available in Fall 2020

Book two in the Moron Series

"West"

ISBN-13: 978-0615857145 (Custom)

"There is no instance of a nation benefitting from prolonged warfare."

- **Sun Tzu, The Art of War**

# Table of Contents

## Moron

## Dedication

For Paula, who followed me around the world for thirty-four years, never complained and despite twenty moves and multiple foreign assignments, somehow raised three incredible children. I have been in love with you since you were fifteen.

For Jamie, the number two woman in my life. My daughter, businesswoman, mother, editor, proof-reader and recommender extraordinaire.

Moron

## Introduction

Imagine a nation so hard up for soldiers that government leaders would fill its military ranks with 354,000 young men between the ages of eighteen and twenty-five who were mentally retarded, criminals, or just plain rejects from society. There is no way that any country would ever be desperate enough to do anything this stupid, especially if that country was introducing, for the first time in its history, an all-volunteer professional Army. The country I'm describing would have to be a third world country on the verge of collapsing, right? What if I told you that was exactly what the elected and appointed leaders of the United States decided to do in the early 1970s, anticipating the end of the draft, which officially occurred in July 1973?

I know most Americans wouldn't believe that our country would do something so asinine, but it is part of our history, and I guarantee you it happened. Of course, if you read the official version, the one that our politicians and leaders would have you believe, it was a great political success. Well, the story I'm about to tell you is not based on the official version; it's based on the truth, so you're going to get the unvarnished truth, with all the warts and none of the revisionist history that turned it into a political success.

The Army in the 1970s was in such bad shape that it's a miracle you're not reading this in Chinese or Russian instead of English. When you put it in perspective, it's hard to imagine that the American Army that won World War II—and was manned by the best that America had to offer, our often quoted "greatest generation"—had degenerated to the pitiful state that it was in the 1970s. If the American people had known the severity of the problems within the Army, and how screwed up its soldiers and leaders were, many of them would have lost a lot of sleep.

The only reason we were never attacked by the old Soviet Union was because they were as screwed up as we were; that and the fact that both sides had so many nuclear weapons that the shared fear of worldwide destruction kept both sides in check. Years later, when the Cold War ended, we discovered that the Russians were hoping we didn't attack them because they thought the U.S. Armed Forces were better than we really were, and we didn't attack them for basically the same reason.

What happened? How did America's powerful World War II Army become such a mess? What led to the complete dismantling of the great Army that saved the world? Aside from years of budget cuts and neglect, we have one man to thank, our Secretary of Defense, Robert McNamara, and his ill-conceived Project 100,000, initiated in 1966.

Let me tell you how the McNamara 100,000 plan worked or was supposed to work. I know, as soon as you hear the concept you are going to say that I made this all up. Clearly, no one in America would allow such a crazy plan to be put into effect. Who in his right mind would put a program in place that would result in the complete and utter dismantling of our country's ability to defend itself? But, it did in fact happen, and somehow everyone in a position of leadership in our country bought into this concept.

In 1973, with great fanfare, our elected officials officially ended the draft. While everyone was proclaiming that the all-volunteer force would make our nation's armed forces stronger and better, it was all basically an effort by politicians to remain in office. By the time the all-volunteer Army was announced, America had been engaged in the unpopular Vietnam War, and everyone in the country was tired of the fighting. Many Americans were taking it out on the Army and, unfortunately, on individual soldiers. Draft dodging had become a national pastime and young Americans were willing to face jail time or had fled to Canada to avoid military service.

During the turbulent late 1960s, desperate for an immediate solution to military manpower concerns, Project 100,000 was born. Even during the worst days of the draft, a potential recruit had to score at least thirty out of a possible 100 points on the standardized intelligence test and have no felony criminal arrests or convictions. Under project 100,000 the minimum score was lowered to ten, and criminal and moral waivers became common place. A score of ten meant that a potential recruit was in the bottom ten percent of intelligence in the country and was slightly lower than what was considered mildly mentally retarded by the American Medical Association. Basically, the plan was to allow mentally retarded individuals to carry weapons and fight America's wars. Despite the obvious concerns with McNamara's 100,000 program, the plan went into effect and remained in place for several years. Unfortunately, it did not end at 100,000. Conventional estimates put the final number of low mental category soldiers brought onto active duty at closer to 357,000, and there is no accurate count of how many criminal deferments were granted. Imagine an organization with 357,000 illiterate men and criminals. Well that was America's Army in 1973.

OK, its early 1973. We have an American Army that has almost a third of its force made up of the lowest mental category available in America. Add to that an unknown number of criminals and young men with moral issues and sprinkle in about 40,000 draftees who never wanted to be there in the first place. Take this concoction and mix it thoroughly with an American population that is tired of war and disgusted with the Army and add in the tensest racial atmosphere in our nation's 200-year existence. You couldn't have concocted a greater mess if you had planned it.

Well, this my friends, is the Army that is the background for my story. This is the story of a group of twenty-four high school students who volunteered to join the Army as the Wolverine platoon, the first mass volunteer group to join the new all-volunteer Army.

Moron

# Chapter 1

## Home

It was the spring of 1973, the first year of the all-volunteer Army, a bold new experiment for America and her armed forces. Many issues were plaguing the county in the early '70s: drugs, race riots, seething inner cities, forced school integration, a growing distrust of our government, a long-running recession, the Vietnam War, and an Army that was literally hated by the majority of the citizens of this country. In the middle of all this turmoil, twenty-three young men from Northern Michigan volunteered to enlist in the Army as the Wolverine platoon. They were from the furthest North you can get in the Continental United States—the northernmost point in Michigan, more specifically the Upper Peninsula, or to those of us who live there, the UP.

Because of the isolated area they came from, by no stretch of the imagination could the Wolverines be considered your average American teenagers in 1973. The lifestyle and environment were such that they were all just a little bit different from the rest of America, and from the soldiers they would end up serving with.

The small town that I come from in Northern Michigan's UP is called Iron City.  While the UP is technically part of the state of Michigan, no one who lives up here ever says that they are from Michigan. When asked, they usually respond, "I'm from the UP."  The UP is separated from Michigan by the Great Lakes, and you have to cross the longest suspension bridge in the world, the Mackinaw Bridge, to get up here. And I do mean up here. We lived on the shores of Lake Superior. Detroit was more than six hundred miles to our south.

Our hometown was named Iron City because of all the iron ore discovered here by the first settlers. If not for all the ore, I doubt that the town would even exist. Other than snow, the mines, lakes, rivers, and lots of trees, there is really nothing else up here.  I don't know a whole lot about the history of the UP, but when you consider that the nearest town of any size is Green Bay, Wisconsin, and that is almost 150 miles away, it should tell you something. It's cold up here. If you went any farther north, you would be in Canada. You have to be a little bit crazy to travel this far north to find a place to live, so I guess the first settlers were just lost. The long winters, cold, and snow actually play a significant role in how we think, how we act, and what we believe in. If you don't like deep penetrating cold, ice, and snow, then the UP is not the place for you.

It starts snowing here toward the end of September, and it is not unusual to have snow flurries at the annual Fourth of July picnic out at the local lake. You know you live in a cold place when you realize that every other house on your street has an extension cord hanging over a pole where you park your car. These cords are for the electric heaters attached to our car engines and oil pans. We have to plug in our cars every night during the winter months, or our engine blocks will freeze solid. If this occurs, you won't be able to start your car until the spring thaw. Oh yeah, if you don't like snow then don't live anyplace where you see orange balls on the top of car radio antennas or orange flags on fire hydrants. The orange balls and flags are so you can find your car or the hydrants after snowstorms. When they talk about summer up here, they are talking about a few short weeks sometime between the middle of July and the middle of August. A lot of people who come here in the cold of winter think that we are nuts to live this far north, but if you are a kid growing up, especially those of us of the male persuasion, you couldn't ask for a better place to be from.

Ice fishing, skiing, snowmobiling, hunting and fishing (both ice in the winter and regular in the summer), ice rinks in every yard, and, of course, lots of woods for exploring, hiking, and hunting everywhere. And do I mean everywhere. You could walk out my back door and walk north all the way to the North Pole and not cross a highway, or see a telephone line unless you went out of your way to find one. If you didn't play hockey or ski jump, then you were not an athlete, and everyone in the UP over the age of five knows how to drive a snowmobile. It's considered an essential skill in the UP.

Hunting is not just a sport up here; it is our national pastime. Deer, bear, quail, and turkey, frankly anything that moves and can be eaten is hunted. Everyone has a freezer packed to the brim with fresh fish and wild game. We have venison hamburger, venison sausage, venison steak, and venison barbeque, you name the cut of meat, and we make it with venison. While we enjoy consuming wild game of any type and regularly do so, hunting was not about the meat; it was more about getting into the woods and away from civilization. Hunting was such a big deal up here that it was not unusual for most of the pickup trucks parked at the local high school to have rifles and shotguns hanging in the racks in the back windows. No one worried about terrorists and no one even conceived of the possibility of a shooting at the school. Surprisingly, even with all the weapons and ammunition, no one ever got accidentally or purposely shot, and we had no fear of crime or criminals. I can't remember many of my friends or my parents ever locking their house doors. No one knocked; you just opened up the door and yelled out, "Is anyone home." If no one was home, you shut the door and went on your way. We left our hunting cabins unlocked in case someone got lost or stranded in the woods and needed food or shelter. The only thing we asked is that whoever used your stuff replaced what they took as soon as they could.

The people who live in the UP are referred to a Yoopers, which is short for Upper Peninsulites. I know you can't find either word in your dictionary, but, trust me, they are common terms up here. People who live up here are true individualists and a lot like the early explorers in America must have been. They don't like to be told what to do with their property or their lives, they want guns, and they are incredibly patriotic. The unofficial motto of the UP is, "If you don't mess with us, then we won't mess with you." Yoopers don't need or want any help from the government, they take care of themselves. Even during the peak of the Vietnam War when most of America had turned its back on our returning combat veterans, they were treated with honor and respect in Iron City.

The population of Iron City is made up of a combination of Welsh, Swedes, Finlanders, and Italians. Talk about a melting pot. Our melting pot was different from other parts of the country because the contents of our pot were from Northern and Southern Europe. No blacks, no Hispanics, and only one Asian family lived in Iron City in 1973. I think that we were just too far off the beaten path and too far from any major metropolitan areas for anyone to want to move up here. There wasn't anything to draw in any immigrant populations. The mines had all gone dormant, so the only economy was small-town businesses, hunting, fishing, and snow removal. We didn't consider ourselves racist, because as far as we were concerned, as long as you were a Packer fan, you were welcome in our community.

Our favorite food is a pasty, and if you're not from here, you have probably never heard of or tasted one. Well, let me tell you, you are missing a treat. Pasties are mostly venison and potato and onion pie with a hard, outer pastry shell that is baked to a golden brown. They are delicious and incredibly addictive. The story goes that they were invented by the Welsh miners whose wives cooked a fresh week's supply every Sunday evening. Once they were cooled, they would be placed in snow banks to freeze overnight. The miners would carry them to work every day. They would carry them inside their hard hats resting on top of their heads. In the early morning hours, it would help keep them cooled down while they were working their asses off in the mines. During the rest of the day, the lamps on the outside of the hard hat, combined with the heat from their heads, heated up the pasty and sometimes even warm it up a little by lunchtime. I know it sounds a bit weird, but once you try one, you will be hooked for life. There is nothing like it.

There are no professional sports teams in the UP, so for entertainment, we focused on high school sporting events, bowling, and all manner of winter sports. Support for our local high school teams in the UP rivaled that of Texas communities for passion and enthusiasm. The environment impacted our lives. There is no high school baseball or fall track in the UP. It is just too cold up here, and there is too much snow on the ground to be able to count on getting a full season in. Even during the spring track schedule, most schools in the UP had to plow the snow off of the tracks for the majority of the season.

In 1973, it was the pre-cable television era here. The only channel we could pick up on our TVs in the UP was Channel 6 from the bustling metropolis of Marquette, Michigan. At the time, it was the only channel that could be picked up by residents of the UP. Sporting events on Channel 6 consisted of the Green Bay Packers football and the Detroit Tigers baseball; there were no other sorts. When the Packers played ball, even in pre-season, everything in the UP shut down. You couldn't even purchase gas because everyone was at home, either watching or listening to the game. If you had an emergency, you were merely going to have to wait until the game was over. If you weren't a Packer fan, then you lied about it, because to deny the Packers was to welcome an ass-kicking and maybe even being run out of town.

If you were looking for someone on a Friday night and there wasn't a high school game going on, everyone could be found at one of the numerous local bars. No, not drinking, but rather socializing and enjoying "fish fry." In the UP, you go to bars to meet with friends and family; it is a must on everyone's social calendar, not just for adults but for the entire family. Fish fry on Fridays consisted of a heaping plate of freshly caught deep fired perch, homemade French fries, and coleslaw. Not the type of coleslaw that you all eat down south, but rather slaw with an oil and vinegar base. This was all served with as much fresh bread and butter that you could eat. If you were not at fish fry on Friday nights, you would be eating at a local supper club, having a steak dinner. Yep, you heard it right; we didn't have restaurants, we had supper clubs.

In case you haven't figured it out already, we even have our own language. Visiting the UP is almost like going to England on vacation. While the people you meet are actually speaking English, you have to listen very carefully to understand what is being said. The dialect that is used in the UP sounds a lot like how they were talking in that movie *Fargo*, but a whole lot worse. We don't say, "Hello," we say, "Hey, youse guys." We don't cheer at ball games, we yell, "Rahoo, rahoo." We don't say, "You're correct," we say, "You betcha, by golly." The language up here is a mixture of English, Finnish, and Swedish, with a little bit of Italian sprinkled in. Sometimes it's hard to figure out what anyone is saying. "Say yah to da UP hey" translated to English would read, "I'm proud to be from the Upper Peninsula of Michigan." Even today, when I speak to one of my relatives from the UP on the phone, it takes about four or five minutes of assimilation before I can fully translate the conversation in my brain. If you're from the UP, then everyone else in the world has a weird accent.

This is the part of the country where twenty-three young men were born and raised, and who as a group decided to volunteer to join the United States Army.

Moron

Chapter 2

An Idea is Born

I can vividly remember the last sane night of my life. It was a crisp, almost cold Friday evening in Northern Michigan. A bunch of seniors from the Iron City High School were hanging out at the lake, standing around an out-of-control campfire in the woods, drinking beer out of Dixie cups. To be entirely truthful, it wasn't all seniors; our Friday night keggers included a smattering of underclassman. They had to be female and reasonably good looking or, if not good looking, easy. Of course, the perfect combination would be pretty and easy.

Several half kegs of beer along with bottles of Boone's Farm strawberry wine chilled in metal trash cans filled with ice that were positioned around the fire, along with stacks of Dixie cups stolen from the local Dairy Queen. The beer was Hamm's, ten dollars a keg plus a fifty-dollar fully refundable deposit. It was a young man's dream. The beer was cheap, and we usually got our deposits back. Normally, because many of our keggers got raided by the police, and you can't run far or fast with a keg of beer in your arms. There was an ongoing competition between the high schoolers and the local police in Iron City to see if the weekly kegger would be raided or not. We spent the entire week scouting out a location where we wouldn't be discovered while the police spent the week trying to get students to disclose the planned site.

If I had paid better attention at the time, I would have realized that I was preparing myself for my future occupation. My buddies and I would head out after school and scout the back roads of the community, looking for the perfect place for the next kegger. The location would have to have reasonable access from the main road, preferably only one primary route so it could be monitored during the party, but would have to have multiple secondary exit routes. These "exit" routes would be in the form of dirt roads or trails that would allow a car full of teenagers to get out of the woods without being caught by the police. It was to our advantage that our cars were old and beat up because we could go places where the police couldn't without tearing up their cruisers. A lake or river location was preferred; we wanted to encourage skinny dipping.

The exact location of the weekly kegger was kept secret until the very last minute of the very last hour of school on Friday afternoon. Nothing about the site was to be written, and information was passed by word of mouth, and then only to trusted agents. We didn't have to worry about anyone emailing, texting, or cell phoning the location of the party; none of that stuff existed in 1973.

When we arrived at the location, we would place an outpost on the entry route. The responsibilities of the team manning the outpost were to make sure that a dollar per person would be collected to defray the cost of the beer and wine. The outpost also served as an early warning in the event of an attack by the local police. We didn't worry about a cross-country invasion. The cops in town didn't want to mess up their cars, and most of them were too fat and lazy to get out and walk through the woods to apprehend a bunch of kids drinking beer. The only cross-country incursions were by students trying to avoid paying the dollar entry fee. We all knew who the deadbeats were, and they were caught later in the evening and forced to pay up.

Our early warning device was a large handheld bullhorn. Not one of the electronic types, but one of the big metal cone types that they use at college football games. Danny Mussio, my best friend, affectionately known as Penis Brain—he thought with his penis and not his brain—could make a sound like a submarine diving, and his job was to sound the alarm at the first sign of danger. It was a great plan, but Penis Brain was addicted to women and beer, so more times than not we got caught unawares because he had left his post unmanned to sniff after some young freshman. Not the best system in the world, but I am proud to report in four years of hosting keggers, no one ever got arrested at any of my events. We lost a lot of kegs but never lost a man.

The evening was going precisely as planned. Guys were all chugging beers while the girls were sipping from bottles of Boone's Farm Strawberry Hill, and there was a haze of cigarette and marijuana smoke filling the air. Cars were parked in every possible space, all with their radios tuned to the only radio station in the Midwest that played decent music, the rock station out of Chicago. Lucky for us, it was a cloudy night.  On clear evenings, it was impossible to pick up any stations farther than fifty miles away, much less the Chicago rock station almost 350 miles south of us.

I was sitting on a log drinking a beer and trying to convince Paula that it was a perfect night to go skinny dipping, despite the chill in the air, you know, being my usual charming self. I liked spending time with Paula and was worried about what was going to happen when I graduated. Paula was only a junior and had another year of high school. I knew I wasn't going to college; my parents couldn't afford it even if I had the grades. But I did know I was going to leave town. I didn't want to be one of those guys that hung around forever talking about the good old days in high school. Frankly, the only reason I had stayed in school was Paula. In the middle of my latest plea to separate Paula from her clothes for a dip in the lake, up walks Danny, who was supposed to be manning the outpost, with a beer in his hand and, of course, someone else's girlfriend on his arm.

"I got a great idea … let's join the Army."

My immediate response was, "Are you out of your mind, there is a war going on in a place called Vietnam, and we could get killed.

"Hell, don't you remember that just last summer we went down to Ann Arbor and participated in an anti-war demonstration."

Well, actually, we went down there to visit Danny's brother who was in his ninth year at the University of Michigan. Yep, you heard me right, nine years of college and still a senior, and purveyor of some of the best grass that could be purchased in the state of Michigan. We got involved in the demonstration because we were stoned off our asses one night, and these two hot chicks from some religious convention convinced us to become part of the peace movement. Ann Arbor was one of the strangest places I had ever visited. The police warned us not to drink beer in public while all around us, everyone was lighting up joints. Ann Arbor was light years ahead of its time in the area of marijuana reform. Even in 1973, possession of marijuana within the city limits was only a misdemeanor, but having a beer was an arrest-able offense. Go figure.

I was sure that this Army thing was just another one of Danny's juvenile jokes. "Don't be an asshole, we are not joining the Army."

"Roger, I'm not kidding," Danny said. "I've thought about this a lot, and I think this is a good deal for us. I went to the picture show last week and saw a movie about the Army. Ever since seeing the movie, I can't get the Army out of my head. I have been meeting with the local Army recruiter, Big John. He told me that the new all-volunteer Army isn't anything like the Army of the past. Everything has changed for the better, and they aren't sending any more soldiers to Vietnam because the war is almost over. In fact, Big John said that the Army is the best-kept secret in America, and we better hurry up and enlist before everyone finds out and there are no more slots left."

Danny continued his spiel, "After spending some time at the recruiting station, I realized that Big John is a pretty neat guy. Did you know that he has killed people with his bare hands? He told me that chicks love guys in uniform and that a soldier can get laid every night of the week if he wanted to. Eh, eh," Danny said, nudging me with his shoulder and attempting to wink. Paula looked at him like she was going to kill him, but this didn't even slow Danny down. "Big John told me he is going to stop by the school tomorrow for career day, and he told me to tell everyone I know that he has something that is going to knock our socks off. He said anyone who doesn't join after seeing what he has to offer is brain dead."

"Besides," Danny added, "all of that stuff that everyone has been telling us about the Army is total bullshit. In the

Army, you get to shoot the most modern guns in the world, blow shit up with plastic explosives, parachute out of airplanes, and spend a lot of time in the woods. When soldiers are not in the woods practicing, they get to travel around the world, drink lots of beer, and hang out with beautiful women. Big John also said that soldiers are getting ready to get the biggest pay raise in Army history and that if we sign up, we will be paid more than college graduates."

Yeah right, I wasn't falling for his BS. "Danny, you're just a drunk asshole, no way I am joining the Amy. If you want to go somewhere and get killed then go ahead, but you will be by yourself. Don't you realize, Big John's job is to sell you on the Army like your Uncle Jack sells those shitty used cars he gets from the auction house in Green Bay?" But, even while I was ridiculing Danny, part of me was just a little curious to see what Big John would be bringing to school tomorrow. Big John was a salesman, but he could always be counted on to put on a show. At the very least, it just might break up the monotony.

My junior year I had come to the realization that there was no way my parents were ever going to be able to afford to send me to college, and based on my grades, there weren't going to be a whole lot of colleges standing in line to offer me any scholarships. That is, if I even wanted to go. At this point, I was so tired of school that I never wanted to see another classroom for the rest of my life. There were only two places to work in Iron City, the paper mill or the factory, and both were laying off, not hiring. So, unless your parents were wealthy or owned a business in town, you were not going to be able to get a decent paying job. Sure, there was always the government jobs at the post office and the police department, but those jobs rarely came open because once a guy got a government job, he never left, so there was always a long line of applicants waiting for a job whenever a vacancy came around.

My future plans at this point consisted of hitch-hiking out to the West Coast, partying all summer, and then heading up to Alaska. I had heard you could make big money working on the fishing boats up there. There was this one guy from Iron City who did that several years before, and rumor had it he was making fifty thousand dollars a year fishing. Imagine getting paid to fish, now that's a dream job. One thing for sure, there was no way in hell that I was going to join the Army. I had spent eighteen years with my father, teachers, and coaches telling me what to do, and there was no way I was going to get a job where someone told me what to do every minute of every day. It would, however, be nice to have women drooling over me. I could see how chicks would be attracted to the whole uniform thing. John Wayne never had a problem in the movies. Come to think of it, I had all the attributes of a good soldier. I was in fights all the time, and mostly held my own, and since I had grown up hunting most of my life, I figured that I would be a better shot than most.

By the time I was eighteen, I had shot over forty deer. Most of the deer I shot were for people who came up north to go hunting but didn't know the first thing about the woods or weapons. I would go to the bars at night, take orders for deer from drunk guys who had never hunted in their life, and then deliver them the following evening. I got so good at it that by the time I was sixteen, I was making enough money during deer season to pay for gas and beer for the rest of the year. I would walk into a bar at night, and start up a conversation with some overdressed clearly inexperienced hunter, and during the interview, ask him how big of a deer he wanted to bag that year?

The next question was, "How much are you willing to pay for a deer that size?"

Most of these hunters didn't want to be out in the woods and snow in the first place. For them, deer season was heading up north, drinking and partying with the guys for a week. If they were lucky enough to get a deer, then it was just icing on the cake. I can't tell you how many hunters went home with a beautiful trophy, bragging rights, and a cooler full of venison steaks courtesy of yours truly.

The way I figured it, I was performing a valuable public service. I was helping to control the deer population so that the herds would not be too big to make it through the brutal Northern Michigan winters, and I was keeping a bunch of idiots with rifles from killing themselves or someone else. A pretty good deal for all concerned. One minor glitch; I was always just one jump ahead of the conservation officers. They knew what I was doing and had a pretty good idea of where I was going to do it, but damned if they could catch me. They came close several times but were never able to close the deal. If you are young and willing to lay in the snow overnight, or at least long enough for them to give up and head home, you always win. I learned most people have no patience. One of my friends, who later became a conservation officer, told me that there was talk in the county that the deer population went up dramatically after I left town. I put this down to coincidence; obviously, global warming or some other unexplainable phenomenon must have coincided with my departure.

Suddenly my daydreaming was shattered by the sound of someone screaming.

"Pigs, pigs, pigs!"

Our impromptu little gathering at the lake quickly disintegrated as the woods became filled with the sound of cars starting up, people yelling, red and blue lights flashing, and a general roar of confusion and panic. People and cars were going everywhere, guys and girls were jumping into open windows of cars or into the back of trucks. Most of the cars and trucks, sticking to the prearranged bug-out rules, were driving away from the party with their lights off. Luckily there was just enough moonlight coming through the clouds to allow us to navigate our way through the back roads and trails. The moon, combined with the fact that we had partied here several times before, gave us enough of a head start to make a clean getaway. Everyone who had a car was driving through the woods to a series of old logging roads down by the dam. From there it was a short two miles to a gravel road, then five more miles to the blacktop. There was no way the police would try to follow us; they weren't about to risk their precious police vehicles.

Until you have observed a mass evacuation of teenagers at a UP kegger in the woods, you are missing one of the wonders of the modern world. Escape comes down to one crucial question. Can over a hundred semi-drunk high school kids with cars in the middle of the woods evacuate a location and not allow the enemy to take any prisoners?

I told Paula to get in my pickup and get the engine running while Danny and I pulled our standard rearguard action to allow the others to escape. We would move a little slower and act a little bit more rude and obnoxious, to draw the attention of the police away from our quickly departing comrades and get them to focus their sights on us. This was easy to do. All you had to do was act so arrogantly that the cops would see red, lose control, and do everything to get their hands on you. We had copied this technique from a Saturday morning episode of Wile E. Coyote and the Road Runner. Don't laugh, there is a wealth of knowledge to be gained from a classic cartoon. We learned from years of experience that a joint in the mouth combined with an "I don't give a shit" pose was more than adequate to enrage the Iron City Police Department. In the past, our antics had resulted in police cars driving into trees and, at least on one occasion, getting stuck in a giant mud hole. We didn't want to get caught, but we honestly didn't want to see anyone hurt, especially us.

The most important part of our escape plan was to make sure you were not recognized by the police. Harder to do than it sounds. Remember, this was a small town, everyone knew everyone, and the cops knew all our parents. Besides, everyone removing the license plates from their vehicles as they drove into the Kegger, once the alarm was sounded, they were required to immediately don camouflage, in the form of a black-knit Yooper hat. This hat, commonly worn by almost everyone male and female in the Upper Peninsula, was basically a black stocking hat with eye and mouth holes. It was so popular that the police and sheriff departments issued them. It was a staple of Yoopers of all ages in the 1970s. The hat was designed to keep your face and head warm in the cold UP winters, but in a pinch, it could be pulled down to conceal your features. This worked exceptionally well at night. The hats, and the fact that everyone male and female wore jeans and flannel shirts, made it impossible for the police to recognize anyone.

Unfortunately, even the best-laid plans can fall apart in the execution. This was going to be one of those nights. For some reason, unknown but to God, Danny Mussio and Steve Wilson had decided to really piss off the cops. I realized that something was wrong when the wail of police sirens suddenly pierced the night air. The police never used sirens in the woods. When I looked behind me to see what was causing this heightened level of excitement on behalf of our city's finest, I came face to face with not one but two "full moons." Danny and Steve had pulled down their pants, which were now stretched between their ankles, and were bent over with their pale white asses facing the oncoming police cars. The image of those two white assess with dicks and balls hanging down will haunt me for the rest of my life. Both were bent over at the waist and were looking through their legs, flipping off the cops and shouting, "Here, piggy, piggy, piggy."

I knew that this was not going to end well, and let me tell you, there is nothing pretty about man-ass. It was a disaster. The final tally for the evening's entertainment included one light bar ripped from the top of a cruiser by a low hanging branch, two busted tail lights on a sheriff's vehicle—the result of backing into a log barrier across the road—and one squad car partially submerged in Lake Marie. We had some really pissed-off cops and one out-of-his-mind chief of police, who declared in the morning edition of the local paper:

"I will not rest until I locate, apprehend, and punish the deviants who caused this city so much pain and damage."

The article went on to talk about devil worship complete with drugs and unnatural sex acts by the light of campfires deep in the woods. Nothing in the section was right. It was just a kegger, but the seeds of a legend had been planted. That kegger and the stories that surrounded it, mostly untrue, took on a life of their own, and over the years, the stories got bigger and more and more bizarre. Of course, every male between the ages of sixteen and nineteen at the time took credit for being one of the two full moons. In reality, only three people know the truth, and we aren't talking. Thank God, technology in the 1970s was such that the police couldn't make a positive identification from an ass and a dangling dick and balls.

Despite the strangest kegger on record, there were some high points. Everyone at the kegger got away clean. We didn't even have to risk life and limb hauling ass to escape. The cops were in such disarray, and we had caused so much damage, that it took them the rest of the evening to get their act back together. By the time they got out of the woods, everyone had dispersed, and there was no one to question. As soon as the police untangled all their vehicles, they contacted the state police and the local sheriff's department who came out in force, stopping carloads of kids all over the county, questioning them as to their whereabouts, and threatening them if they didn't confess. It was impossible for them to single out anyone from the kegger, as we quickly merged our cars into the hundreds of vehicles pounding the main drag in town. Once we mixed in with the Friday night crowd, we were all but undetectable. By the time Danny, Steve, and I arrived downtown, the story had already been passed up and down the street and had already begun to grow in size and description. For at least one night, we were gods.

Moron

# Chapter 3

## The Show

After a weekend of swilling beer and retelling and embellishing the story hundreds of times by the first bell on Monday, the events being told of the Friday night kegger no longer bore any resemblance whatsoever to what had actually taken place.

"There were over a hundred police cars from all over the entire UP, and the entire senior class, females included, mooned the police. Shots were fired, and the police let their dogs loose on the crowd. At least two police officers were punched by students in the mad dash to escape, and there were felony warrants out for indecent exposure for the individuals who mooned the police. The state was going to bring in occult experts to determine if the fire in the woods was actually a cult meeting." No wonder history is continuously being revised, and history books get changed so many times; people just can't keep facts straight.

After one of the most exciting weekends in our senior year, it was back to the drudgery of the final month of school, and do I mean drudgery. No one wanted to be here. It's hard to concentrate when the weather outside is beautiful. All you think about twenty-four hours a day is graduation; finally, the accumulation of twelve long years of boring, senseless, never-ending classes. Couple the excitement of graduation with the anxiety of not knowing what you were going to do for the rest of your life—especially for those of us who were not going on to college—and you have a perfect cocktail for disaster.

The only reason I hadn't wholly skipped Monday morning classes and gone fishing was because I needed at least three more Cs to graduate. I knew I was on the borderline in several of my classes. The last thing I wanted or needed was to receive a graduation certificate instead of a diploma. Earning a certificate meant you were going to spend your last free summer going to night classes to get a diploma instead of hanging out with your buddies. The only saving grace of the morning was that I had a ninety-minute government class taught by the school's conservative rebel, Colonel Trump.

Colonel Trump was a retired Army colonel who had fought in Germany at the end of World War II, Korea, and then Vietnam. He was, as he said, "An officer of infantry."

He decided that when he left the Army, he was too young to retire and quietly go someplace to die. Instead, he dedicated his life to teaching high school students' government and history, and he did it with a flair that only a combat veteran could bring. His class was not too bad. If you got him going on his war stories, he would drop the standard curriculum and allow the students to bullshit for the entire ninety minutes of his class. He called this 'group discussion' and felt that we learned more from these conversations than from lecturing us. A lot of his stories were unusual, and all were exciting. He never made himself out as the hero in the stories, but you could read between the lines, and we came to realize that he had lived an incredible life. Indeed, a lot more exciting than the lives of anyone we knew around here.

The most important aspect of his class was that you were guaranteed a B if you participated in the discussions and showed him proof that you had registered for the draft and signed up to vote. The government had just passed the 18-year-old voting law in 1971, and he wanted to make sure that we all took advantage of our Constitutional rights. If you decided to enlist in the Army, attempt to qualify for West Point, or sign up for college ROTC, you would be the proud recipient of an A+ from the colonel. The plus was for living up to your civic responsibilities as an American citizen. The colonel thought that every young man should be required to serve in the military and applauded those who did so. Colonel Trump was singularly responsible for a lot of guys in Iron City being able to graduate.

Colonel Trump didn't stick to the approved curriculum. In fact, I don't think we ever read or discussed a subject out of the school issued book. And while we were not learning about government the way the administration intended, I contend that we were getting a far better education. We were learning more about our country and how the government ran than we ever could have sticking to the lesson plan. I probably learned more about the "real world" from Colonel Trump than any other class I ever took.  Through his stories and reminisces, and his years of working at the Pentagon in Washington, D.C., we learned how and why wars were really fought. He regaled us with tales of Special Forces, Airborne Rangers, the infantry, and, most importantly to a bunch of eighteen-year-olds, stories of honor, sacrifice, death, and destruction. His talks of death and destruction were concentrated on enemy forces, but occasionally the colonel would become sentimental and talk about the loss of close friends and comrades, and how significant their sacrifices were to our way of life.

The colonel didn't care for politicians, and he often explained to us in detail why office-bearers, even those with the best of intentions, all turned bad sometime during their first term. Hint … it's all about money and power. More significantly, we learned how important it was for the average American citizen to hold both our government and politicians accountable. His favorite saying was that bad things happen when good men stop paying attention and, especially, fail to act. His theory was that elected officials were mostly bureaucrats, and rarely leaders. Bureaucrats can keep things running and on time, but they can't effect change, and they rarely have the best interest of the country or the citizens in mind when making decisions. Free-thinking men, he declared, built and defended this country, and free-thinking men willing to fight will keep it free.

We were smack dab in the middle of one of his Korean War stories and group discussions when the air was suddenly shattered by the sound of a semi-truck's air horn blasting through the windows that had been left open to allow the spring air in. This sound was quickly followed by the hissing of airbrakes being applied. Everyone in the class jumped out of his seat and rushed to see what was going on outside. As we crowded the windows, we saw a big rig was pulling into the school parking lot, and we were stunned by the image that flooded our senses.

Pulling to a stop in the center of the teachers' parking lot was a brand-new Cummins semi. It was painted dark black and outlined in bright silver chrome with U.S. Army, and "Be All You Can Be," written in large gold letters on the sides and front. Directly behind the semi cab was something none of us could have imagined even in our wildest dreams, much less believe we would ever see with our own eyes. There behind the semi on the attached vehicle carrier were eight jet-black-and-chrome 1973 Pontiac Firebird Trans Ams. On the doors of each of the cars was the Army emblem, and on the hood of each Firebird was the easily identifiable flaming eagle—or, as we referred to it in 1973, "the screaming chicken."

For those of you not familiar with cars or, in this case, "muscle cars," these were not ordinary vehicles. These were the hottest, fastest cars that had ever come out of Detroit. The 1973 model of the Pontiac Firebird Trans Am would, in fact, become the best and the last model of the most potent—yet still street legal—vehicle ever made in an American factory. According to car magazines at the time, a stock Pontiac Firebird ran the quarter-mile in under fourteen seconds. This car was a teenage boy's wet dream.

There we were, staring out a classroom window with drool running down our collective chins. Quickly realizing that his herd of wild horses was about to stampede, the colonel, with a grin and a nod, declared, "Class is over, go on and see what game Big John is playing out there." The ensuing mad rush to the parking lot must have set some national speed records.

Within seconds of arriving at the foot of the transporter, the school lunch-period bell rang, and we were quickly joined by every male in school in our mad flight to get to the parking lot. All were scrambling to get a look at the cars on the truck. Along with the male student body, there was a smattering of girls. Several older guys from town also showed up. They had seen the truck on the highway, followed it to the school, parked across the street, and walked into the parking lot to get a better look. As we were all clamoring to get closer to the truck, the air was suddenly filled with the voice of Sgt. Barry

Sadler singing his hit song, "The Ballad of the Green Berets." The music was so loud that people downtown told us they could hear it several blocks away. The Army must have had hundreds of speakers hidden all over that truck.

While the music was playing, and everyone was fighting to get a closer look, Big John opened the truck door and climbed down from the cab of the semi. He was decked out in a crisp, sharp, fancy blue Army uniform that none of us had ever seen before. The sleeves of his uniform were encircled from top to bottom with a series of bright gold stripes. His chest was covered with medals that were glinting in the bright, midday sunlight. On his feet were shiny black boots that were polished so brightly that you could see your reflection in them. His pant legs were sharply creased, and there was a bright gold stripe running down the outside seam of each leg. His pants were tucked into his boots. On his head, he wore a green beret. None of us had ever seen Big John in anything except the Army green pants, a pinkish shirt, and an old-looking flat hat. This was the first time any of us had seen his beret. I had no idea he was a Green Beret.

All in all, it was making for one hell of a show, and it quickly began to achieve its desired results. Big John had us exactly where he wanted us, under his spell. When I think back on it, Big John would have been one of the top marketers in the world of advertising had he devoted his considerable showmanship and psychological talents to the private sector instead of the Army.

Continuing to play for his ever-growing audience, Big John climbed up onto the top deck of the transporter and slowly walked down the outside rail beside the cars.  When he reached the end of the trailer, he bent down and grabbed a large lever at the end of the deck. Booming out, "Stand clear," he pulled the lever forward, causing the heavy metal tailgate to slam down into the ground. As soon as it hit the pavement, the music shut off. The sudden absence of sound caused the crowd to go silent, and you could hear a collective gasp. The show was getting better and better. With a curt "Heads up," Big John tossed his bullhorn down to one of the kids closest to the truck and jumped down.

As soon as his feet hit the ground, he spun around, marched up the waiting ramp, and climbed into the last Trans Am on the transporter. You could have heard a pin drop as the engine started and the parking lot was filled with the growling sound of a finely tuned, high-performance engine. Even today, decades later, I can still hear that engine as clearly as the day Big John fired it up. Nothing, and I mean nothing, can replicate the sound of that engine. The Firebird he was in then began backing down the ramp onto the pavement of the parking lot. When all four tires touched down, Big John hit the gas and the brakes at the same time. The engine roared, and the tires squealed.  The pungent smell of burning rubber and clouds of dark white smoke filled the air. Big John killed the engine, and for a moment, silence once more filled the air. As quickly as it began, it all ended. Only for a moment, because the silence was quickly replaced by the roar of applause and screaming of awed teenagers.

Once the applause had died down, and Big John had somehow regained possession of his bullhorn, he announced:

"Gentleman, I am going to set up shop in the high school counselor's office for the next two hours. The first eight seniors who come to see me and tell me they are interested in serving in the Wolverine platoon, an all-volunteer platoon to be made up of young men from the Upper Peninsula of Michigan, can put your name on one of these 1973 Trans Am Firebirds. Yep, you heard me right, no gimmicks, no strings attached. You volunteer to serve your country in the greatest Army in the world, and Uncle Sam signs over the title to one of these brand-new Firebirds to you and only you." He then paused, slammed his hand down on top of the car he had been driving and said, "Well, unfortunately, they are all not actually brand new. This one here now has about a tenth of a mile on it." After the laughter died down, Big John continued. "OK, step back and give me some room, so I can head up to the counselor's office. I'm going to start taking applications in about ten minutes."

If I had a brain in my head, I would have stopped right then and walked away. My father had preached to me for as long as I could remember, "If it sounds too good to be true, then it probably is."

But you know how it goes, eighteen years old, women and fast cars on the mind twenty-four hours a day, living in a perpetual state of horniness and the fastest muscle car in America—brand new and so close I could touch it—being dangled in front of me. I clearly was not thinking with my big head. As soon as Big John departed, I, along with just about every other male in my class, raced to the counselor's office. I already imagined how many girls I could pick up if I owned one of those Trans Ams. They would be fighting to go out with me.

It was elbows and assholes as we raced upstairs. I was one of the faster guys in school, so I was one of the first eight to be able to make it to the counselor's office. Iron City High School was a relatively small school, and there were only fifty-two males in the graduating class. A hallway full of anxious teenagers were lined up outside the counselor's door. Along with the rowdy senior crew were most of the males from the junior class and at least one freshman, who at the time I was sure was no more than fifteen years old. He didn't even have his driver's license yet. But I admired his guts, go big or go home. The line stretched all the way down the hallway. The only members of the senior class who were not in line were athletes who had already been notified that they had full rides to play sports, mostly at Northern Michigan University, and those whose parents had enough money that college was not going to be a problem. You know, the sons of doctors and lawyers, those kids who had been living the privileged life since birth. Heck, many of them had even been on real summer vacations. It didn't seem fair, but it was what it was. You had to get over it and move on.

As you can imagine, things were not going very well in that hallway. All of us could count. People realized where they were in line and started to argue with one another. There were a few shoves and pushes, and at least one punch was thrown. The pressure was building, and an explosion was imminent. Just when it appeared that there was nothing that could be done to stop the flood of male juvenile hormones from being released, the door swung open and into the fray walk Big John and the counselor.

Quickly assessing the situation, Big John looked us over, and in his loudest voice, he boomed:

"I told headquarters that this was not a pussy town and that I was going to have more than eight volunteers, but you know how bureaucrats are, they wouldn't believe me. Everybody calm down, give me a few minutes to make some calls, and I will see what I can do about getting the Army to send some more cars up here. You guys know me, I've never lied to any of you (yeah right). Quiet down and hang out here for the next ten minutes, and let me see if I can work something out. One thing though, I am putting my neck out on this one. If you leave this hallway without talking to me, the deal is off. Also, any fights and you're done."

He then went back into the office with our school counselor and shut the door.  For the next fifteen minutes, which for an eighteen-year-old felt like a lifetime, we waited in the hallway. Yeah, sure the arguing continued but at a significantly reduced decibel level and all the pushing and shoving ceased. No one wanted to lose an opportunity to own a brand-new Trans Am. Those poor guys in line behind number eight waited in dread.

After the longest wait in my life, the door burst open and Big John strode out with a big shit-eating grin on his face.

"Gentleman, I just got off the phone with the general in charge of recruiting in Washington. I explained the situation to him and convinced him to divert some money from some of the big city programs downstate to purchase additional Firebirds for you guys. They are not having much luck in Detroit, Chicago, and Milwaukee. Those city pukes don't have the balls to fight for their country. I told him he was wasting his time trying to find soldiers in the cities and to put his money where his patriots are."

He went on to explain to us that he had been given permission to provide every senior in the school who signed up one of the new Trans Ams. He said he was authorized to make a special deal for the juniors, who would be allowed to sign up for a delayed entry program with a guaranteed opportunity to join the Army after they graduated the next year. The lone freshman, the fifteen-year-old, had his hand shook by Big John, who apologized to him and said, "I'm sorry, there is nothing I can do for you right now, but come back and see me in two years."

One by one, the seniors went into the counselor's office and signed up for appointments at the U.S. Armed Forces recruiting station just outside of town. We were followed by the juniors, who also signed up for interviews. I guarantee you none of us got any sleep that night. We were the talk of the town. Everyone wanted to talk to us to see if we were really going to get brand new cars. Everyone in the city went to the local stores to purchase car magazines to find pictures and stories about the coveted vehicle we chosen few would soon be driving. By six that evening, there wasn't a copy of a magazine with a photo of a Trans Am in it available within a hundred-mile radius of our little town. A lot of fathers and mothers were not too happy, and the school was getting a lot of calls, but for twenty-four lucky seniors, life was good.

Moron

.Chapter 4

The Sale

After speaking to all my buddies the following morning, it was clear that the past twenty-four hours hadn't brought any relief to our level of excitement. Most of them, like me, had stayed awake all night fantasizing about the Trans Ams. Adrenaline was pumping through our veins, and we were all still on a new-car high. There was no way that any of us were going to show up for class that morning. We were too amped up to even attempt going to school. There were only three weeks left anyway, and at this point school mostly consisted of practicing for the graduation exercise and trying to get teachers to give you high enough grades to prevent you having to attend summer classes. I had worked my schedule hard to make sure that none of the courses required a final exam. For me, it was merely a matter of getting a high grade from the colonel and then coasting until summer.

We spent the morning driving slowly past the recruiting station and looking at the Firebirds that had been removed from the transport vehicle and were now strategically parked out front. As tempting as it was, there was no way we could stop and get a closer look because if Big John caught us cutting class, we were dead meat. He wasn't a teacher or a cop, but we knew from experience that he wouldn't hesitate to grab us by the collar and escort us back to class, and I can tell you from personal experience, it wasn't a pleasant trip. I was driving a 1961 rusted-out blue Impala that morning, but in my dreams and fantasies, I was already behind the wheel of a 1973 jet-black Trans Am.

As soon as two o'clock rolled around, the earliest we could claim that we were legitimately out of class, all the seniors who signed up for a car showed up at the recruiting station. Our appointments were scheduled at thirty-minute intervals, but no one wanted to miss anything. It would be just my luck to miss my meeting and have the last available Trans Am go to someone else. I wasn't going to take any chances. Some of the guys had evening appointments, and they were going to be waiting until nine o'clock that evening; but for them, it was worth the wait. By the time of the first scheduled appointment, the recruiting station parking lot had taken on the persona of a carnival. People all over town had heard about the new cars, and they wanted to get a good look at both the new cars and the "idiots" who were about to volunteer to join the Army.

The overriding question in everyone's mind was, "Why would anyone in his right mind volunteer to be drafted?"

At a time when a great number of the young people in America were out protesting both the war in Vietnam and the Army, it didn't make sense to have almost the entire senior class of the local high school fighting to sign up to enlist. In larger cities across the country, you wouldn't want to even be seen in a military uniform. Respect for the military in America was at an all-time low. The older people in town, for the most part, couldn't understand why something as simple as a car had caused such a frenzy. I guess they underestimated the effect of a new car on a teenage boy. The only adult in town who had not underestimated the impact was Big John. He knew exactly what he was doing.

When Big John realized that we had all shown up at the same time, he decided to change his tactics and had us all come in and talk to him in one massive group session. He said he was doing this because he valued our time and didn't what us to have to wait late into the evening when he knew we had school the next morning. I believe Big John didn't want a bunch of teenagers sitting out with the crowd that had come to see the cars and any chance of us being negatively influenced by naysayers. He had put too much time and effort into his plan to allow casual bystanders to take charge and risk losing all his potential recruits.

Can you say "sucker?" I can't believe we all didn't just walk away when Big John began his pitch. For an offer with no strings attached, it seemed like there were going to be a lot of little threads for us to untangle and fight our way through before we could even touch the new cars. You know how it is, you're eighteen years old, you have the world by the horns, and no one, especially an adult, is smarter than you. Our impulsive teenage brains had caused us to underestimate the cunning and expertise of Big John. He had every move planned, right down to having extra assistants standing by to help us complete and sign our contracts. How helpful! The guy was a master of psychology, particularly the psychology of the American teenager.

Big John started his sales pitch by talking to us about the Firebirds, and how cool we would look driving around town in them with our girlfriends and buddies, and how jealous everyone else would be. He stated that he wished he was young enough to join the Army again because we were going to be getting some significant tail. What, with the new cars and our Army uniforms, and war decorations, what woman in her right mind was going to be able to resist us? Unfortunately, there were only going to be enough cars to ensure that the volunteers for the new Wolverine platoon each got one. The vehicles were so rare that it would be impossible for an average guy to buy one even if he could afford it. In Iron City, if you weren't part of the Wolverine platoon, then you weren't going to be able to own a new Firebird. The closest you could come was to feel the rush of air and smell the exhaust as we flew past in our new Firebirds.

As Big John went into his sales pitch, I could practically feel the cool leather of the Trans Am's seats cradling my ass as I eagerly anticipated the moment when Big John handed the keys to my new car over to me. I could envision it in my mind already. It would be an evening of driving my new car up and down the main drag and all-around town for everyone to see and envy. Can you imagine all those black Trans Ams in a row, going down the main drag of Iron City? The local police were going to have a nut. I had even brought proof of insurance and copies of my driver's license along with me in case they needed some kind of paperwork before signing for my new car.

Wait a minute! Slam on the brakes! Wake up, Roger. Pay attention. What was it that Big John just said!

"There are a few minor details ..."

Now, I admit I'm not the sharpest tool in the box, but I am smart enough to know that when someone is offering you the keys to paradise, and he says, "There are a few minor details," everything is about to go to hell.

The first detail, and this was a big one, "You guys don't actually get to drive the cars away today. For me to legally allow you young men to take possession of the beautiful Trans

Ams parked in my parking lot, the Army requires me to have you complete a few little housekeeping things first. Nothing big or complicated, just some simple procedures that we are required by law to complete to make this perfectly legal. It's important that we do this right. We don't want anyone coming back and trying to take one of your cars away, do we?" According to Big John, the first thing we would have to do was to enlist in the Army as members of the new Wolverine platoon. We already knew that. We were then going to have to wait a short period of time before we could take possession of the Firebirds. "The Army," he said, "has to make sure that you will all stick to your contracts and serve on active duty as promised, so you will have to successfully graduate from basic training at Fort Knox, Kentucky, to fully qualify for the new cars." Don't worry, it's only eight short weeks of training. According to Big John, in less time than it takes to complete a high school football season, we would be able to take possession of our new cars. He assured us that the time would go by fast, and the Army always lets you come home for thirty days after training. Big John told us that driving home in our new cars after basic training would be the highlight of our lives.

In addition to driving back to the UP in our new cars, we would all be wearing brand new Army uniforms, courtesy of Uncle Sam. "Imagine returning to town as highly trained killers, in the best shape of your lives, wearing lady killer uniforms, and driving the hottest car in America.

"Guys, that's like a double dose of Spanish fly. The women in this city don't stand a chance; they will be fighting one another to get to you. After all, why would any women in her right mind want one of the local weaklings when they could have a soldier?"

We were being sucked into his web, and I, for one, believed every word he told us. It's not hard to convince a bunch of teens who have sex and cars on their minds twenty-four hours a day that a car and a uniform will make them irresistible to women.  Hell, we were teenagers, we already thought we were the coolest things on the planet. Something about being a senior in high school makes you believe that you are about to conquer the world.

Oh yeah, one more "minor detail." We would all be enlisting under the combat arms option. We would be signing up to join the infantry. And here's the kicker, we would be signing up for four years. *Four years*! He had to be kidding to an eighteen-year-old just out of high school. Doing anything for four years seemed like a lifetime. It was practically a quarter of the time that we had been alive. Signing a contract for four years at eighteen was tantamount to signing a contract for the rest of your life. Big John quickly picked up on the growing hesitation and went full tilt into his pitch.

"You guys are going to love the Army. Four years will go by so fast that I bet most of you will ask them to let you stay longer. As part of this deal, the Army is going to send you all to Fort Lewis, Washington, for your first assignment. Hell, while all your buddies you leave behind are back here trying to find work flipping burgers and driving their old rust heaps around, you gentlemen will be living in the best hunting, fishing, and scuba diving location in the world. That's right, scuba diving. The U.S. Army is going to teach you how to scuba dive, and we are going to buy your equipment for you. This is all part of what the Army calls adventure training, a new program specifically designed for the all-volunteer Army."

As he was speaking, he showed us pictures of mountains and oceans. He regaled us with stories of skiing down the slopes, rappelling off cliffs, and paddling rafts down roaring rapids and steep mountain streams. All this adventure, of course, would be paid for by the United States Army. He also told us that there were five major colleges within twenty-five miles of the Army post and that three of them were women-only colleges. We would be living in brand new barracks, with brand new furniture, and would have free access to some of the finest gyms and exercise facilities in the world. Once again, all these claims were backed up with a series of glossy pictures. You know what? This Army stuff doesn't look half bad.

"Now wait a minute," shouted Steve Wilson, aka Long Stick. Parents and teachers thought we called him that because of his stature, six foot two and no more than 120 pounds soaking wet. What they didn't know was that he had the longest dick that any of us had ever seen, and that included those twenty-five-millimeter porno flicks that Danny Mussio stole from his dad's lockbox and was always bringing to parties.

"Big John, you know this is all bullshit. I spoke to my brother about this, and he wouldn't lie to me. He was drafted three years ago. He said you can't trust the Army, especially recruiters, and that the Army will promise you anything to get you to enlist, but once you get in, they treat you like shit and that they don't do crap for soldiers." Steve continued his rant. "Soldiers are treated like garbage by the officers and lifers who make them do all the shit work. My brother said he once had to clean all the bathrooms in his unit for a month, just because there was nothing else for them to do. He told me that he was hit, yelled at, and basically treated like a slave. Hell, he was only in the Army for two years and said it felt like a hundred. He also said these cars are nothing but a scam, that there is no way that the Army is ever going to let us have brand new cars."

Big John immediately interrupted. "Hang on for a minute, Long Stick. How long have you guys known me? Don't

I come to all your ball games? Haven't I helped coach each and every one of you on your football and basketball skills? Don't I talk to your parents, the cops, and the judge when you guys get into trouble? Listen, guys, I'm never going to lie to you. What Stick says may have been true when his brother served in the Army. In the old draft, Army things were bad, but in the all-new, all-volunteer Army, everything has changed. The government didn't change the rules because they wanted to or because the Army wanted to. We changed because the government realized that they couldn't have a volunteer Army unless they changed the way they treated their soldiers."

Big John explained to us that the laws the government had passed had created something called the VOLAR Army. Project VOLAR was short for Project Volunteer Army, and it was really a "bill of rights" for all the men volunteering for the first all-volunteer Army in the history of the world. He passed out a sheet entitled "VOLAR ARMY" and began to explain what he referred to as "the new reality" to us.

"First, the Army realizes that to get people to volunteer, they have to treat them better. No one in the Army is allowed to treat soldiers like second-class citizens. No one can touch you in any way, and more importantly, you cannot be degraded or made fun of by any of your superiors. If someone violates these new rights, there is a very clear process that allows you to file a formal complaint against them. Let me tell you, no one in the Army wants to have a VOLAR complaint filed against them because that could mean jail time. Guys, the Army is very serious about this."

Boy oh boy, if I only knew then what I learned a short six months later. I would have just hauled off and hit him right there and then.

"Gentlemen, the Army is going to spend a fortune training you, paying you, and making sure you have the best food and housing. Volunteer soldiers are too valuable for the Army to waste their time doing menial tasks. You are going to spend most of your time at work, learning to use the most modern weapons and the deadliest fighting skills available. You won't be cleaning bathrooms because you will be America's warriors. In fact, I predict that many of you are going to end up coming back here in a year wearing green berets. That is, of course, if you're good enough and tough enough for the challenge." He paused to let that image sink in, then went on. "I almost forgot; let me tell you about the new pay raise. The Army's not stupid. They know that they are going to have to pay top dollar to get quality volunteers. Now, the information I'm getting ready to tell you is so new that it won't even be in the papers until the end of this summer, so please don't spread it around. To ensure the success of the all-volunteer Army and allow the country to end the draft, Congress has proposed a massive sixty-percent pay raise for all soldiers."

In case you missed the slight nuance, the key word here is *proposed*.

"Guys you will be making more money than your teachers here in high school or one of your friends who has graduated from college and has been working for four years, and you won't be working your ass off at some demeaning job. You'll be getting paid for having fun.

"Not only are you going to get the biggest pay raise in the history of the Army, but you don't have to use your money to pay for anything except having a good time and, of course, entertaining the ladies. While your buddies back here in Iron City are paying rent, you will be getting your room and all your utilities for free. Hell, the Army will even provide the sheets, blankets, and pillows for your beds for free. All your food is free. Not the same old Army food that your friends and relatives have told you about. You guys are going to be served by gourmet cooks. You're going to get three-plus meals a day. I say plus because the Army now serves brunch on Saturdays and Sundays to allow soldiers a little more time to sleep in and enjoy the weekend. Most Army posts have at least one steak and a lobster meal every week. I don't know about you, but until you have lived on a diet of steak and lobster, you just haven't lived. The food is so good now that we are starting to get worried about how much weight some of the soldiers are gaining.

"What's one of the biggest expenses for a young man starting out in life or going off to college? You might be surprised, but the answer is beer and women. You are all going to spend more money on beer and women than you do on any other single item, except of course on car expenses. Oh, I almost forgot, that doesn't matter to you, because the Army is giving you all free cars. Wait a minute, did I forget to tell you that in the VOLAR Army, good ole Uncle Sam is going to provide your beer for free. The new law requires the Army to put free, ice cold beer on tap in every dining facility in the Army. Of course, you can't have a beer for breakfast, and at lunch, you are limited to two glasses. Big glasses but try to keep it to two. But, in the evening it's as much as you can drink. Hell, you can get wasted every night if you want to, and then head downtown to see the ladies. Think about how much money you are going to save."

Note: I know this is hard to believe, but the Army did have beer on tap in the dining facilities and beer machines in the barracks. Talk about stupid, it was a disaster waiting to happen.

"I know that some of you are thinking about going to college but can't figure out how you and your parents are going to pay for it. Well, here's the best thing about the all-volunteer Army. When you are ready to start college, the Army will send you for free and allow you time off work to go to classes. More importantly, when your four-year hitch is up, you can leave the Army, and they will pay for four straight years of college for every one of you. Imagine not a penny of your or your parents' pockets, and you can go to any college you want to. You don't even have to look at the tuition costs because Uncle Sam is going to pay it for you.

"You know what the biggest complaint we get from our new soldiers is? They complain that they get paid more than they can possibly spend. In the Army, so much stuff is free that you are going to have to look for places to spend your cash.

"Not a bad problem to have.

"If I were you guys, I would start myself a nice savings account and save up for a business, or a home on the beach someday. After all, you're not going to be in the Army forever."

The little voice in the back of my mind kept saying, "Roger, if it sounds too good to be true, then you need to be careful."

Unfortunately, my eighteen-year-old ego and testosterone overruled my good sense and drowned out that little voice.

Big John went on for an hour straight, hardly pausing to take a breath. He talked about how we could get off work half a day every day to attend college classes. How the Army would let us decorate our rooms anyway we desired to include painting to our individual tastes. No more stupid barracks inspections. Officers and NCOs were now required to honor your personal privacy and could not come in your room without your permission.

"Now, when you think about it, it's only fair. After all, it is your private residence."

The most attractive aspect of the new all-volunteer Army was that you would receive some of the best training and job skills available anywhere in the world.

"Yeah right," interjected Stick once again. "I'm sure we're going to get a whole lot of valuable job training in the infantry. Why just yesterday I saw signs in the stores around town: Wanted, a person with experience in shooting people, and throwing hand grenades, please inquire within."

Big John responded as quickly as Stick ended his little speech.

"I'm sorry, you must have misunderstood me. You don't have to stay in the infantry for four years, you only must enlist in the infantry. As soon as you get finished with infantry training and arrive at Fort Lewis, you can apply for training in over three hundred different skills. There is no limit to the types of training you can get.

"I personally recommend something like x-ray technician or helicopter pilot. Both of those careers pay great money in the civilian world and are highly sought-after skills by companies everywhere. Under the Army's new high school to flight school program, I fully expect to see some of you flying helicopters by this time next year. Can you imagine being the pilot in command of one of the most lethal weapons in the world, or for that matter how about being a tank commander in one of the Army's newest tanks?"

I think you get the picture. One by one, Big John overcame each one of our objections and somehow portrayed a four-year stint in the Army as the greatest adventure we could possibly undertake. He described the Army as an adventure rather than dangerous or monotonous. In all fairness, most of what Big John told us that evening had some element of truth, not much truth in some cases, but in others a little. There was, in fact, an experiment going on called the VOLAR Army, and Fort Lewis was one of the sites they were testing it at. The Army was attempting to make some historic changes. They really were trying to change some of the old rules and regulations. For example, they did allow volunteer soldiers to sign up for college while they were assigned to Fort Lewis, and they did allow soldiers a half day off to attend classes. They called it Old Reliable University.

Bottom line, by nine o'clock that evening, all the seniors in the recruiting station signed an intent to enlist, and we were all scheduled to head down to Milwaukee for testing, medical examinations, and processing at a place called the Armed Forces Entrance and Examining Station (AFEES). We were supposed to pick up our bus tickets, hotel vouchers, and meal tickets on the first Thursday after school let out for the summer. The following morning, we would be heading down to Milwaukee on the bus.

We were young, and we were stupid. We all signed up to be soldiers under a program called the delayed entry program. This program would allow us to finish high school and hang out in town until the end of the summer. A little time to relax before we bit the proverbial bullet. No pun intended.

All the juniors could take paperwork home for their parents to review. Most were under the age of eighteen and couldn't sign up for themselves. Their version of the enlistment program allowed them to sign up and be in the delayed entry program for their entire senior year of high school. They wouldn't have to join the Army until the end of the summer after they graduated. They, of course, would also be receiving the 1974 version of the Trans Am when they successfully finished basic training. Little did any of us know at the time that 1973 would be the last year "the screaming chicken" would be manufactured. We were so hypnotized and manipulated by Big John's pitch that we had no idea what we had just done. My father, to his benefit, never tried to talk me out of my enlisting in the Army but did ask me to talk to the Air Force and Navy recruiters before I went to Milwaukee. He thought I should take the time to weigh my options if I was serious about going into the military. "Maybe," he said, "just maybe you will change your mind after hearing what they have to offer." I, of course, did not do that. At my age, I thought I knew everything, and I had made my decision. It should have been a clue to me that there was a waiting list to join the Air Force and the Navy while the Army and Marines were scouring neighborhood schools and courts looking for anyone they could get their hands on.

# Chapter 5

## The Deal Explained

All right, I know everyone is going to ask: How in the hell could the U.S. Army promise a bunch of potential recruits they would get brand new Trans Ams as part of an enlistment program to attract high school students to enlist in the all-volunteer Army?

If you had said, "There was no way the government could do this because it is illegal," then you would have guessed right. It was against the law at the time for the Army to promise anything more than the new signing bonuses that had been authorized by Congress.

Don't get me wrong; we indeed were promised new cars by our recruiter. In addition to his incredible oratory skills, Big John was a businessman and apparently didn't mind bending the rules just a little bit.

In the early seventies, the Army had just initiated the first of what would be a series of enlistment bonuses. These incentives to enlist were designed by McNamara and his crew and approved by Congress. Twelve years of war had created such a mess in this country that eliminating the draft was about the only platform that an aspiring politician could use to get himself elected. Of all the military services, the Army had the worst reputation. Its standing was so bad that government leaders knew large sums of money needed to be thrown at potential recruits if the country was going to have any hope of success in creating an all-volunteer force. The all-volunteer Army's initial goal was a lofty one. They wanted to require all recruits to have a high school diploma before they could enlist. They knew if they wanted to have a highly educated force, they were going to have to pay to get it.

When the all-volunteer force began, the Army offered, for the time, extremely lucrative bonus payments. Unfortunately, they very quickly had to lower their sights and were forced to forgo the high school requirement. No amount of money seemed to be enough to get high school graduates to sign up in the numbers required to make it work. The government thought that over time, the new program would work. The strategy was to pay as much as possible to attract kids about to graduate.

In the spring of 1973, the Army had just come out with the highest bonus in its history, offering $4,500 to anyone who would volunteer to enlist for a period of four years and agree to serve in a combat arms specialty (infantry, field artillery, armor, or air defenses artillery). Four years of college tuition was also part of the deal if desired. Today, $4,500 doesn't seem like a whole lot of money, especially when you are talking about four years of your life. But in 1973 it was more than a young man fresh out of high school could make in a year, and definitely more than enough to make a teenager salivate.

To put it in perspective, today's Army is offering up to fifty thousand dollars in a signing bonus plus a payoff of any existing college loans and assignment to the station of your choice. Sounds just a little bit desperate, doesn't it? If they're offering that much, I guess the all-volunteer Army is still facing a lot of problems.

You could purchase a lot of stuff with $4,500 back in '73. Not by coincidence, one of the things you could buy was a brand new 1973 Trans Am. Big John was smart enough to realize that a new car, something you could feel and smell and sit in, was more enticing to a young man than cash. He contracted with a buddy at the local Pontiac Dealer to purchase every new Trans Am he could get his hands on. They concocted a deal to get us to sign over our bonus money to them, and they would use the cash the Army would pay us as an enlistment bonus to purchase the new cars. The dealer and Big John split the commission on the cars and both made out like fat rats. Big John felt that it was a win-win for everyone. The Army would get its new high school graduate recruits, the dealer would have a record year, and Big John would put some extra cash in his pocket.

The only thing they had to do was get some suckers to sign over their bonuses in the form of powers of attorney to the car dealer. Big John was able to work this deal two times before he was caught by the Army. I believe his overall plan and concept were brilliant. Where he failed was in the execution. If he had worked out something with the Army attorneys and explained the deal to them, they might have bought off on it. I even think that it would have opened up an entirely new form of bonuses. If the Army can sponsor NASCAR and Professional Bull Riders, then using cars as bonuses is not a bridge too far. While many things have changed, one thing has remained the same, and that is the thinking pattern of young men. A new car is still a powerful enticement.

Chapter 6

Road Trip

I have forgotten a lot of incidents in my past, but I can still remember clearly in the sharpest detail everything about the morning I headed down to the local Greyhound bus station. Not because it was a hallmark in the growth of a young man but because of how naive I was at the time. I had no idea how my decision to enlist in the Army was going to change my life forever. When I think back, I realize that this was a pivotal moment in my journey into adulthood. A simple shift of direction would have changed everything I am today. You have all heard stories about the path untaken. Well, this was one path that, had I made a different choice, would have dramatically changed the course of my life and the lives of many of those close to me. Just by missing or electing not to take that bus, I would have become a completely different person.

School was out for the summer, but for many us, it was out forever. Forever is a big word and an even bigger concept for an eighteen-year-old. Along with the end of school, we were contemplating the end of the community that had tied us together and comforted us every day of our lives up to this point. Family, friends, community, church—nothing would ever be the same again. Like every other high school graduate in America, I was spending my time hanging around, attending endless graduation parties, and waiting for the inevitable end of summer and the end of my childhood. I don't think it had really soaked in that I had enlisted for four years in the Army and that I had chosen the Army as my first job out of high school. I hadn't taken the time to think everything through, so for me it wasn't real yet. Talking about becoming a soldier made for some great stories to tell my girlfriend, but I still hadn't entirely accepted the consequences of my actions or considered the magnitude of what I had done. Joining the Army and leaving home were concepts that I just hadn't come to terms with yet.

As I headed out of the house that morning, the last morning of my innocence, my father, who was against my decision to join the Army, made a final appeal to change my mind. My father had served in the military, in the Air Force, and was very proud of it. While he had never been assigned to an Army base, he had visited many and had a lot of Army friends, so he knew a lot about the Army. He didn't go into all his arguments against the Army that he had been posing to me over the previous weeks, the same arguments that had monopolized the conversation at every family meal since that fateful day at the recruiting station. Instead, he summarized his objections in a story that he told me as he walked me out the front door that final morning.

"Roger, I'm proud and honored that you have decided to serve your country," he began his cautionary tale. "I think it admirable that a young man just out of high school is so eager to serve. I'm not so dumb as to not realize that your decision has a lot to do with those black Trans Ams, but regardless of the reason, I'm am proud of you, son. Please, take the time to think through your decision, and if you still want to serve, then please consider joining the Air Force, or the Navy. I know you don't think I know what I am talking about, and when I was your age, I didn't pay much attention to my father either. But, before you sign a permanent contract with the Army, there is one final thing that I wish you would consider."

He paused, took a deep breath, and continued his final plea. "In the Air Force, the officers go off and fight the war every day in their airplanes, and at night, they come home and sleep in their own beds, take hot showers, and eat in their own homes, and, more importantly, sit on modern toilets. The enlisted men in the Air Force never get shot at and are never in any danger. They work on the flight lines, preparing the airplanes and making sure they are ready to fly. Most remain in the United States and can serve close to home. For example, if you joined the Air Force, you could get assigned to K.I. Sawyer Air Force Base. It's only eighty miles from here, and you could come home to visit your friends and family on weekends.

"Just like the Air Force, in the Navy, it's primarily the officers who fight the wars. Hell, I know a lot of guys in the Navy, and they don't even get issued weapons, much less having ever to fire them. They even have Marines assigned to their ships to protect them. If you are assigned to shore, you have the same amenities as the Air Force guys. If you are assigned to a ship, your bed and your food, and your toilet, go with you wherever you go, and you can take a hot shower every day. You could get assigned to Great Lakes Naval Station in Chicago and be able to return home on the weekends. If you decide to go ahead and enlist in the Army, everything changes. The enlisted soldiers in the Army are its primary fighting force. They fight the wars while the officers stay back and direct them where to go and how to attack. Everyone in the Army carries a weapon, all the time, and you better know how to use it, and use it well. You never know when you are going to get shot at. All your meals and your bed get carried by you on your back. More importantly, while it doesn't seem like a big deal now, you may go for months at a time without a shower or even the opportunity to sit on a toilet that isn't a hole in the ground that you dig outside of your tent or foxhole.

"Please," he reiterated, "reconsider and at least speak to the Navy and Air Force recruiters before you make your final decision. In both of the Air Force and the Navy, you'll get some real job training, and the pay and benefits are the same no matter which military service you decide to enlist in. More importantly, if you enlist in the Air Force or Navy, you will probably never get shot at. In case you haven't read a newspaper lately, we are still fighting a war in Vietnam. I don't care what Big John told you, I don't think this is going to end soon, or well, and if history has taught us anything, it's that as soon as this war ends, another is going to start somewhere."

Of all the things my father ever told me, this was going to be the one that I had wished the most I had paid more attention to, especially the part about sitting on a toilet.

Years later when I was digging a foxhole in the woods or scraping a hole in the sand in some desert to do my business, my father's words would flash into my brain, causing me to smile and shake my head. You have no idea what a luxury it is being able to sit in a bathroom, on lovely warm porcelain in a private setting, until you have it taken away from you. Of course, like most teenagers, I completely disregarded everything my father had to say to me.

By the time I arrived at the bus station, most of the guys were already there, and by eleven a.m. everyone, all 24 of us had arrived. Big John had given us a choice of taking the six a.m. bus or the eleven thirty bus. Not much of an option to a bunch of teenagers. No chance any of us were getting up that early in the morning just to catch a bus leaving at six. Besides, we were on summer vacation. Our last summer vacation, and it was rare to see any of us out during daylight hours. A typical day consisted of getting up around one or two in the afternoon, watching TV until early evening, and then running around drinking and getting into trouble until early the next morning, and then starting the cycle all over again. Most of our parents referred to us like vampires. The fact that we had a hard time getting out of bed before midafternoon to catch a bus should have been an omen of things to come. Here we were getting ready to sign up for the Army, and we were barely able to get out of bed before noon. Life as we knew it was going to get a whole lot tougher.

The bus station in Iron City wasn't really a bus station in the real sense of the word. It was actually the Sing-Along Café. This was way before Starbucks, so if you wanted coffee twenty-four hours a day, this was the only coffee house in town. It was open 365 days a year, and none of us had ever remembered a day when it had been closed. The food was greasy, the coffee was strong, the waitresses and staff were friendly, and a perpetual blue fog of cigarette smoke hung in the air. Ah, the good ole days when you could smoke whenever and wherever you wanted to. The Sing-Along was a great place to sober up after a hard night of drinking, a good place to hide out when cutting classes, and a place to meet buddies to discuss life's pressing problems. The waitresses were old but sweet and would always listen to your problems and offer good motherly advice. No one criticized, and all were welcome. In many ways, it was a lot like a church. The Sing-Along was on Main Street and occupied the only corner with enough road space to temporarily park or turn a bus around; therefore, it was the bus station. The "station" part of the coffee house consisted of two tables by the front door and some benches on the sidewalk out front. Of course, the benches could only be used in the summer. In winter, it was too cold to wait outside, and even if you wanted to wait outside, you couldn't find the benches under the snow. The station inside provided a place to sit and drink coffee while waiting for the next bus to arrive. Tickets could be purchased on board the bus from the driver or from the local post office. In our case, Big John got the tickets, and he met us at the door of the café, handing them to us as we staggered in by ones and twos.

The latest bus schedule and the price list for trips were posted on a yellowed cardboard sign in the window. The yellowing was a combination of sun fading and cigarette smoke. The sign was useless because the buses didn't run on anything close to a regular schedule. The scheduled times, as with all schedules in the UP, were merely recommendations. The weather and road conditions caused so many delays that arrival and departure times were more guesswork than science. There are no four-lane highways in the UP or in

Northern Wisconsin. We would have to travel to Green Bay, over a hundred miles away, before we hit anything that resembled a highway. On the UP highways, you could always count on delays. A single piece of farm equipment, a slow-moving semi-truck, or lousy weather would wreak havoc on any schedule. A noon departure from Iron City meant you should be there at noon just in case, but the bus could arrive as late as six in the evening depending upon what was happening on the roads. There were four busses scheduled between Iron City and Milwaukee five days of the week. It was not unusual for the six-a.m. bus to arrive just when the noon bus was scheduled to depart. It was a little confusing, but we were used to it.

That morning, I figured it was a good omen that not only did the bus arrive on time, but it was also almost empty, so I took a full seat to myself. There was a bathroom on the bus, but it smelled like ass, and no one wanted to sit in any of the seats near it. We all wanted to drive down to Milwaukee in a couple of cars instead of the five-hour bus trip, but Big John quickly nixed the idea and told us that allowing us to take POVs, (privately owned vehicles) as he called them, would be against Army regulations. The Army wanted us under complete control. And, as we all knew, following the rules was very important to Big John.

All of us brought a change of clothing and basic toiletries. We would be arriving late in the evening and would be spending the night in the Milwaukee YMCA before processing into the Army the following morning. The Army was too cheap to spring for a real hotel. We would spend all day Saturday processing and would return on the late bus Saturday night. This crazy schedule was designed to keep us out of trouble. Frankly, I can't believe they even tried.

We were excited about spending a night in Milwaukee; Milwaukee was the proverbial big city. To us, it was more of an adventure than a processing trip for the Army. The drinking age in Wisconsin at the time was eighteen, so most of us would be able to drink in bars legally for the first time in our lives. Not that we hadn't been drinking illegally for years, but something about being able to walk up to a bar and order a drink intrigued the hell out of us. More critical than drinking was the fact that there were strip clubs in Milwaukee. Not the topless ones like they have around the UP during deer season, you know the ones where the girls wear bikini bottoms and those sticky stars on their nipples. The clubs in Milwaukee were real honest-to-goodness totally nude strip joints. Friends had told us that they had some of the most beautiful women in the world in some of those clubs and that one guy had met a Playboy centerfold who was dancing at a club.

With that in mind, imagine a smelly, hot bus filled with a bunch of boisterous, drinking, teenage boys, full of anticipation and on their way to the adventurous city. The bus smelled like a combination of fresh puke mingled with an overfull shitter and combined with the odor of wet socks. The only thing that saved us from being overcome was that it was early summer, and we could keep all the bus windows open as far as they would go. It was windy, but it beat the hell out of suffocating. The open windows, coupled with the fact that a half hour out of town we were already wasted, made the trip tolerable.

The bus stopped at every location with a population over fifteen, and most were like the bus stop at Iron city. They were a combination of restaurants, bars, and gas stations. The bus would stop to drop off mail and items that the driver was ferrying from town to town. Occasionally, there was a new passenger, but for the most part, the bus picked up packages rather than people. The guy driving our bus appeared to be at least a hundred years old. He wore glasses with lenses thicker than the bottom of coke bottles, and he was utterly oblivious to what was happening on his bus and sometimes even to what was happening on the highway. I don't know how he managed to keep the bus on the road half of the time. I guess years of routine and driving the same route every day had steeled him to the noise and commotion on the bus to the point that nothing fazed him. We were apparently not his first Milwaukee Army group. Young men from Northern Michigan had been making the trip since World War I. It didn't matter what we did on the bus—yelled, puked out the window, or sang raunchy songs at the top of our lungs—he merely stared straight ahead and kept the bus moving down the highway to the next stop.

The other passengers on the bus were mostly the hard-core bus riders, and they slept through everything we put out. Word must have gotten out about the rowdy teenagers because by the second or third stop, the bus in front of us was full of passengers and we were down to the Wolverine platoon. For most of the trip, we had the entire bus to ourselves. The regulars probably knew from experience that this was the time of the month that the idiots joining the Army would be traveling the Milwaukee route.

The bus finally pulled into the Greyhound station in downtown Milwaukee, the second real bus station on the entire route, the first being the Greyhound Station in the bustling metropolis of Green Bay. By the time we arrived, we were all too wasted to walk straight, and couldn't find the strip map to the YMCA that Big John had provided to us. The United States Army anticipated this and not wanting to lose their fresh fodder, had a plan to ensure that we reached our destination on time and in one piece. The minute we began to disembark, or more accurately roll off the bus, a sergeant and five privates appeared and began to organize us. After getting us all off the bus and identifying all our belongings, they started the task of getting a bunch of drunken teenagers down the street and into the YMCA. Knowing we would more than likely be arriving in a condition that would prevent us from being able to walk and carry our stuff at the same time, they brought along rolling suitcase holders, the kind you see porters using at the airport, to help us transport our bags. Between the six of them, they were able to corral us and herd us down the street to the Milwaukee YMCA. Staggering and arguing all the way, we somehow made it down the street and through the front door of our overnight home.

The entrance to the YMCA had more signage than any place I had ever been in my life. I learned from the signs on the wall as we entered the Y that they did not tolerate drinking, drugs, or drunks. The signs let us know that if we were using alcohol, we would have to find somewhere else to spend the evening. It should have been clear to even the casual observer that we were all drunk off our asses, but they let us in anyway. I guess having a military escort, and the government maintaining a large account with the YMCA, provided the staff with the necessary incentive to ignore our inebriated state. We were surprised at how friendly and accommodating the sergeant was acting. I began to relax a little. I believed none of those stories we were told about screaming, yelling sergeants were true after all.

## Chapter 7

## Milwaukee

The YMCA wasn't exactly the Ritz, but it was a place to get some sleep and sober up. That is, if we ever got to bed that night. Although we were all drunk, we agreed to shower and meet back in the lobby in thirty minutes. It was already early evening, and we didn't want to waste time sleeping that could be used for bars and strip clubs. To make sure we knew where we were going, Stick had brought a strip map with him that listed all the strip clubs in downtown Milwaukee. His older brother, who had processed through the Army Milwaukee processing station several years prior, gave it to him. Stick gained a lot of prestige from being the "keeper of the map" because to us, it wasn't just a map. It was the Holy Grail.

The rooms at the YMCA were basic institutional rooms: concrete block walls and a metal bunk with yellowed sheets, a pillow with no pillowcase, and an old Army blanket. Every room had a sink on the wall and a window that was sealed shut, protected by black twisted iron bars on it. I wasn't sure if we were in a hotel or in prison. When I laid down on my bunk, I could touch both walls by stretching out my arms. There were no televisions, radios, or phones in any of the rooms.

These luxury items could be found in the lounge down on the first floor. The TV in the lounge of the Y was a thirteen-inch, black-and-white with an old set of rabbit ears wrapped in tinfoil on top of it.

The showers were communal and were located at the end of each of the floors. No big deal because we had all been playing sports together since grade school and sharing a shower with a bunch of guys was nothing new. But someone forgot to warn us about the number of sexual predators that hung around the YMCA in Milwaukee. In retrospect, they should have called this place, "The Milwaukee Gay Predator Hunting Lodge," instead of the YMCA. You wouldn't believe how many had infiltrated the Y and were hitting on the mostly unaware rural boys from Wisconsin and Northern Michigan who were visiting Milwaukee to enter the military. For most of us, this was our first introduction to the world of alternative lifestyles, and we didn't take to it very well. I might have been fairly described as "a raging homophobe" at the time.

One good thing about arriving as a group instead of individually, the fags, as we called them, quickly realized that if you messed with any one of us, you messed with all of us. It only took two or three bloody noses before they got the message, and the word was spread to beware of the Wolverine boys. Word must have traveled fast because, after the few encounters, they pretty much backed off us for the remainder of our visit.

The front door of the Y was guarded by an ancient black man with more wrinkles than I'd ever seen on a human being. He was wearing a jet-black suit, a crisp white shirt, and a bright red bowtie. He sat on a gray metal chair holding a worn out, dog-eared bible with gold lettering on the spine in his hands. He sat there like a statue holding that bible. He never opened it, just held it and stared straight ahead. His main job appeared to be to control the entrance to the Y and to hand out board games, books, and balls for the pool table to anyone who wanted to use them in the lounge. It was an easy job because there were only two board games and all the books were bibles or religious handouts. It would be tough if you wanted to play pool. The cue ball and eight balls were missing, and there were no cue sticks. In a pinch you probably could have used a broom handle as a substitute.

For an establishment that purported to be run by people of religious persuasion, they sure had a lot of severe morality issues at the Milwaukee YMCA. I'll give them the benefit of the doubt. I'm sure most of their problems stemmed from the location and proximately to the bus station and the ghettos of Milwaukee, but still, they didn't try very hard to control things. I got offered more drugs and pornography than I even knew existed. Before I made it up the stairs and down the hallway to my room, I had been offered cocaine, marijuana, and any type of acid I wanted. There was even one person in the hall who said he had a girl in his room and that we could each spend ten minutes with her for ten dollars. If we weren't into girls, he said he could find a nice boy for us.

The city of Milwaukee at that time reflected seventies America. LSD was still popular, but most people had migrated to the various forms of acid, and all the marijuana, at least the good stuff, was laced with some type of chemical.

One of the great things about living in the UP, "in the woods," was that you could always find a sweet spot to cultivate your own crop of marijuana. Everyone had access to some potent marijuana, and we had a pretty good trading network going on. For the trip to Milwaukee, most of us brought along a little of our own private stashes. You know, to help us relax when it came time for us to take our Army tests.

Good thing we did. The crap they were attempting to sell in the halls of the Y was mostly dried out stems and seeds. I couldn't believe that the people down here were willing to spend good money on this crap. When the local sellers and users had the opportunity to view and sample some of the stuff we had grown up North, we became instant celebrities. Most of them had never experienced the quality of weed that we had brought with us. Thanks to a little entrepreneurship on my part, I left Milwaukee with a lot more money than I had arrived with and ensured, at least for the next couple of weeks, the potheads in Milwaukee would be smoking some good stuff. If I were smart, I could have set up a lucrative business and dropped my Army plans.

Somehow, chalk it up to the resilience of youth, we managed to make it down from our rooms to the front desk. All accounted for, and it only took forty-five minutes. Surprising what a hot shower and a couple of cold beers will do for you. Some of the guys had already checked with the front desk clerk and determined that the local Ponderosa Steak House would be the best place to get something to eat before we headed out for our evening's entertainment. Everyone was starving. The Ponderosa was cheap, had lots of food, and was only a block away. It was close to the local strip joints, they accepted the meal coupons the Army had given us, and, best of all, they had an all-you-can-eat buffet.

I don't know how, but once again we managed to bumble and stumble our way down the street, and somehow we made it to the restaurant. The Ponderosa was great; we were able to use our meal coupons, and there were tons of food.

Unfortunately, within thirty minutes of our arrival, the manager on duty walked up to us and said, "We have a problem. Could you please leave?"

It wasn't our fault, and to his credit, he did say please. We were not even making a scene or acting like assholes; we just wanted to eat. According to the manager, the problem was we were eating the food at the buffet so fast that they couldn't keep it resupplied, and some of the regular customers were complaining.

How could we be held responsible for them running out of food? For God's sake, it was a Saturday night. They should have anticipated something like this. From what we had heard, the Ponderosa had been serving kids coming to Milwaukee to join the Army for the last ten years. They accepted the Army's meal tickets and were a favorite feeding place for the new recruits.

I just don't think they ever encountered this many country boys starving from a seven-hour bus trip before, and, of course, a few of us did have the munchies from the marijuana. I thought some corporate bigwig at those restaurant chains was supposed to plan for every possible contingency. The manager also accused us of hiding food. He just couldn't believe that we had cleaned out the shrimp bowl, not once, but four times. We were just getting started when they asked us to leave. Before we knew it, the cops had been called and were in the restaurant trying to resolve the altercation. As soon as they realized we were from out of town and there to join the Army, they told us to get the hell out of the restaurant or they would take us to jail. My shouted question to the cops as we were hustled out the door was:

"If all you can eat doesn't really mean all you can eat, then just what the hell does it mean?"

We didn't get more than twenty feet from the front of the Ponderosa before Danny, Stick and I were approached by three black guys. They were wearing long dark coats and wool-knit hats with their Afros stuffed inside. This was a little strange because even though it was early evening, it was still seventy degrees outside. It was hot for an early summer night in Milwaukee. As they approached us with their hands in their pockets, one of them spoke.

"Hey, white boys, what you doing in my city? You all best give my boys and me some money so we can buy dinner or it's going to be a very short night for you farm boys. Reach into your pockets and come up with forty dollars, so I can buy me some supper. Let's just call it a tax for being on my personal property without my permission."

"Be careful," Danny whispered. "I'm pretty sure those guys are packing."

The others in our group were scattered around at this point. Looking over my shoulder and seeing the cops who had rousted us from the restaurant standing by their cars, I was feeling safe. They were only twenty feet away and could easily overhear our conversation. I couldn't believe that these guys were stupid enough to attempt to rob us right under the noses of the local cops.

Frankly, I was pissed off. We had just been kicked out of the restaurant, I was still hungry, and now these assholes were trying to shake us down.

"Fuck you and get a job if you want money."

Danny tapped me on the shoulder. "Don't be stupid, Roger, let's just leave, this is not worth getting shot over."

Still feeling brave, because of the proximately of the police, I just couldn't help myself. "Get out of my face before I kick your ass and mail the pieces back to your mama, black boy. That is, of course, if you even know who your mama is?"

All three pushed out their chests and shoved their hands deeper into their pockets.

The same one who did the talking before said, "You wouldn't be so brave if you didn't have a whole fucking Army standing beside you, cracker. You all better have some firepower because my boys and I do, and we ain't afraid to spill some honky blood. I don't even know why I'm wasting my time talking to you," he sneered. "We should just waste your white ass and be done with it."

I'd never been known for my caution or discretion, and with the recklessness of an eighteen-year-old, what the hell, I decided to push it just a little bit more.

"I don't need anyone to help me out, you fucking lowlife scumbags." I yelled over my shoulder, "Guys, no matter what happens, no one interferes."

I sure hoped they weren't taking what I said seriously because, to be perfectly honest, these guys looked like they could truly hurt me if they wanted to.

"OK, ass wipes," I said as I removed my jacket. "How do you want to do this? Do you want to fight me all at once or one at a time? Don't be shy, cocksuckers, you decide, and I'll comply." The talker for the group walked up to me and put his face about an inch from mine. He looked me in the eyes and then turned to his friends.

"This mother-fucking white boy is crazy, let's blow."

With that, they turned and walked away.

Sensing victory and feeling quite full of myself, I immediately began to push the envelope even further and yelled, "Go ahead, you chicken shits, I bet ..."

I never got to finish my killer final line, because Danny and Stick had grabbed me, thrown me to the ground, and were holding their hands over my mouth to keep me from causing any more trouble.

"What the fuck were you thinking, you crazy asshole," Danny said. "Are you trying to get us all killed on our first trip to Milwaukee? I thought that was the Army's job. At least let them send us to a combat zone before we get shot at. The way you're going, we are all going to be dead before we get to the first strip club."

"I don't know what you were all so afraid of? Didn't you see the cops were right behind us. Those boys weren't going to nothing with the police so close."

Danny began to laugh. "Yeah," he said. "I saw the cops. I also saw them get into their car and hightail it out of here when they saw our welcoming party. You dumb shit, you were getting ready to go up against three guys that the cops didn't want any part of, and I am positive they had guns with them. But no, tough guy Roger has to challenge three ghetto boys to a brawl, not one at a time, but all at once. Those guys were right about one thing, you are one crazy son of a bitch."

The others who moved in afterwards agreed, and as I dusted myself off, all the while continuing to exclaim that we could have taken them quickly, even without the help of the cops, I was silently thanking the Lord for not letting me get into a fight.

Danny, seeing right through my bluster, said, "Cut the shit, Roger, we don't believe you and I don't think even you believe you. This ain't home, Bubba. No one here is going to get in a fist fight and then walk away. You have to remember you're in the big city now."

He was right. I didn't really know why those guys walked away, but maybe they did think I was a crazy white boy.

Next stop and the highlight of the trip, the reason we had endured the bus ride. Strip clubs! This was the payoff for the long miserable journey down here. We quickly discovered that there was a whole lot about strip clubs that we didn't know. I thought, how hard can it be? Go to a club, watch naked women dance, and put some dollar bills in their G-strings. Boy, was I ever wrong. Some clubs charged an entry fee of twenty bucks just to get past the front door. As soon as we discovered this fact, we quickly eliminated these clubs from our list.

Other clubs required a three-drink minimum at ten dollars per drink, and that didn't include the requirement to purchase three drinks for the dancers. The dancers' drinks weren't even real drinks, they were ice tea or coke, but they charged you the same price as the alcoholic drinks. That's sixty dollars shot right there, and that was just the overhead fee; it didn't count the money you would need in the club.

I was beginning to think that none of the clubs on our list would be in our price range, which was not very much.

A lot of the clubs we stopped at wouldn't even consider letting us through the door, something about an Army of rowdy kids. One club appeared to be open to the public but claimed it was a private club, and you had to be a member to gain entry. To become a member, we would have to purchase a club card, which was a paper business card, and it would cost us each $150. While we stood outside the entrance and argued with the bouncer, we watched several older guys in suits be given complimentary membership cards and welcomed inside.

Oh well, another club off the list. There were a lot of clubs that didn't have high entry fees, but they required a coat and tie for entrance. Most of us didn't own a suit, and if we did, we certainly hadn't brought them on an overnight trip to Milwaukee. I was starting to get a little confused. Why did you need a tie to watch naked women dance? It almost seemed counterproductive.

One of the clubs in town was featuring Miss January 1973, but the closest we got was a glossy brochure from one of the bouncers as he told us to move along. At least it provided some excellent whacking-off material that we didn't have to pay for, not to mention how many lies we were going to be able to tell the guys back in town. No, for us, the recommendation of the day was hamburger. We were destined to wander the bottom of the capitalist heap with cheap beer, watered down drinks, chicken wings, French fries with chili, and older, or should I say, more mature women.

After what seemed like hours of endless searching, we finally ended up at one of Milwaukee's premier strip clubs, the Nasty Lady. I think the name says it all. We agreed that the dancers of the Nasty Lady shattered our raised expectations, but as the booze flowed and the joints got passed around, the dancers magically started getting better and better looking. Must have been fairy dust in that place.

The evening began with us joking and harassing the dancers about how old they were. I would bet that many of them were easily old enough to be our mothers. We just kind of watched, drank, and made cruel jokes as we sat off in a corner a little way from the stage. As the evening progressed, we found ourselves starting to interact and enjoy the company of these women. By the end of the evening, despite our lack of funds and discretion, they had assembled around our tables. We were having a blast, and no one wanted to leave when the bouncer announced that it was closing time.

I must admit, they weren't the best-looking women I've ever seen naked, and they were a little older than I expected, but all in all, they turned out to be a lot of fun and quite exciting ladies. During my life, I have been to many strip clubs in many countries and met all kinds of strippers. In summing up my first experience that night at the Nasty Lady, I would have to say, honestly, the people in the club, both the crowd and the strippers, were real people. What you saw is what you got, no pretenses and no false promises. It was as real as it gets.

Just to set the record straight, I did, in fact, get to meet Miss January eventually. Or should I say, see her. She appeared in a club in Seattle in 1976. I suppose that I only saw her because the bodyguards that accompanied her kept everyone at least twenty feet away. It was like they were afraid that you would contaminate her or something if you got too close. I had to wait in line for an hour just for the opportunity to stand beside her and have my picture taken. The picture cost twenty-five dollars, and to have her sign the picture and write, "To my friend, Roger, all my love, Miss January," cost ten more dollars. Thirty-five dollars to get a five-second picture and autograph only to be told to move along so the next guy could take my place. Miss January didn't even have the courtesy to smile or say hi. I wish I would have taken the money and went to one of the strip joints down on the waterfront. I can't even tell you where that picture is. I think I stuck it in one of my files and put it away the following week. Haven't thought much about it or even pulled it out since.

The combination of booze and marijuana had gotten to us pretty good by closing time. It was almost three o'clock in the morning. We didn't have to be at the Army testing center until eight. We still had nearly five hours to find the Y, get sobered up, have breakfast, take showers, and make our way to the testing center. Well, one out of five wouldn't be bad.

While we were in front of the Nasty Lady arguing about breakfast or finding more beer, we were approached by the same sergeant who had met us earlier in the evening at the Greyhound bus station. This was apparently not his first rodeo. From years of experience and dealing with thousands of drunken recruits, he knew precisely where and what time to find us. The U.S. Army, ever vigilant, was not taking any chances of us getting lost and not making it in for testing and processing. With his assistance, we were summarily led, dragged, and carried back to the Y. By the time we arrived, it was almost five in the morning. The sergeant told us that he would be in the lobby at seven a.m. to pick us up and take us to the station. That was in two hours. He was going to need a lot more than the force of the United States Army behind him if he expected us to make the deadline.

Moron

## Chapter 8

### AFEES

The dumbest guy in the world could have figured out that none of us would make it to the lobby on time. The sergeant who had escorted us back to the Y several hours earlier showed up and began banging on our doors at six thirty, but as soon as he got one of us up, the others were back in their beds. Realizing that he was facing a no-win situation, he gave up and went back to the testing station to get some reinforcements. Returning with a band of privates to assist him, the Army physically dragged us from our beds and threw us into cold showers. Even with his privates to help, the sergeant had a tough time making his deadline.

No one had even bothered to change from the night before; we crashed wherever we ended up in whatever we happened to be wearing when we passed out. The Wolverines had fallen asleep everywhere—floor, bed, or chair, it didn't matter. We looked and smelled as you would expect a bunch of drunks to look and feel. We all needed real showers, coffee, and breakfast, but none of that was going to happen. We were so far behind schedule that it looked like we would not be able to make it in time to test. One by one, the sergeant and his privates carried or led out wet, smelly teenagers, hungover or drunk, to several vans that were parked in front of the YMCA. Most of us were put in the vans still asleep. There was a lot of morning-after puking and dry heaves, but somehow, we all made it to the Armed Forces Entrance and Examining Station (AFEES) in time for the first battery of tests. I was utterly intoxicated and sick to my stomach. I had one swollen eye shut. To this day I couldn't tell you how I got that black eye, and even in my drunken state, I realized that I was stinking to high heaven of booze, sweat, and vomit.

All in all, I was in perfect condition for testing. It is not a good idea to take any kind of test after less than an hour of sleep and forty-eight hours of drinking and pot smoking. It was now irrelevant. I was there and somehow made it on time to start testing, and Big John told me that there was no way anyone could fail the Army entrance test. How bad could a bunch of tests be anyway? I was not thinking very clearly that morning, but I seem to remember that there were a whole lot of tests that morning. It all passed in a coffee drinking, sleeping, head aching blur. Drink two large cups of lousy coffee, stumble through the explanations of the test reporting process, show your driver's license, and let the guy in charge know that you were competent and sober enough to be tested. For the Army, responsible and sober meant showing them that you could walk and breathe without falling down too many times.

No one seemed concerned that we couldn't walk in a straight line and that most of us were sleeping in the chairs as soon as we took our seats in the testing room. We were asked to read a form that said we understood why we were there and that we were prepared to be tested. From what I could see, there were guys I was sure were going to have to put their "mark" on the form, as there was no way some of these boys were capable of reading and writing. I was a little confused. Was I testing to get into the Army or to get into a grade school? Based on the looks of the guys around me, I thought that a mental institution made more sense. At least I could relax a little. If these morons could pass the Army test, then I would have no problems

After the reporting process was completed, we were led into another room, the testing room, to take our first test of the morning. The Army made a big deal about everyone being awake for the instructions at the beginning of each test. For some strange reason known only to the Army, you had to be awake and alert for the reading of the instructions, but after the instructions were given, they didn't care what you did during the test. When everyone had told the officer in charge, some second lieutenant, that he understood the instructions, he could do whatever he wanted. For me it was to go back to sleep and try to soothe the massive, throbbing headache that was tearing me apart. The only rule the testers enforced was that you couldn't leave your seat or the room until everyone was done with the test. No problem. After each set of instructions, I would immediately place my head on the desk and drop into a deep sound sleep until the testing officer woke me up with his two-minute warning.

"Gentlemen, you have two minutes to complete this portion of the test. Two minutes!" the officer would scream before the end of each test section.

When it got down to the last thirty seconds, he would count off the seconds from thirty down to zero, and when he got to zero, he would yell: "Gentlemen, this phase of the test is complete. Place your pencils on the table and turn your exams over."

This part of the test was apparently as crucial as the instructions. The lieutenant made a big deal of making sure that all tests were turned over before telling the sergeant to pick them up and pass out the next test. This was pretty much how my day went. I resented all the interruptions to my sleep and wished they would just go away and leave me alone. I needed to rest up for the trip home.

I had no clue how I was doing on the testing, and frankly, I wasn't too concerned. Big John had told us that the only way you could fail would be to die during the exam. Looking around me, I figured dead drunk I could do better than most of these losers. Remember McNamara's 100,000? I suspected that many of them had joined us in Milwaukee that morning. My strategy was to wake up every time the lieutenant yelled out, "Two minutes," and then blacken out as many of the little test blocks as I could in the final two minutes. I was using what I like to call my "middle of the road strategy." Since there were only three or four answers for each question, I decided to fill in all the middle blocks. I figured I had a twenty-five to thirty-three percent chance of getting the right answer on every block I filled in. What I didn't understand at the time was that just being able to figure out the odds of getting the right answer made me a fucking genius compared to my fellow test takers.

The sergeants at the testing center clearly knew how low the intelligence was of the people trying to join the Army under the McNamara plan. To make sure they made their monthly quota of new recruits, they used some protective measures to get the recruit numbers needed. After the sergeant came in and collected the tests, he would tell the lieutenant it was time for him to take a short rest while he passed on some administrative information to the recruits. The instant the lieutenant left the room, he gave the tests back to us. The sergeant would then have us check every fifth answer on the test. It would go something like this:

"Go to question number five, if you didn't mark C, then change your answer to C now. Go to Question number 10, if you didn't answer B, then change your answer to B now."

I think you get the point. Now I knew why no one would fail unless he were dead. Even with this added assistance, the sergeant had to go around the tables and help some of the recruits by pointing to where they should put the correct answer. From where I was sitting, it looked like we were all going to pass the Army entrance test. This discovery made my test taking a whole lot easier. I abandoned the middle of the road strategy. I went to sleep at the start of each test and waited for the sergeant to come after the test and give me enough answers to obtain a passing score. I could deal with this.

The sergeants had their jobs cut out for them because, I swear to God, they actually had to fill in the blocks for some of these guys. I assumed that most of my fellow test takers had spent the last forty-eight hours the same way I had. They all appeared tired, stoned, and hungover. I didn't realize at the time that some of these guys were, in fact, mentally retarded. I would run into many of them later in the Army, and, in some cases, I would have supervisors who were illiterate, mentally retarded, unstable, and sometimes all three.

If I hadn't been so drunk, maybe I would have realized what a monumental mistake I was getting ready to make. Perhaps that's why the Army makes you go to Milwaukee. I don't know how many of us would have gone through the testing procedure had we been sober enough to understand the consequences at the time. Drug addicts, alcoholics, illiterates, more than a handful of criminals, and a smattering of mentally retarded guys were all there to be tested. This was going to be America's all-volunteer Army. We even had one homeless guy processing with us. He was either homeless or just enjoyed carrying all his shit around with him in a shopping cart.

However, I was so naive back then that I probably would have continued even without the alcohol. I really wanted that car. At eighteen, you tend to ignore the bad and only see the good or what you imagine to be good. For my fellow Wolverines and me, getting a new Trans Am was excellent.

After a grueling day of testing, during which I assumed we had all passed, it was time for a quick box lunch and onto the medical examinations. During lunch, they allowed us to use a game room with pool tables and foosball tables in it. No one was using them because they were coin operated and cost a dollar a game. Everyone at the testing station had, like us, spent all their money the night before. The Wolverines quickly rectified the situation and provided an opportunity for some free lunchtime entertainment. The strategic placement of some plastic cups in each pocket of the pool table and sandwich boxes stuffed in the foosball goals provided a no-cost alternative. Within a few minutes, all the tables in the room were in use, as our fellow test takers picked up on our money-saving techniques. I can't believe they couldn't figure it out themselves.

I'm sure the government lost some income, but it made for some happy young men. I had the opportunity to visit the testing station many years later. It had, of course, been remodeled many times over the years. One thing that hadn't changed was the recreation room. There were more pool tables and foosball tables, and there were the new electronic games. I had to smile when I noticed that the potential recruits placed drink cups in the pockets and sandwich boxes in the foosball goals. Some traditions are just too good to end.

For the medical and physical portions of the examination, once again breathing and walking counted for a lot more than the actual medical condition of the individual. Many of the guys trying to process had obvious physical issues. It certainly didn't take a doctor to notice them. The Army was mainly concerned about the number of teeth you had and the condition of your feet. These were the only reasons I saw anyone get washed out. I understood the feet part because of all the marching you must do in the Army, but for the life of me, I couldn't understand the teeth issue. It should be cheap to fix teeth so you could keep more guys in the Army. They sure had some strange rules.

Just like in the testing phase, the Army made sure there was a sergeant in each of the physical exam rooms so that as many of us as possible got through the physical phase. The Army doctor was so old that he could have examined George Washington during the American Revolution. He was hard of hearing and often couldn't hear anything we said, asking us to repeat ourselves several times before he figured it out.

He would ask, "Have you ever broken any bones?"

The typical response would be, "Yes, Doctor, I broke my arm playing football ..." or skiing or some other activity. The doctor would look at the sergeant who would yell in the doctor's ear, "Sir, he said no broken bones."

If anyone looked back at those exams, I'm sure he would have found us to be the most perfect human specimens in existence. According to our physicals, none of us had a hint of a blemish, and we were all in excellent condition.

One of the guys who was in-processing came from Chicago to enlist. That should send up all kinds of warning signs. Why come to another town to get into the Army when there was a testing station in the city you came from? We heard that the Chicago station was bigger than the one here. When this guy took off his shirt, I understood why he had to come to Milwaukee. He had bullet wound scars down the side of his back. There were three of them, and they were fresh. I had been hunting for years, and I knew a bullet wound when I saw one.

You guessed it. The doctor asked, "Any scars or wounds?" The sergeant yelled in his ear, "No, sir, no scars or wounds."

I learned his name was Spider, and he was only sixteen. The Chicago police shot Spider during an attempted armed robbery. Since it was his fourth felony arrest, the judge was going to sentence him as an adult. Lucky for Spider, but unlucky for America, a recruiting sergeant happened to be in juvenile court that day and told the judge he thought the Army could straighten Spider out. It would save the city and the courts money and keep a kid out of adult prison. The judge, according to Spider, said he would "sponge," I think he meant to expunge, his record if he joined the Army and stayed out of trouble for two years. The judge said he would give Spider to the Army if they got him the hell out of town that day. The sergeant transferred Spider up to Milwaukee to process into the Army. Spider was scheduled to ship to Fort Knox for basic combat training the minute he got through the testing station. His training was expected to start the following Monday.

Even though this was the all-volunteer Army, not everyone at the testing station was a volunteer. Yes, it was true that the military was no longer drafting, and they had lowered the physical and mental standards as low as they could go. However, even with these lowered standards, there were still shortages that had to be filled at all cost. That was where the American legal system came into play. I would estimate that one out of five young men in-processing with us that day were sent there by courts, police officers, or the juvenile system. I am confident of this estimation because these guys were not shy about telling everyone they met that they were forced to come to the processing center against their will.

The phrase, "Enlist in the Army or serve time in jail," was thrown around a lot in the early seventies. Some of them even had guards assigned to them to make sure they didn't run away. Many of the judges gave them a little bit of an out if, for some reason, they were not physically qualified. The courts would let them go if they passed all the other tests. No one in the legal system wanted to waste time sending a kid to jail because he wasn't physically qualified to enlist. The only way you could get out of joining the Army if you were court-directed was to fail the physical part of the examination. Based on the lack of rigor on the part of the doctors and misdirection of the sergeants, it would be nearly impossible for anyone to fail the physical.

One bizarre guy at the Milwaukee center even concocted a plan that he was sure would prevent him from being selected for the Army. Before the rectal exam, he crammed some chunky peanut butter into his ass crack.

When he bent over and spread his cheeks, the doctor jerked back and declared, "Young man, do you realize you have shit all over your ass?"

The kid reached back, scraped a hunk on his finger, and put it by his nose to sniff, then placed it in his mouth, saying, "Your right, Doc, it is shit."

The sergeant in the room, not missing a beat, yelled out, "Excellent cognitive abilities, good sense of taste and smell. Next."

Needless to say, not only did he not get out of the Army but was doomed to forever be known as "peanut butter ass."

All afternoon I stumbled from station to station to complete my Army in-processing. If your breathing was bad, the sergeant substituted someone else's breathing test. If your eyes were terrible, some sergeant told you what to say when the doctor pointed to the eye chart. Even if you tried to fail, the sergeant would read the eye chart for you. It seems like they spent more time and money preparing fake physicals and tests than they would have spent if they'd just sent everyone directly into the Army.

One of the more interesting testing stations was for the Army hearing test. At this station, a medic ushered us into a large room with ten chairs on each side. On each chair were a headset and a cord with a plunger attached to the end. The doctor who provided us the instructions told us to place the headset on our heads and hold the plunger in our right hands. When we heard a sound on the earphones, we were told to push the button on the plunger and hold it down until the noise stopped. As soon as the doctor finished providing his instructions and left the room, a sergeant came in and told us:

"The testing procedures have been changed. I need you all to look at the big red light at the end of the room. When you see the light go on, push your plunger and hold it down until the light goes out."

How interesting. Unbeknownst to modern science, the Army invented a method of measuring hearing by using vision.

The final station at the testing center was the urinalysis. The sergeants were taking no chances at this station. The law at the time required that all personnel involved in the urinalysis testing process sign to verify that the urine belonged to the guy with his name on the bottle and that the container was sealed when it was turned into to the testing officer. No way was I going to pass this test. I had been drinking and smoking pot all night long. I was surprised that Big John hadn't warned me about this part of the test. I peed in my little bottle and passed it to an examiner. He put his initials on the bottle to verify that he had observed me peeing into the bottle and had me sign on the label as a cross check. What he didn't do was place the unbreakable, tamper-proof seal on my bottle. This was to come later.

When I was done, and the examiner left the room, the sergeant poured my urine into a sink and rinsed out the bottle. The container was refilled from a large plastic bladder, the type you find in those boxes of wine. When my bottle was refilled, he recapped it, placed a seal over the top and had me initial the seal. Perfect. A urine sample with the examiner's initials and the person being tested verifying that it had not been tampered with, all topped off with an unbreakable tamper-proof seal. This made it clear there was no way that these bottles had been altered.

I wonder how they ever explained to the Army laboratory why everyone had pissed the exact same amount in the sample bottles. Or, more importantly, how all of us had exactly the same blood type and same chemical makeup. It's funny that I pissed O positive, but when I got my dog tags, it said AB negative. I guess they would take chances with paperwork but didn't want to risk someone getting the wrong type of blood during a transfusion. Come on, they did have some ethics, didn't they?

Notice the trend here? I don't know why the Army bothered to test anyone. It would have been cheaper and more efficient just to eliminate the guys that couldn't get through training.

After pissing in a bottle, being stuck for blood, and having a doctor look up my ass and feel my balls, the ole turn-your-head-and-cough, I only had one more processing station remaining. That was the psychological exam. Talk about weird. We went into a room one at a time, and the examiner asked four or five of the stupidest questions you could possibly imagine. The only problem from the test that I remember was, "Would you rather kill a cat or slap your mother?"

I have no idea what answer they were looking for or why, but I must have answered it correctly because they allowed me to move forward in the test. Depending on your answers, you got to leave the room, or you had to move on to a shrink who would make you look at a bunch of inkblots on paper cards. I am not a shrink, but I can tell you those tests were worthless. You wouldn't believe the psychological issues that some of the people I met in the Army had. The Army was full of nuts, weirdos, criminals, and mentally retarded soldiers. Maybe this is what the Army had intended all along. Perhaps I had gotten it all wrong and the purpose of the testing was to ensure that the Army could bring in psychopaths. If that was their intent, they did an outstanding job.

Following the psych exam, I was told to get dressed and take a seat in the main waiting room. For me, it was more like a crash-and-take-a-nap room. The alcohol and drugs in my system were wearing off, and weariness was beginning to set in. After about an hour of waiting around, a sergeant came in and read off the names of those who had not passed on the examinations that day. There were not many of these, probably only twenty or thirty out of about 550 to 750.

Unfortunately, two of the Wolverines were eliminated, one for flat feet. We could have saved them the time it took to conduct the examination. His nickname since the first grade had been Penguin. He walked like a penguin, and his feet slapped the ground as he walked. Even though he had flat feet, I still didn't understand why they wouldn't let him enlist. Back home he played football and ran the two-mile event on the track team. He was in better shape than most of us, and his feet never stopped him from doing anything athletically. Years later, I heard he was competing in and placing high in marathons across the country. The Army missed the boat on this Penguin.

Our other no-go was Paul Schmidt. Sadly, Paul's blood sample came back positive for leukemia. It was good and bad. Good in that they caught the disease in time to provide him with some treatment that allowed him to live for five years. Five years with his family that he wouldn't have otherwise. Bad, obviously, because cancer is terrible. They didn't tell Paul or us at the time. We didn't find out until several months later when we got a letter from his mom letting us know he was in the hospital. It was tough on Paul and his family as well as a shock for all of us. At that age you think that you are invincible and expect all your friends to be the same. He was the first person our age we knew who had any kind of significant disease.

One of the things I regret the most in life was how bad we teased Paul over that summer about failing a chicken-shit Army medical examination. There are a lot of things that I said or did in my younger years that I wish I could take back. One thing I've learned in life, you can't take anything back.

As soon as the guys who failed were removed from the room, a team of soldiers came in and divided us into three groups. Those who would be leaving in the morning for Fort Knox, those who had to return on Sunday to select job training and assignments, and the last group, those who had signed up for the delayed entry program. We would be going home and waiting for assignment instructions, which would arrive later that summer. The sergeant told us that since the Wolverines had signed up for the combat arms option, we didn't have to select any job training. The Army decided it for us; we were all going to be in the Infantry. The Army did offer us the opportunity to move to the line that was going directly to Fort Knox, but none of us were dumb enough to take them up on it.

When we were all in our groups, a lieutenant in a fancy green uniform with one medal on his chest, sauntered in, climbed up onto the stage and stood before us. While he was standing there, a couple of soldiers came in and set up and American flag and an Army flag.

Then a sergeant in the back of the room yelled: "Attention! Quiet down and listen to the lieutenant."

Reading from a three-by-five card in a monotone voice, the lieutenant said, "Congratulations, men of the all-volunteer Army. You are all patriots. You are part of history. Your nation thanks you for your service, and for being America's first volunteers."

That wasn't quite right. I knew a little bit about history, and we were not the first volunteers. What about the original Minutemen?

"Please raise your right hand and repeat after me.

"I, state your full name (Roger Berlin, I said), do solemnly swear that I will support and defend the Constitution of the United States against all enemies, foreign and domestic; that I will bear true faith and allegiance to the same; and that I will obey the orders of the President of the United States and the orders of the officers appointed over me, according to regulations and the Uniform Code of Military Justice. So help me God.

"Gentlemen, welcome to the United States Army."

With that, the lieutenant turned and walked from the room, the soldiers removed the flags, and we were handed enlistment documents to sign. All the forms had been pre-signed by the lieutenant and one of the sergeants. Those of us who could read began to scan through the ten-page enlistment document; however, we were quickly stopped and told, "Just hurry up and sign the goddamn documents. Your buses are waiting to take you to your final destinations, and we don't want you to miss them. Don't waste time reading. … There is nothing to worry about, the government doesn't lie and always keeps its promises. … You can trust us that everything is OK."

As soon as we had our enlistment documents in our hands, the sergeants hustled and prodded us until we had all signed the papers. This wasn't hard because most of us still weren't thinking very straight from the night of hard partying. We were not allowed to keep any copies of our documents. They promised us that they would send copies to Big John, and we would be able to pick them up in his office any time next week. We were then all sent in separate directions to board buses to the airport or head over to the ID card section.

The last stop in my day-long journey into the all-volunteer Army was to be issued an ID card. No, these were not the typical military ID cards. I wasn't officially in the Army yet, so technically they couldn't give me an identification card. I was told that I would be issued my real Army ID card when I got to basic combat training (BCT) at Fort Knox. The card I was getting was a small, white, cardboard card covered in plastic. On one side of the card was the Army seal and on the other was my name and serial number, along with the following statement.

"The individual carrying this card is a member of the United State Army. Before arresting or booking on any charges, please contact Sergeant First Class John Bagwood at the following phone number 906-774-2356."

Bagwood was Big John. The phone number on the card was for the recruiting station back in Iron City. The Army was not going to take any chances. No way were they going to risk any of us disappearing before we got to basic training. It looked like they had covered all the bases.

One more thing. I'm sure you will appreciate the humor in this one. My serial number was US6275798. I had just received my "scarlet letter" (US62 was the Army's designation for an individual of marginal intelligence, one of the

100,000.While I never got the best grades in high school, I had graduated and had a near photographic memory. When I took the college entrance exams at the end of the school year, I scored one of the highest scores in the history of our high school on the ACT. I was what they called smart but lazy. I prefer smart but not sufficiently challenged. I was now a full-fledged member of the United States Army's "Moron Corps" and didn't even know it. I had the dubious honor of achieving the lowest possible score you could get and still be allowed to enter the Army. Chalk one up for drugs and alcohol. How ironic one of the smartest to join the new all-volunteer Army was considered to be in the lowest possible intelligence quadrant. This was going to be an exciting ride, to say the least.

The Army was not going to let us spend a second night in Milwaukee and allow us to get into any more trouble. We were marched straight from the testing station to the Greyhound bus station where the bus for the Upper Peninsula was waiting for us. Our gear was already loaded on the bus, and there was an MP on board who was supposed to make sure that no one went through any of our bags. On each seat of the bus, there was a box lunch. This was Saturday evening dinner. Unfortunately, we were not provided the opportunity to hit a liquor store before departure. I wasn't concerned because most of us had a little bit of booze and smoke remaining in our bags. At least I thought we had. What I didn't count on was the MP who was supposed to be guarding our bags had gone through them and stolen our goodies. He didn't take any valuables. He only stole things that we couldn't complain about because they were illegal. I wondered why he had such a big smile on his face as we pulled out of the station.

The trip back to Iron City was uneventful. No booze, and no drugs. Just a bunch of tired, worn-out, hungover Wolverines. It hadn't sunk in yet that I was in the Army. I looked and acted the same as when I had left for Milwaukee, but something had fundamentally and irrevocably changed. I was now, for all practical purposes, a soldier. The whole oath-and-contract signing thing had happened so fast that it was just a blur. I crashed as soon as the bus began to move and slept the entire return trip. I was so out of it that it seemed like just a few minutes had passed before we were pulling back into town, entirely oblivious to the future ramifications of my forty-hour trip to Milwaukee.

Chapter 9

Departure

My last summer at home was a complete haze; it was like I was living in a dream. When I think back on it, no matter how hard I try, I just can't seem to remember what I did. I spent the entire previous year looking forward to completing high school and doing whatever I wanted to do. Now that I was here, I didn't know what to do. My friends and I had all kinds of plans and schemes for that summer. We had agreed that nothing was going to be off the table, and I can't for the life of me recall anything outstanding. I do know that it included a lot of drinking and smoking dope.

Of course, there were the exaggerated stories about what we would be doing as soldiers, especially to Paula. You just never know when the "This could be my last summer, you know I'm going to war" trick might work. I kept up a tough exterior. After all, I was going to be a soldier. But I was starting to worry that I was going to miss her a whole lot more than I thought I would.

I do remember a summer of apprehension and fear of the unknown. For the first time in my life, I didn't have someone else to rely on to take me into the next year of my life. I was going to be on my own, finally. Whatever my future was going to hold, I was going to be the one who molded it. What I did or did not do would dictate my future.

At some point in our lives, all of us go through a significant change. We graduate from high school and really don't know where we're going or what we're going to do. High school graduation is a turning point in the lives of young people. Nothing will ever be the same again. You realize that for the first time in your life, your friends are all going in different directions, and you don't fit in at home anymore. You have outgrown your family, your community, and your friends. It's scary and exciting at the same time. You would rather be back in school playing ball or fishing with your buddies, but at the same time, you want to be independent and strike out on your own.

Before I was ready, it was time to leave. I was frightened to death, and I am sure the rest of the Wolverines were as afraid as I was, but at eighteen you don't show fear to your friends. You just suck it up, pretend all is fine with the world, and move forward. My mind was filled with thoughts of all the things I had never got around to doing, and all the things I had never got around to saying, especially to my parents and friends. Something told me that my friends, who I graduated from high school with, whom I had assumed would be friends for life, would soon be distant memories. Everyone promises to stay in touch, but it never happens. The only guys that ever keep in touch are the ones who get stuck in town and hang around the bars or work in the mills together. None of us really wanted to be those guys.

I don't think that I realized I was really leaving home forever. I wasn't sure I wanted to go, but, you know how it is, you talk about something so much that you back yourself into a corner and you can't back out no matter how frightened you are.

Not all the Wolverines had the same issues that I had, or the same level of concern about letting people down. Some guys can back out of anything. On the day that we met up at the airport to depart for the Army, three Wolverines never showed up. Big John didn't miss a beat. He told us that the missing Wolverines had some last-minute issues to take care of and that they would be joining us later and that everything was going as planned. I never saw the missing three in Army uniforms, and despite being best friends before joining the Army, I never again spoke more than a few words to any of them. To this day, I honestly don't know what caused them to change their minds.

Forty-five years later, whenever I would run into one of the three who dropped out, he would awkwardly say hi, make some quick small talk, and then come up with an excuse to disappear. It's clear they were ashamed or harbored regrets that they had not gone through with the deal. From what I could tell, they just hung around town, got jobs, and continued the same lifestyles that they had in high school. They'd go to the same bars, eat at the same restaurants, and maintain the same boring, mundane lives that they lived when they were teenagers.

The tiny Iron City airport was a madhouse that final morning. It seemed as if the entire town had turned out to see the Wolverines off on our adventure. Big John had the mayor and local congressman there to give speeches, shake hands, and provide an official air to the event. No self-respecting politician would miss an opportunity for free press. Between the political groupies, the high school band, and family members, there were quickly 250 people at our grand departure. Not bad for a small town, but as far as I was concerned, the quicker we got out of there, the better off I would be. I just wanted to get going before I changed my mind.

Big John worked it so that both the local newspaper and radio station were there to send us off, and to get himself some additional "free" publicity to help with the next batch of recruits that he was working on back at the high school. As a dramatic backdrop, the Trans Ams were parked in a semicircle at the entrance to the airport. It was a breathtaking sight, and I often wonder how many people came to see the cars one last time, compared to those who came to see us off. I bet that if we had taken a poll, the vehicles would have won.

I don't remember any of the speeches or even the subject of any them. I don't even remember saying goodbye to my family and my friends. The first memory I have of that day was being in the air in a small puddle jumper airplane on my way to the Chicago airport, so I could transfer to another plane for the connection to Fort Knox, Kentucky. It was interesting to see the Trans Ams from the air because of the way they were arranged. They looked like a frowning face.

I have flown on hundreds of flights since that day. That was the quietest flight I have ever been on. The only sounds I recall on the airplane from takeoff to landing in Chicago was the pilot giving his spiel over the intercom and the sound of the engines as we sped away from home and family toward the unknown. You would have thought that the excitement of our new adventure would have me talking like a jaybird, but that wasn't the case. I was in my own little world, thinking my own private thoughts, and facing my own secret fears.

Moron

Chapter 10

Arrival

The time spent on the flight to Fort Knox gave me the last calm moments I would have for a long time. It was about eight in the evening when we finally landed at the airport in Lexington, Kentucky. When we got off the plane, we were met by an Army sergeant who told us where we could pick up our bags and then directed us to stand in the parking lot in front of the airport along with hundreds of other young men arriving. Everyone looked the same, confused and worn out.

After about thirty minutes of waiting, a long line of big, ugly, green buses came down the road and pulled into the parking places at the airport. Before they came to a complete stop, Army sergeants in perfectly pressed uniforms and wearing ranger-style hats started jumping off. They soon began screaming and attempting to gather and control the several hundred young men standing in the parking lot, herding us onto the waiting buses.

Everything began to happen at once, including sergeants yelling and Army recruits trying to ask questions. Everyone was bumping into one another, hoping to comply with the insane commands of the sergeants. There were guys from all over the country, all sizes, all colors, and some with accents that I couldn't even begin to place. Some of these guys couldn't speak English. The Army had several Hispanic sergeants on hand to control the Spanish-speaking recruits. I even saw several Asian guys who spoke Chinese or Korean, I'm not sure which. To get them on the buses, the sergeants pointed in a general direction and then pushed them along with the crowd.

Each ugly, green Army bus had a letter of the alphabet painted in bright red on the passenger side of the windshield.

A drill sergeant would scream at us, "Get on the bus with the letter that matches your last name. If you don't know your last name sit down, and we will assist you, now move it and get your slimy civilian asses on my buses. Move! Move! Move!"

Now if you thought, this is simple, all we had to do was get on the bus that had the same letter as the first letter of our last name; no way could we could screw this up, you would be wrong. We began boarding the buses at nine in the evening, but it was close to ten before the sergeants could get everyone sorted and on the right bus. Along with the yelling and screaming, bags were getting lost and some guys were crying or begging to go home. We would later discover that during this madness, some of our fellow future soldiers were busy going through everyone's bag, stealing anything of value.

The bags that guys brought to Fort Knox were as varied as the people carrying them. I saw everything from a set of polo leather bags with a guy's name embossed on them to a kid with long hair and torn clothing carrying two paper bags. One young man was barefoot and had no bags. Now, I thought, I have really seen everything. I had no idea how he got onto an airplane without shoes, but maybe it was considered normal in some parts of the country. I was reasonably naive at the time, but this was nothing compared to what I would see before this little adventure was over. When everyone was finally on the right bus, the sergeants took the bags we had left in the parking lot and tossed them onto a waiting Army trailer. It was total chaos, but finally, we were on our way.

The bus ride to Fort Knox was nothing like the subdued atmosphere on the plane. Because we were separated by the first initial of our last name, the Wolverines ended up on different buses. Although it was late at night and everyone was worn out, everyone on my bus seemed to get a second wind. All the recruits were trying to talk at the same time. You would have thought there was a prize for the guy who could out-yell the guy next to him. The best I could tell from the jumble of conversations going on around me was that these guys were all experts on the Army. They were offering their sage advice to anyone they could out-shout.

Only one not letting everyone around him know how important and tough he was sat in the seat directly in front of me. He was about five foot seven, a small, thin guy with bright red hair and freckles on every inch of his exposed skin. He stood out a little because he was a little older than the rest of us and didn't look anything that you would expect a soldier to look like. I guessed he was in his late twenties or early thirties.

He only spoke when I held out my hand and introduced myself. He shook my hand and said his name was Bob Bradley, then he immediately put his head down and went to sleep. I have no idea how he slept. There was too much going on in the bus, and the volume was too high for me to even think about sleeping. But nothing seemed to faze Bob. He slept through the turmoil. I knew he wasn't faking because I could hear his snoring mixed in with the roar of voices. Unlike the rest of us, he had refused to let anyone take his bag and load it onto one of the waiting trailers. He had his bag lying across his lap and used it as a pillow to rest his head as we headed down the highway.

When our bus passed the front gate at Fort Knox, I knew I was in trouble. Nowhere was there anything even remotely resembling the flashy recruiting pictures of the Army that Big John had shown us. Even though it was late at night, it was clear that we were entering a broken-down, beat-up area. Everything looked old and drab, and as far as I could see, I couldn't make out a modern building or any type of infrastructure. It was as if I had just entered a black-and-white World War II movie.

As the bus drove through the front gate, we passed a large sign that read, "Welcome to Fort Knox, home of Basic Combat Training." The sign itself was a statement on the state of repair of Fort Knox. It was made from cheap plywood, and the painting and wording were faded and began to peel. Across the bottom of the sign were three hand-painted black letters, "FTA." It didn't take me long to learn that these three letters were the unofficial motto of the Army, "Fuck the Army."

I had a sinking feeling in my stomach and thought, how about "welcome to hell?" One of the guys in the back of the bus summed it up for all of us. "Toto, we're not in Kansas anymore."

The bus continued past the front gate and weaved through a series of dilapidated, old wooden buildings. We would later come to know them as World War II Wood. These structures were built as part of the Army's build-up to house all of the soldiers called up to active duty to fight in World War II. There wasn't enough room in the existing barracks to accommodate the millions of extra soldiers needed to fight the war, so they constructed these temporary wooden buildings to house them until the war was over. Now correct me if I am wrong, but I thought the war ended in 1945. If this is the new modern all-volunteer Army, then why were they still using barracks that were temporary thirty years ago? How long is temporary?

The bus finally pulled to stop in front of a building with a giant white sign on it labeled, "Welcome Center." Talk about an oxymoron, nothing was welcoming about this place. When the bus stopped, a large sergeant with a Smokey Bear-style hat burst through the front door of the center and started screaming at the top of his lungs:

"You pussy civilians, get your stinky cunts off my bus now. Move! Move! Move! I don't want you on my bus; I don't want your shit on my bus, GET OFF! Get your motherfucking pussies off my bus."

After the long trip to Kentucky, and the emotions of leaving home for the first time, most of us were too startled to move. Soon this wild man was joined by an army of sergeants who boarded the buses and began to grab guys and propel them out the doors. Witnessing the first of my fellow recruits flying through the air, I got the message and scrambled the best I could down the steps and out the doors of the bus. I think I was in a state of shock and froze in front of the bus door when Bob Bradley grabbed me and said, "Come on, kid, follow me, keep your mouth shut and your head down, this is all for show."

In the scramble to get off the bus, more than one guy got knocked off his feet and landed face first in the dirt, and before he could get up, another sergeant would run over to him screaming, "As long as you're down there, give me ten, trainee."

Although that meant ten pushups, you never got to ten before the sergeants were screaming at you to get up and move before they kicked your ass. I was desperately looking around to see if I could spot some of the other Wolverines but could only see Moose and Stick, both of whom were in the push-up position and getting yelled at. It was common to see another drill sergeant waiting to yell at someone and make him do pushups.

Somehow, in the middle of all this melee of screaming and confusion, the drill sergeants got everyone off the buses and lined up alphabetically by last name in front of the welcome center. Several sergeants walked down each row of recruits with index cards and black permanent markers. They would ask us our last name, write it on the card in bold black print, and then pin the card to the front of our shirts. A second card with the first initial of our last name was pinned to our backs. I was now B or Berlin, depending on which direction I was approached. Most of the recruits had shut up by now. Who wouldn't with the continual shrieking in your face?

One drill sergeant was still screaming at Moose.

"Shut your pie hole, son, or I will knock you on the ground and stick my dick in your mouth to shut you up. No, on second thought, I wouldn't do that, you'd like that too much, wouldn't you, sweetheart? I can spot a fag a mile away and, son, you're my fag now."

Moose was asking for it. The entire time he was being yelled at, he kept a big-ass grin on his face. He wasn't trying to be an ass; he was just one of those guys who smiled a lot when he was nervous.

The shock-and-awe technique used by the drill sergeants worked because we eventually shut up. The sheer overwhelming force of the assault wiped out our defenses. Even the guys with the smart-ass comebacks and comments finally subsumed to the onslaught. When we were under their complete control, the drill sergeants marched us into the welcome center, which was a large auditorium with hundreds of old-fashioned school desks lined up in rows. You know, the kind with the small, round table attached. How did they expect grown men to get into those tiny chairs? We were told to move behind a chair, ground our equipment, and keep our mouths shut and eyes forward. It didn't take a lot of yelling and screaming this time. For anyone who didn't move fast enough or couldn't keep his mouth shut, the response from the drill sergeants was fast and violent. Offenders would be rushed by several screaming drill sergeants who would knock the offender's desk over with one yelling:

"Don't you understand English, trainee? Are you here to fuck with me? You must be some kind of communist infiltrator."

This was the first time I was hearing the term "trainee," but it wouldn't be the last. It would become the name I responded to every waking moment and in my nightmares for the next eight weeks.

The room was as silent as a morgue, and we each stood behind a desk staring straight ahead. A monster of a man with more stripes than a zebra appeared on the stage. In a voice way too calm and soft for his stature, he told us to take a seat. He introduced himself as "Sergeant Major God." That's right, "God." He explained to us that referring to him as God was not sacrilegious because he was, in fact, greater and more powerful than any god that any of us had ever prayed to. He was more powerful because not only did he have the power of life and death over us, but God, he declared, had a fatal flaw. "God shows mercy." The sergeant major assured us that he did not possess that flaw and had never shown mercy to a trainee in his entire life.

The sergeant major went on to say, "I knew the minute I was born that it was my destiny to become a soldier. I love everything about this Army. This is my Army, and I jack off every night while rubbing my M-16 so that I can have a good night's sleep.

"There are only two things on this earth that I detest. One is anyone who disrespects my Army, and the second is civilians. I hate civilians so much that as soon as I was old enough to realize that my mom was a civilian, I killed her and ran away from home."

I think I believed him. He was capable of killing someone, and from the way he was talking, there was no doubt in my mind that he was certifiably insane.

After the sergeant major's "I love everything in the Army" speech, he told us that despite what our recruiters had told us about bringing prohibited items to basic training, he was confident that many of us had shown up at his Army post with contraband items.

"Contraband," he said, "consists of the following: pornography, guns, knives, razors, brass knuckles, nunchucks, blackjacks, alcohol or drugs of any kind to include aspirin and women's underwear." He continued, "At the four corners of this room, you will see that the Army has taken great pains to provide you with four large wooden boxes. Each box has slots in the front to allow you to place your contraband inside. My drill sergeants and I will leave this room for exactly thirty minutes, not one second more or one second less. During that time, you trainees will deposit any contraband you brought with you in those boxes. We will not be watching, and we will not ask any questions about anything we find in the boxes. You do not want to have any contraband in your possession when we return. Is that clear?

"When we return to this room in exactly thirty minutes, we will conduct a strip search of you and your gear. The search will include drug dogs. Anyone caught with contraband will be arrested, tried, and found guilty, and should be on your way to federal prison before lunchtime tomorrow. I assure you that the Army does not waste time on criminals. Don't even think about your legal rights. You gave all your rights away when you dumb shits joined my Army. The only rights you have from now until the day you're discharged are the rights I give you, and that will be zero."

When he ended his speech, he and the drill sergeants in the room suddenly vanished. I was nervous because I had a stash of marijuana with me, and I knew that the dogs would be able to smell it as soon as they walked in the door. I believed every word the sergeant major had said and decided that this was not the time to take any chances. As soon as I started to get up and head to one of the boxes, Bob put his hand on my shoulder and said, "I wouldn't do that if I was you. If you got something with you that will make this place a little better to tolerate, I would hang on to it. Trust me, it's going to be OK."

I was scared to death and, I don't know why, but I listened to him. A lot of the guys in the room got up and started shoving stuff into the boxes, but arguments ensued throughout the place.

How could they possibly search everyone? Send my ass to prison in one day, bullshit. I have been arrested a hundred times, they can't use the stuff against us as evidence. It's unlawful search, and seizure.

One black kid from Detroit was particularly outspoken and extremely loud. He was attracting the attention of the entire room.

"Shit, those knuckleheads are too stupid to find my stash. I been hiding drugs from cops smarter than these guys my whole life. If the Detroit cops couldn't catch my ass then, how are a bunch of dumb soldiers gonna?"

That's right, buddy, I thought, if the cops never caught you, then what the hell are you doing here?

The Army was nothing if not punctual. Precisely thirty minutes to the second, all the doors in the room burst open and a stream of drill sergeants poured through. Along with them were a contingent of MPs in shiny silver helmets with large MP armbands and, most disturbing of all, four snarling and snapping German shepherds. I went into panic mode. Why did I listen to a guy I had just met on the bus? I'm screwed. My first day in the Army and I'm going to jail.

As soon as the MPs and dogs entered the room, two of the dogs began barking and acting crazy. They dragged the MPs holding their leashes over to where Detroit was standing and knocked him to the ground. I couldn't believe it. Detroit was lying face down with two dogs snarling over him and the MPs and remaining dogs surrounding him. Within ten seconds, the MPs had jerked Detroit to his feet, stripped him naked, and had everything he owned pulled out of his bags and piled on the floor in front of him. Several drill sergeants began to rip through his now discarded clothing and belongings, then tossed them in a pile. The MPs released the two dogs, who went nuts and started tearing his clothes and belongings. One of them began pushing a can of shaving cream around the floor with his nose.

This was the most thorough search I had ever witnessed, and I was scared shitless that I was going to be next. The MPs ripped apart everything Detroit owned. They turned every pocket of his pants and jackets inside out, pulled the souls off his shoes, tore his books apart, and systematically destroyed all his stuff. Every time they encountered a lump or bulge in anything, they would cut it open with a large bayonet-style knife that one of them carried with him. In less than thirty seconds, they had amassed a pile of contraband from Detroit's belongings, which they presented to two drill sergeants who carried the collection up to the stage and placed it on the floor in front of the sergeant major. The MPs then dragged the stunned and still naked Detroit up to the stage and had him put his hands on a table, spread his legs, and lean forward. There in front of all of us was a naked black boy from Detroit with his bare ass facing us and the two German Shepherds snarling and snapping at him.

The pile of stuff they had taken from Detroit was being thrown on the stage in an ever-growing collection for all to see. Some of the items I could make out included a knife, a straight razor, and decks of cards, "marked," according to the sergeant major, who quickly flipped through them. The MPs, who had grabbed the can of shaving cream from the dogs, screwed off a false bottom and declared it to be filled with cocaine.

The sergeant major told the MPs, "Great work, guys. My drill sergeants will put everything in evidence bags. Take the prisoner away."

The MPs threw the now sobbing, totally nude Detroit to the ground, cuffed him, dragged him back to his feet by the handcuffs, and marched him, dick waving and crying, out of the room in front of all of us. I was stunned. As fast as it had begun, it was over. The sergeant major retook the stage and, in his calm voice, let us know that the contraband they had removed from Detroit's person and belongings would typically result in a prison sentence of about ten years. However, since the crime had occurred on federal property, the punishment would be doubled to twenty years' confinement with hard labor.

"The Army," he said, "maintains its own prisons and we still believe in hard labor. Anyone ever hear of Leavenworth?

"In case you haven't, that's where soldiers are serving time, breaking big rocks into little rocks. That's where your fellow trainee will be calling home for a large part of his life."

The sergeant major bowed his head and moved slowly across the stage. After several audible sighs, he turned to us said, "I just hate this shit. Every class it's the same thing. I have to send twenty or thirty of you young men to prison. I know what happens to young men in prison, and it just makes me sick to have to send so many of you there every training cycle. This doesn't have to happen if only they would have listened to me and taken the opportunity I provided them to dump their contraband in the amnesty boxes. What a waste of a life. I just wish there was some way to avoid all of this, but I guess it is what it is. You trainees never learn."

Sighing one more time, he raised his head and yelled out, "Sergeant Smith, commence the individual searches."

As the MPs and drill sergeants began to get us out of our seats and lined up, one of the sergeants hollered, "Everyone stands down for one minute," and then he ran up to the stage and whispered something to the sergeant major. For the next three minutes or so, they engaged in some type of argument, adamantly debating something. Because the trainees were now talking to one another about how to get rid of contraband, I couldn't hear a word the two men were saying, but from the gestures that were exchanged and from their body language, it was clear that there was some type of disagreement going on. At the end of the conversation, the sergeant major shrugged, and the drill sergeant left the stage.

The sergeant major looked up at us and, with a great sigh, said, "Gentlemen, I have been informed that I made a mistake in my earlier briefing and maybe you did not fully understand the contraband instructions or the implications of not taking advantage of the boxes in this room. So, I am going to repeat my briefing one more time."

He then went on to repeat his amnesty box briefing from earlier word for word. At the end, when he got to the part about thirty minutes, he said, "Gentlemen, I have never given a group a second chance before. Don't make me think that I have wasted my time. All of my drill sergeants will now leave the room. We will be back in exactly thirty minutes."

Once again, he, the MPs, and the drill sergeants disappeared from the room.

The millisecond the doors clicked shut, there was a mad dash by almost everyone in the room to the amnesty boxes. Guys were fighting one another to get rid of contraband and stuff it into the boxes. They were so shaken up that some were even tossing away items that were apparently not on the contraband list, but no one wanted to be the next guy caught with anything illegal. I was part of that mad rush, and I began tearing through my stuff, looking for my stash. I was not going to prison for a bag of grass. I had to get rid of this stuff at all costs. How was I going to explain to my family and friends back home that my Army career had lasted all of one day and that I would be spending the next twenty years of my life in a military prison? Hell, I would be thirty-eight when I got out. I didn't think guys' dicks worked once they got past thirty. I had to get rid of my stash and fast. Bob once again grabbed my arm.

"Not so fast," he said, "everything is not always what it appears in the Army. Leave it be, you're going to be OK."

"No way!" I replied. "I can't spend twenty years in jail for a couple of bags of dope."

Bob just looked me straight in the eyes and said, "Relax. Look, if you don't trust me, give me your stash and I'll hold it for you, but for God's sake, don't throw that stuff away." Once again, still not knowing why I trusted him, I decided, against all common sense, to hang on to my dope and hope that my faith in Bob was justified.

The amnesty boxes were overflowing, and stuff was piled up on top of each of them, spilling over onto the floor. I don't know how these guys had hidden that much stuff in their gear. Once again, the Army was right on time. The second thirty minutes were up, and all the sergeants and the sergeant major returned. Climbing back on the stage and looking at the amnesty boxes, the sergeant major declared:

"Trainees, I see you didn't waste your second chance. Because you didn't waste my time and have restored my faith in young soldiers, I am not going to waste your time. I believe we have a good group here."

With that, he marched off the stage, and he and the MPs departed the room.

"Told you so," Bob whispered.

I assumed I would never see Detroit again, unless I screwed up and ended up in Fort Leavenworth with him. But I was wrong. About a year later, I was back at Fort Knox and happened to run into Drill Sgt. Detroit at one of the snack bars on post. It struck me as appropriate that the Army had used the stage in the welcome center when they set up the amnesty box show for us new trainees.

The remainder of our processing for the evening (now early morning) was spent signing for the things we would need to survive for the next few days, or as the drill sergeants informed us, until we moved into our permanent units and the Army could provide us a full issue of equipment. We were issued blankets, sheets, a pillow, a towel, toothpaste, soap, shaving cream, deodorant, a safety razor, and a toothbrush. We were then broken into groups of one hundred and marched out of the processing center, down the street to some old barracks buildings.

Each building had fifty metal bunk beds and could accommodate a hundred trainees. Accommodate is a term we learned in those first days at Fort Knox. To the Army, accommodate means, "How many people can you cram into the available space?"

The stuff they issued us was useless because there was no time for grooming. We couldn't even take a shower or brush our teeth. The drill sergeants allowed us a quick bathroom break, and we were told to hit the sack. One of them told us, "Tomorrow we will be waking you cockroaches up at five a.m. to finish processing. The Army is going to let you sleep in because it will be Sunday morning and, because it's your first day, we want all you precious little soldiers to be comfortable." As he shut out the lights and walked out the door, he turned his head and said: "Don't get used to these luxury accommodations because when you maggots get to your training units, life is going to get really tough and you will not be allowed the luxury of sleeping in until five a.m." Little did we know that he was not kidding.

It was so late when we finally got bedded down that at best, I was only going to get three or four hours of sleep that first night. That is, if I could sleep in a room that sounded like the inside of a machine shop at full production. Who knew a hundred sleeping guys could make so much noise? Everyone was in bed, but between the heavy snoring and the sobbing from someone who wanted to go home, I thought I was never going to be able to fall asleep. But somehow the mind overcomes all objections, and along with most of my fellow trainees, I dozed off and got a solid three hours of sleep that night.

One thing about the Army, when they give you a time, they meant it. At precisely five a.m. the following morning, a drill sergeant came into the barracks and walked down the row of bunks, banging two metal trash can lids together.

"All right, scumbags, wakey wakey time. Drop your cocks and grab your socks. Welcome to your first day in the service of Uncle Sam."

No one should have to feel the way I did that morning. I was disorientated, confused, and bone tired, and those were just the good things. My nightmare was just beginning.

I didn't know it at the time, but I was looking at my future life. This was what my life was going to be like from now on. No more sleeping in, no more six hours of school and then an afternoon of relaxing, no more hanging out with my friends, no more doing what I wanted to do whenever I wanted to do it. My life as I had come to know it was over. If this was what being an adult was all about, then maybe I would have been better off if I had figured out some way to go to college and stayed a kid just a little bit longer. I wasn't sure the privileges of adult life were going to be worth what I was going to have to give up obtaining them.

My first day in the Army, and it was a Sunday for God's sake, was complete madness. I spent the day standing in lines and waiting for stuff to happen.

The first thing I learned on my first day in the Army was that the official motto of the Army wasn't "Be all you can be;" it was, "Hurry up and wait."

In addition to being world-class experts in making you wait, the Army didn't like to waste gas on using vehicles for anything less than two miles. They marched us everywhere we went. Gone were the days of going anywhere by myself.

From now on every time I moved, I would be taking my entire unit with me. That morning we marched to breakfast, and then we marched to church. No one asked me if I wanted to go to church or even what denomination I was. The drill sergeant told us, "Every last one of you swinging dicks is going to attend church today. The Army doesn't care what God you believe in. Everyone in my Army goes to church. Only communists don't believe in Jesus, and there are no communists in the Army. If you don't believe in God, then keep your mouth shut and don't tell me. I don't want to know if I have any goddamn heathens in my Army."

After morning church, the afternoon was spent attending classes given by a bunch of Army attorneys. They called them all-volunteer indoctrination briefings. At the first briefing, some Army attorney gave us background on what to expect. Remember what Bob told me, "Everything is not as it seems in the Army?" The first briefer was a young Hispanic captain.

"Hello, my name is Captain Juan Diego Gonzales, I am an Army lawyer, and I am here to talk to you about the all-volunteer Army. The Army calls its new force the all-volunteer Army or the VOLAR Army."

He went on to explain to us that we were all going to be part of history. "For the first time in two hundred years, there will be no conscripts joining the U.S. Army. The draft is over, and you trainees are the first volunteers. Besides becoming an all-volunteer force, the Army will be making some fundamental changes in how it treats its all-volunteer soldiers. Drill sergeants can no longer swear at trainees, they cannot lay their hands on you, and they cannot demean you in any manner." Someone forgot to tell those guys that we met last night that there were some new rules.

Capt. Gonzales gave us his building number. He said, "If any of you trainees ever feel violated or uncomfortable, ask your drill sergeants to release you, and please stop by my office so we can talk. I will make sure that things get straightened out." He went on for about a half hour on how there were new rules and regulations to protect us.

As soon as he left the building, the biggest, ugliest, but certainly not the tallest, man I had ever seen, strolled to the front of the classroom. He stood about five foot five and was nearly as wide as he was tall. His arms were so big that his shirt had slits with extra fabric sewed to them to accommodate his massive biceps. His neck, if you could call it that, was twenty-eight inches around if it was an inch.

He said, in a deep bass voice, "My name is Drill Sergeant Guimanymanalmana, but none of you white boys, spics or niggers can pronounce that, so you can call me Drill Sergeant G.

"I'm from the island nation of Guam, and I'm the worst motherfucker on my island. What did you pussies think of the captain's excellent briefing?"

Uh-oh, I thought, this is not going well.

Slowly walking over to the edge of the stage like a lion stalking prey, he singled out the biggest trainee in the room. Everyone who joins the Army acquires a nickname, and this guy had earned the moniker "Mountain." He was from a farming community in Louisiana and was a big, strong farm boy. He was one of those guys who was quiet most of the time, but you didn't want to piss him off because you knew if he ever lost his temper, you were dead meat. Guys who came from Louisiana with him and had seen him mad said if he turns red, the safest thing to do is run. Drill Sgt. G asked Mountain to move to the front of the room for a small demonstration. Drill Sgt. G jumped down from the stage and slowly walked around and around Mountain while continually speaking.

"The captain say in the new volunteer Army, I can't touch you. The captain say in the new volunteer Army, I can't use naughty language. The captain say in the new volunteer Army, I can't demean you or your family. The captain give you his building number and say you can come and see him if you have any problem. Do you understand the captain's briefing, big boy?"

Mountain immediately said, "Yes, Drill Sergeant."

As soon as the words left Mountain's mouth, Drill Sgt. G spun on his heels and delivered a powerful punch to the center of Mountain's chest. Mountain's knees collapsed, and he crumpled to the floor. As he lay gasping for breath and puking on the floor, Drill Sgt. G, with veins popping out of his neck and arms and with spittle leaking from the corner of his mouth, began his tirade.

"You stupid fucking nigger, your mother is the biggest whore in Louisiana. I've had her about a hundred times myself. DON'T BELIEVE NOTHING YOU HEAR," he screamed, "especially from officers. Those stupid pussies don't know nothing about nothing." Spinning back to face the rest of us, he straddled the prone and gasping Mountain. With spit spraying from his mouth on every word, he said, "There ain't no fucking VOLAR Army. Me and my fellow drill sergeants run this Army and we own your body and soul. Anyone complains to anyone, and I will personally rip your head off and skull fuck you. Is that clear?"

"Yes, Drill Sergeant," we responded loudly in unison.

"I can't hear you!"

"Yes, Drill Sergeant," we repeated even louder.

Several trainees went to Mountain's aide to help him back to his seat but were immediately stopped by Drill Sgt. G, who demanded, "Don't touch that trainee, unless you want to join him. Allow him the dignity of crawling back to his seat like a man."

While Mountain was trying to recover and get back to his seat, another drill sergeant accompanied by three official looking MPs walked in to give us the rest of our VOLAR Army legal brief.

The sergeant started, "This is an all-volunteer Army, and we only want the best soldiers in our new Army. When you signed your enlistment documents at the Armed Forces entrance station, you signed a document that said that you were free of drugs and alcohol and had no arrest records, warrants or court appearances pending. The document that you trainees signed is what we call an official government document. It is a federal crime to lie or mislead anyone on an official government document knowingly. If you lied about taking drugs, you would be arrested, and you will go to jail. If you lied about alcohol, you would be arrested, and you will go to jail. If you lied about your arrest record or any pending court appearances, you would be arrested, and you will go to jail. Now, does anyone here want to tell me about anything they might have lied about on this official government document or does anyone have any changes they want to make?"

The entire time he was speaking to us, three large MPs stood at attention behind him, looking very stern and eager to arrest someone. I wasn't surprised in the least when no one had any changes to make.

The final briefing for the day was another boring legal briefing about the enlistment process for the VOLAR Army. This briefing concentrated on the role of the recruiter in assisting us to join the volunteer Army. The briefer, another drill sergeant, passed out a pile of documents to each of us when he made a series of statements, followed by a penalty if we had, as he said, violated any federal laws. The three MPs remained at the front of the room throughout the briefing.

"If anyone here received any incentive from your recruiter other than an authorized bonus, that is against the law. The punishment is confinement for up to five years in federal prison and a fine not to exceed twenty thousand dollars. Did anyone here receive any such incentive? If you did not, please check the no block, that would be the black block on the front of your form."

Surprisingly, or maybe not, all the no blocks on our forms had already been checked in advance to save us time. How nice of the Army to help us like this. I guess they had a lot of confidence in their recruiters.

The Wolverines already knew about this part of the briefing. Big John had given us a heads up before we left Iron City. He told us to answer every question, "No." We wouldn't be lying, he said. He was just worried about the other trainees who would be jealous of the deal we got. "You see," he told us, "I'm afraid if the other trainees found out, they would all want new cars and the deal I have with the Wolverines could be at risk. Frankly, there weren't enough Trans Ams to go around, so it will be better for you guys if you just keep quiet and make sure that you say no in every place it asks a question on the form."

The rest of the briefing followed the same format.

"Did your recruiter ask you to lie on any forms you completed for the Army?"

"Did your recruiter assist you on any of the entrance examinations before you came in the Army?"

"Did your recruiter coach you on any portion of the medical examination before you came in the Army?"

"Did your recruiter assist you with any law enforcement officer, judge, parole officer, or juvenile officer before you came in the Army?"

"Did your recruiter coach you in any way on how to pass a drug test before you came in the Army?"

The questions went on and on like this. It seemed that there would never be an end to the questions. After every series of questions, the drill sergeant giving the class told us how much time we would spend in jail, and how much money we would be fined.

When he was finished, he asked, "Did anyone yes on any answer?" If so, he said, "Please step forward so that you can be read your rights by the MPs and be arrested."

Of course, there were no yeses. I guess that we all had great, honest, ethical recruiters.

When we were finished with all the briefings, Capt. Gonzales came back into the room and passed out some more forms to everyone. The Army had a form for everything, and if they didn't have one, then they would make one up. When we all had our forms, he asked us to raise our right hands.

"Please repeat after me," he said.

"I, state your full name. Do solemnly swear that the affidavit I am signing is true and accurate. I have not been promised anything or threatened in any way to elicit my signature on this document.

"Please sign your name at the X on the bottom of the form."

I noticed that the legal officer had already signed all the forms as the officer administering the oath and that a drill sergeant had already signed as a witness. I was comforted knowing that I had joined an organization with such high integrity. After all, they went to great pains to make sure no one had interfered with the recruiting or testing process.

Thus ended my first full day as a soldier, hours upon hours of boring briefings, getting screamed at, degraded, and pushed around. Everything came at me so fast and confused that I was just a little off balance all the time. I wanted to check on my fellow Wolverines, but I was unable to make contact with them, much less be able to speak with any of them. I was the only B in our group, so I was on my own. At least the Ms had some hometown company. There were three of them. I was hoping that when I got out of the welcome center and to my actual platoon, we would all be moved back together as the Wolverine platoon. At least that is what we had been promised by Big John when we signed our enlistment forms.

My second night in the Army was no better than the first. After all the bullshit briefings and thousands of pushups, coupled with the stress of being screamed at for everything little thing I did wrong or not fast enough, I was utterly exhausted by the time they called lights out. It was only ten p.m., early by teenage standards, but I didn't complain as I collapsed into my bunk. I remember hearing the snoring and wondering once again how I could possibly fall asleep with all this racket, but I was so exhausted that I immediately crashed. The next thing I remember is the pounding of a metal garbage can lid. Oh my God, it's only four a.m. It's funny how your mind and body can become acclimated to something. Within a few days, I began to think of the sound of garbage cans as an alarm clock. I still sometimes wake up to the sound of my alarm clock and wonder why I didn't hear the trash can lids being banged together.

Moron

## Chapter 11
## BCT

Four a.m. is too damn early. Nothing living gets out of bed this early. Roosters are still sound asleep, and the early bird isn't even thinking about worms yet. I don't know why the Army insists on getting up so early. We don't get any more done, and you always end up with a bunch of pissed-off, tired, and exhausted young men. I'm sure anyone who ever conducted research into early risers would discover that most of the Army's disciplinary problems occurred because people get woken up too early in the morning. It pisses people off to get up so soon.

Boy, I missed home. Instead of Mom yelling, "Hurry up, you'll be late for the school bus," some asshole caveman in a Smokey Bear hat was screaming:

"Get your hands off your cocks and get your stinking asses out of my beds. Today is your lucky day, faggots. You are all moving to the United States Army basic training location. May God have mercy on your soul, because no one else gives a shit whether you live or die. Move! Move! Move!"

This was the beginning of basic combat training, or BCT.

I was up, dressed, had already run two miles, worked out, cleaned my barracks, made my bed, showered, and lined up outside of the mess hall at 0530 hours—that's five thirty a.m. The Army used terms like mess hall and chow for a reason. It didn't want to associate eating or anything you do in the Army with anything even remotely similar in the civilian world.

You will never hear the word culinary or fine dining associated with the Army. Army eating is nothing like you would expect or ever see anywhere food is served. I include serving food to animals in this statement. I firmly believe the Army went out of its way to find the rudest, most surly individuals to serve as cooks. Most Army cooks had been fired from other jobs in the Army. The mental requirement to become a cook in the Army was even lower than the mental criteria to become an infantryman. I would like to meet the guy who decided that the health and nutritional needs of the Army should be left to the Army's lowest mental category soldiers.

An Army basic-training mess hall was a small, wooden building that seated about seventy-five soldiers comfortably. The problem was there were over a thousand of us sharing this mess hall. The drill sergeants moved us through the chow line in groups of a hundred. Seventy-five would be eating while twenty-five would be rolling in or out. As soon as the last person in the group got twenty feet from the door, the next group of a hundred was lined up directly behind them.

Drill sergeants roamed up and down the line, screaming at you to run in place or drop for pushups or sit-ups. Just because you were waiting to eat was no reason to allow you a moment to relax. The last obstacle before entering the building was to climb up on a chin-up bar and complete five chin-ups. If you were unable to do the pull-ups, you went to the back of the line and kept trying until you could. Eventually, you would be allowed in, but not without a lot of harassment. If you wanted to eat without a lot of bullying, you had better figure out how to get your five chin-ups done, or it was going to be a long eight weeks. That first week, none of us could complete the chin-ups to the drill sergeants' standards, but we got better fast.

The turmoil didn't end when you entered the mess hall. You immediately yelled out your serial number and your status. You were RA, Regular Army; NG, National Guard; or AR, Army Reserve.

I had to yell out, "RA US675798 Drill Sergeant, request permission to enter the mess hall."

When you were granted permission, you signed your name on a sheet of paper and moved to the serving line. In basic training, it didn't matter what you wanted to eat because you were going to get what they served, and you were going to eat it. The servers behind the line were fellow trainees who had been unlucky enough to be tagged for KP (Kitchen Police) duty.

This duty sucked because you had to get up before everyone else to set up, serve the food, later clean everything, and get ready for the next meal. A typical day of KP started at 0200 hours (two o'clock in the morning) and ended about 2200 hours (ten o'clock at night). When you finished pulling your KP, you stunk of grease and food for three days. No matter how many showers you took, you still smelled like a walking French fry.

Breakfast in the Army was a massive pile of scrambled eggs and seven to ten strips of burned bacon; it depended on how many the server grabbed. To this they added two slices of cooked ham and four slices of toast with creamed chipped beef poured on top of the pile. This was referred to as shit-on-a-shingle, and that is what it tasted like. In addition to these somewhat traditional breakfast foods, you were also served a heaping spoonful of grits. Who in the hell invented this as breakfast food? Grits, I learned, was something that everyone in the South ate for breakfast, and they loved it. Grits are ground-up hominy.

I had never heard of hominy or grits before. At Fort Knox grits were served with butter, salt, and pepper. For some reason, all the Southern guys couldn't get enough grits. At the end of the chow line, there were cold cereal and sweet rolls in case you needed more food. Everyone had to take one roll and at least two biscuits; cereal was optional.

This culinary delight was topped off with as much coffee, milk, and juice that you could drink. There was no limit, you just had to fit the glasses and cups on your tray. The Army didn't believe in plates or bowls. Everything was served on a large metal tray with indentations to hold the food. They didn't need the indentations because everything ended up in an enormous big pile. The servers threw the food wherever they could find space on the tray. I had never seen so much food before, and I was not a big breakfast eater, so I didn't know how I was going to eat this mess.

The Army was cramming as many calories as possible into our bodies to help us make it through the long days of training ahead of us. By the end of basic training, I could eat all they gave me and more. Despite the large breakfast serving, we were starving every day by lunchtime. For every calorie they pumped into us, they burned off two. Despite these outrageous artery-clogging meals, I lost weight and gained muscle mass while I was there. I got bigger and stronger, no more baby fat.

Imagine trying to keep thousands of young men fed and somewhat contented with Army meals. The Army knew from years of experience it could screw with you in a lot of ways but messing with your food was not one of them. The Army would occasionally force you to eat cold or canned meals; however, as soon as you got someplace where a meal could be prepared, hot food was served as quickly as possible. I guess somewhere back in history, the Army must have had a mutiny over cold food. The three things the Army did not mess with were hot food, mail, and pay.

Another problem with eating in basic training was you couldn't possibly eat all the food they gave you in the time the drill sergeants allotted for you to eat. To make sure they could push all of us through a small mess hall in one hour and ten minutes, the Army evolved the feeding of trainees into a science. Forty-five seconds through the chow line, forty-five seconds for drinks, sixty seconds to get to a table and find a seat, seven minutes to eat, and forty-five seconds to drop off your tray and get out the back door to make room for the next group of trainees.

There was no time for any special preparation. Having it your way was not going to happen. You got what they had, the way they cooked it, and you ate it. They provided a variety of choices in food, but there was no choice in seasoning or level of doneness. To make sure we didn't get sick on undercooked food, everything was overcooked. The Army cooked, baked, or boiled everything for as long as they could. All steaks were well-done, and all eggs were over hard or scrambled. You got used to it because you really didn't have time even to taste what you were eating. This wasn't eating; it was refueling at its most basic and primitive level.

It didn't take me long to figure out how to eat in the Army. As soon as I got my tray, I would begin to shovel food into my mouth as fast as I could until I got to the drink area. When I moved from the drink area and was walking to my table, I would again shovel food into my mouth. When I got to my table, I ate everything that could be eaten with a spoon first. I used a spoon because Army spoons were the size of small shovels, and you could get more into your mouth with less effort. I didn't have time to cut, so if I got any meat, say a slice of ham or a piece of steak, I ate it with my hands. Anything that could be made into a sandwich was put on bread, and I mean anything. Ham, eggs, potatoes, corn, gravy, it didn't matter. If it fit on bread, it became a legitimate sandwich. To this day, I get flak from friends and family because I insist on turning everything I eat into a sandwich.

No food of any kind is allowed outside the doors of the mess hall. I had to make sure anything I wanted to eat was crammed into my mouth before exiting the building. Every once in a while, someone would try to slip out a roll in a pocket or inside his shirt, but the Army always posted a drill sergeant outside the door who I swear could smell food a mile away, and he invariably caught everyone who tried.

You had to eat everything on your plate. Drinks were the hardest part of the meals because you had no time to sip, so the liquid was taken in large gulps. I quickly learned to tilt my glass up and drain it as fast as I possibly could. None of this was natural and did not come easy. It was a learning process, and it took me about four or five meals to perfect my feeding technique. I swear, by the end of the first week, I was an eating and drinking machine. Not pretty to watch but highly effective.

Years later, I still have a problem with my eating. My family is used to how fast I eat and make fun of me in a good-natured way, but more than once at restaurants, I have had people stare at me when I put mashed potatoes, gravy, and green beans on a roll to make a sandwich. I say, 'Don't knock it until you've tried it.' Whenever I go to dinner with a group of friends, I find that I am done before most of them have even started. It certainly hasn't done much for my digestion. I always have stomach problems that I blame on basic combat meal training. Almost everyone I know who has served in the Army or the Marine Corps has the same problem. The ground troops of America have become a legion of Prilosec junkies. Whenever I see someone wolfing down his food, I invariably ask, "When did you go through basic training?"

The only trainees who were not required to eat everything on their plates were the ones the drill sergeants considered overweight. These were our designated fat boys; they were harassed and treated ruthlessly in the mess halls. It was harder for them to get in the front door. Even if they were in good enough shape for the chin-ups, the drill sergeants felt it was their God-ordained responsibility to force them to burn off as many additional calories as possible while they were waiting in the chow line. It was not unusual to see fat boys running in place or doing sit-ups and pushups while waiting to eat. The drill sergeants never allowed them to stop moving.

No one was allowed to miss a meal. Army regulations said we had to eat three times every day in basic training, but the drill sergeants made it impossible for the fat boys to get much, if any, food into them. A drill sergeant was assigned to the serving line. His job was to ensure everyone received an equal serving of everything on the line. This could be a real problem, especially since the serving trainees tended to give their friends extra of all the good stuff, leaving little for the other guys. I learned within a day or two that the drill sergeants would not tolerate favoritism, but people kept trying to find ways to give friends a little bit of an edge.

No matter what race, religion, or color we were, the drill sergeants were, for the most part, fair to everyone. They treated all of us like shit. They never allowed or condoned favoritism and would severely and quickly punish those they caught extending favors or treating people differently for any reason. I never saw a drill sergeant giving an advantage to one trainee over another. Sure, they treated us like crap, but at least it was fair. The only people we allowed to make fun of us or demean us in basic training were the drill sergeants, and they did it to everyone.

Now, the sergeants did have an exception when it came to the fat boys. They didn't get the same amount of food. The fat boys were not allowed potatoes, gravy, bread, or deserts of any kind. They got half the meat than the rest of us, and they were prohibited from eating bacon, hot dogs, hamburger, or pizza. They were fed large plates of vegetables and all the salad and milk they wanted. For the big guys, it was not unusual for a drill sergeant to put a cigarette out in their food just to keep them from eating what was on their plates. On more than one occasion I watched some poor guy trying to eat around a cigarette butt smashed into his food. On top of these non-verbal insults, fat boys were continually harassed by every drill sergeant in the mess hall.

I have to admit that the fat boys who made it through the gauntlet of abuse generally tended to lose a lot of weight; unfortunately, most of them also lost a lot of their humanity. It was like watching someone breed dogs for fighting. No matter how gentle their spirit when they started basic training, by the time they finished, they all came out with mean, nasty dispositions. It's surprising how humiliating an individual three times a day can break their spirit and alter their personality.

It was also scary how easy it was to get the other trainees to join in on the abuse. I don't know if it was relief that the drill sergeants were picking on someone else or just the dark side of human nature that made so many of us eager to join the crowd and jump in. It does, however, make you think long and hard about your own humanity and realize how screwed up we can become.

After finishing breakfast that first day, we were broken down into what would be our platoons and companies for the remainder of our time at basic training. Unfortunately for the Wolverines, the Army stuck to the tried-and-true alphabetical method of dividing us up. I ended up with the A's and B's. Since none of the other Wolverines had last names in that series, I ended up as the only Wolverine in my platoon. I was pissed because this was not what we had been promised when we enlisted.

Mussio, ever the problem child, decided that he was going to do something about this injustice. At the next formation, he asked Drill Sgt. Guimanymanalmana, "Drill Sergeant, I and my fellow recruits from northern Michigan enlisted under the platoon concept where we are all members of the Wolverine platoon.

"We were guaranteed in our legal contracts to all be assigned to the same platoon for both training and later for our permanent assignments in the Army. With all due respect, I request that we be immediately reassigned to the correct platoons. If you do not assign us together, it would be a violation of our contact, and you would have to let us all go home immediately."

Drill Sgt. G put his face right in Mussio's and screamed at him.

"Don't tell me how to do my job, you dumb fucking civilian. The Army doesn't make mistakes. There is nothing in your contract about being in some pussy platoon with all your faggot buddies from back home. When and if you graduate and become a real soldier and move on, you can get your pussy platoon back together again so you and your buds can all start butt fucking each other again. Now shut your pie hole and give me some more pushups. Next time I want lip from you, I'll scrape it off my zipper ..."

This went on for at least five minutes. No one had any more questions after we saw what Mussio went through. Mussio kept a big grin on his face the entire time he was doing pushups, but those of us who knew him knew that he was seriously pissed off and was already planning his revenge. It was going to be a battle of wits. Drill Sgt. Guimanymanalmana wasn't going to give up, and Mussio wasn't going to admit defeat.

I was assigned to Alpha Platoon E-18-5-A. This was Echo Brigade, 18th Battalion, 5th Company, and Alpha Platoon. This was to be my home, my address, and my very existence for the next eight weeks. The rest of the Wolverines were assigned to the same brigade, battalion, and company, but to a multitude of different platoons. We wouldn't be bunking or training together, but at least we were all going to be on the same street. After getting our platoon assignments, we were lined up once again and a lieutenant accompanied by two armed guards set up a small folding table in front of the welcome center. We were told that the lieutenant was the paymaster and that we would be getting a partial payment from the Army. We were called forward one at a time, once again alphabetically, and were each issued one hundred dollars in twenty-dollar bills. I didn't realize it at the time, but along with giving you money, the Army also told you what you could spend it on.

When we had received our partial pay from the paymaster, the drill sergeants marched us over to the post barbershop one street over. The line in front of the barbershop was about a half-mile long, but it was moving a lot faster than the chow line. We marched in the front door twenty at a time, took a seat in one of two rows of antique barber chairs, and prepared for our first Army haircuts. Because I was toward the front of the line, I was one of the first trainees from our unit to get into the barber shop. By the time I got in, the floor was already a foot-deep carpet of shorn hair made up of every possible shape, color, and texture.

On the wall of the barbershop were two sets of posters, one for black trainees and one for white trainees, depicting the various haircuts that you could ask for. The barber would ask you which style you wanted when you sat down in your chair. Many of us had come through the front doors with hair down to our shoulders, so we picked the style that would leave us the most significant amount of hair. Once I made my selection,

Danny G. I. Pummill

the barber laughed and said, "Who do you think you are, Jody?" He then proceeded to shave our heads completely bald. I had no idea who Jody was. It reminded me of an old movie I had seen of farmers shearing a herd of sheep. The entire experience took less than two minutes per head. When I looked around at my fellow trainees outside the barbershop, I saw that more than one guy had blood on his scalp from a botched cut job.

As soon as our heads were shorn, and everyone was outside, we were lined up and trooped through a small building with a cashier's cage in it. The drill sergeant inside told us that we were each required to pay the cashier five dollars for our new hairstyles: two-fifty for the haircut and two-fifty for a tip. This was highway robbery. I wondered how they got away with it because after basic training, we could get our haircut on any military post in the world for a dollar. Someone was making a lot of money. During basic training, we were required to get a fresh haircut every week. We paid five dollars every time we went to the barber shop during training. I think the bank accounts of the drill sergeant and barbers did quite well while we were assigned to basic training.

When I was finished overpaying for my bad haircut, I waited outside for the remainder of the trainees in the brigade to exit. While we waited we milled around, rubbing the fresh stubble on our now bald scalps. It was strange to observe. A thousand young men were quietly standing around, rubbing their heads and staring at one another. A completely shaved head is a weird feeling. I just couldn't stop rubbing my head and marveling at the unusual texture. It felt like thousands of needles sticking into your head. I was sure I looked goofy as hell, but at least if I looked stupid, then the entire battalion looked the same way.

Freshly shorn and looking like a bunch of cue balls, we were marched by the sergeants back to our barracks where we were ordered to strip down to our undershorts or "underdrawers," as Drill Sergeant Guimanymanalmana called them. When everyone was down to his underwear, believe it or not, we were marched out the door and down the street to the clothing and equipment issue point. We must have made quite a sight, a thousand bald-headed guys in underwear and socks. I hoped no one got any pictures. I was starting to get a good idea of how cattle felt when they were being moved from location to location. Come to think of it, don't they get slaughtered when they arrive at their destination?

After a short march, we arrived at a group of large metal buildings at the end of the street. On the road in front of the building were white footprints with a number beside them. One of the drill sergeants yelled out, "Everyone get on a pair of footprints and stand there until I tell you what to do." After a short wait, the drill sergeants began to move us into the building in groups of one hundred, based on the numbers that we were standing on.

When my number was called, I was marched through the front doors of the largest building where two green canvas duffle bags were shoved into my arms.

"Put one bag over your back by the strap and walk down the red line that is painted on the center of your floor," I was told. "On the red line are green arrows. Continue in the direction of the green arrows. Hold the second bag in your hands with the mouth of the bag open. Follow the red arrows. Do not step off the red line."

Once more, I felt like a cow as I was herded through the building, carefully following the red line and the green arrows. Every three or four steps, someone would hold up an item of clothing, look at me to guess my size, and shove some article of clothing into my bag.

"First station, boxer shorts," a quick look at me, "size large."

Ten pairs of boxer shorts shoved into your duffle bag.

"T-shirts. Large." Ten more in the bag.

"Socks, olive drab, green, size ten." Ten pairs in the bag.

This went on and on until both my duffle bags were bulging at the seams and my arms were full of the extras that I couldn't fit into the bags. I had hats, belts, underwear, uniforms, and all the medals, stripes, and some things I had never seen before and had no idea what they were.

One interesting detail. During my trip through the supply warehouse, this was the first time that anyone in the Army took the time to tell me that I had already been promoted. When I got to the man who passed out the stripes, he gave me ten sets of gold single chevron stripes and said, "Congratulations. You have just been promoted, and you are now officially a private E-2." It turns out that all trainees who had signed up under the delayed entry program got promoted to private (E-2) on the day they arrived at basic training. Good deal. I hadn't done anything yet, and the Army had already promoted me and given me a pay raise. All the trainees who came directly to basic training from the processing stations were private (E-1). They were what we called slick sleeves; they had no stripes. These trainees would be E-1s for six months before they could achieve the lofty rank of private (E-2). I rather liked being a superior officer.

The staff in the Army's uniform issue building didn't measure anything. Somehow, they managed to get most of it right. Many trainees didn't fit exact sizes; they were in between sizes. You know, the ones that are a little too small, a little too skinny, or oddly shaped. But the Army only stocked standard sizes, so these poor guys got saddled with some stuff that was never going to fit them. When they complained, they were told to shut up and suck it up. The guy passing out shirts said, "Just shut up and take it. Anything hanging out can be tucked, cut, or folded."

Several of the trainees in my platoon ended up looking like scarecrows stuffed with cornhusks. It was ridiculous but functional, I assumed.

The only item of clothing that we were measured for was boots. The Army viewed footwear very seriously, taking great pains to ensure that all the shoes we were issued were perfectly sized. They had us walk around a little to get the feel of them. We were issued two pairs of black combat boots with metal islets and two pairs of low quarters (dress shoes). Despite the care they took in measuring us for proper footwear because the boots were brand new, ninety percent of us would be sporting blisters and raw feet by the end of the first week of training. The Army didn't believe in tennis or running shoes. Boots were for combat training.

In addition to our clothing and boots, we were issued some essential combat gear. Helmets, helmet liners, web belts, backpacks, a small shovel, canteens, mess kits, I'm sure you get the idea. The strangest item we were issued was the helmet liner, which was made of spun green nylon in the shape of a helmet. It only weighed about a pound or so and fit inside your helmet. It provided the cushioning necessary to protect your head while the metal portion on top of it contained the bullet and blast protection.

The helmet and the helmet liner together probably weighed six or seven pounds. If you had to wear it for any period of time, your head would be pounding within hours, and by the end of the day, only handfuls of aspirin and Motrin could stave off a throbbing headache. The Army decided that it would be best not to have us wear the full weight of our helmets during most of our training, but we had to have something on our heads, so they made us wear the helmet liners. The only time we had to wear the full combination was when training would include any kind of live weapons or explosives. It took a load off, literally, allowing us to train with only a liner, but it made us look like a bunch of turtles when we were walking around the training areas—those turtles you see in *National Geographic* marching across the sand to the ocean.

There we were, a thousand young men in various types of civilian underwear with wool green knee socks, black boots, and green plastic helmet liners. I still didn't get the whole underwear thing. They either wanted to humiliate us, or they were a bunch of closet homosexuals who enjoyed watching young men in underwear. Each of us was dragging, carrying, or pushing along two pregnant green duffle bags. For some of the smaller guys, the bags were bigger than they were. The drill sergeants wouldn't let anyone help his fellow trainees and insisted that everyone carry his own stuff, so it was every man for himself. Somehow, we made it back to our barracks with all the items we had been issued.

When we got back, we were told to, "Get the fuck out of those queer bait civilian tighty-whiteys and get some real drawers on."

Real drawers in the Army meant the white oversize boxer shorts we had just been issued. We were told to throw our old underwear in a large metal trash can at the end of the barracks. Drill Sgt. G told us, "Get out of those contaminated civilian drawers. I know they're all infected with all kinds of diseases that you picked up from Susie's rotten crotch. The

Army is going to help you all stay healthy and burn all that civilian shit."

As soon as we got dressed, we were given what the drill sergeant called our most important piece of equipment, dog tags. Drill sergeants walked down the aisles, called out our names, and handed each of us four shiny metal tags and two beaded metal chains. On each of the tags were our last name, first name, and middle initial. Directly beneath our name was our service number. Yep, good ole number US675798. Below that was our blood type and our religious persuasion. We were each issued four separate dog tags. Two would always be worn around our necks, and two would be placed in the shoelaces of the boots we were wearing at the time. This, we were told, was in case our upper body was destroyed in an explosion so they could tell who died by the dog tags on the boots or vice versa. Drill Sgt. Guimanymanalmana told us:

"Until the day you leave the Army or die, under no circumstances will you be caught without your dog tags around your necks. If you are caught without them, I will make you wish your body had been destroyed in an explosion."

When everyone was finally dressed, and we had our dog tags around our necks, we were told to place all our civilian belongings in our suitcase, bag, or whatever we had brought with us from home. For those of us who knew how to read, we could keep four books. Porn didn't count as a book, so a lot of guys were out of luck. All our belongings were packed up and were given preprinted labels with our name and our new units on them. Mine was labeled E-18-5-A. Attached to the outside of each of our bags were our name tag and a white tag on a string with our valuables listed on it. I have never been able to figure out why the Army wanted us to register valuables on the outside of our bags. It seemed stupid, but they did it all the time. I guess it was to let thieves know which bags to break into. The only two groups in the world who sign over personal belongings must have been soldiers and prisoners.

The drill sergeants stripped us of anything that could possibly remind us of our former civilian lives. No cards, no letters, no pictures, no food, no jewelry, we were not allowed to keep anything that we had brought to basic training with us except for four books, a wedding band if you had one, and one religious medal, but you were not allowed to wear the religious medal while you were at Fort Knox. You were told to keep it in your locker. We were stripped of anything that would make us an individual or differentiate us from a fellow trainee. When the drill sergeants were done, we all had the exact same clothing, the same equipment, the same haircut, and were all treated the same, like shit. To the naked eye, there was no difference between any of us. For all practical purposes, we were all now Army clones.

Dressed in our new uniforms, we were told to put on our combat belts, called web belts, and fill our canteens with water. This was another basic training rule to have a full canteen at all times. It would become a real dilemma because whenever you drank from the canteen, it wasn't full anymore. Once we had belts affixed, and our canteens filled, we were marched up the street to the final portion of our in-processing.

Inside the final processing building, we were met with another line and another long wait. After about an hour of standing around with a thousand other trainees, I was given a batch of forms with all my personal information and asked to verify the specifics. It didn't matter if it was right or not because when I found a mistake, they blew me off and told me not to worry about it. The common refrain was, "The Army will fix it later."

Why did they even take the time to ask? It was apparently another rule. The Army sure had a lot of rules. I was quickly learning that Soldiers did what they were told, no matter how stupid or ridiculous the task. During basic training, I discovered the Army did things that didn't make sense to the average person, but to the Army, it was critical.

After verifying the forms, for whatever good it did, we were taken to the identification desk where they took pictures of us from the waist up. This was my first official picture. Bald head, oversized clothing and all. This picture would be on the card that was to be my personal identification for the next two years. While we were waiting for them to glue my photo to my new Army ID cards and cover it with plastic, the picture clerk yelled out my serial number. A drill sergeant came over with a small can of white paint and a paintbrush. He verified the number was correct and said, "Turn around, dumb shit."

Then he put a small white dot on the back of my helmet and one on the end of each of my boots. He then said, "Moron, if you can remember this when you get back to your barracks, I want you to march right up to your drill sergeant and tell him that you need to be dotted. You think you can remember that, dumb shit?" This I later learned meant I would have white dots placed on the back of all my shoes and all my headgear. Since you always had to be wearing at least your boots or some type of headgear while you were at Fort Knox, this meant you would always have a visible white dot for everyone around you to see. On my new green Army helmet and shiny new black boots, those white dots stood out like a deer's eyes in the headlights.

About twenty percent of the guys going through the ID card section received the white dot treatment. I didn't know it at the time, but I had just been marked as an official member of the Moron Corps.

At the time, I thought the white dots were cool, and I had no idea of how significant an impact this was going to have on my future at Fort Knox. I assumed that they were marking me for some special type of leadership role because they had recognized my obvious leadership potential. Yeah, right.

Our administrative processing now complete, we marched out of the final processing building and into the medical building directly across the street. The medical building was a long hallway with ten stalls inside. The booths were roped off with white cloth tape, five stalls on each side of the hall that the drill sergeants referred to as "medical stations."

Soldiers wearing armbands with red crosses stood in each of the medical stations, ready to stick us. One solder in each station was holding some type of metal gun in his hand. A flexible metal tube was attached to the gun and ran into a large glass bottle with liquid in it. It looked like something out of a science-fiction movie. The other soldiers in each station were lounging around and had a green canvas stretcher with them, more like a green blanket attached to two sticks. They wore the Red Cross armbands and had longer hair than the trainees. I immediately started to look for the nearest exit as a loud murmur carried through the room, and imaginations began to run wild picturing the punishment that was about to be inflicted here.

Drill Sgt. Guimanymanalmana screamed for everyone to hear.

"At ease and shut your pie holes. Trainees, at this station you will be inoculated against every disease known to modern man. Uncle Sam does not want to let you get killed by a disease. When Uncle Sam wants you dead, he will send you to war. The corpsmen on each side of this building are holding the latest marvel of modern medicine, the inoculation gun. Those guns they are holding are not just any inoculation gun; they are U.S. Army air gun inoculation systems. Their purpose is to quickly and painlessly pump every known vaccine into your disease-riddled civilian excuses for bodies. No need to be afraid; there are no needles. The guns shoot a stream of high-pressure air that will open a tiny hole in your arm, at which time the vaccine will be automatically pumped into your system. When you are getting your shots, you will stand perfectly still. It will not hurt. However, any movement on your part is extremely dangerous. If you move, my guns will rip open your arms. Trainees, if you move, it will be like slicing your arms open with a bayonet. Do not move, is that clear?

"Are there any questions about the procedure that I have just briefed?"

About a thousand hands went up at the same time, mine included. Drill Sgt. Guimanymanalmana looked at us disgustingly.

"Put your fucking hands down, I don't want to hear any of your stupid questions. Just move forward and take your shots like men. If any of you move and gets cut, then you just proved you're a pussy. OK, trainees, five shots each. Move! Move! Move!"

OK, I know I'm not the smartest guy in the world, but how about …

"Are any of you allergic to any medications, are you sick at this time, have you had any of these inoculations before?"

Once again, the Army treated everyone the same. Better to treat all of us, regardless of allergies or problems, than take the time to treat everyone as individuals. I only wish there had been at least one doctor present. These corpsmen didn't seem very well-trained or very interested in our well-being.

Of course, people panicked, and a lot of the trainees moved. No torn arms but a whole lot of blood. Good thing this was the pre-AIDS era because I never saw them wipe off a gun between trainees. By the time I got my shots, I bet the blood of at least fifty guys was built-up on the end of that gun. A surprising number of guys fainted. They were thumping to the ground left and right. It was more like a prairie-dog shoot than a medical processing center. The medics would just scrape them up, roll them onto a stretcher, and carry them outside in the street to get some fresh air. On the way outside, however, they stopped at every station to ensure that, conscious or not, they all got the shots the Army wanted them to have before they left the building. The drill sergeants took great delight in dumping anyone lying on a stretcher for more than five minutes off the stretcher and yelling at him to stop malingering.

To the best of my knowledge, no one died from any adverse reactions, but all of us had sore arms for the next couple of days. The drill sergeant cure for sore arms was, of course, more pushups. "It will circulate your blood, trainee, and you will feel better."

Moron

Chapter 12

## New Home

Sore from all the shots, confused by the paperwork, and sporting sunburned heads, we marched back to the reception station barracks for the final time. Today was the day we were scheduled to move to our permanent homes. When we got back to the barracks, everything was gone. They had taken our personal items and told us they would be locked up for the duration of basic training or, as the drill sergeant had told us, until we graduated, went to jail, or died. Those were the only ways out of here; so much for an all-volunteer Army.

Drill Sgt. G informed us, "All of your military gear has been shipped to your new home. Board the cattle cars outside, and once you arrive, you will find all of your gear neatly stowed in your private air-conditioned rooms."

Private, air-conditioned rooms sounded pretty good to me, but what the hell was a cattle car? I assumed it was merely a military name for a bus or something. In the short period that I had been a soldier (two days), I had already learned that the Army is not satisfied with the names that ordinary people give to items. For some reason, they have this inexplicable need to make up their own names for everything.

They also liked reducing names to letters. For example, basic combat training was BCT, physical training was PT, and Kitchen Police was KP … you get it. I thought a cattle car was just another fancy name for something ordinary. Was I ever wrong. A cattle car was precisely that. Parked in the narrow street between the barracks were ten honest-to-God cattle cars. Ten semi-trucks each hauled a large green trailer that looked like the cars they haul cattle to the slaughterhouse. The containers had a large opening in one side with a set of metal steps welded directly below the opening. Windows consisted of cut-out holes along both sides of the trailer. There were no doors on the opening or glass on the windows, just holes. The perfect conveyance for hauling farm animals.

The insides of the trailers were large open spaces with a metal bar along each wall, the same kind you find in ballet studios, and metal bars suspended from the ceilings. The concept was to cram as many human beings as you possibly could into the back of each trailer, and then ask them to hold onto a metal bar. The door opening was secured with a series of nylon straps woven into a web shape that locked on the outside of the trailer.

Once you entered your cattle car, you could not exit until a drill sergeant unlocked the webbing and released the passengers inside. There was no emergency exit, and no one except the absolute smallest of us had any chance of getting out one of those holes referred to as windows. There was no air-conditioning/heating system. You had to rely on whatever the wind blew in to cool you off or keep you warm. It was exactly as advertised, a cattle car.

My first ride in the cattle car was a nightmare. A thousand of us trustingly entered these vehicles and tried to survive the journey over to our permanent homes. No one knew how to hold on, how to balance, or how to keep from being slammed into the metal sides of the trailer. It took most of us four to five trips before we figured out the best stance and best places to stand to protect our body from serious damage. You had to decide on the outside wall, where you were guaranteed to be slammed into the sides of the trailer but at least could get some fresh air, or the inside, where you would be cushioned by the bodies of the other recruits but had no fresh air.

After being crammed into our modern Army transport, it was only a short twenty-minute ride to our new home. Ah yes, home for the next eight weeks. Home for my new closest friends and me.

Home consisted of a paved street with fourteen World War II wooden buildings, seven on each side of the road. The Army built these buildings as a temporary measure during

World War II. There was no room to house the massive buildup of troops, so the Army requested money from Congress to build new housing for the influx of new soldiers. Congress figured that the war was not going to last forever and didn't want to spend precious resources on permanent facilities. One of the drill sergeants told us that all the thousands of buildings on Fort Knox had been built in only 90 days. It showed. Well, here it was 1973, and the buildings were still here and still being used. It looked as though the Army had not performed any maintenance over the years. I thought the only thing holding them together was floor wax, white paint and cleaning fluid.

The buildings were two stories high and sat on brick stilts that kept them about four feet off the ground. Rusted metal pipes, I later learned were stove exhausts, protruded from the top of every building. Entry into the buildings was through a single set of concrete steps at one end. The steps were painted white. You could see into some of the buildings through gaps in the wood. They were all freshly painted a bright white. As a matter of fact, everything on the street not alive was painted white. Signposts, telephone poles, electrical boxes, and sidewalks. The sides of the street were lined with large rocks, and large stones encircled each of the buildings. You guessed it, all the stones were also painted white. I had never seen anything like this before. It was as if someone had found an unlimited supply of white paint and didn't know what to do with it.

Ten of the buildings were barracks. This was where we would live for the next eight weeks. Fifty trainees to a building, twenty-five to a floor. For the remainder of basic training, my world would consist of rows of bunk beds and wooden lockers. They were approximately six feet apart with two wall lockers, the kind you see in high school gyms, between the rows. Top bunk lockers were on the right and bottom bunk lockers on the left. At the foot of each of the bunk beds were two green wooden boxes the size of an old steamer trunk. These "footlockers" were provided for additional storage space. We were going to have to neatly stow all our new green military gear in our assigned wall and footlockers. For spoiled kids from the '70s, this was a rude awakening. How could we possibly keep everything we owned in these two small spaces?

Contrary to Drill Sgt. G's description, there were no private rooms, no air conditioning unless you counted the large industrial fans on each floor, no running water, and no toilet facilities in the barracks. The heat was provided by a sizeable diesel-burning stove located at the end of the row of bunks on each floor. These heaters were so dangerous that whenever they were on, we were required to have someone guarding them to make sure that if a fire started, the trainees would have enough time to exit the building safely. The stoves were watched twenty-four hours a day when they were on.

The floor layout of the barracks was simple and basic. Bunks on one side and more beds on the other. Wall lockers neatly lined up in between. Each floor had eight wooden pillars, four on each side of the room that ran down the center of the hallways. The empty space between the wooden posts was outlined with a dark-black painted line about two inches wide. The area in the outlined space was the most highly polished piece of wood I have ever seen in my life. It was polished so intensely that you would swear it was pure glass. We learned that this space was referred to as "no man's land."

While floors in all the buildings were highly polished, special care was given to no-mans land. Under no circumstances could any trainee ever dare to set foot here. This was probably the most serious rule in basic training, and we didn't even want to contemplate the punishment for an infraction of this rule. We were required to clean and buff no man's land several times every day. We accomplished this by standing outside of the black line and running a buffer with a special polishing cloth across the floor while carefully ensuring that human feet did not touch this precious territory.

No one knew the penalty for violation, but there were a lot of rumors, and most of them ended with a trainee being found dead in his bunk. At the end of the top floor of each building was a single locked room that was approximately twelve by twelve. These were the drill sergeant's private room and office. Each room had a bunk, a locker, a small wooden desk, and a chair. Only drill sergeants could sit on the bed or chair in these rooms. If a trainee was called into one of these rooms, he was supposed to remain standing. You didn't want to be called into one of these rooms.

Lighting consisted of twenty bare bulbs screwed into the ceiling and controlled either by individual pull strings on each bulb or all at once by a switch at the end of the hall. Only drill sergeants could use the master light switch. There were no electric outlets in the barracks. There was no need because none of us could have any electronic appliances, including electric razors. The Army believed that the only way to shave was with a blade. Anything less was just not considered manly.

In addition to the ten two-story wooden buildings used for living space, there were four one-story buildings, two on each side of the street. One was the mess hall for all our meals. One building was the battalion and company headquarters where the first sergeants, sergeant major, and officers hung out. This was another place you never wanted to be called to; you never even wanted to see these people. One building was the logistical building. This building was used to store equipment, gas masks, and weapons; it was also where all our mail came in. The final structure was the only building that was not constructed out of wood; it was a cinder block building, our own "private" latrines for five hundred men.

So much for private rooms. The only thing private about our new home was our military rank. We were all a bunch of brand-new Army trainees, looking forward to eight weeks of this.

Now, you're going to think I'm a little anal, excuse the pun, but it's important to tell you about our bathrooms, or latrines, as the Army called them. Of course, Army latrines have a different connotation than bathrooms in the civilian world. Private to the Army consisted of a cinder block building with a metal roof. The building was about 120 feet long and forty feet wide. Once again, no heating and no air-conditioning because why would the Army want to spend any money to make a latrine a pleasant place to spend your free time, especially if it was being used by trainees?

Every day, millions of Americans routinely use bathrooms and frankly take showers, privacy, and personal hygiene for granted. We pop into the john, grab our daily newspaper, and do our business. Now imagine this: forty toilets in an open room arranged twenty in a row about one foot apart. The rows were directly behind each other with the backs of the toilets touching one another. No walls, no privacy, just you and thirty-nine of your best friends taking a shit together. On the sidewalls, directly in front of the toilets for your viewing pleasure were forty sinks with mirrors, arranged twenty on each wall. At the end of the building was an open space, not a separate room, just a space with multiple drains and approximately twenty to thirty shower heads protruding from the walls. For the next eight weeks, there would be no privacy. Anything you ever imagined—some that you could have never thought of—was going to happen in this building.

Words can't explain or describe the chaos that reigned every morning at four thirty and every evening at seven. These were the designated latrine times for our platoon, a hundred guys trying to shave, shit, and shower at the same time. And don't forget, we were sharing that building with four hundred other trainees who also had designated latrine times. If you had a shy bladder, you had better get over it quickly.

When it was hot outside, you sweated your ass off in the latrine, and when it was cold, you froze. It was that simple. I'd heard stories of BCT during the winter where it got so cold that there was frozen water in the toilet bowls. To use them, they had to first break the ice with the back of a toilet plunger or risk overflow. Those guys were happy to share the latrine. Especially if someone before them had taken the time to break the ice and, if they were fortunate, the seat would still be a little warm from the last ass.

Take the worst thing that you ever did or smelled in a bathroom and multiply it by five hundred. Add to that the problem of a lot of people who had no clue about proper hygiene and didn't care what other people saw them do. During platoon latrine hours, there were books and magazines all over the place. It was not unusual to see a guy jacking off on the toilet while reading a magazine. When you attempted to ridicule him, he would simply accuse you of being gay. The hardest thing to comprehend was the guys who would sit on a shitter and eat with all the chaos going on around them. I must have been raised in a protected environment because there are some things that I simply couldn't get used to. That latrine was the foulest, strangest place I have ever seen. To this day, I go out of my way to ensure that I am left alone with complete privacy to do my business. On the positive side, the Army teaches you to appreciate the little things in life.

There were no toilet paper dispensers in the latrine. All the toilet paper was kept on the shelves under the mirrors. So, you had to go over to the sink and get what you thought you needed before you took your seat. Army TP wasn't like the toilet paper that ordinary people use. This was a rougher, thinner version, but it didn't matter because there was hardly ever any toilet paper in the latrine. Between the guys who took it and hid it somewhere to have some the next time and the permanent party guys who stole it to sell to the hotels downtown at the end of training, there was a critical shortage.

To find innovative places to hide it, it was not unusual to see toilet paper in phone booths, under cars, or in drains; it was utterly insane. Trainees always tried to keep a small supply in their pockets to take care of business.

By the end of training, most of us had resorted to using the brown paper that came with the hand washing dispensers by the sinks as toilet paper. This presented some major problems; one was a constantly sore and scratched ass, and the other was consistently backed up toilets. It was a good thing that toilet plungers were one of the few items that seemed to have no supply problems in the Army. In the entire time I spent in the Army, the lack of TP was always the hardest thing to accept.

The only thing worse than using the latrines was being placed on latrine duty. Just do the math: eight weeks of basic training equals fifty-six training days; ten guys per day on latrine duty means that you were going to have to clean the bathroom from hell at least three times during the time you were at basic training.

It would have been a horrible, miserable duty had we just been required to clean the latrines, but in the Army, we were required to clean the latrines to a standard that no one outside of the Army could hope to emulate. When we were done with latrine duty, the drill sergeants had to be able to see their reflection in every piece of chrome and brass in the latrine. This required us to use gallons of Army brass cleaner (Brasso) and a polishing cloth on sink handles, toilet handles, mirrors, traps, shower and sink grates, and even pieces of metal in the shower heads.

We were given small metal rods and Q-tips to ensure that every nook and cranny in the latrine was cleaned and polished to the highest possible standards. Latrine duty was so bad that some guys vomited their guts out while performing it. When we were finished, there could not be a single smudge on any window or mirror, and, according to the drill sergeants, you had to be able to eat off the toilet seats.

Cleaning latrines required the use of about five gallons of disinfectant. The damn place always smelled like a chemical factory. When a drill sergeant inspected the latrine, he would put his head in each toilet bowl and look for any dirt or crud under the rim of the bowl, and he would push Q-tips in the holes on the shower heads to make sure there was no rust inside of them. I had never seen anything as clean as those latrines when we were finished with them. During latrine duty, we transformed the bathroom from hell into a work of art, at least temporarily.

As soon as a platoon was finished with latrine duty, there was a mad rush to be one of the first guys into the latrine. Everyone wanted to have a fresh bowl and, for at least a short period, some fresh air to breathe with a halfway decent place to do your business. You had to be quick because the clean and fresh latrine didn't last long. Within thirty minutes of re-opening the latrine, it was right back to the hell it had just come from. But for that brief thirty minutes, the nastiest place on Fort Knox became a thing of beauty.

At the end of our unit street was a large field with a dirt quarter-mile track along the outside of its perimeter. In the center of the track, there were multiple obstacle course objects, ditches, walls, rope climbs, and logs that we learned would be used by the drill sergeants daily to test our physical fitness and to torture us. Directly across from the exercise field were two rows of pay phones mounted on poles. There was a total of twenty phones available for each group of five hundred trainees.

You were not allowed to touch a phone for the first week, and after that, each platoon of fifty was allocated a twenty-minute window once a week. Twenty minutes was not enough time because half of the phones didn't work, and it sometimes took five to ten attempts to get in touch with an operator. The close vicinity of the phones to one another, loud voices, and fights for good phones caused more than one major riot during training. Unfortunately, in 1973 the pay phones or the mail were our only two options for getting in touch with or speaking with loved ones back home.

This brigade street, its buildings, and the adjoining field would be our entire existence for the next two months. There were ten streets like it on Fort Knox, so I assumed there were at least five thousand of us trainees going through basic training at the same time. To supplement our little community across the street was a movie theater, a church, a small store called a PX, and a snack bar.

These facilities were shared by the ten streets, so a strict rotation schedule of use was enforced. For the first two weeks of training, all the trainees in our block were restricted from visiting any of these facilities. The only thing we knew about the PX and snack bar was that it was rumored they served large Dixie cups of ice-cold beer for twenty-five cents a cup. Of course, there was no way we could find out for sure for two more weeks. We could only watch and drool as we saw fellow trainees who had passed the two-week point, walking down the road with their slices of pizza and Dixie cups of what we fantasized was ice cold beer.

Moron

# Chapter 13
## Drill Sergeant

Every basic training platoon was assigned two drill sergeants whose primary mission was to keep an eye on the trainees and to guide them through the training process. The Army assigned an experienced combat veteran and a younger, usually newly promoted sergeant, to every platoon to provide both leadership and guidance. The first platoon, my platoon, was assigned Sgt. First Class Harper, whom we referred to as Drill Sgt. Harper, and Drill Sgt. Bond, whom we referred to as "Little Hitler."

Drill Sgt. Harper was a tall, skinny man. Skinny but scary strong with those ripcord muscles that warned you, despite his lean stature, he could kick your ass whenever he felt like it. This was topped off by his piercing blue eyes, the kind of eyes that froze you in place when they settled on you. He walked, talked, and moved slowly. Nothing he did was in excess, and no movement was ever wasted. It was clear to all of us that this man could kill you as easily as he could shake your hand, and he wouldn't lose a second of sleep thinking about it. He was also a man of few words; he seemed to ponder every question before answering.

Talking to him was a little bit like talking to someone on tape delay; this was a bit unnerving, and it forced you to always be on your guard. He controlled every conversation because no one could maintain his slow pace; he simply wouldn't let you.

He was what the Army called a combat junkie and had done six tours in Vietnam, all voluntary except for the first tour. His first tour was shortly after he had been drafted. He apparently liked it so much that he volunteered for all the subsequent assignments. At one point, he admitted to me that he felt more comfortable in combat than living a civilian life in America. Most of the other drill sergeants in our battalion considered him "certifiable."

He liked to be in combat because, he said, you knew what everyone's role was, how they were supposed to act, and what to do if they didn't. To him, battle was predictable. Life in peacetime America was simply too difficult, he said. "Everyone is pretending to be something they're not, and no one has any idea of what it's like to be a real human being, experience real emotions, or make real decisions." He contended that the only way to truly measure a man was to observe him and his actions in a combat situation.

His pet peeve was corporate "wimps," as he called them, male or female who thought that because they had nice cars and clothing that they were somehow essential and were something special.

"When everything goes to shit in this world, and it will," he would say, "these people will be the first to die. They have nothing to offer anyone. They can't fish, they can't hunt, they can't farm, they can't do manual labor, and they can't even repair their cars or homes. When it all goes wrong, they die."

He couldn't understand how these useless people could achieve such high status in our society. He used to tell us that when the world went to war, a gardener was going to be a hundred times more valuable than a banker. America had just gotten it all wrong.

We learned that while at first, his decisions seemed arbitrary, over time, most of his choices turned out to be fair and well thought out. He didn't believe in making us do crap just for the fun of watching us suffer, and he didn't believe in belittling anyone. His favorite expression was, "Don't underestimate anyone."

He explained, "Everyone has something that they do very well; you have to find out what that is and work it to your advantage. Underestimating the enemy or someone on your team or not using them to their full ability costs lives in combat. There is nothing stupider than an officer or NCO who writes off someone in their command as useless. Everyone, no matter how stupid or different, has something they can provide to the fight. You have to find out what it is that they bring with them."

His one flaw, and it was a big one, was that he was a confirmed alcoholic. He knew it and didn't care, nor did he care who knew it. He made zero effort to hide it from anyone. He said it was his money and his life, and he could spend both anyway he wanted. He said when he retired, his master plan was to go somewhere where there were very few people and keep drinking until one day he didn't wake up. "Everyone," he said, "has to die of something." He felt that his excessive alcohol consumption was just as good as a lot of other ways to die, and probably a whole lot less painful than how many of those he had known had died.

It was not unusual for us to come back from some training and find him passed out on one of the bunks on the first floor. If we saw him passed out in the daytime, we would leave him alone because we knew he would wake up as soon as it got dark, so he could go out drinking again. If we found him in the evening and we needed the bed, several of us would carry him to the room at the end of the hall, use the keys in his pocket to open the door, and deposit him in the bunk in the drill sergeant room to sleep it off.

Everyone in the unit was aware of his affliction, including the command sergeant major, but no one ever mentioned it or even spoke to him about it. There were a lot of Vietnam veterans just like him all over the Army and talking about them was taboo. Despite the massive amount of alcohol he consumed every day, he was probably the highest functioning alcoholic I have ever met. It was not unusual for us to see him put away two full bottles of booze. I'm not talking about beer or wine. He drank the hard stuff—vodka, whiskey, brandy. The brand didn't matter as long as it was potent and had a high alcohol content. In a pinch, he would drink beer. He just said he was not a big beer drinker because it took too much time to consume enough to get genuinely wasted. For some reason, he refused to touch wine of any kind. He said that only fags and women drank wine. I guess even alcoholics have their standards.

He never talked about his time in Vietnam, and unlike some of the younger NCOs who had served combat tours, he never told war stories, and he refused to discuss his extensive awards and decorations. When we saw him in his dress uniform for the first time, we were shocked that one guy could have so many awards. His included four Purple Hearts, a Silver Star and at least five Bronze stars. He must have seen some heavy-duty combat. Today he would have been diagnosed with severe PTSD (post traumatic stress disorder), but back then stress and mental problems were just something that combat vets were expected to deal with.

As far as the Army was concerned, it was, "Do your damn job, fight the war, get over it, and then get on with your life."

You couldn't help but like him. He was tough, and he took no shit. He expected us to do what we were told when we were told, but he was fair. Unlike some of the other sergeants, he never picked on a trainee solely for the fun of picking on him. If Drill Sgt. Harper was on your case, then you deserved it because for him to be on your case, you had probably screwed up big time. He was brilliant. Not intelligent in the sense that he was the kind of guy who knew he was smart and let you know it, but knowledgeable in the way his actions and outcomes always seemed to be the right ones.

He was the kind of guy who would make subtle recommendations, give you time to figure out how you would do it, and then let you take credit for the great idea. He had a unique way of allowing everyone to feel he was smart, from one of the lowly Moron trainees all the way up to the colonel in command of the unit. I couldn't understand why he was in the Army. I was sure that he would have been successful in whatever endeavor he attempted.

Drill Sgt. Bond, "Little Hitler," on the other hand, was the complete antithesis of Drill Sgt. Harper. The only reason he existed was to torture and humiliate people. His specialty was seeking out everyone's weakness and exploiting it until you broke. If he couldn't break you, he would move on in search of weaker prey. He was so relentless in his torture and abuse of trainees that he quickly earned his nickname.

He was a lot like a spoiled child in that whenever he didn't get his way, or his abuse failed to create the desired effect, he would go into fits of rage. When he went into one of these tantrums, it was like watching one of those old black-and-white documentaries of a Hitler speech during World War II. He had it right down to the foot stomping, the worried look on his face, and the hand waving. The guy was so full of himself that I was convinced he was either mentally unbalanced or deranged.

He was a mean little guy; he only stood about five feet seven. Whenever he was speaking with anyone, he invariably had to look up at them. He had thinning, dark brown hair that he combed over his bald spot, the most prominent ears I have ever seen on a human being, and beady little, rat-like brown eyes that were constantly darting from side to side and never seemed to be entirely focused on you when he was talking to you. His looks and stature probably had a lot to do with his temper and disposition.

I was sure that he possessed the classic Napoleon complex. To Little Hitler, all trainees were nothing more than idiots. He didn't think that any of us deserved to serve in his Army. As far as he was concerned, no one in the Army was smarter than him. He was convinced that he knew everything about everything. If you doubted that premise, all you had to do was ask him and he would be glad to fill you in.

Like many small guys, his favorite subject was women, and he incessantly talked about all the women in his life and his conquests. I figured he was probably one of those guys who talked just a little bit too much, always bragging about his conquests but more than likely never getting anything that he didn't pay for. None of us could imagine any women wanting to talk to him, much less sleep with him for free. We joked that he would have to find a whore who was as ugly as a dog, blind, and stupid, and then he would only have a chance of getting her to sleep with him.

To round out his perfect disposition, he was a pervert, a bigot, and a gigantic homophobe. He was so paranoid with the possibility that one of the trainees may be gay that he regularly monitored the showers to make sure that no one was messing around with another trainee, or at least that's what he said he was doing. Just having him hanging around the latrines was creepy enough. The trainees weren't the only ones weirded out by Little Hitler. Several times we heard the other drill sergeants teasing him about how much time he spent monitoring the latrines. They would ask him if he liked looking at naked men, and did he go back to his room and jack off after each one of his informal inspections. This teasing by his peers only pissed him off, and then he would come back to the barracks and take it out on us.

We had a couple of guys in the platoon who were a little on the feminine side of the street, and he made life miserable for them. He constantly harassed them and tried to get them to admit they were faggots. While I'm sure we had some guys who were gay serving with us during basic training, I can guarantee you that these two weren't gay. They both had hot girlfriends and were two of the biggest horndogs in the platoon. Once again, Little Hitler had gotten it all wrong.

There was a rumor that during the previous training cycle that Little Hitler had encouraged several of his recruits to beat up a guy that he suspected of being gay and had put the trainee in the hospital with serious injuries. I believed the story was much more than a rumor. He was so homophobic that when he thought he had caught someone, he went crazy attempting to humiliate them and get them drummed out of the

Army. He was such a coward that you just knew he would never try to beat anyone up by himself. He would be the one to direct the action but allow the trainees to take all the blame while he came out clean. He was just that kind of a guy, basically a scumbag.

Little Hitler had been in the Army for two short years, and although he wore a Vietnam ribbon on his chest (you know, the one that said, 'I was there') and he had a Purple Heart, something about him didn't say, "combat veteran." The only reason he was a sergeant was that the Army was short of personnel and promoted everyone who agreed to reenlist after his initial two-year stint. The story we got from the other drill sergeants was that when he was a private, right out of basic training, he got orders to supply school and then went to Vietnam. He wanted to be in the Infantry, but they told him he was too small, so the Army trained him as a supply clerk.

When he got to Vietnam, he was assigned not to a combat unit, but a supply unit in Saigon. This supply office was in a major city about as far from the jungle as you could get. He was a REMF (rear echelon mother fucker). One night when he was in a bar trying to pick up a whore, someone fired a mortar into the city. Even though the mortar landed about a mile from where he was, he panicked and during the "mortar attack," he fell a flight of stairs while running to a bunker and shattered his foot. Because he broke it so badly, he had to be medically evacuated back to the U.S. for treatment. Back in the United States, he convinced the medical authorities that he had been wounded in the actual mortar attack and got the Purple Heart for wounds received during combat action with the enemy.

He had only been in Vietnam for four weeks and was supposed to go back after his hospital stay, but by the time his foot was good to go again, they had stopped sending troops into the country. Some of the sergeants said the only reason he got a Purple Heart was that he paid the unit administration clerk to fabricate a story about how he was trying to return fire and the mortar blast knocked him down the stairs of his firing position.

For a four-week combat veteran, who never left the big city, he had thousands of stories about his combat adventures in the dense bush fighting Charlie, and, of course, he knew everything about booby traps, fighting communists, Vietnamese women, and poisonous snakes. Most of us knew that he was full of shit, but there were always gullible guys in training who would willingly listen to his stories.

The other drill sergeants never said anything in front of him or directly to the trainees, but the looks on their faces said it all, especially the ones with real combat patches on their uniforms. The only guys in the barracks that could stand him or would even talk to him outside of an official requirement were the toadies and bullies. Every platoon in the Army had at least one or two of them. He seemed to attract them, and once he did, he began to influence them into his way of thinking. We called these assholes "Little Hitler's Brown Shirt Army."

Hitler reserved a special hatred and saved his worst punishment for the Morons. The fact that he thought he was smarter than everyone else in the Army made us Morons the perfect targets for his abuse and ridicule. It seemed that every time he came around, I got placed in a position where I was forced to protect the rest of the Morons in the platoon. I found myself always playing mind games to fuck with Hitler, which, surprisingly, wasn't that hard to do. It didn't take much of a mental push to keep him off balance. Hitler couldn't believe the Army would allow people of "marginal intelligence" into his fighting force. Where Drill Sgt. Harper saw the best in everyone, Hitler saw only the worst.

One of Hitler's favorite pastimes was to humiliate trainees during physical training. One ploy was to wait until we were completely worn out from an hour or so of tough, physical training, usually under the control of one of the other drill sergeants, and then he would volunteer to take over the formation. He was as fresh as a daisy and raring to go, because he had been standing on the side, watching us while we got physically torn down by the other instructors. When he took over the formation, he would push us as hard as he could to see how many of us would drop out from sheer exhaustion. He typically arranged his little show in front of the sergeant major. The dumb fascist didn't think the sergeant major was on to what he was doing. We would run by, and he would yell out something inane like, "Sergeant Major, can you believe how weak the youth of America is getting? These young guys should be kicking my ass. I'm a wounded combat vet with a damaged leg, and I can still kick their asses."

Of course, the only person he was fooling was himself, but in the process, he kicked our asses and caused us a lot more suffering than was necessary.

For his size, his upper body was in pretty good shape; he must have worked out regularly. Every time he walked past a mirror or a window, he would glance at his profile and flex his arms a little. The only problem was that he only worked out his arms and chest and neglected his legs and lower body. The result was a grotesque troll-like body. His body, just like everything else about him, was just a little off balance and not quite right. He might have thought of himself as a ladies' man, but the women wouldn't think so.

The Army couldn't have picked two more opposites to serve as drill sergeants. I suppose someone in the Army figured that if they assigned them both to the same platoon that they would cancel each other out. Drill Sgt. Harper, ever the professional soldier, never said a word about Drill Sgt. Bond; he just gave him strange looks, would shake his head, and move on. Hitler, however, hated Drill Sgt. Harper's guts, and he took every opportunity to let us know that Harper was a has-been alcoholic who shouldn't be in the Army anymore, much less training soldiers.

He probably did this because Harper was everything that Hitler wanted to be, a combat soldier. Hitler constantly reminded us that if he had his way, he would court-martial Harper and put him in prison for being a disgrace to the sergeants of the Army. He claimed it took every ounce of his willpower not to kick Harper's skinny ass. The only reason he didn't was because poor Sgt. Harper was too old to fight, he told us. We knew the real reason was that he feared for his life. Harper would have killed him in a fair fight.

So much for drill sergeant personalities. When we first arrived at our new barracks, we were met by Drill Sgt. Harper and Drill Sgt. Bond. They were standing in front of the barracks, and behind them was a large, unorganized, pile of duffle bags. This is what Drill Sgt. G meant when he said we would find our stuff neatly stowed in our private rooms. Harper's first instruction to us was to give us five minutes to stow our gear and to get back in formation and lined up on the street.

"Listen up, dog faces," he said. "Every bunk has a number; the same number is on the wall locker and a footlocker. Those numbers match the last two numbers of your serial number. Find your bunk and put your shit in your lockers. I don't care how you do it; I'll show you the right way later. Just stuff your shit in and when you are done, help someone else get his shit stowed. Do it any way you can and get back out here."

He continued, "On the street in front of this building are fifty sets of painted white footprints. In five minutes, you will be standing on a pair of those footprints. Move it, trainees, I only want to see assholes and elbows."

After four minutes of rushing and shoving shit into lockers, we were nowhere close to stowing our gear and moving out of the building and back into the street. I was pretty sure that I was going to miss my first official Army deadline.

It didn't help that Harper was standing by the door, giving us one minute and then ten-second intervals, and finally a second-by-second countdown for the last thirty seconds.

"Ten, nine, eight, seven …," and finally, "one!"

Instead of helping us to complete our mission quicker, it only made us more nervous and more frantic in our efforts.

"I knew you dumb, fucking civilians couldn't get out of my building on time. Everybody outside now! Drop whatever you are doing wherever you were doing it, and get your asses out of my building. Now! Move! Move! Move!"

As we scrambled to get out of the building, I realized a lot of the guys had a hard time matching their Army serial numbers to their bunk numbers so that they couldn't put their stuff away. Several of us did our best to help them, but it took us a lot longer than five minutes, and once we got back outside, it took another five minutes to get everyone on the footprints. It was more like a Chinese fire drill than an organized Army maneuver. A quick look up and down the street confirmed that we were not the only platoon going through the same shit storm and having the same problems. No one, it seemed, was going to be able to make his first deadline. I took the opportunity to quickly wave at some of the other Wolverines in the next platoon. Big mistake. It cost me twenty pushups.

"Who are you waving at, Gomer? Are you a faggot? Are you trolling the other platoons for some fresh meat? Stop being mister fucking mayor. You're not running for re-election, you dumb shit. Drop and give me twenty."

We spent the next forty-five minutes in the stifling ninety-degree heat doing pushups, squat thrusts, and sit-ups. In between drills, we were constantly yelled at and forced to run back into and out of our barracks. Most of the Wolverines had played high school football, so a forty-five-minute workout would not typically have been such a big deal; it was just that none of us had ever done it in combat boots and on hot asphalt while getting screamed at.

And do I mean hot? The Kentucky asphalt in front of our barracks was getting so hot that the road was melting and starting to get soft and mushy. When we were told to drop for twenty pushups, we killed ourselves in a mad effort to complete all twenty as fast as we possibly could. Failure to speed through your pushups meant remaining in the prone position for a longer period and risking blisters on the palms of your hands from the heat of the street. When it was clear that we could no longer keep our hands on the ground, the drill sergeants would order us to roll over onto our backs and command, "Die, you cockroaches."

The "dying cockroach" was the first military position we learned. As soon as we heard this command, we were to fall to the ground, roll over on our backs, and then put our arms and legs up in the air, wiggle them vigorously and shout, "I am a dying cockroach, the lowest form of life on earth. Please kill me, Drill Sergeant, please kill me."

So went my first afternoon of basic combat training. Lots of pushups, lots of sit-ups, acting lessons (I was becoming an expert at being a cockroach), and getting acclimated to the constant screaming in my ears. So far, I didn't think what I had learned would help me in combat or could even be considered training. After sufficiently amusing our new drill sergeants with our cockroach antics and our inability to follow even the simplest of instructions, we were told to "Fall in," meaning to get on your white footprints and keep your mouth shut.

I was so busy being miserable that I hadn't had a chance to see how the other platoons were doing. A quick sideways glance and the absence of noise showed that they were all as exhausted as we were and standing on their footprints as well. The entire street became very still and for the first time was quiet, except for the sound of heavy breathing and vomiting. When I took a glance around, I realized that somehow the sergeants had gotten us all facing the same direction.

I should say most of us were on our footprints because on both sides of the street lay trainees who had been overcome by the exercise and the heat. Drill sergeants were pouring water over their heads and yelling at them to get back on their feet. The Army cure for severe heat exhaustion at the time was cold water and a loud voice. Pouring water on a trainee's head was the Army's number one first-aid technique. Pass out, they pour a canteen of water over your head and tell you to get up. Have a heart attack, they pour a canteen of water over your head and tell you to get up. It was a simple, low-cost remedy and seemed to be highly effective for a bunch of eighteen-year olds.

When the noise died down, loudspeakers from the tops of all the buildings began to blare the Army song.

Immediately, the drill sergeants simultaneously screamed at us to "Stand at attention."

When the Army song ended, the biggest, fattest soldier perhaps in the military walked to the center of the street and climbed up on a six-by-six wooden platform. The groan of the wood on the platform echoed down the silent street as he jumped up on it. There was a bullhorn on the platform that he picked up, and it immediately began to screech and wail as he attempted to adjust the volume.

"Good afternoon, trainees. My name is Command Sergeant Major Adams, but you can call me Your Majesty. You will soon discover that I am more powerful than any man living in this country to include the president of the United States. Many of you will drop to your knees and pray to me before basic training is over. I am your judge and your jury. I am the man who decides if you pass or fail here at basic training. I decide if you live or die. If I don't like you or your attitude, I'll tell one of my drill sergeants to kill you in your sleep. When they come to investigate, I'll blame one of the many trainees assigned to this battalion for killing you. That way, I will have solved my problem and made my life better here at Fort Knox. One trainee dead and one trainee in prison for life. Bottom line, with two of you gone, my life has just become a whole lot easier. If you think I'm kidding, check out the local paper at the library when and if you get permission to leave this street. You'll find evidence of more than one strange death that has occurred here on Fort Knox. I'm proud to say that my battalion has the highest graduation rate and the highest death rate at Fort Knox. Trust me, don't fuck with my drill sergeants or me. You have a choice. You can become one of my statistics or one of my graduates. Your choice, and either way I could give a shit.

"I don't know why you joined my Army, and frankly, I don't give a shit. If you joined to serve your country, then you are an idiot. If you joined for the glory, then you are an idiot, and you will soon be a dead idiot because you will be killed the first time you go into combat. No matter why you think you joined, I'll tell what you are not here for. You are not here for America ... family ... honor ... devotion ... money ... the education they promised you ... or that goddamned bonus. You are here for one thing and one thing only, that is to fight America's wars, and to win them. Look to your left and your right. The men you just looked at are why you are here. These men here with you today are your brothers. At this moment, they are stupid fucking brothers, but they are your brothers. From this day forward, you need to realize that they are the only ones who give a fuck if you live or die.

"You can only trust a brother soldier, and from this point forward, you only trust brothers who serve in my Army. Everyone else is full of shit. Politicians are all liars, your parents are dumb fucking sheep, and America is a corrupt nation, and the only thing that makes living here even halfway worthwhile is my Army. You will learn to hate and mistrust civilians. They are not like us. They want to be like us, but they can't. They and all like them suck. The only civilians that are even a little worthwhile are women, and only if they fuck. So fuck them and leave them. Do not marry them, or they will fuck you over the minute you leave home.

"You have one and only one job. That is to kill the enemies of this Army. Destroy their countries, kill their families, and keep your brother soldiers alive. The life of a brother soldier is worth a hundred civilian lives. We would all be better off without civilians, and the only reason we do not kill American civilians is that they pay us. My job is to teach you to kill, and let me tell you, my drill sergeants and I are damn good at our jobs. Don't fuck with us and we won't fuck with you. Learn your job, which comes down to one simple thing, kill the bad guys and don't get killed yourself. Learn how to become a great killer and you will be a great soldier. Please, no one ask me to be your friend. I will never be your fucking friend, but when I go to war with you, we will be brothers. I want to know that my brothers won't run away, piss their pants, and get me killed. If I think you will let me or my Army down, I'll kill you here and now and get it over with. It will save us all a lot of time and save the country a lot of money.

"Oh yeah, I almost forgot, welcome to the all-volunteer Army and Fort Knox. Have a nice day, assholes."

# Chapter 14

## Routine

After the sergeant major's wonderful and inspiring welcome-to-the-Army speech, we were marched out of the battalion area and across the street to the small post exchange building that was in our brigade area. The post exchange, or PX, was just a Walmart or Kmart type of store. The PX sold everything: bars of soap, alcohol, cigarettes, candy, electrical appliances, stereo components; you name it and it was for sale in the PX.

On this trip, however, we wouldn't have time to look around the store. When we arrived at the PX, we were marched in the front door where the store clerks handed us each a large paper shopping bag with handles. The sergeant in charge directed us to walk down the aisles and follow the red line and the green arrows on the floor. Talk about a lack of imagination. As we walked through the aisles, several clerks stationed in each aisle dropped various items into our bags.

Sgt. Harper told us, "Don't screw this up, faggots. Don't touch anything on the shelves, don't put anything in your bag, and under no circumstances are you to let go of your bag handles. Don't even think about getting anything that is not put in your bag." One of the guys in my platoon asked if he could pick out his own toothpaste because he only liked a particular type. "You don't get to pick out anything anymore, Susie. The Army will make all your decisions for you and make sure that everything you need is placed in your bags. The Army doesn't pay you to think, so keep your traps shut and keep moving."

The clerks tossed all kinds of items into our bags. Everyone received precisely the same articles in the exact equal quantities. This was a store, so I assumed someone was going to have to pay for all this crap, and I was hoping it wouldn't be me because I had absolutely no idea about the price of anything. Once again, our friendly drill sergeants filled us in.

They informed us not to worry about the money because Uncle Sam would take it directly out of our next paycheck. I had only been in the Army for three days, and I had already lost track of how much money I owed the government. This had a scary resemblance to the old company store concept that I read about in the mining towns of West Virginia. The only thing that I knew for sure, I was going to end up owing the Army money at the end of the month. I had a sneaking suspicion that I was in the negative already.

While it probably made sense for the Army to ensure we all had the items we required for personal hygiene, I resented the fact that I was forced to purchase what they wanted me to have and not allowed to shop around for better prices. What about those useless combs and hairbrushes? Come on, none of us had any hair. What the hell were we going to use them for?

In my first three days of basic training, I discovered some of the guys here had never brushed their teeth in their lives. It was funny when they gave us the floss because most of the guys had no idea what it was for and were astounded when I explained it to them. At first they thought I was making fun of them or something, they just couldn't get the concept. Even scarier, some of these boys had never heard of deodorant before. It was a real novelty, and when we got back to the barracks, they had a blast spraying it all over themselves, one another, and all their equipment. It was a mess, but it did mask all the odor. Some of them had not taken a shower in the three days we had been at Fort Knox. I was getting worried they were going to try and go the whole eight weeks without a shower. With all the physical activity, we were being forced to do, they were already starting to get ripe.

The Army didn't take anything for granted and planned everything down to the tiniest detail back at the barracks. A team of corpsmen and medical specialists were waiting for us and began to instruct us on how to brush our teeth, how to take a correct shower, how to shave, and even how to properly wipe our asses. When the instruction was done, the drill sergeants had us all strip and marched us buck ass naked to the latrine. In the latrine, we were given long handled brushes with stiff, coarse hairs and instructed to get in a line and scrub each other.

I don't know about getting clean, but we came out of the shower bright red and sore all over. Harper said, "I hope this will be the last time that you will have to use the brushes on each other. I don't intend to make you go through this again, that is unless anyone is caught not taking a shower and completely cleaning their nasty bodies at least once a day. If I catch one of you dickheads not taking a shower, I will make the entire platoon take group brush showers every fucking day for the rest of the time that you are here at Fort Knox.

"The same thing goes for brushing your teeth and using deodorant. Anyone misses one day, and all your asses are back in the group shower routine. Besides, everyone will put on a fresh uniform to include socks and underwear every morning. All the drill sergeants will conduct surprise inspections of your laundry, and I better not catch anyone cheating. The Army will do your laundry for you, so you goddamn well better change every morning. If you think I am kidding, I dare one of you to test me. Now get your nice clean, red asses back to the barracks. Run, you shitheads. Move! Move! Move!"

Wow, for an organization that spent so much time trying to root out gay recruits and eliminate them, they sure made us do a lot of faggoty stuff, I thought. I hoped no one back home ever found out that I washed another guy's back while someone else was washing mine while we were all buck ass naked. I don't think they would understand the training nature of this event. As a matter of fact, I wasn't sure I understood the training value either.

When we got back to the barracks and dressed again, we were provided charts of wall and foot lockers with pictures of where everything we had just purchased or had been issued should be placed in our lockers. Not only were we told where in our storage areas to put our new items, but we were also shown exactly how they would be folded, how they should be stacked, and even which way everything should face.

Harper said, "OK, children, look at the pretty pictures and place all of your items in your lockers precisely as shown in the displays. You're not home with mama anymore. From now on no one gets to be different. Having it your way is now a thing of the past, I want every one of these goddamn lockers to look identical."

Sgt. Harper then pulled five other trainees and me over to the side (all white dot boys) and worked with us for over an hour, taking great pains to ensure that we understood exactly where and how all our equipment and supplies were supposed to be stored and how they were supposed to be placed.

I enjoyed the relaxing hour of one-on-one instruction and was starting to get a better idea of what it was going to be like to be a Moron. This wasn't half bad. While my platoon-mates were getting screamed at to move faster and were required to finish their displays in a few minutes, the other Morons and I were allowed to sit on our footlockers and take all the time we needed to get our stuff together. When they were done with their personal gear, they were quickly and violently assigned to various details, sweeping and cleaning up the barracks. The drill sergeants disappeared into their private room at the end of the hall and left us to our own devices.

This, I realized, was going to be my lot in basic training; while the "smart trainees" worked their tails off, my fellow Morons and I would be left alone to take all the time we needed to figure out where to place our shiny new things in our lockers. An hour of storing gear and cleaning the already clean barracks went by, and Sgt. Harper stuck his head out of his room long enough to yell out, "You maggots have thirty minutes to get your stuff together. Drill Sergeant Bond and I will be back to inspect to ensure you all got it right. Remember, the key is making sure that everyone's shit looks the same, no exceptions."

As soon as he shut the door, I quickly assisted the Morons in placing their items in the correct positions, and then we took a twenty-five-minute break until it was time for our first inspection. I did, of course, make sure that we messed up a few items. I didn't want everything to look too perfect on the first try. No sense in setting expectations too high. After all, we still had eight weeks of this shit to go.

We stored all our Army gear in this same slow, meticulous, manner. The key to success in the Army is to make sure that everything looks the same. It was like living in the house of the cloned lockers. The only difference between lockers was the name tags on the uniforms and the books we could keep on the top shelf. In the spirit of pretending that the Army valued intelligence, on the top shelf of our lockers, trainees could place the four books we had been allowed to retain. Most shelves were empty. Not a lot of readers in this group, except the religious guys that had brought Bibles with them.

I had brought along a lot of books, as I was an avid reader, and I had a hard time selecting the ones to bring when they told us we could just take four at the welcome center. I wanted to bring them all but had selected ones that comforted me and made me think of things other than the Army, the kinds of books you just like to read over and over again, the ones that become like old friends. On my top shelf rested:

*The Foundation Trilogy* by Isaac Asimov

*The Cosmic Connection* by Carl Sagan

*Carson of Venus* by Edgar Rice Burroughs

*Final Blackout* by L. Ron Hubbard

While I loved my books and could claim some solace in my ability to lose myself in them in the few free moments that I was given in basic training, they made my life a little miserable. For some strange reason, drill sergeants hate any book that doesn't have graphics or pornographic pictures. In their small minds, they didn't expect any of us to read books with actual words. They particularly detest any book by an author whose name they couldn't pronounce. Every once in a while, you would come across a higher functioning sergeant who had some level of literacy, but these guys were few and far between. The "intelligent" drill sergeants could be identified by their pornographic novel collections. Yep, you guessed it, no pictures. They had to use their imaginations.

At our first locker inspection, both drill sergeants made a point of tearing our stuff apart, looking for the smallest errors in placement. When Sgt. Bond saw my books, he said, "Holy shit, we have a fucking Einstein in the barracks. I believe this boy actually thinks he can read."

Sgt. Harper tapped him on the shoulder, pointed to the white dot on the back of my helmet liner, which was sitting on top of my locker exactly two inches off center as prescribed by the Moron white-dot placement chart, and said, "Let it go, Sergeant."

This was my first interaction with Drill Sgt. Bond, and I could tell by the gleam in his eyes that there was no way he was going to let it go. He was just dying to humiliate me in front of the entire platoon. I knew what was coming next.

"Jesus Christ," he exclaimed. "Who the fuck is kidding who? Private Berlin, the only thing you do when you display these bullshit, highfalutin books is proving to everyone in this barracks what a stupid fuck you really are. You, I, and everyone on this fucking Army post know that you can't read, and I doubt you can even write your own name, so why pretend? Just admit you're a fucking idiot and we will all get along just fine."

Finishing his tirade, he reached up to the shelf and pulled *The Cosmic Connection* off the shelf and shook it at me.

"You Moron, you weren't even smart enough to get a book written by an American. This shit is written by some communist faggot foreigner named Sagan. Hell, I bet he's a Christ-crucifying Jew. Berlin, I'm going to do you a favor and toss all this crap into the nearest garbage can. I know you thought this little display would make people think you were smart, but I'm going to save you a lot of heartache and humiliation over the next eight weeks. Learn your place in this here Army and don't pretend to be something you're not. Christ, I hate fucking Morons."

"With all due respect, Drill Sergeant," I calmly replied. "Carl Sagan is a famous American astronomer, astrophysicist, and author. He has played a leading role in our space program, advising NASA since the 1950s. Are you aware that he briefed the Apollo astronauts before their flights to the moon? He is involved in the search for extraterrestrial intelligence, or SETI, for those who like smaller words."

Whoops, big mistake.

Drill Sgt. Bond turned bright red with his veins popping and his eyes bulging. Saliva dripped from the corner of his mouth as he screamed in my face.

"Who taught you to speak like that, you fucking monkey. How long did it take you to memorize that speech, Moron?" He turned and screamed to everyone in the barracks, "This just proves my point that anyone, no matter how goddamned stupid, can be taught to memorize a few short phrases. This fucking book goes in the garbage right now."

I couldn't resist. As he raised his arm to toss my book into the trash can I said, "Excuse me, Drill Sergeant, request permission to speak?"

"Speak, dumb shit," he replied.

"Drill Sergeant, Army regulation six thirty-thirty, paragraph four, subparagraph three B, states, under no circumstances will a superior deny a subordinate access to his personal property. For the purposes of this regulation, personal property includes but is not limited to personal jewelry, religious items, Bibles, letters, pictures of family, and *books*."

I continued, "Being that the book in question is neither pornographic nor on any Army banned reading lists, you realize that the Army could court-martial you for throwing it away. Drill Sergeant, I don't care, either way, I would just hate to see you lose your job over a silly book, especially one written by a Christ-crucifying Jew."

I have never in my life seen a face turn such a bright shade of purple. The veins in his neck were throbbing, and he looked completely out of control as he screamed and threw the book at me. The book sailed across the bunk beds, hit my chest, and bounced onto my bunk. Still out of control, he started to come at me, but Sgt. Harper grabbed his arm and said:

"Relax, Drill Sergeant, we have an inspection to finish. Let the dummy have his little piss-ant library. It's not going to hurt anything for him to pretend a little. You know what headquarters said, we have to go out of our way to accommodate the special soldiers. Not worth losing a stripe over. Let's just move along."

Drill Sgt. Bond took a deep breath, attempted to calm his shaking hands, and slowly backed off as he said to me, "Don't ever tell me what to do, you stupid fucking Moron. If you know what's good for you, you will make the books disappear before the next inspection. You are on latrine detail."

He then spun around and stomped down the hall to the door. Just as he got to the door, he turned and said in a loud voice, "Fuck this inspection, I'm going over to the club to get a beer. I want this barracks spotless when I return."

I had a big ass smile on my face because I figured I had just won a small battle in the war called basic training, but I didn't have time to enjoy it because Sgt. Harper was staring at me, fuming.

"Get your ass into my room now, Private, and bring those fucking books with you."

Damn it, my first day in actual basic training. My goal was to keep a low profile, and here I was heading to the one place in the barracks where a trainee never wants to be. I was nervous as I walked to the room at the end of the hall with books in one hand. I knocked loudly and requested permission to enter.

"Shut the fucking door," ordered Sgt. Harper as I entered. He was sitting in his chair and reached out to take my books. He asked, "How in the fuck did you know that Army regulation?"

"Actually," I confessed, "I don't know any regulations, Drill Sergeant. I made it up, but I guess Drill Sergeant Bond doesn't know them either, because he believed me."

He stared at me with a blank expression on his face, and then his eyes lit up like he had just discovered something. "Oh shit," he sighed, "we have a big problem here."

He then began to question me about my books. To my absolute astonishment, he was an Isaac Asimov fan. After the first few questions, he pulled up his chair and sat about a foot from me, staring up at my face.

"OK," he said, "no bullshit, who do you work for?"

I replied, "I have no idea what you are talking about."

"You know exactly what I'm talking about. Do you work for the office of the inspector general, or are you assigned to the criminal investigation command? Look, buddy, you blew your cover, and I mean you blew it bad. Just tell me who you work for, and we can figure out how we're going to work this situation."

"Drill Sergeant, I have absolutely no idea what you are talking about."

"Look, that white dot on your helmet liner and boots designates you as a soldier of deficient intelligence. You and I both know that's not true. If you want to keep your job, just be straight with me."

I said, "I admit that I didn't get the highest scores in high school, and I'm a little bit of a wiseass sometimes, but I have never been accused of being of limited intelligence. When I took my SATs, I got one of the highest scores in the country. Anyway, how would the Army know what my intelligence level was anyway, I don't think they ever tested me?"

When he heard that I had not only graduated from high school but had taken the SATs, Harper almost fell out of his chair. According to him, I was probably the only guy in the platoon who could spell SAT, much less have taken the tests. He spent the next ten minutes explaining to me the Army testing process and how all the trainees had been cataloged and graded while in Milwaukee. I spent the same amount of time explaining to him what had happened in Milwaukee and why my test scores were so low. He wanted to know how I had qualified to get in the Army if I had a hangover and had slept through all the tests. When I told him that the sergeants in Milwaukee had given us all the answers, he said. "I knew something was going on down there. There's no way half of these guys should even be here."

"Look," he said, "I've never run into a situation like this before. This is my last stint as a drill sergeant. When this class ends and you dumb shits graduate, I plan on retiring and sitting on my ass and drinking beer for the rest of my life. I don't want or need some smartass little shit blowing it for me. This is how we are going to work this."

He then informed me that he expected me to do everything I was told to do, keep my mouth shut, and, of course, lose the books. He said he would hold them for me until graduation. He also told me that I had to dumb down as much as possible.

"From this point on, I want to see just another dummy when I look at Private Berlin. From this point forward, you are the dumbest soldier at Fort Knox, is that clear?"

I was told that I would be expected to accomplish every task given at the minimum level required for me to move on to the next stage of training. No talking back, never ask questions, never volunteer for anything, and, for God's sake, no more games with drill sergeants. He also expected me to make sure that every Moron in the platoon graduated on time. If I didn't follow these instructions, it would be my ass. I was now the King of the Morons, and I was expected to act the part.

If I could follow the simple rules that Sgt. Harper had laid out for me, then he and I would get along great, and I would graduate and get my car. If I didn't play along, he promised to make my life a living hell and to do everything that he could to lock me up for something.

"If you don't do anything worthy of being arrested, then I will make something up and blackmail you," he promised.

As the session ended and I was walking out the door, I heard him say, "*Final Blackout* is my favorite book. In another life, I would have loved to discuss it with you. I bet you have an interesting take on it."

With that, he opened the door and yelled so that everyone in the building could hear, "Now get your slimy ass back to your platoon."

He slammed the door behind me as I left his office.

It was a confusing confrontation, but I got it. I now knew the ground rules and had gained a new level of respect for

Drill Sgt. Harper. The rest of the drill sergeants were still a bunch of assholes, but at least under the surface, I knew one of them was an intelligent man. He couldn't display that intelligence in the company of his fellow drill sergeants or us trainees, but somehow just knowing made me feel a little better.

To my fellow platoon members, I had just had my ass chewed and lost my books. None of them believed that I could read anyway. Oh well, I had spent the first eighteen years of my life holding back and taking it easy; why should I change things now? Eight weeks of acting like a dummy should be a cinch for me. I had been fooling teachers and parents my whole life. It was going to be tough, but I was just going to have to do the best I could to take it easy. Hey, it was an order, what could I do?

When I got back to my bunk, Bob, the guy who had befriended me at the reception center, was standing by my wall locker waiting for me. As I walked up to him, he put out his hand and introduced himself,

"Bob Bradley," he said, and firmly shook my hand. Before I could respond or introduce myself, he stopped me and, still tightly holding my hand, said:

"Look, I think you and I are going to get along just fine. Frankly, I like your style, but let's get one thing straight before you tell me who you are and make our nice introductions. You and I both know that you're not one of the Morons. As a matter of fact, you are one of the smartest guys here. So, what's the fucking deal?"

Uh oh, I thought, here I go again. I'm really going to have to dumb it down to prevent this type of shit from happening, but I trusted Bob.

I laid out the conversation I just had with Sgt. Harper and explained to him that I had been ordered to play a game and to keep a low Moron profile. Bob shrugged.

"I get exactly where he is coming from," he said. "If it were to come out that you had been illegally spoon-fed answers at the Milwaukee reception station, it would cause a lot more problems than anyone in the Army wants to deal with right now. They're better off keeping you a Moron. I think you can live with that. Hell, it will actually make your life a whole lot easier here."

Once the strange introductions were out of the way, we began to talk. I had never met anyone like Bob. Like the old saying, "Never judge a book by its cover," there was more to Bob than met the eye. He had been in the Army before and served for almost four years. He informed me that he had gotten out of the Army about eighteen months prior. He left because he was going to get married and had been promised a dream job with his future father-in-law in the family-owned furniture manufacturing business.

Bob told me that everything in his life was going well. In fact, he was having the best period in his life. He figured that he had finally arrived. His fiancée's daddy was a millionaire, and he was impressed that Bob was a soldier and was infatuated by his Vietnam service. He had guaranteed Bob a high paying position, and it was decided that Bob would quickly work his way up through the company to become the senior vice president and eventually the president of the company when his father-in-law retired. Bob said he was pretty sure he had a good chance of inheriting everything when Daddy died or decided to retire from the furniture business permanently. Talk about a sweet deal; besides, the daughter was a real looker, so it wasn't going to be too hard to take.

Bob said he was living the life he had always dreamed of and everything was going great. Daddy had ordered a new home to be built for the newlyweds as a wedding present. It would be finished and ready to move in on the day of the wedding. Bob had started working as a foreman on the night shift, but his future father-in-law was paying him at the executive level. Even though he was considered middle management, everyone in the plant knew who he was and whom he was getting married to. They would have been crazy not to treat him like the president of the company because that was what he was destined to become someday.

Bob shook his head. "Some people have to go to college and work their asses off to become successful. Lucky for me, I have a big dick, and a rich woman fell in love with me. Everything was going great; frankly, too great.

"You see," he admitted, "I have this strange affliction, whenever everything in my life is going perfectly, I seem to find some way to screw everything up. It's not that I want to have everything go bad, it just happens. It's almost like that old cartoon. I have this little devil sitting on my shoulder, and his only job is to make sure that I never get a break in life. I just can't seem to shake him, no matter how hard I try. In addition to my own personal devil, I am also extremely addicted to Asian women. I think I picked it up in Nam, but regardless, you put a tiny Oriental chick in front of me, especially one with a tight little ass and long legs, and I am destined to go down and go down hard.

"About a month ago, Daddy Big Bucks hired a new secretary for his front office work. You guessed it, an Asian chick. Not just any Asian chick, I'm talking about one of the hottest little pieces of ass you have ever laid your eyes on. About five feet tall, dark almond eyes, silky black hair that fell to her waist, legs that went on for miles, and the tightest little body that you could possibly imagine. I was smart enough to know that I would be in trouble if I got anywhere near her. I knew I wasn't going to be able to control myself. So, I went out of my way to avoid all possible contact with her. Hell, I only saw her one time and just thinking about her in that front office just about drove me crazy. I wish I could describe to you how incredibly beautiful and exotic she was. She was truly a once in a lifetime beauty.

"I thought that as long as I stayed away, I would be able to maintain control, but then that damn little devil had to go and get involved. One night I had to stay late to get some equipment repaired for the morning shift. I finally finished around ten o'clock and stopped by the office to check out with Daddy Big Bucks and give him a status on the equipment. I figured, there was no way the Asian princess would be in the office this late. Wrong. Not only was she still at work, but she was holding down the fort for Daddy and informed me that Daddy had asked her to go over the final assembly line repairs with me so she could pass the information on to him in the morning. My future father-in-law was taking his wife to the theater that evening and had left the Asian princess in charge of collecting all the evening reports. I was totally screwed, and I knew it.

"While we were working in the office, she started putting some documents into the filing cabinet. Bent over in one of the tightest, shortest skirts I have ever seen, my eyes were immediately drawn to her beautiful long legs ending in a pair of four-inch heels. The sight caught me so unaware that I was speechless. Turning to see if I was watching, it was obvious to her that I was totally befuddled and infatuated with her. I guess the lumps in my throat and pants were a dead giveaway. There was no way that she could miss the fact that the bulge in my pants was throbbing in time with my heartbeat, and, as you recall, I do have a big dick.

"Now, you have to know that I in no way planned this. I really wanted to get married, settle down and, in my own way, I really did love Daddy's little girl. But one minute we were talking about Vietnam and the next minute she was bent over the desk with her skirt hiked up to her waist, and I was going at it from behind like a sixteen-year-old getting his first piece of ass. I was literally in heaven. Now picture this, Miss Vietnam screaming and moaning, and me behind her going like a steam engine with my pants around my ankles and my bony ass going a million miles a minute.

"You know how it is when you reach that point in sex that no matter what happens, you're so far gone that it's impossible to stop. Well, we were at that point. Hell, your mother and the pope could walk in on you, and you're not going to be able to stop. The next thing I remember is hearing the door open behind me. I glanced over my shoulder, and guess who had walked in? Yep, you guessed it, my future father- and mother-in-law coming back to the office to pick up the theater tickets they had left on the desk.

"Now, no disrespect intended. I really wanted to stop, pull out and hike my pants up immediately. I just couldn't do it. I couldn't for the life of me stop. Hell, I was in midstream. The only thing my body would allow me to do was to finish the act. Unfortunately, it was one of the best climaxes of my life. I yelled out loud as I finished, and I fell to the floor. Well, I don't have to explain the rest of the gory details to you. Bottom line, it was the end of my future marriage and the end of my new life. I no longer had a high-paying job, and I had to get the fuck out of town before Daddy Big Bucks had me hung. The last thing I recall that evening was me trying to run out of the office with my pants around my ankles and Daddy Big Bucks throwing staplers, paperweights, and anything else not tied down at me as I dove out the front door. I had just fucked it up again. Thanks, devil.

"Sitting in a hotel room a week later, I contemplated my options and figured that the only place I was ever able to do anything worthwhile was when I was in the Army. I was done in this town and frankly was running out of options and money. I was actually pretty good at being a soldier, and I kind of missed it. I called the local recruiter and explained to him what I wanted to do. After telling me I was completely nuts, the recruiter told me that because I had been out of the Army for such a long time that I would have to go back through basic training all over again. If I were stupid enough to go back in the Army, then he would be stupid enough to sign me back up. I figured I had done it once and it didn't kill me, so no big deal, I could do it again. What the heck, after two tours in Vietnam, I can do and put up with just about anything. I could stand on my head in a pile of shit for eight weeks if I had to. So here I am, yours truly, back in the saddle again."

He told me that he tried to get in touch with Miss Vietnam for weeks after the office-rutting event but was never able to reach her. "The few people at the furniture factory who would talk to me after the incident told me that Daddy Big Bucks had run her out of town," Bob continued. "My fiancée was devastated and said that she could never show her face in town again. She kept the only thing I paid for, the ring. Daddy Big Bucks sent her on a European tour to get her mind off the traumatic events, and hopefully she would meet a nice guy and get married. I wished her no ill will. It was my dick that cheated on her, not my heart." Bob guessed that the Asian chick had gotten absorbed back into one of the Vietnamese American communities. He hoped that she had hooked up with some sugar daddy somewhere because someone should be paying for that stuff. It would be a shame to give it away for free.

"I have thought about it a thousand times since that night," Bob said, "and I keep asking myself repeatedly, was it all worth it? I consider what I lost and how I threw away a perfectly planned future with tons of money at the end, and, you know what, after considering everything I have to say, fuck yes! Daddy Big Buck's daughter was a frigid little shit when it came to the sex department, and I knew that it would just be a matter of time before I strayed, and she caught me anyway. At least this way there were no children involved, and we didn't have to go through any big drawn-out messy divorce. As for the Asian princess, it was a once in a lifetime event and by far the finest piece of ass I have ever had or imagined."

Bob was a unique character. I learned that in addition to serving two tours in Vietnam and being wounded three times, he had been awarded the Bronze Star for valor and the Silver Star for bravery. The Army is not in the habit of handing out the Silver Star to just anyone. You have to be one badass motherfucker to earn a Silver Star.

You would never know from just looking at him that he was a real live American hero. Hell, it was hard to imagine that he was even a soldier. Bob just seemed like a little kid that lived down the block from you, quiet, unassuming, and friendly as could be. I don't believe there were more than two or three people on Fort Knox who knew about Bob's combat service and his awards. He was not the type of guy who would talk about his exploits. He only told me because he trusted me and knew I could keep my mouth shut. I think he needed to tell someone because it was eating away at him. I was, if nothing else, an excellent sounding board. It wasn't until graduation when we were required to wear our full-dress uniforms, and he showed up decked out with all his awards and decorations, that the rest of the guys realized his background and combat experience.

The drill sergeants almost shit when they discovered how highly decorated Bob was. A lot of them felt terrible when they realized they had been treating a guy with this much combat experience like a typical trainee. I'm pretty sure that he had more medals and campaign ribbons than any drill sergeant in the command except Sgt. Harper. The Army should have had a better system for tracking people who came into the Army. Under no circumstances, should Bob have been going through basic training with all of us idiots. With all the training and experience he had, there should have been some way of bringing him back on a specialized advanced program or something. If the Army had done a better job of screening recruits, they could have used people like Bob to help train their fellow soldiers.

The next two weeks went by as usual, up at four a.m., exercise and training for sixteen hours a day, and collapsing into bed at ten every evening. I have to admit things were a lot easier for my fellow Morons and me. We were given a little more time, a little more instruction, and the drill sergeants accepted more mistakes from us. I quickly adapted to my role as an underachiever and with a little practice was able to make enough stupid mistakes to keep from standing out in the crowd.

It was kind of fun, figuring out ways to manipulate both the drill sergeants and the other members of my platoon without them realizing that someone was playing puppet master with them. In the few minutes a day that I got to spend with my fellow Wolverines, I would get my comeuppance. They were all over my case about my path down the road of least resistance and gave me a hard time.

Danny and Stick told me that it wasn't funny anymore; they were afraid that when the Army found out how smart I was, they were going to put me in jail or something. Danny, who knew me best, warned me, "Don't be stupid. You're acting so dumb that even some of the Morons are trying to figure out what the hell is going on. I'm telling you, this is not going to end well. Stop now while you have the chance or at least tone it down a little." Frankly, it didn't matter, and I put it down to sour grapes. I was getting the same pay as they were and did a lot less. Morons couldn't be trusted or expected to complete even the most menial of tasks.

The training was unusual in the Army. To teach to the lowest level, which would be the Moron level, the Army had resorted to some strange training techniques. You have probably heard of the comic-book training program the Army instituted in the '70s. Instead of training manuals, the Army provided soldiers with comic books. A lot of pictures and very few words. When we got to the maintenance training, the Army gave us coloring books with pictures of the vehicles and all the parts. The instructors would tell us to color specific parts certain colors so that we could learn to recognize them. They also provided larger-than-life mockups of all the equipment that they were teaching us how to use. Twenty-foot-long M-1 rifles, a six-by-six-foot radio, and five-foot-long bayonets. It was like being one of the actors in the *Land of the Giants* TV show. Someone spent a lot of the taxpayers' dollars figuring out how to train dummies for America's Army. Kind of ironic using dummy equipment to teach the dummies.

We had comic books for everything. The most humorous was "The Use of Weapons" series. Imagine a comic book with picture instructions on how to properly stab an enemy combatant. It was hilarious. At that time, the enemy soldiers portrayed in the comic books still had exaggerated Asian features to represent the Viet Cong.

About two years after I completed basic training, I caught wind that the comic book training series had become one-hundred-percent politically correct. The Asian American community put so much pressure on the Department of Defense that they eliminated all Asian faces from the training comics. America was changing fast. The Army blanked out all the features of the enemy. The comic books ended up with a shadow figure with a black or white silhouette. I guess I should have been insulted because the Army had decided that all enemies our country would face in the future would be black or white. I bet some Chinese guy was responsible for publishing the new training manuals, and he is probably still laughing at us.

Moron

# Chapter 15
# Race Relations

Race relations class. The very thought makes me cringe. The Army, like our nation, had some serious race issues in the early seventies. In fact, many people in the Army honestly believed that racial tensions and problems were going to destroy both the Army and our country. Many of us thought that it was just a matter of time until the country imploded. At the very least, I was sure that racial pressures would doom the all-volunteer force to abject failure. The Army had not been integrated for very long, only since the Korean War, and many of our senior leaders still believed that black and white soldiers had no business living and working together.

It didn't take a brain surgeon to figure out that some of the Army's senior leaders were out and out racists. Most were so secure in their positions that they didn't even make an effort to hide it. In the seventies many schools in the South were still segregated, and cities across the country were still smoldering from the race riots of the late sixties. Race-related crimes and attacks were rampant in the Army. It seemed as if nothing the Army did was going to change anything; things just kept getting worse. Soldiers, for the most part, kept themselves racially segregated. They attended events and activities with those of the same race and, when not at work, did everything they could to stay in their own groups. At work, some units even allowed all-black or all-white squads. It was still a mess.

Most of the problems and issues the Army was facing were restricted to black and white interactions. No one gave much thought to the Hispanics, Asians, or other races; these guys seemed to be able to move back and forth between the black and white populations at will and took up sides when it was in their best interest to do so. The only other group that seemed to be able to remain out of the argument were the drill sergeants. I don't know how they did it, but they instilled in these guys the need to treat everyone the same, like shit. If your job allowed you to be a bully, and you got to push everyone around, you tended to ignore skin color. The Army would have been better off if all its leaders had emulated drill sergeants.

The Wolverines were caught right in the middle of the entire racial conflict. Due to our isolated upbringing, we were more than a little naïve. None of the Wolverines had any experience with people of different colors or religions. No minorities were living in or near Iron City. The only thing we knew about different races was what we had seen on TV or read in newspapers or books. To us, racial tensions were a problem with the Indians back home, fighting for better access to hunting and fishing areas. In Iron City, there were no blacks, no Asians, no Hispanics, and no Arabs. We didn't know anything about other races, so we figured we weren't racist.

We had grown up in one of the whitest communities in America. I don't know why we had no immigrants or people of color in the UP, but most people speculated that it was because of how isolated we were, and the long, cold, hard winters tended to drive all but the hardiest of newcomers away. Everyone who lived in the UP said that the black families didn't stay because of the cold and the snow. I believe it had more to do with not having anyone like them living nearby. It's tough to live in an area where you are one of a kind, and no one really understands you. I can't imagine living in a town of all black people and being able to feel comfortable.

In the early seventies, the Army, like every other institution in the country, was caught amid racial tensions that were tearing America apart at the seams. Tensions were erupting in the form of race riots and killings in major cities. The news was full of horrific race riots and towns being burned to the ground. Many of my friends and family members back home were stocking up on guns and ammo in anticipation of the inevitable race wars. A lot of black guys from the cities had big chips on their shoulders and spent a lot of time thinking about what was happening back home. We had white and black soldiers who wouldn't eat at the same tables or use the bathrooms at the same time.

For the most part, the drill sergeants were able to keep a lid on the simmering racial tensions, but occasionally, something would cause tensions to boil over, and all hell would break loose. Unbeknownst to us, while we were at basic training, the Army was dealing with all out-race riots on Army posts all over the world. It was so bad at some posts that the Army broke down units by race and kept the soldiers apart from one another. Because the Army is a closed society, they were able to keep it hidden from the press and from the average American.

We were going to be facing a whole new world when we got out of basic training and arrived at our first duty assignment. If we had known in advance what we were going to experience, we just might have called it quits and gone home. I wonder how the people of America would have felt had they known the guys with all the guns and ammunition were getting so close to fighting it out with one another.

Just to show that truth is stranger than fiction, our biggest problem at Fort Knox occurred when we were training to respond to race riots. The race riots happening all over the country prompted the Army to add mandatory riot training to its training regimen. To prepare us to be riot policemen, they issued us clear plastic shields, wooden batons, and black football-type helmets with face guards. The drill sergeants would form us up in lines and force us to remain still and calm with our shields up and our emotions under control. Meanwhile, other soldiers acting as rioters in civilian clothing threw bottles and rocks at us, pushed us, yelled obscene comments, and generally did everything they could to make us lose control.

The worst part of the exercises would be when they spit on us or threw cups of urine over our shields. We knew that it was only a training exercise and that the rioters were fellow soldiers throwing iced tea. Even with that knowledge, it sometimes got to be too much for us to handle, and we lost control more times than we remained calm. God help any rioters if we were called in to calm things down. If we couldn't control ourselves in a situation that we knew to be a test, what chance did we have in the real world?

Clearing a city street of rioters required two hundred soldiers in full riot gear, taking small controlled steps all at the same time. Every time we took a step forward, we would stomp our feet, strike our shield with our Baton, and yell,

"Ugh." The theory was that two hundred young men in riot gear shouting in unison and moving steadily toward you would make even the bravest rioter turn tail and run. The problem was that being in a riot formation was such a power rush that the longer we practiced, the harder it became for the drill sergeants to control the formation.

As soon as we realized we had the power over the imaginary crowd in front of us, we wanted to rush forward, force them to run, and just bust some heads. There is something about seeing people flee before you in a panic that caused even the most liberal of young men to lose control and start to swing for heads with his baton.

On one particular day, the drill sergeants had assigned about thirty black soldiers to rioter duty and ordered them to oppose the riot formation and to generally raise hell with us. The Army must have assumed any riot that we were going to face on the outside would be made up primarily of black people. After some heavy taunting and swearing, shoving and spitting, some of the guys in the riot unit broke loose and began to beat our actors to the ground with batons, adding a few well-placed kicks whenever they thought they could get away with it. Seeing that things were about to get out of hand, the sergeants rushed to intervene and almost had everything back under control when one of the black guys in our unit began to yell.

He screamed at the drill sergeants, "This is bullshit; the man wants us brothers to use our training to beat down young black men from our cities. Where are all the white rioters? Why are all the rioters always young black men? How come it all got to be about us beating the shit out of our black brothers and sisters? This is nothing but more Army bullshit. We don't have to take this abuse."

Things were starting to heat up, and you could hear the stirring of complaints from other voices in the crowd. It began as a whisper but quickly started to get louder and louder. It was as if someone had a large stereo system and was slowly turning up the volume. It looked like we were about to have our first official race riot, at our first riot training class. In the seventies, no one cared about being politically correct. The word "nigger" was often thrown around, and no one really gave a shit who it offended.

"The entire time we have been here the white motherfuckers in charge have been trying to brainwash us into hating all black folks," the black guy continued. "Well, this is bullshit. I'm not your puppet or your pet attack dog. I'm not taking any more of this white racist bullshit. We are men, we have brains, we can think. I refuse to go against my black brothers. No more! No more! No more!"

Finishing his impromptu speech, he thrust his right fist into the air and screamed, "Black power! Down with the slave masters. Brothers, are you with me?"

Like a virus infecting its host, one by one and then in groups, the black guys began to throw their batons on the ground and thrust their right fists into the air. Since almost half the trainees at Fort Knox were black, we had us the beginnings of a stalemate on our hands. There we were on the practice field, approximately one hundred guys on each side with a smattering of Hispanic and Asian guys wondering where the fuck they fit in. We were supposed to be training to stop riots, and it looked like we were going to have one of our own. For a while, it looked like the drill sergeants were going to be able to control the situation, and I figured it was going to end with them breaking up the formation and sending us all back to the barracks to cool down. After all, the black soldiers were just standing at attention with heads bowed and right fists thrust into the air. No one was fighting or causing any problems.

The drill sergeants were running around, doing what they do best, screaming at the top of their lungs. They were trying to get things back under control, but it was clear to even the most naive trainee that they had lost command of the situation, and nothing they were doing was going to get things back in hand. No one wanted to back down. The black soldiers refused to move, and some of the Southern white guys were starting to egg them on. Unfortunately, no one was paying any attention to the drill sergeants, and their screaming was doing more to escalate the situation than it was to calm things down. Nothing good was going to come of this. You know how the air gets right before a badass thunderstorm is going to hit when you can feel and smell it coming? Well, that's how it felt on that training field.

There was a definite feeling of electricity in the air. Tensions were rising, drill sergeants were screaming, and hotheads on both sides of the standoff were doing their best to ignite a confrontation. I had never been in combat, but I felt sure that this must be precisely how it felt right before the big assault takes place. I didn't know what was going to happen, but I did know it was going to be fast and furious, and there were going to be winners and losers.

Realizing the drill sergeants weren't going to regain control of the trainees, the sergeant major directed one of his drill sergeants to call the military police and tell them to get a team over to the parade field ASAP. When the military police arrived, I felt sorry for them. Even though they had guns, there was no way in hell they were going to be able to do anything against agitated trainees with clubs, helmets, and batons.

Things had escalated past the point of no return. The head MP was doing his best to browbeat us into laying down our clubs and returning to our barracks. He had one of those bullhorn things and was saying whatever he could think of to convince us that if we didn't obey his orders that we were all going to go to jail. You could tell from his voice that even he didn't believe what he was telling us. He knew he was screwed, and we knew that he knew.

People can see through bullshit, and it always makes things worse. Ten MPs weren't able to lock up or control a mass of trainees. Things went from bad to worse. Four black MPs with the team dropped their helmets and joined in the protest and raised their fists into the air in support of the black trainees. Things were deteriorating fast.

I was beginning to think that this might be the start of the big racial civil war that all the people had been talking about on TV and in the news. Those nut jobs waiting for the race war back home were going to be surprised when they discovered that the Wolverines were part of the spark that started it. It wasn't too much of a stretch to imagine a conflict in the Army boiling over into the general population. What a shit storm.

There is still a lot of argument about who finally ignited the fuse that day. Every time the Wolverines get together for a beer or two and reminisce, we argue about whether it was the blacks or the whites who pushed the button. Some say one of the Mississippi rednecks called one of the brothers a "nigger" and smashed him in the head with his baton. Others say one of the black guys grabbed a baton from a white guy and yelled, "Let's kill these white motherfuckers!"

As for me, I have no idea. The only thing I know for sure was that one minute we were all yelling at each other while the MPs and drill sergeants were trying to break things up, and the next minute it was a free-for-all with everyone swinging batons and fighting one another. The MPs, true to form, ran for the cover of their cars. Guns or no guns, they wanted no part of this mess.

I had never seen anything like it before, or since. Several hundred young men were trying to kill one another with short wooden batons. Many of the guys were going down, and the smart ones were dropping their batons and running for the shelter of the drill sergeants. Sgt. Harper was herding up the ones that had been knocked down or exited the melee. He had them in the front-leaning rest position doing pushups while his fellow drill sergeants were slowly culling the herd. Slowly but surely, they were able to regain control of the situation. It helped that most of the guys wore themselves out swinging at each other.

There were a lot of minor injuries that day, but thankfully they were mostly superficial, and no permanent damage was inflicted. I figure it was a lot like watching a bunch of football players in a fistfight on the field. While everyone throws a lot of punches, no one really gets hurt because they are all wearing too much protective gear. In our case, we all had helmets, gloves, facemasks, shields, and batons. We couldn't do much damage, and if you were dumb enough to hit someone in the head with your bare hand, then the helmet would usually win the battle.

When it finally ended, we realized the last ones on the field of battle were the Wolverines. Not because we had any deep-seated racial hatred but rather because we had quickly sought out one another, formed a perimeter, and fought as a team. We had instinctively formed a circle and were defending each other's flanks and backs. No one, white or black, was getting inside that circle or taking down one of the Wolverines. No one wanted to leave and let his fellow Wolverines take a beating. So, we just stood our ground and fought. The other trainees, both black and white, realized that to take on one of the Wolverines meant taking on the entire group, and it would be a big mistake. More than one trainee of both races went down that day when they mistakenly attacked our group. The smart ones stayed as far away from the crazy white boys from the UP as possible. Not a good idea to try to fight an entire platoon, especially a platoon of crazy boys from Northern Michigan.

It ended as quickly as it started. What looked like World War III had suddenly become a bunch of tired, worn-out trainees. Lots of scrapes and bruises but that was it. The black guy who gave the speech was kicked out of the Army, but nothing was done to the rest of us. The only tangible outcome was the elimination of riot training and a substantial increase in race relations classes.

For some unknown reason, the Wolverines were particularly targeted for extra classes on race relations. They must have thought that because we had fought together and wouldn't walk away from the field, we were all racist or something. At first, it was no big deal, but it became a pain in the ass when we realized that it would follow us wherever we went for the remainder of our time in the Army. The Army leadership probably maintained a bigot list somewhere, and the Wolverines were on the top of it.

The drill sergeants responded the same way they did to any infraction by trainees; they dramatically increased physical training for our brigade and upped the harassment, but they never spoke about the near riot and our failure to follow orders or instructions. The Army figured as long as we were engaged, we would be too tired and worn out to even think about fighting one another. I know the whole event must have sent shock waves through the Army training command and, naturally, they elected to ignore the situation, rather than take any steps to rectify the problem or attempt to prevent a reoccurrence in the future. By ignoring the problem, the incidents at basic training only escalated in both size and scope. They should have remembered, "Those who fail to learn from history are doomed to repeat it."

# Chapter 16
## Moving Day

It was our third week at Fort Knox, and I had mentally and physically locked myself into a monotonous routine of training. The days were rolling by quicker than I could have imagined. The Army had us so busy that we hardly had time to think, and we lost track of time. Every day was another day of training and another day of sore muscles and chronic fatigue from the oppressive Kentucky heat and humidity. When I got back to the barracks after one particularly rough day, I found that Sgt. Harper had once again passed out dead drunk on the first bunk on the bottom floor.

This was easily the ninth or tenth time someone in the platoon had found him in this position and in this condition. It happened so often that at this point, no one was even surprised. Poor Sgt. Harper. It was as if he had used every ounce of his willpower and energy to make it back to the barracks and into the front door, but he just couldn't seem to get past that first bunk and had collapsed on it. Well, at least this time he made the bunk. Most times he just ended up on the floor.

What I could never figure out, because no one had ever seen him enter the barracks, was how he got down the street and into the barracks without being caught. He was drunk out of his mind, and nothing we could do could rouse him from his heavy snoring and deep trance-like sleep. He must have had a perfect sense of timing because the trainees were always out when he got wasted, and he never seemed to run into any of the battalion leadership. He had a way of materializing out of thin air.

While others in the barracks, used to the scene, stood or sat around, Bob and I, per our usual routine, each took an end, one on the head and one on the legs, and hauled him up the stairs and down the hall to his private room. It was a good thing he was so skinny because we could never have dragged a larger man up those narrow stairs and, even with his thin frame, you would be surprised how hard it is to lift and carry someone who is dead drunk.

Unlike most of the drill sergeants, I think Harper lived in his small room more than he lived at his quarters over on the main post. I don't believe the Army intended for the drill sergeant rooms in the barracks to be lived in; they were mainly small offices with a cot on one side. The cot was in the rooms to give the drill sergeants a place to rest occasionally and to allow them to get away from trainees. It certainly wasn't designed to be slept on for long periods.

No one ever saw Sgt. Harper eat, only drink and only alcohol. He didn't own a car, and the room the Army provided him was rent-free. Other than boot polishing, laundry for his uniforms, beer, and cigarettes, he was living a money-free existence. One of my theories was that he was saving all his money for the island retreat he kept telling us he was going to move to and drink himself to death on when he retired.

We carried Harper's limp body to his room and laid him on the floor. I propped his head up against the wall, while Bob, our resident burglar, pulled out a lock pick from his wallet and quickly popped the lock on the door. I kept asking him to teach me how to pick locks because I was sure it was a trick that would come in handy someday. But Bob steadfastly refused, stating that once you learned how to do it, you couldn't resist trying tougher and tougher locks, and that would only lead to getting in trouble with the police.

"It becomes a challenge you just can't resist," he explained.

As soon as the lock popped free, we opened the door and hustled to get Sgt. Harper into the room and onto his cot. We had to move quickly, not because anyone cared that he was drunk again. Hell, everyone knew he had a drinking problem, but whenever Sgt. Bond realized that he had no one around to countermand his orders, he would take the opportunity to make our lives a living hell. Unfortunately, this was not to be our lucky day. As soon as we got Harper into his cot, Sgt. Bond walked into the room. I just knew we were dead.

"All right, Moron, how did you and your butt buddy get into this room?"

Not being born yesterday, I immediately replied, "The door was open when we got here, Drill Sergeant."

Bob backed me up. "We found Drill Sergeant Harper lying on the floor, and the door was already open."

I chimed in, "He must have been so drunk that he unlocked the door and then just passed out before he could get into his room. Bob and I were just putting him on his bunk so he wouldn't get a crick in his neck from laying on the floor all day."

Drill Sgt. Bond looked at me like I was crazy. "No way," he replied, "I've been here through four trainee cycles and have never seen him make it past the first bunk."

I said, "Well, maybe he was drinking a new kind of booze, you know, one of them delayed alcohol type drinks."

Bond stared at me, and I gave him my best idiot look, then he just shrugged and said, "Moron, you're too fucking stupid to make any sense. Hurry up and get him in his cot and get the fuck out of his room. I never want to see you two trainees in a drill sergeant's room ever again. Is that clear?"

"Yes, Mr. Drill Sergeant, clear as a bell," I replied.

That was easier than I thought it would be. I figured we were home free, but as I closed the door to Harper's room, Bond puffed out his pitiful little chest and began to scold us.

"I don't know how you trainees can stand to live in this pigsty of a barracks. The living conditions here are so pitiful that they make a Vietnamese rice paddy full of shit look like a palace. What the fuck is wrong with you people? Are you trying to spread disease all over this entire post? Do you realize how many of the world's epidemics started at Army posts because people like you failed to follow regulations and decided in your little minds that you wanted to live like pigs? Are you purposely trying to kill everyone who lives here? I could give a shit if you want to kill each other, but I don't want me or my fellow drill sergeants to get sick because of you pigs."

We knew we were in for it. He was just starting, and it was going to get worse. He knew that Sgt. Harper was not there to stop him. He was in his element, and we were about to get screwed.

What drove me crazy was the fact that the barracks were the cleanest place that most of us had ever lived in. Despite being built in World War II, they were cleaned so often and so thoroughly that everything in them gleamed. This was the only place I had ever been where we cleaned the light bulbs and made sure that the pull strings on the individual lights were removed, washed, bleached, and then reattached. The windows had been cleaned so many times that it was not unusual for birds to fly into the glass. None of this mattered to drill sergeants. They were always able to come up with dirt from somewhere. I don't know how they did it. I swear they carried dirt in their pockets and threw it into a corner or on a bed whenever we weren't looking. Sometimes they used that imaginary dirt that only drill sergeants could see. The worst asshole of them all at finding imaginary dirt was Drill Sgt. Bond.

When he was finished berating us for living like animals, he screamed at the top of his lungs, "I want everyone in this building standing at attention on the company street in ten seconds.

"Ladies, I have something special for you to do."

Once we scrambled out into the company street and were standing at attention, he let us sit and simmer in silence for a while. When he felt we had been waiting for the appropriate time, he began to address the platoon.

"Ladies, it has come to my attention that the living conditions in this platoon's barracks have become so unhealthy that the United States Army might actually be putting your health and very lives at risk. These abysmal living conditions were brought to my attention by one of the Morons in your unit, Private Berlin, and if someone as stupid as Berlin notices how unsanitary it is in the barracks, who am I to argue? You know I am the last person in the world who would want any of my trainees to get sick and die because I wasn't doing my job and paying close attention to the living conditions. But don't worry, my little piggies, I won't let you continue to lay in your own filth. Luckily for you, I have come up with a plan to make sure the situation is rectified and restore this barracks to its proper state of cleanliness.

"It's a well-known fact that in the civilian world, the only time that most homes get truly cleaned is when the occupants move to a new home. Something about moving everything you own out of one home and then moving it all into a new home forces people to take stock of their surroundings and really do that deep-down cleaning. Well, shitheads, I have decided that today is going to be your very own moving day. I'm going to go home, take a nice long nap, maybe take a hot bath, and drink an ice-cold beer. While I'm gone, you are all restricted to the platoon area and will conduct house-moving exercises. I expect everyone on the first floor to move to the top floor, and everyone on the top floor will move to the bottom floor.

"Now, piggies, this is not going to be a moving day like you are used to. This is going to be Army-style moving. You are going to move everything you own, and as far as I am concerned, you own everything on your floor. I want beds, lockers, clothing, bedding, boots, Venetian blinds, hell, I even want the fucking light bulbs moved. If you find a speck of dust on the top floor, I better find it moved to the bottom floor. I'm leaving for three hours. When I get back, I expect to see this move completed and everyone living comfortably in their new, clean homes. Now move your asses and let's get this place fit for human habitation."

The worst part of all Bond's crap was that we had nothing to do that evening, and we were all looking forward to some much-needed sack time without the harassment of the drill sergeants.

As soon as he departed the area, we immediately got to work. Now 'get to work' means different things to different people. As was our platoon's standard routine at Fort Knox when we got ready to go to work, we gathered together, rolled some joints, and began planning and bitching. We could usually figure out some way to get out of stupid work, but in this case, we knew that we were getting screwed. There seemed no way out of our dilemma. Sgt. Harper was passed out cold, so he wouldn't be of any help to us, and if he remained true to his regular schedule, we wouldn't be seeing him until he woke up for PT the next morning. Well, if we were going to be working our ass off, at least we would be high while we were doing it.

Right at the point when we were all reaching that mellow state from the smoke, and as we were commiserating and trying to find some way to get out of all the work we knew was coming our way, Bob suddenly sounded off.

"I don't know if it's just my vastly superior intelligence or just the dope talking, but I think I have a way out of this mess. Look, we know for sure that Hitler left the company area and probably won't be back until the three hours are up. We know from experience that he will more than likely get back here about half an hour early, so he can nitpick and harass us for the last thirty minutes or so. Why do we have to move everything? Why don't we just move our clothing from the top floor to the bottom level? We will just leave all the equipment, all the furniture, hell, even leave the bedding in place exactly where it is.

"To make it look good, we will dismantle two or three of the bunks up here and a couple on the first floor, just in case he stops by to check on our progress. That dumb fuck isn't going to figure out that we really haven't moved any of the heavy stuff or any of the equipment. Gentlemen, we sit around and bullshit for a couple of hours, and when we know we are being watched, we pretend to work our asses off for as long as it takes to make an impression on that idiot Bond."

Everyone was in immediate agreement. Bob was our new hero. We should have thought it out a little bit more, but what do you expect from a bunch of guys who were getting high? Clearly, the decision-making functions in our brains were not working at full power at the time, and, besides, we would do just about anything to get out of work. We were the perfect example of the old saying, "If we worked as hard doing shit as we did trying to get out of work, we would have been the most successful soldiers in the world."

We had the perfect plan, what could possibly go wrong? All we had to do was create a little camouflage, stage a diversion, and then sit around and get high for a couple of hours while Bond thought we were working our asses off. The best thing about the plan was that Bond was nothing if not predictable. I wouldn't want to go into combat with that idiot. The enemy would be able to figure him out in about two minutes. Just like clockwork, thirty minutes before our designated completion time, we got word from the lookouts that Hitler was on his way back to the platoon area.

As he came down the street, we went into full mobilization mode. Everyone began to play his role in the excellent moving day deception. Before Bond returned, we had stripped down to our t-shirts and splashed water on our faces and chests to make it look like we had been sweating our asses off. A little water here, a little dirt here, some dazed expressions, lots of slow-moving trainees. We hoped we looked like a totally worn-out and disillusioned moving crew that had been working hard for several long, grueling hours.

As soon as we had all the camouflage in place, we made a big show of moving the 'last' pieces of equipment down and up the stairs at the same time. We wanted it to appear as if we were rushing as fast as we could to make the final adjustments. All the guys who were not moving the furniture pretended that they were sweeping, mopping, dusting, and doing touch-up work. We even had one of the guys standing on a chair twisting in the "last light bulb" and then making a big show of dusting it off when he was done. I was pretty sure that we had everything covered. There was absolutely no way that he could know we had moved only our clothing. The only thing that we had a hard time hiding were the smiles on some of the guys' faces.

When Little Hitler came into the first platoon barracks, he merely stood off to one side and watched us moving and reassembling the last of the bunk beds and wall lockers. We played our parts to the max, huffing, and puffing, dripping fake sweat, and complaining about all the hard work. Hitler just stood there and watched us, never said a word. He had his feet apart and arms folded, staring at his watch once in a while. This worried me a little because being silent was not in his nature. He usually just screamed at us, yelling at us to hurry up and calling us names. He enjoyed the screaming because it allowed him to exert his authority over us, and he liked to see us squirm under his control. He got to be the big man. The more he belittled us, the bigger he felt. With overexaggerated and entirely overacted tiredness and hustle, we finished the final act of our little show.

Drill Sgt. Bond waited until the last bunk was in place and checked his watch once again; we were one minute ahead of schedule, so we weren't concerned. When we were finished, Bond had us all standby our bunks for inspection. We figured that he was going to check for cleanliness, which didn't worry us because the damn place was spotless before we began, so it hadn't required much effort on our part. We also assumed he would be going through wall lockers to check name tags and personal items, just to make sure that we had performed the move. It looked like we had finally won a battle against the biggest asshole of a drill sergeant in the entire battalion.

Not so fast. Sgt. Bond decided to start his inspection on the top floor and work his way down. When Hitler got to the first bunk, he pushed a wall locker over on its side and then made a big show of flipping the bunk bed on its side. He then bent over, looked at the bottom of the wall locker and the bunk beds, and, with a bright red face and drool coming out the corner of his mouth, screamed:

"This is not my first rodeo, you dumb fucks. Did you really think that you were the first group of trainees to try and pull a fast one on ole Sergeant Bond? I think you forget that I am a combat veteran, trained to deceive and overwhelm the enemy. I notice everything. I find everything. You all messed with the wrong drill sergeant this time. When you decided to match wits with me, you lost the battle before the first shot was fired."

Pointing to me, he yelled, "Dummy, get your ass over here and tell me what you see on the bottom of that wall locker?"

As I bent down to look at the bottom of this wall locker and saw what he was pointing at, I realized that the son of a bitch had won again.

How could we have been so stupid? We had just let the biggest idiot in a uniform get one over on us. I blamed the weed; we were usually smarter than this. There on the bottom of the wall locker was a white dot painted in the center of the base.

"You see that white dot, dummy, a dummy mark, a white dot, just like the one on your helmet." Pointing to the bottom of the bunk bed, he said, "Oh look, more white dots."

He then knocked the footlocker on its side. "More white dots. Oh my goodness, now how did all of these white dots get on all of this equipment?" As he was smiling and gloating, I kept thinking, how in the fuck did we miss them all? Now that I looked at them, they were as plain as the nose on my face.

"You know what?" he shouted. "I bet if I go downstairs, none of the equipment has any dots. Now let's recap, pussies. When I left several hours ago, all the gear up here had white dots, and all the gear downstairs had no white dots. Now that I am back, I find that none of the dots have moved, but you all tell me that all the furniture was in fact moved. Now, without thinking so hard you blow a gasket or something, how do you suppose that happened, dummy?"

I immediately replied, "Gosh, I don't know, Drill Sergeant, do you think someone painted these dots on here when we were sleeping last night?"

At this, Hitler exploded. "You stupid shit, you know exactly what I am talking about. You and your friends here moved your personal gear and didn't move one single piece of furniture. You have all broken the cardinal rule in basic training. Not only have you failed to follow instructions, but you have lied to a drill sergeant. I could have understood if you were trying to deceive that old drunk Harper, but how in what world did you think you could get the best of Drill Sergeant Bond?"

As I said, we were fucked. Little Hitler went into a full-blown rampage, or should I say tantrum? He got everyone assembled on the first floor and walked up and down the barracks with his hands behind his back like Napoleon. Every few minutes, he would stop, grab someone's gear out of his wall locker and throw it out one of the windows. By the time he was finished with his rampage, half of our equipment was in the street, and everything else was thrown in piles in the center of the floor, no man's land.

There would be hell to pay if we couldn't get our clothes out of there without stepping on the floor. He kicked over all the footlockers and whatever fell out got kicked, shoved, or tossed into the ever-growing pile of gear and clothing. He ripped the blinds from the windows, upturned the trash cans at the end of the floors, and generally destroyed the barracks. When he was done upstairs, he headed downstairs, and for the next thirty minutes, we heard him doing the same thing down there.

When he was finally finished, he stomped back up the stairs and pointed to me.

"Dummy," he said, "tell your dumb-fuck platoon buddies to try it one more time. This time move everything exactly as I told you to do it the first time. If you fuck this up again, we will be conducting platoon-level moving exercises for the next two weeks. Is that clear enough for you? Next time it won't be upstairs, downstairs. Next time it's going to be a mile down the street. Am I making myself clear or do I have to write it down in crayon so you can understand?

"Two more hours, girls. I'm going back to my quarters."

OK, time to get to work again, which for the first platoon translated to, let's get high again. There had to be some way we could work our way out of this shit without working. Bob apologized over and over to everyone. He was convinced that all the extra work was his fault.

"I know better than that," he said. "I committed the cardinal sin of an infantryman. I underestimated the enemy, and frankly, I'm embarrassed that Hitler nailed us. That Hitler is a little bit smarter than I gave him credit for. I guess my mistake was thinking that he was a complete idiot and not giving him any credit at all."

I told Bob, "Calm down and don't take this personally. This isn't all your fault. We all agreed to the plan, and the blame should be shared equally. Besides, we really haven't lost anything, because we really didn't do anything." I continued, "It wouldn't have mattered anyway. You know that asshole. Even if we had moved everything, he would have made up some shit to make us do it all over again."

We began the arduous task of sorting through the various piles that Hitler had created and collected our shit from outside of the building. We were exactly where we started when this horrible day began. So much for getting some shut-eye.

Bob said, "I guess we need to get moving."

It was going to be a long two hours. None of us saw any way out of moving this time. We were resigning ourselves to our fate.

As we sat around complaining and finishing up our last joint, it suddenly hit me. "Hey, guys, not so fast. I'm pretty sure we can still convince Hitler that we moved everything without really moving."

I knew I was taking a big chance because if he caught on to us messing with him a second time, there was no telling what he would do to us. I knew he would figure out some way of destroying us, but we just had to try. I couldn't stomach that asshole beating us at anything. I asked Luney, one of my fellow Morons, to go down to the cleaning closet and get some rags and rubbing alcohol. We always used rubbing alcohol to clean the brass and metal in the bathroom before polishing them with Brasso to make them shine. I then sent Bob over to the unit headquarters to borrow as many bottles of White-Out as the company clerk could spare. Everyone was curious as to what I had up my sleeve, and no one was in a big hurry to work, so they agreed to at least hear me out.

As soon as Bob and Luney returned with the supplies, I took stock of what we had. A box of rags, two bottles of rubbing alcohol, and five bottles of White-Out. I took a small tape measure and a notebook out of my locker and told the platoon, "Watch and learn, gentlemen. This is phase one."

I measured exactly where the white dot was on the bottom of the wall locker and carefully copied the information onto a page in my notebook. I didn't know if Bond had any idea of exactly where the white dots on the furniture were, but I wasn't going to take any chances.

"OK, guys, let's go downstairs for phase two."

When we got downstairs, I pushed over a wall locker, used the tape measure to find the exact location that I had measured on the wall locker on the second floor, took out the White-Out, and painted a white dot in the same place.

Voila, instant moving. "OK, guys, same plan as before. I'll take all of the measurements and paint all of the new dots."

The last thing we needed was more than one person involved in the painting portion of the plan. We needed to make sure that we maintained consistency. I was convinced that Bond had done this by himself, so I wanted to make sure that every dot was in the same place when he looked at them.

This was not my first forgery attempt. When I was done painting all the new dots and had double checked to verify that they were in the correct positions, we used the alcohol and rags to completely erase the dots from the furniture on the second floor.

Before we started, I formed a team of four individuals whose job it was to search every piece of equipment from top to bottom to make sure that there were no additional dots or marks anywhere on any of the furniture that might trip us up a second time. It was a good thing that we had, because we found small white dots on the third bed spring from the top on every bunk. "No problem, just one more simple measurement."

A few guys were still not convinced and didn't want to take a chance at pissing off Hitler more than we had already. They were paranoid that if we got caught again that we would end up moving our barracks equipment a mile down the street next time. I carefully explained to them that even if we did get caught, it wouldn't be more work, because we hadn't done the job he had told us to do in the first place.

Besides, Hitler was such an asshole that it really didn't matter what we did or didn't do. He was going to make our lives miserable. We might as well put up a good fight. Worst case scenario, it could only last as long as Sgt. Harper was passed out or until early the next morning. He wasn't going to let us get out of training to play moving games with Drill Sgt. Bond.

Lookouts were posted down the street while the survey team meticulously checked every inch of every piece of equipment. The alcohol team cleared the dots as soon as I certified that every piece of equipment had been measured, and the drying team made sure the new dot was dry and reset the furniture. All in all, it was the perfect military operation. While the teams were hard at work, the rest of the platoon returned all our clothing to the correct lockers. It looked like everything was going great. We were able to finish the job in less than thirty minutes. We were going to win the battle after all.

The whole time that we were working, a lot of the guys just wanted to get high. They didn't understand why they had to remain straight just to move clothing. Trying to control the guys in the platoon was a whole lot harder than figuring out how to get out of work. It was one of the hardest things I had ever done, but I managed to keep them away from the pot long enough to complete the move. I hoped I would never have to be in charge of anyone in the Army. We checked every single inch of the barracks to make sure that no White-Out had spilled anywhere on the floor or left any telltale marks.

Just to make sure we had covered all our tracks, we took all the empty Whit-Out bottles to a trash can four blocks away, and then we topped off the alcohol bottles with water so it would appear that they had not been used. We traded our rags with the platoon across the street because ours reeked of alcohol, and we didn't want to have to answer any questions in case Bond smelled them in the closet.

All the bases had been covered. Because this whole plan had been my idea, I felt responsible, so I took every possible precaution to cover our tracks. I didn't want everyone to suffer more on my account. This was a precision operation, and one small mistake could blow it. As soon as everything was back in place, and I had verified that we had made no mistakes or left anything out of place, we finally took the time to do what we do best. We sat around, rolled another joint, and got high.

Right on time, about thirty minutes before our time was up, we got a heads-up from the lookouts.

"Little Hitler is on his way."

By the time we got the word, we were prepared for an Academy Award-winning performance. Looking tired, discouraged, and worn down, we stood by our bunks for inspection. Some of the guys had even run around and around the building a couple of times so that they would be sweating for real and breathing hard when Hitler arrived. Those of us who didn't run sported good, but fake, water-induced sweat marks on our clothing. This performance was going to be better than the last one; it had to be. The key to this fake-out would be convincing Hitler that he had broken our spirits and that we just couldn't take any more of his harassment. He had to believe that he was the tough drill sergeant and that he had utterly outsmarted the entire platoon. The only thing that could screw us now was a stupid mistake or a weak member of our conspiracy spilling his guts.

Just like he did during his previous inspection, Hitler knocked over wall lockers, footlockers, and bunk beds. He checked all the visible spots first, and then pulled the mattresses and looked in detail at the bed springs to see if the marks he had placed on them had also moved from floor to floor. I only hoped that he hadn't been smart enough to have hidden more identifying marks somewhere we never thought of looking. It looked like our luck was holding. He was apparently satisfied with what he saw on the equipment. Our extreme fatigue and our broken spirit act seemed to be carrying the day. This was one time when being stoned out of your mind was an asset. We looked so utterly lethargic that he assumed he had beaten us down and that we were moving slowly because we were beat to shit.

With a smug look of satisfaction on his face, Hitler informed us that he hoped we had learned several lessons that day. The first lesson, he said, was to keep his barracks spotless and prepared for inspection always, and to stop living like civilian pigs. Another lesson was that on his worst day, he was smarter than all of us put together and that to try and match wits with him was a futile effort at best. He claimed that in his many years in the Army, thousands of trainees had tried to outsmart him, but he had won every time.

He boasted, "I'm not a has-been soft leader like Drill Sergeant Harper. I am a modern leader, intelligent, highly trained, and honed in combat. You would all be wise to pay attention to my leadership techniques and try to emulate them. If you want to survive in combat and get promoted in my Army, you would be wise to walk in my footprints. Guys like Harper are dinosaurs, and the Army is going to replace them with modern intelligent NCOs like me. Harper will never get promoted again. He will end up retiring in a year or two, if he doesn't die of alcohol poisoning first. I am going to end up as the command sergeant major of the Army."

I just couldn't resist.

"You're right, Drill Sergeant, we did learn a lot of lessons today.

Bob was glaring at me, and his eyes were saying, *Shut the fuck up before you piss him off, and we have to do this all over again.*

Bond, on the other hand, seemed to soak it all up. He thought I was paying him homage.

As Drill Sgt. Bond left the barracks for what we hoped would be the final time that evening, he suddenly stopped, turned around, pointed at me and said, "I don't know what you're going to do when you get to the real Army, dummy. You're so stupid that everyone you meet is going to take advantage of you. You're the kind of soldier that they send out ahead of the patrol to find out where the land mines are. In my estimation you won't last a month."

I thought to myself, "If everyone is as stupid as you, I will be promoted to general in a month."

Moron

# Chapter 17
## Mail Call

Any Soldier will tell you it doesn't matter if you have been in the Army for twenty days or twenty years—soldiers live for daily mail call. In the seventies there was no such thing as personal computers. No one had even conceived of the cell phone or email, and there were no twenty-four-hour news channels, or even cable TV in many areas. Long distance phone calls were so expensive that they were not within the means of most soldiers. The minimum wage was only $1.60, and a long-distance phone call was ten dollars for three minutes. If you wanted to call home, you would have to work for nearly three full days just to make a ten-minute call.

The only news soldiers got was in the mail sent by friends and families. Long letters from home, love notes from girlfriends and wives, Dear John letters, and care packages with homemade cookies and candy were routine. Some of the guys even had their local newspapers mailed to them every day so they could keep up on hometown news. More than once in my time with the Army, I heard senior leaders say:

"You can make a soldier walk a hundred miles in the rain and snow, you can treat him like shit and make him sleep in the muck and mud, but the one thing you never do is mess with his mail. If you do that, you will cause a mutiny in the ranks."

Mail was our religion, and mail call was our holy communion.

Our lifelines to our hometowns, family, and, more importantly, girls were in the form of pen and paper. Our only connection to humanity and to home was through the good ole U.S. Mail. Mail call in the Army was an exciting time; it was like Christmas every day. You never knew what you were going to get or who you were going to get it from. You were always hoping for something good and wanted to be able to impress the other recruits with the fact that people cared enough about you to send you something, especially women. No one wanted to be that guy who never got anything.

Mail call was also one of the few things that you could count on. No matter how hard the training was or how abusive the drill sergeants became, they always made sure that all trainees were present for mail call. Mail call was held at noon every day except for Sunday. Wherever we were or whatever we were doing, the unit halted for mail call at noon.

Nothing stopped the mail; weather, war, famine, you name it, we still got mail. If we were away from the unit area, say at the range or the obstacle course, the command carted the mail out to our location. It was comforting to know that there was one thing we could count on, and it was the one equalizer in basic training. Everybody attended mail call to get mail, from the lowest ranking private to the highest-ranking sergeant major. Everything came by mail—bills, news, letters, food, bad news, good news, everything.

Mail for soldiers was sent directly to units. Soldiers were not allowed to receive mail at private addresses. I was never able to figure this out, but maybe the Army just had to have control over every single aspect of your life. This made it a little hard for many wives who had to rely on their soldier husband to bring home bills, packages, and letters. The Army ran its own post offices and had a unit mail address for every unit in the Army. It was one of the few systems in the Army that worked.

Mail call was the same no matter where in the Army you were assigned, basic training or Vietnam. The unit was called together, and the mail clerk would stand in front of the formation and yell out names. When your name was called, you stepped forward, and the mail clerk would toss you your letter or package. A lot of guys bought stuff through the mail just so they could get packages and have their name called. The only difference between mail call in basic training and other units in the Army was that our mail was censored by the drill sergeants.

Now, the Army told you that unless you were in Vietnam, under no circumstances did they censor mail. But there was censorship. During basic training, the Army censored our mail in a way that ensured they maintained control over us while ensuring they could not be accused of tampering with the U.S. Mail.

The Army didn't want us to have anything that could possibly undo the mental conditioning that was being pounded continuously into us twenty-four hours a day, seven days a week. They had worked too hard to let some crap from home upset us or cause our training to become ineffective. The rules for mail call were simple but strictly enforced.

If you received a package from anyone, you were required to open it immediately. I mean right then and in front of all your fellow trainees. If you got food, you had a choice: you could eat it yourself, or you could pass it out to the other members of your platoon and allow them to share your bounty with you. Once again, this had to happen immediately. Under no circumstances could you leave mail call formation with anything that was considered edible. If you had any drugs or contraband, then everyone would be able to see it, and you would be hauled away, and the Army would confiscate whatever it was that got sent to you.

We learned that it was always best to share the food with the rest of the platoon. Not only did it prevent you from choking down ten dozen homemade chocolate chip cookies, but it also helped to bring the platoon together and create a stronger bond of brotherhood.

Nothing brings a group of young men together than sharing food that was prepared by loved ones. Guys would write home to their mothers and beg them to make the best possible goodies to share with their buddies. It became a contest, and guys achieved bragging rights based on the quality of the food that was sent to them. There was one guy from Oregon whose mother sent the best brownies I'd ever tasted.

There were fights when guys tried to take more than their fair share of those brownies. At one point during training, several of us wrote to her and thanked her for the brownies to let her know how much we enjoyed them. This turned out to be a perfect tactic because the following week, she arranged for several of the women in her neighborhood to bake a bunch of goodies, and they sent us more than five hundred brownies.

That was a great mail call. We were stuffed, but everyone was happy.

There were a few other rules, unspoken rules but rules nonetheless. If you got underwear or any type of pornography from your girlfriend or your wife, and believe me many of us did in the first couple of weeks, the mail clerk would call for a volunteer. The first person to volunteer would be allowed to take the underwear or item from you. Let me tell you the last thing that you wanted was some of those perverts having a pair of your girlfriend's underwear. God knows what was going to happen to them. Within two weeks, there was no more underwear in the mail.

There were lots of items we were not allowed to keep. Anything considered inappropriate in a package or letter was tossed in a large trash can that was brought out especially for mail call. You would be surprised by how much marijuana was mailed to trainees in 1973. The drill sergeants didn't make a big deal of it, they just made sure you tossed it into the trash. No one asked any questions, and the MPs were never called. I'm sure the mail call clerk had a lot of fun with the stuff we were forced to throw away. You could keep all your bills, letters from girlfriends, spouses, and parents because no one wanted them.

There was one catch with letters from women. If you got a letter that smelled like perfume, was addressed in feminine handwriting, had little hearts or flowers on it, or, worst-case scenario, had lipstick kisses all over it, you were a goner. The drill sergeants would make you open your letter and stand beside you while you read it out loud to the other trainees in your platoon. I had more than one letter from Paula read to the entire platoon. I sent her a letter to have her use code words as soon as I could. Some of the guys got real steamy letters in the first couple of weeks, and they were a lot of fun to listen to. The sexy messages, just like the underwear, quickly dried up when guys wrote or called home and explained what was happening.

The Army wanted to make sure we were concentrating on our training, and they were going to do whatever they could to eliminate any and all distractions. By the end of basic training, the letters were mundane, except for the occasional girlfriend who seemed to get off knowing that a bunch of guys were listening to her mail. For the first couple of weeks, mail call was a blast. It was like listening to *Penthouse* forum letters. Some of these guys had some wild women back home.

In our platoon, a lot of guys complained about letters from girlfriends being opened before they got them, and many of us were missing pictures that our girlfriends had told us they had sent to us. Specialist Ford, the mail clerk, told us that there were no problems with the mail and that they probably got opened by mistake in the crush of all the mail. He said if we were missing any pictures, they might have gotten thrown into the trash can by mistake in the mad rush of opening and reading mail every day.

Besides, he said, "Drill Sergeant Bond inspects the mailroom daily, and he has never found any discrepancies."

Since we couldn't check, the trash can was off limits, we had to take him at his word.

"After all, it would be a federal offense to mess with the mail," he said. "The Army would never allow anything like that to happen."

Specialist Ford was the biggest doper on Fort Knox. Since he knew how mail call was run, he made sure that he intercepted any packages that he thought might contain excessive amounts of dope. He said he did this to make sure we would not be arrested and was trying to protect us. He would open these packages before we got them and if they had drugs in them, he would contact the person that was supposed to get the package and then he would split the drugs with them. He could have kept it all, but that would mean the dope would have dried up pretty fast. If people thought the dope would be intercepted, then they would stop sending it.

Ford wanted to make sure the supply kept on coming. It worked out well for everyone. There was a steady supply of good dope in the barracks, and Specialist Ford kept out of our business and kept our drugs out of the trash can. We heard that he was running a significant drug operation on the side. The military police were some of his best customers, and while many of the mailrooms on post were raided, they never bothered to raid his mailroom.

The Army spent a lot of time preparing us for the loss of girlfriends and spouses during basic training. The minute we arrived, we were told by our drill sergeants that our girlfriends and wives would soon leave us and it was to be expected. The Army degraded all women, especially the women we had left behind. Even the marching songs we sang reminded us that there was a good chance our girls were going to take off while we were at basic training.

They didn't want us married, and they didn't want us to have any connections back home. The Army created a persona called "Jody," the stereotypical guy back home who was going to fuck your girlfriend or wife the minute you left home and joined the Army. Jody was a civilian enjoying the comforts of home while the soldier sweats it out in the field or overseas. Soldiers love to console themselves by singing about Jody, the main character in most of our marching songs:

> *Ain't no use in going home;*
> *Jody's got your girl and gone.*
> *Ain't no use in feeling blue;*
> *Jody's got your sister, too*
> *Ain't no use in lookin' back;*
> *Jody's got your Cadillac ..."*
> *Ain't no use in going home*
> *Jody's got your girl and gone*
> *Gonna get a three-day pass*
> *Just to kick old Jody's ass.*

Mail call also served as a valuable psychological tool for the Army. Somehow Sgt. Harper could identify a Dear John letter from a mile away. He had some kind of sixth sense that allowed him to catch them almost one hundred percent of the time. There were a lot of Dear John letters. You can imagine the promises that a lot of young teenage girls had made to young men going off to join the Army. Most of these promises were forgotten before our airplanes landed in Kentucky. Harper would always catch them and force the trainees who received one to read it out loud. You would think that this would be incredibly traumatic, but it has a strange therapeutic effect on both the individual trainee and the unit.

When the trainee was reading his letter to the rest of the guys in the platoon, we would all chime in at the appropriate places. It was a lot like a church service. We instinctively knew our parts and knew when to add our voices.

"That bitch! You just can't trust women. Hell, she's probably pulling train for every guy in town. You wouldn't want that disease-ridden cunt anyway."

"When we're done with basic training, we will all go home with you and help you to cut Jody's nuts off. They'll make a nice coin purse."

By the time the trainee was done reading his Dear John letter, everyone was clapping and cheering. It made you feel better because you knew everyone was going through it, and the other guys all blamed the women. It also gave you a chance to talk about it with the other guys and get it off your chest. Because they knew what was going on, the guys would be asking you questions later, and in answering them, you would begin to feel better.

There were so many Dear John letters that we became numb to them after a while. The Army convinced us we were next, so no one was surprised when he finally got his letter in the mail. After several weeks guys were proud to read their Dear Johns to the rest of the platoon.

The strangest package we ever saw at mail call contained a shriveled-up penis and testicles. We guessed that it had come from a deer or a horse or some other type of animal. I sure hope it wasn't human. Whatever it was quickly became a primary source of discussion and amusement for the rest of basic training, and the guy who got the package became a legend at Fort Knox. The letter inside the box was addressed to "Private Mother Fucking Simpson." It read:

"Tommy, I trusted you, you son of a bitch.

You and I were going to get married when you came back home.

You told me you were going to war and that you might die, so I gave you my virginity.

You swore that I was the only woman you had ever slept with and that I was your first.

I have clap, ass hole.

The doctor is giving me shots.

Everyone in school is making fun of me.

I went to church and prayed to God that he would hurt you as you hurt me.

I hope your dick and balls dry up like the ones I sent you.

I hope your cock falls off.

I hope you can never get hard again.

Fuck you."

We laughed our asses off. Pvt. Simpson had to go to the medic to make sure that he got treated for clap right away. He was now a basic training legend. None of us could believe any girl would be dumb enough to fall for the "I'm going to war" story that only happens in movies and on TV. His new nickname was "Broke Dick Tommy."

Moron

# Chapter 18
## Church

The Army didn't care what your religious preference was, as long as it was Christian. It didn't matter what religion you had been raised or what your affiliation was before you got to Fort Knox. Your new faith was Christian with a heavy dose of U.S. Army. Army leaders made it clear to us that the sergeant major of our battalion was God and the drill sergeants were his disciples. They told us the Army tolerated all religions and respected any deity we wished to worship. What they really meant was if you want to survive in the Army, you have to be a Christian, preferably Southern Christian. Oh yeah, according to the Army, Catholics were not really Christians, and Jews, Muslims, and, God forbid, atheists were worse than the enemy.

No one forced us to attend religious services, but we were highly encouraged to do so by our drill sergeants. How much pressure they put on you varied from platoon to platoon; it depended on the religious affiliation and intensity of belief of the drill sergeant assigned to your platoon. In our case, we were lucky because Harper and Bond could have given a shit if we believed in God or not. Bond didn't tolerate Jews, Catholics or any of the other, as he said, "heathen" religions, but he did pretty much leave us alone.

We were, however, encouraged by other drill sergeants in the battalion to go to services on Sunday morning. Every Saturday evening, the sergeants circulated through the barracks asking if anyone in their platoons was interested in attending services the following morning and encouraged us to become God-fearing soldiers. In our platoon, the sergeants simply yelled through the front door, "If any of you assholes are interested in church tomorrow, the bus leaves at 0800. Don't be fucking late."

Like soldiers throughout history, we learned on our first day in the Army that only fools volunteer for anything, and since going to church was voluntary, the collective response from our platoon was usually negative. This was part apathy and part the fact that the drill sergeants were required to leave us alone for four hours every Sunday morning. Four hours without a drill sergeant in your face meant four hours of much-needed sleep.

Only one or two guys per platoon would ever volunteer to attend services. They were our Jesus freaks or the guys who were just a little bit odd. The rest of us, being typical teenagers, usually made fun of these guys and considered them to be mama's boys or weaklings. Besides, we all knew the chaplains were ordered by the Army to try to get us to give up sex, dope, and alcohol. You know, all the good things in life. We were young and invincible, and nothing could hurt us. We certainly didn't need any Army chaplain trying to convert us into some holy-rolling celibates.

One of my fellow Morons in the first platoon, Pvt. Homer Luney, I shit you not, was one of those Bible-carrying religious types, and he definitely met the 'I'm a little odd' criterion. Homer couldn't really read a word and could barely write his own name, but he had extensive knowledge of the Bible and what he figured religion was all about. Someone, somewhere in his life, had brainwashed him to the point that he was able to quote phrases from the Bible to fit almost any situation life threw at him. The fact that he mostly got the quotes wrong was lost on most of the guys in the platoon. They just considered him to be a hick and a general pain in the ass. While everyone took every opportunity to make fun of him, no one really disliked him; he was just too simple to hate.

I liked Homer. He had a childlike honesty that made it impossible to stay mad at him for very long. It was clear to even the casual observer that he was mentally challenged, but he didn't have a mean bone in his body. The only thing that kept him from being continually harassed by the other trainees was his sheer size. Homer was six feet four, and he weighed about 240 pounds, and every ounce of that was pure country boy muscle.

Homer came from a small farming community in the hills of West Virginia and had spent his entire life working on the family farm. He told us that he began full-time work for the family when he was five and that the first time he left home was when he joined the Army. It was also the first time he had ever ridden in an automobile. Hard to believe there were still people in this country who lived like that, but here he was, a member of our platoon.

There are in life, places, and times where stereotyping is accurate, and you can perfectly nail the personality of individuals. Homer was exactly like you would expect someone raised on a farm in West Virginia to be. He literally believed everything everyone told him and was always being surprised by modern marvels, and by modern marvels, I mean things like television and shoes. Whenever someone in the platoon attempted to provoke him, he would respond with "The lord sayeth; an eye for an eye and sticks and stones don't hurt me, but if you don't stop, I'll knock your teeth in."

No one knew for sure if he was misquoting or threatening, and no one had the guts to call him out, because he apparently had the raw strength to tear any of us apart whenever he wanted.

Every night just after the bugle sounded taps, Homer would drop to his big ole knees beside his bunk, fold his hands, bow his head and squeeze his eyes shut as he said his nightly prayers. He was proud to be a Christian and didn't mind sharing it with everyone in the platoon whether they wanted to hear it or not. Every night we went to bed with his innocent voice booming out across the barracks. He would entertain the platoon as he had his nightly conversation with God. He always started, "Hey, God, Homer here. Please say, 'Hey,' to Baby Jesus for me."

He would then go into his prayer for the day, and then end by asking God's blessing for everyone he came into contact with that day, including those who had teased him or tried to hurt him. I don't know for sure, but his prayers might have shamed a lot of guys. By the end of the first week of basic training, the members of the platoon were defending him against our fellow trainees in the other units. None of us would ever admit it, but we looked forward to the routine every night at lights out. He may have been a big dummy from West Virginia, but he was our big dummy.

Homer insisted that all of us come together for a minute of prayer before any tough training event. He did this so he could ask the Lord to keep us safe. We made fun of him and tried to make light of it, but you know what? We all joined in every time.

"Oh, great and powerful God ..."

He sounded like the Wizard of Oz in that scene behind the curtain.

"We soldiers ask you to keep us all safe. Please watch over all of us, even the heathens in this platoon and Drill Sergeant Bond, cuz they just don't know better. Thanks, God. Amen."

I admit I did eventually end up going to Sunday services during basic training, and it was Homer who talked me into going to my first Army church service. No, I wasn't a religious guy. I wasn't against organized religion, I just never considered myself a church-going kind of guy. Hell, I had spent most of my early childhood Sundays trying to find a way out of going to Mass with my family. There were too many things in the world that our family priest had told me were sins that I just loved doing and wasn't willing to stop.

The idea of attending Sunday service in the Army began to form in my head when I overheard Homer trying to talk several other guys into going to Sunday service with him. I really didn't pay too much attention to all the talk of God, prayers, worship, fellowship, and so on. What caught my attention was this:

"After service, they serve juice, pancakes, and cookies to all the soldiers from basic training, and there are some really pretty girls over there who are serving the food and talking to you. Good Christian women," he said.

I could have cared less about the Christian part. What caught my immediate attention was the "women" part. After two weeks of smelly, farting, snoring men, I was aching for the sound of a female voice, the whiff of some nice perfume, and the opportunity to just look at some honest-to-God, non-male human beings. The minute I overheard Homer's comment about women, I made the first major religious decision of my Army career. I immediately converted from a non-church going Catholic to an 'I'm going to Sunday services tomorrow Christian.'

Trainees who went to services on Sundays were referred to as "Cookie Christians." They were the guys who went to church just to get some cookies and take a break from the drill sergeants. Hey, I could live with that title. Cookies and women, what could possibly go wrong with a combination like that? Worst case scenario, I would get some sleep in the chapel, eat a couple of cookies, be free of screaming drills for an hour or two, and with any luck at all, I might get the opportunity to hit on some lovely young ladies. The light of God must have shined on my soul at that point because I decided I was going to church. At chow that night, I told Danny about the church and the women. He was immediately in. We agreed to meet at the church bus in the morning.

You should have seen the look on Harper's face Saturday night after he yelled into the barracks, "Anyone who desires to attend religious services tomorrow raise your hands so I can put your name on the list for the bus. It's leaving at 0800 hours." I raised my hand.

"In my office, Berlin," he yelled.

When we got in his room, Harper slammed his office door so hard the entire building shook. He immediately got in my face and screamed, "I warned you! You're about as religious as I am and that is exactly zero. You're up to something, and I want to know what it is right now."

I calmly looked at him in the eye and with my most condescending voice said, "Drill Sergeant Harper, how can you doubt my sincerity? I just want the opportunity to share in fellowship and worship with my fellow trainees Sunday morning."

"Bullshit, you don't want to share in anything. There's an angle here somewhere, and I'm going to find it. You're not going, you're not on the list, you won't get on the bus, and you're not going into the chapel, end of story."

"But, Drill Sergeant," I replied, "I'm serious about this. See right here on my dog tags it says that my religion is Catholic, which in case you didn't know is a Christian religion. When I went to bed last night, I had a sudden epiphany. Every day we talk about combat. I'm a soldier, and I suddenly realized that I wasn't immortal and that I could get killed or wounded in combat someday. All this combat training and talking of war and death have got me contemplating my own mortality. I really think I need to renew my relationship with the Lord."

"Contemplate this," he said as he grabbed his crotch. "You're up to something, and you're not going. The only epiphany you had is that you are working a scam on me. Get out of my fucking office, and I don't want to hear any more of this crap."

I pulled out my ace in the hole. "Drill Sergeant, I know that no one in the chain of command would understand a drill sergeant denying a trainee the opportunity to worship, especially a Christian soldier like myself. I feel so strongly about my newly discovered need to find the Lord that I feel obligated to take my case directly to the chaplain's office should you deny my request. The post chaplain gave us a phone number and told us to call it if anyone attempted to block us from attending service or seeking the assistance of a chaplain. I know you wouldn't want to be accused of denying a trainee his opportunity for Christian fellowship."

I may have pushed Harper just a little too far with my last comment. He went nuts. Grabbing me by the front of my shirt, he screamed directly in my face.

"You little maggot, who the fuck do you think you're threatening? I've been dealing with little shits like you my entire military career, and if you think your little smartass threats have any impact on me, you're dead wrong."

I didn't want to tell him I already had an impact on him because he was out of control. Pushing me away and pounding his finger into my chest, he continued:

"OK, wiseass, you got your fucking church. But remember, asshole, I have eyes everywhere on this post. I guarantee you that someone will be watching you every second that you're out of my sight. You even come close to crossing the line, and your family back home won't be able to recognize your remains when the box with your body in it arrives in your hometown."

I couldn't resist. "Bless you, Drill Sergeant," I replied. As he stared back at me like he was ready to commit murder, I added:

"Look I've been straight with you so far, right? I give you my word, the only thing I want to do is relax a little, have some cookies and Kool-Aid, and get away from all this military shit for a couple of hours. I'm not planning anything, I just thought that it might be good to get a little break from the drill sergeants, present company excluded, of course."

"Fuck your present company," he said.

I had conveniently left out the part that there was a good chance there would be women present at the service. I figured what he didn't know wouldn't hurt him. I had no intention of screwing this up. Hell, this could turn out to be a good thing.

"Get the fuck out of my office, Berlin, and remember, there is nowhere on this post where I don't have someone who will report your every move back to me."

It was hard for me to hide the grin on my face as I left his office. Looked like I would be going to services the following morning.

Look out cookies and ladies, here I come. Praise the lord!

Bright and early the next morning, and much to the surprise of everyone in the first platoon, I lined up with all the other Bible thumpers to board the bus to Sunday services. As I boarded, I saw that Danny was already onboard. Boarding a bus was an unusual event for trainees at Fort Knox who usually traveled in cattle cars. The chapel was only four blocks away, so it really didn't make sense to take a bus when you could walk over.

In basic training the standard rule was, if it's within five miles, it's within humping distance. We marched everywhere. I assumed that because the head chaplain on post was putting so much pressure on the training leadership to get more trainees to Sunday service and that services were open to everyone on post, the Army wanted to make a good impression and pretend they were treating us humanely.

There were ten chapels on Fort Knox, so soldiers had a lot of choices when it came to places to attend Sunday services. The Church for Basic Training Soldiers was located on the main post. A lot of people from downtown and from the military housing areas attended services at that chapel because it was closest to their home. Besides, I think they got a kick out of seeing all the panicked young men every Sunday. This was also the chapel where the senior chaplain on post, Chaplain Jackson, held services. All the big brass came to this chapel so they could, as they say in the Army, "eat cheese." For you civilians that means suck up to the boss. I guess the Army is no different from civilian communities in this respect because everywhere I have ever lived, all the assholes suddenly became religious adherents on Sunday mornings.

Army chapels were unlike the usual religious buildings. Even though the Army did not care for non-Christians, all religions were accommodated on its installations. The Army came up with a house of worship that could be quickly modified to fit the needs of those attending services. The outside of Army chapels looked like a church, but there were no religious symbols to indicate what denomination worshiped inside.

Once inside an Army chapel, the non-denominational theme continued. Army chapels resembled many of the civilian churches I had been in minus the denomination-specific paraphernalia. For instance, when you enter a Catholic church, you expect to find crucifixes and Stations of the Cross. In other Christian churches, you expect Bibles and crosses. In a synagogue, you see the Torah and Star of David. The chapel on Fort Knox was completely nondescript. It had plain wooden pews, an organ, and a stage up front. In the pews were four different versions of the Bible, a Torah, and some religious tracts from other religions I had never heard of before.

When Danny and I walked into the chapel on Sunday, the chaplain's assistant was at the front pulling a long rope, which caused a large wooden cross to slide from behind a curtain to a position in the center of the front wall of the church. This same pulley system allowed for a crucifix or Star of David to take the place of honor, depending on the denomination scheduled next. It was like a fast-food version of a church.

One of the neatest things about religious services in the Army was that no one minded sharing the house of worship. Everyone took it for granted. No one messed with the other denominations' stuff. The community at large in America could learn a valuable lesson from the way the Army handled religion. This was the way our Founding Fathers intended people to worship in this country.

I knew the minute I walked in that I was going to enjoy this. Homer was right, there were real honest-to-goodness women in attendance. When we arrived, we were met at the front door by an Army colonel wearing a white collar who shook our hands and welcomed us to "Gods house."

He told Danny and me, "Sit down anywhere you like, relax, and clear your minds of training and drill sergeants."

This was the first officer over the rank of lieutenant that I had been this close to since becoming a soldier. Up to this point, I figured I would never see, much less shake hands with, a colonel unless I was being court-martialed. Who knew that soldiers, especially colonels, could be preachers? Wasn't the Army supposed to be a place where you learned how to kill and maim the enemy? It seemed to me that might just be a little bit of a conflict for a religious leader.

The service I was attending was what the Army called a non-denominational prayer service. It was basically a worship service for anyone of any of the various Christian denominations. Having been raised a Catholic, the whole thing was more than a little strange to me. It might as well have been a Buddhist ceremony for all the sense it made. I looked for the quietest, darkest location in the church to find a seat. I was looking forward to a little peace and quiet and, who knows, maybe some Zs during the service. Once the service was over, I intended to hit the cookies that Homer said they would serve in the basement and see how well my 'I'm a poor lonely trainee,' line worked on some of the ladies I saw in the church. I hoped that they were all going to hang around for refreshments; some of them were actually pretty good looking.

Danny and I found the perfect spot in the back corner of the chapel. It was directly behind one of the wooden posts that held up the roof, and it did a pretty good job of blocking anyone in the aisle from seeing me while I was trying to catch up on my beauty sleep. It would be the perfect short-term hideout. I pointed it out to Danny, and we hurried over to take a seat before someone else beat us to it.

It was a cool day for Fort Knox, and the pews all had cushions on them. I quickly relaxed and got myself comfortable. Turning to Danny, I smiled and said, "This is the life, peace and quiet and no drill sergeants."

Danny wasn't listening to me. He was sitting like a statue and staring over at the aisle. I tried to nudge him, but he was in a trance or something. When I looked up to see what had caught his attention, I immediately understood why he had become hypnotized. Walking down the aisle was the cutest brunette I had seen in a long time. About five-foot tall with shiny brown hair, she was a tiny little package, but everything was in the right place and was perfectly proportioned. I assumed she was attending services with her family because she was walking with a man in a major's uniform and an older but equally good-looking woman.

Danny, his hypnotic state finally broken, turned to me and whispered, "I have to get closer to that. When she sees a good-looking guy sitting close to her, she won't be able to resist me." I immediately panicked and tried to stop him, thinking this wasn't going to turn out well. I wasn't fast enough, and short of causing a disturbance, I could only watch his back and stare as he dashed out of the pew we were sitting in and followed the family up the aisle. When the family moved into an empty pew, Danny entered the one behind them and sat right behind the cute brunette.

What happened next is the stuff of legends. It was so over the top that I can't even explain to you. This was how Danny described it to me and others in our platoons:

"As soon as I sat down, I tuned out the chaplain's voice and began to concentrate all my attention on the drop-dead gorgeous brunette sitting in front of me. I know that it's sacrilegious, but I couldn't help going into one of those mini daydream/fantasies that are common to men in their teens and early twenties. I'm not going to make excuses, but for me, this period of my life was a time of perpetual horniness.

"The only thing I thought about every waking and sleeping moment was women and sex. Combine the naturally heightened sexual awareness of a young man with the forced two-week abstinence that basic training had imposed on me, and I think you get the picture. I had not even been in the presence of a member of the female persuasion for so long that I had almost forgotten what they looked like. I had been relying upon memories and a stack of *Penthouse* magazines that the guys were passing around the barracks to satisfy my needs. I was a walking time bomb.

"For some reason, the atmosphere of the chapel, the women, and the relaxation all came together in a manner that put me in a heightened state of arousal. My dick was so hard that it ached. At some point, I'm not sure when my fantasies got away from me, and I lost all awareness of what was going on around me. I found myself staring at the brunette several rows in front of me, and unconsciously began rubbing myself through my pants. I could vaguely hear Chaplain Jackson's voice droning on in the background, but as far as I was concerned, it had become merely background music for my personal fantasy. There were only two people in the chapel, the young brunette and me. In my imagination, she was begging me to throw her on the pew and have wild passionate sex with her.

"Did you ever have the feeling when you suddenly realize that something is just not quite right? You don't know exactly what it is, but you have this strange feeling that causes the hair on the back of your neck to stand up. I was having one of those moments. I was deep into my fantasy and oblivious to all that was going on around me, but I just knew that there was a problem. Catching movement off to my left, I glanced over and realized that I was no longer the only occupant of the pew.

"The first thing I noticed was the most beautiful set of legs that I had ever seen."

This was the height of the miniskirt era, and for Danny, those long slender legs represented a monument to the seventies.

"They began in glossy, black, platform shoes and ended in a tiny, tight white miniskirt. It's very rare to see a woman not wearing nylons, especially in a church, but the owner of these spectacular legs was extremely confident in her body because her legs were bare. This only added to her sexiness.

"Topping off the miniskirt was a lightweight, white cotton, sleeveless blouse that opened at the bottom to expose a creamy smooth midriff. Around her shoulders she wore a white macramé shawl. Yeah, she was in a chapel, but everything clse about her was so hot it was almost sacrilegious. Completing my visual exploration of her body, I found myself staring at the most beautiful blonde. She was older than me, about thirty-five to forty years old. She had long flowing blonde hair, ruby red, pouty lips, piercing bright blue eyes and creamy white skin that would have put the air brushers who worked for *Penthouse* to shame. I was sure she was one of the women that I had been fantasizing about in the September issue. She was just too beautiful to be real."

All men have several women they fantasize about when they are growing up. They are usually teachers, family friends, nurses, or whatever. It's often an older woman, and they are always put together magnificently. To an eighteen-year-old, there is just something incredibly sexy about a woman in her late thirties to early forties. They seem more confident in themselves and are not afraid of young men like the younger girls are.

"I thought I'd died and gone to heaven," Danny continued. "While I was heavy into my fantasy and was enjoying the view, I suddenly realized that I had two serious problems. I was still rubbing myself, and the lady who had sat down beside me knew I was staring at her. When I looked at her face, I realized that she was alternating her stare between my eyes and my crotch. I was screwed. I immediately came to my senses, panicked, and grabbed the biggest, fattest hymnal from the pew and placed it on my lap. Usually, a scare of this magnitude would have caused my libido to deflate immediately, but for some unknown reason that did not happen, and I was forced to sit there totally embarrassed and plagued with a throbbing painful member.

"To top it all off, I was starting to get a mind-blowing headache. I think that in my panicked state, all the blood that wasn't in my penis suddenly rushed to my head. In one burning flash, I had gone from 'Fantasyland' to 'oh-shit land.' Of all the places to get caught rubbing my crotch, I had to pick a church.

"At first, I tried to ignore everything around me, stare straight ahead, and concentrate on the sermon, pretending nothing had happened and hope it would all just go away. I was desperately trying to convince myself that she hadn't seen anything and that everything was going to be OK. My head hurt, my mouth was dry, my penis ached, and I had that hollow feeling you get in your stomach when you know you're in deep shit and there is nothing you can do about it.

"I even prayed. 'Please God, let her not have seen me rubbing one out through my pants in church. I promise I'll be good in training and stay out of trouble. I'll come to chapel services every Sunday. Just help me get through this one thing.'

"As I prayed to myself, I stole a quick sideways glance to see if I was going to be able to get away with this or if she was in shock or just waiting for service to end so that she could turn me into the chaplain.

"When I looked over at her, I realized she was still staring directly at me! I tried to look away, break eye contact, and pretend that I was just looking around the church, but like a magnet, my eyes kept being drawn back to her. Every time I glanced back, I realized that her eyes remained locked on me. Oh shit, I'm caught. She's going to tell the chaplain who will report me to the military police and to my drill sergeant. When he finds out how bad I've fucked up, I guarantee you he's going to destroy me. Hell, destruction might be a blessing at this point. How do I get myself in these situations?

"I was sure my worst nightmares were about to come to life. I could imagine it now. Any second she was going to scream and yell out that there is a pervert in the chapel. If the fathers and husbands attending this service didn't tear me to shreds, then the chaplain was going to hold me until the military police arrived. What was I thinking? I was confident that in about three minutes, I would be on my way to prison for the rest of my life. At least it would be a short trial. I had absolutely no chance of getting out of this one. I've heard what they do to perverts in jail, especially military prisons. The way my luck was going, she would end up being the wife of some colonel. Every second that passed, the possible repercussions I was imagining grew in scope and complexity. I guarantee you a young man can create greater punishments in his head than any court could possibly impose.

"Just when I thought that I couldn't take it any longer, and was seriously considering turning myself in before she screamed, she suddenly tapped my shoulder and asked, 'Are you OK, soldier?'

"God, she even had a sexy voice. There was no way in hell that I was going to be able to answer. Even if I was capable of speech, which at the time I wasn't, I doubt I could have formed the words to respond. My mouth was so dry that I could barely breathe, and I didn't dare lick my lips; she'd definitely take it the wrong way. Should I apologize, or should I blow it off and pretend nothing had happened or should I just respond with a simple 'I'm OK.' Before I could make up my mind, she slid over next to me until her bare leg was touching mine and asked, 'Can I borrow your hymnal?'

"What else could I say? 'Sure.'

"I was too numb to pass it to her, so once again she took the initiative. Before I could respond, she reached over with her left hand and removed the hymnal from its strategic location on my lap.

"Once she had the book in her hand, she thumbed through it and seemed to be concentrating on the words on the pages. I couldn't think. I couldn't focus because of the bare leg, which was touching my leg. My situation was getting worse, and I found myself wishing that she would move away. I was afraid to move. Just when I thought that everything would be Ok, my dick betrayed me. Of its own volition, my cock, still in a painfully engorged state, began to twitch and shake. She couldn't possibly miss it. Damn, why won't it just behave? I need to get this under control. I reached to get another hymnal to replace the one I had lost, but my hand hit hers as she was attempting to replace the one she had removed from my lap back in the holder on the pew. When we bumped hands, she laughed and whispered, 'Relax, soldier, Chaplain Jackson actually puts on a pretty good sermon. I think you'll enjoy it.'

"With that, she gently reached over and placed her hand on my crotch. I couldn't believe it and almost exploded on the spot. I was frozen in a combination of fear and excitement. Was it an accident? Did she realize what she was doing? Could she not feel that my cock was throbbing with every beat of my heart? I felt it through every fiber of my being. My blood was pounding from my head to my toes. If she was just trying to be a friendly Christian, then she had badly miscalculated because her touch was worse than the most horrible evil torture I could have imagined.

"When I looked back over at her to see if I could get some kind of clue, she was staring at Chaplin Jackson, seemingly and genuinely intent on every word he said. All the while, her hand, which for some reason was now burning hot, rested lightly on my crotch. I couldn't tell you the subject of the chaplain's sermon. For all I knew, he was speaking in Chinese.

"How much of this was I going to be able to take? I had been living with my penis for almost nineteen years, and for the first time in my life, it was doing things that I didn't even know it was capable of doing. I thought that it was going to bust right out of my pants. For some reason, it had taken on a life of its own and was worse than a drill sergeant who was out control. I was trying everything and using every trick I knew. I tried the multiplication table and the alphabet backward. I tried to imagine blood and gut scenes. I even attempted to picture my grandmother tucking me in. Nothing was working, and the harder I concentrated, the harder it got. The most distressing part of the entire experience was that I couldn't do anything about it. I was simultaneously trying to control myself and keep the lady beside me from seeing and feeling what was going on. Unless she had no sense of feeling, she had to feel the throbbing and twitching that was going on under her hand.

"Maybe, I thought, she was like a nun or something and had never felt a stiffy before. Perhaps she thought what was happening was simply a regular part of male anatomy. I was more than a little confused about the entire situation, and things were reaching a boiling point. Either she was messing with me, or she was entirely oblivious to what was occurring under her hand. This wasn't the first time in my life that I was in a situation with a woman and couldn't understand what was going on. But it was sure different than all the others.

"Just when I was almost at my wit's end, Chaplain Jackson began to lead the congregation in a hymn, and the beautiful lady beside me stood to join in the singing.

"I was both relieved and a little bit saddened when her hand left my lap. She motioned for me to stand, but in my engorged condition, I could stand and join in with the other members of the congregation. I think I mumbled something about having a sore knee and that it hurt to stand, but I honestly can't remember. Besides, I would have made quite a sight, trying to act pious and religious, with a tent pole pushing out the front of my pants. Glancing at the lady beside me made the situation even worse. If I had thought that she was gorgeous when she was sitting down, she was an absolute knockout standing beside me. It didn't help matters that her ass was about six inches from my face, and her essence had engulfed all five of my senses. I remember her smelling of vanilla.

"For the remainder of the hymn, I was forced to stare at her tight ass and creamy white thighs as I contemplated my unusual situation. I was still in danger and still trapped, but at least it looked like she wasn't going to turn me in for being some kind of pervert. Maybe she was just one of those naive women and really didn't know what had happened. Maybe I had dodged a bullet. Maybe, just maybe, this would all work out OK. I don't know what kind of perfume she was wearing, but boy did it ever smell great, and the vanilla smell kept getting stronger.

"I was feeling self-conscious sitting while most of the congregation was standing. The only thing in my favor was that there were a few others in the congregation who were also sitting. I don't know if it was part of their religion or if it was just guys who didn't know the proper protocols. Whatever the reason, I took full advantage of the camouflage that sitting provided me. I immediately grabbed another hymnal and attempted to hide my condition. I was definitely going to need some more time to get myself under control. No chance of that happening any time soon because the lady began to sway with the music, and every time she swayed in my direction, her hips brushed against my shoulder and arm. I swear I almost came three times.

"I wanted to move a couple feet away, and at the same time, I wanted desperately to move closer to her. This was not getting better. I was stuck precisely where I was. At this point, the hymnal I was using to cover my erection was moving up and down of its own volition and I couldn't think of any non-obvious way of covering myself with my hands. I was afraid that if I put my hands on my lap, she would think that I was playing with myself again. No sense in pushing my luck. I was merely going to have to ride this out and hope for the best.

"When the congregation finished the hymn and started on a second, she turned, looked down at my lap and sat down beside me. When she took her seat this time, she sat so close to me that her bare leg was locked against mine. She took the new hymnal off my lap and placed it in the rack on the back of the pew. She then pulled her shawl off her shoulder and laid it gently across my lap. I thought it was bothering her so much that she had to cover it up. I still thought it was possible she was going to tell the chaplain about this when services ended. I looked at the back door of the church and wondered if I got up and quickly ran out of the chapel, would I be able to get away?

"All the while she was draping my lap with her shawl, the lady continued to sing along with the rest of the congregation. Singing in one of the sweetest voices I have ever heard, she suddenly reached under her shawl pulled down my zipper and reached her hand into my pants. Thank God for easy, access Army boxer shorts. I swear there was some divine intervention because of its own will, my cock immediately found the opening and jumped into her hand. I wanted so much for her to just wrap those fingers around me. Keeping me covered with her shawl she began to gently run the back of her hand and then her fingernails up and down the entire length of my shaft, stopping at the top to softly probe the opening of my penis with her nails. I had indeed died and gone to heaven. I wanted this to last forever. Excruciating torture has suddenly transformed into extreme gratification. There was something about the whole church forbidden fruit thing that both frightened and excited me at the same time. Whatever it was, it created the most intense pleasure that I had ever felt in my life.

"The entire time that she was touching me, and it felt like hours but was actually mere seconds, she continued staring straight ahead and singing along with everyone else in the chapel. I, on the other hand, was not capable of singing, talking, or even breathing. I was afraid that if I opened my mouth to breathe that I would let out a blood-curdling scream of pleasure. But discretion being the better part of valor, I merely sat there and bit my tongue and decided that I would simply suffocate.

"I could vaguely hear Chaplain Jackson directing everyone to turn the page and move on to the second verse. As soon as the second verse began, my beautiful antagonist placed her hand around my shaft and, with no wasted motion, firmly gripped me and started to slide her hand up and down my entire length.

"I'm no newcomer to masturbation, and I have had more than one sexual experience with girls back home, so I had always considered myself one of those guys who could maintain a little bit of self-control, allowing the lady to enjoy herself before you lose complete control. Well, this was not going to be my best day in the self-control arena. Maybe it was the abstinence, or perhaps it was just the entire circumstances. Whatever the reason, in less than three strokes, I literally exploded.

"Not just the normal, hey, I haven't had sex in a few weeks explosion, but a genuine and unbelievable oil-well gusher of an ejaculation. I didn't know that it was possible to have so much in me. It just kept coming and coming and showed no signs of letting up. All the while, my new best friend kept a firm grip on me. The only evidence that anything at all was happening was the big smile plastered across her face. I was still holding my breath.

"Every time my heart beat, it caused my penis to pulse, and more sperm shot out. There was no indication of anything stopping it. I began to think that I was going to expel every bit of liquid in my body. After about ten or fifteen seconds of this, it finally stopped. She looked at me in disbelief because instead of deflating as could reasonably be expected, I was getting bigger again. Under the circumstances, this could be a problem.

"Bending over to get closer to me, she whispered in my ear, 'Oh my God, you are a horny soldier, aren't you?'

"I swear to God, when her breath and voice hit my ear, I immediately exploded a second time. No stroking, no manipulation, just her holding tightly to my penis. While I was going crazy on the inside, I was fighting my body to maintain some semblance of composure on the outside. I don't know how successful I was because more than one person looked at me with concern. They thought I might be having a stroke or something. If they only knew what was really happening, they would have all be having strokes. I was in complete disbelief. Nothing like this had ever happened to me. The second explosion, if anything, was more intense than the first.

"When the hymn was reaching its final stanza, and my member had completed its twitching and pumping, she took her shawl and wiped up the mess that had gotten onto my pants and all over her hand. Tucking me back into my pants, she zipped me up, bundled up her shawl, and got up to leave the pew.

"Just before she turned to go, she once more bent down and whispered in my ear, 'Good luck in basic training, soldier. I hope you enjoyed today's sermon. Your girlfriend will be a fortunate lady if you ever learn to control that weapon you're carrying.'

"With that, she gently kissed me on the cheek, exited the pew and walked out the back of the chapel."

After he told me this story, I shouted, "Bullshit. Danny, you are the biggest liar I know. I saw you and her sitting there, and I knew something was going on, but there is no way you got a hand job in the church. Even you are not that stupid."

Naturally, Danny swears it is one hundred percent true, and even to this day, whenever I bring it up, he swears he can still remember the smallest detail, sights, smells, and sounds, as she departed. He was upset that he never even learned her name. He said that during the entire incident, he hadn't even said more than two words. He was pretty sure he held his breath during the whole encounter. He told me he should have followed her out and spoken to her, but to tell the truth he said, "I couldn't have stood up even if I wanted to. My entire body was limp, and my legs felt like rubber bands. It took me the remainder of the service to regain even a small measure of my composure."

It was probably all for the best because it couldn't have possibly turned out well. He had the experience of a lifetime and a lifetime of memories to look forward to. Sometimes it's just best to leave well enough alone.

Maybe Danny had read too many *Penthouse* letters, but he just might have been telling the truth. I had never seen him so worn out after the service and he walked back next to me. He was utterly spent, both physically and mentally. I honestly didn't know if it had even really happened or if it was all a figment of Danny's imagination. Either way, no one was going to believe him. It was too bizarre for me to believe.

After service finished, Danny and I sat in the back of the church for a minute or two. One of the ushers came over to ask us if we were all right. He was concerned because Danny looked a little bit peaked.

Danny told him, "I'm fine, just a little tired from all of the training and exercise they are making us do."

The usher laughed and said that it was standard for trainees and invited us to come downstairs for some snacks, coffee, juice, and fellowship. We told him that we would join him shortly; we just had to thank God for something before we headed downstairs.

Everyone downstairs was friendly, and there were lots of girls. We looked everywhere, but Danny's fantasy lady was nowhere to be found. It was like she had disappeared off the face of the earth. Danny figured that she was probably an angel and had gone back to heaven where she had come from.

As you can imagine, no one back at my platoon or Danny's platoon believed a word of his story, but I guarantee you they all listened intently every time he told it, and Danny told it many times.

I know for sure that some of them must have believed part of his tale or at least they were a little bit curious, because the remainder of our time at basic training, both of our platoons set a new Army basic training record for Sunday service attendance.

Chaplain Jackson even presented the drill sergeants from both of our platoons with a special award at a unit formation. They probably figured that one of them had convinced us good Christians to attend services. At least the chaplain was a happy man. He had a full flock at every Sunday service for the remainder of our training cycle.

Danny told me that although he thought about her a lot, he never saw his fantasy lady again. I attended every Sunday service the remainder of the time I was at Fort Knox. Most of the first platoon attended with me, even the ones who swore Danny's story was bullshit. Sgt. Harper knew something was going on when we all started going to services, but he couldn't quite figure it out. Every Sunday, when the bus pulled out, he would stare at me, as if I were behind some sort of a conspiracy. He finally must have written it off to cookies and Kool-Aid. We ate a lot of cookies, and we drank a lot of coffee and juice, and some of the guys got dates with some of the local young ladies for after basic training. Unfortunately, or fortunately, depending on how you look at things, no one I am aware of ever got another hand job during Sunday services.

As for Danny, it really didn't matter. He came out of the whole episode better off than when he went in, at least in his own mind. A lifetime of memories, a hand job for the ages, and while no one knew who he was, he became a living legend and the stuff of myths at Fort Knox. Not bad for a Moron and a Cookie Christian. Later, in my military career, whenever I stopped by Fort Knox, I made an extra effort to visit the chapel. You never know, if Danny got lucky then maybe I would get lucky someday.

# Chapter 19
## Testing, Testing, Testing

When everything is going so well, you just know something is going to happen to make it all go wrong. That's where I was in the middle of the fifth week of training. Despite the turmoil and the trauma of training, I was doing OK. I was doing better than OK. No one was harassing me, and for the most part, we Morons were pretty much left alone. Drill Sgt. Harper continued to use me to school my fellow Morons so that they could all pass the courses. He didn't do this out of any particular need to help; he just didn't want any of us to be recycled and have to see our ugly mugs for another six weeks. Or at least that's what he said to us. I really think he just had a soft spot for underdogs.

Whatever the reason the harassment and hazing had pretty much been cut in half. The only problems I had were with that asshole Bond. That son of a bitch just had it out for me. I'd learned several weeks back that the best thing I could do was to avoid him.

The non-Moron Wolverines were beat to shit. That's what's supposed to happen in basic training, but the breaks that came with being a Moron gave me just the edge I needed.

While in the land of the blind, the one-eyed man is king, and in the land of the white dot, the guy with half a brain is king. I had the best of both worlds. No one bugged me, and the Morons were mine to command. It was like being a general in my own private little Army. I kept them out of trouble and stopped the other guys from harassing them. They, in return, made sure that no one messed with their king.

Thursday, in the middle of afternoon training, the drill sergeants brought us all into a large air-conditioned classroom. This was a treat for us because we spent most afternoons in the Fort Knox heat, running around like idiots and getting yelled at. As soon as we got in our seats and calmed down, a captain in a fancy-dress uniform walked in. "Gentlemen ..." He paused. I loved it when the officers called us gentlemen; it beat the hell out of shithead or dumbass and infuriated the drill sergeants to no end.

He continued, "... the Army is looking for some soldiers to attend the United States Army's West Point Preparatory School. Today we are going to give all of you a series of tests that will allow us to gauge your ability to attend advanced academic training at the college level. Those of you who score high enough will be processed for background checks, and if you pass the background check, you will be invited to enroll in the Army's preparatory school.

"Attending the school is entirely voluntary, and no one will be forced to join; however, you are all required to take the test. The school is in New Jersey. If you are lucky enough to be selected for the preparatory school, you will be assigned there as a student and be given up to a year to prepare yourself to test for full acceptance as a cadet at West Point Military Academy, this country's finest institution of higher learning.

"Gentlemen," that word again. "This is a singularly unique opportunity. A West Point education is valued at over a hundred thousand dollars and is one of the most sought after in America. Young men from across this country would give anything for an opportunity to attend."

I thought, if it's so sought after, why are they here looking for more people to attend? Uncle Sam was scraping the bottom of the barrel if he thought that there was very much talent in this cesspool. The captain went on and on for about fifteen minutes. He was utterly wasting our time, but at least we were out of the sun and sitting down in an air-conditioned building. In basic training, you learn to appreciate the little things in life.

The captain told us we would be taking a three-part test, each part being one hour in length.

"If you finish early," he continued, "please bring your test forward and take a break in the entryway until the hour that is scheduled for that portion of the test is over, or everyone else finishes that portion of the test. There will be refreshments available outside in the hallway, and no drill sergeants will be in the building to harass you or distract you when you are taking the test. Gentlemen, please open up the first packet on your desk and follow along with me while I read you your instructions."

OK, I could get into this. A three-hour rest from training and not being yelled at was almost as good as hearing, "refreshments available." After five weeks of cramming food down our throats in the mess hall, relaxing in an air-conditioned classroom and eating some snacks sounded like heaven. As soon as we opened the test packet, the captain asked the drill sergeants to leave the room. Sgt. Bond took this opportunity to begin to round up the Morons and start moving us to the back of the room. The captain asked him what he thought he was doing.

"I'm clearing the room of all the dummies so that they won't disturb anyone who is actually capable of completing these tests," Bond replied. "These guys will only waste your time. Hell, most of them can't even write their own names much less understand anything on these fancy tests."

The captain yelled, "Sergeant, my orders were that all trainees would be made available for this test. What part of all trainees don't you understand?"

We were shocked. We had never heard anyone talk back to a drill sergeant, but because it was Bond, and everyone hated him, we all strained to hear how this was going to go. In retrospect, this was a dumb move on the part of the captain. The discipline that the drill sergeants had taken almost five weeks to build had been destroyed in less than five minutes.

Sgt. Bond glared at the captain and said, "Sir, be careful what you ask for because you just might get it." Realizing that he was not going to win this one and seeing the anticipation on all our faces, he added, "Roger, Captain, I was just trying to help some of these trainees who might get upset with having to take a test. But I understand if the Army wants everyone, then the Army will get everyone. All right, Morons, back to your seats, and enjoy your test. We'll talk later."

As Sgt. Bond stomped out of the room, he said under his breath, but loud enough for the trainees near him to hear, "Fucking officers, what does he think is going to happen when a bunch of retards take his stupid test?"

Some of us could still hear him complaining or talking to someone as he got near the door and walked out. "Hell, he might as well be asking them to save their used toilet paper and give it to him for all the good it will do him," he said. "If one of them goddamn Morons even gets a fifty percent on that test, I'll eat my goddamn hat in front of the entire unit."

I was pissed, who did that little runt of a drill sergeant think he was? I would show him what a Moron could do. I would make him eat that fucking Smokey Bear hat in front of the entire battalion. It's time that asshole learned a lesson once and for all and I was just the guy to teach it to him. Mistake. I let my pride override my brain. I should have held my temper and controlled myself. Maybe things might have turned out differently.

Once the drill sergeants had left the room, the captain continued, "All right, gentlemen, now that the distractions are all over, let's get this done. You each have three folders in front of you. Open the folder with the Roman numeral one on the front."

One Moron raised his hand. "What's a Roman numeral, captain?"

The captain sighed and held up the folder.

"Gentlemen, please open the folder that looks like this."

We were told that we had one hour to complete the first portion, the literature portion of the exam.

"You must answer every question that you can in the time allotted. If you want to turn in your test before the end of the hour, you can, but you must answer every question. If you don't know the answer, please make your best guess and move on to the next question. You will not be penalized for guesses. However, you can only receive points for correct answers, so don't be afraid to guess if you don't know the answer."

I could smell the fresh pastries waiting in the hallway, so I whipped through the first part of the exam in about fifteen minutes. When I walked up to the front of the classroom to turn in my test, the captain checked to see that all the questions had been answered. Nodding his head, he pointed to the door, and I was on my way.

As I passed by the guys still taking their tests, I heard someone say: "That son of a bitch probably just filled in a block for every question on the test. Stupid Moron, I bet he didn't even sign his name correctly. He's going to eat all the goodies before the rest of us are done with the test."

Some of the guys in the room were surprised that I waited fifteen minutes before turning in the test.

The rest of the Morons in my platoon, however, seeing me leave the room, tried to follow my example, turning in their tests as soon as they could to get right behind me.

For the next three hours, I repeated my little routine. Fifteen minutes on the test, turn it in, take a short time to eat and relax. They had some good chow. By the end of the testing period, most of the Morons from all the other platoons were turning in their tests soon after I did. They were just filling in the blanks and enjoying the snacks. I don't think anyone in the room had a clue that I was completing each portion the test reading and carefully answering every question on every page. It turned out that this was going to be both my best day and worst day at basic combat training.

When the testing was over, and I had been chastised by everyone in the platoon for screwing around and eating most of the snacks, we headed back out into the Kentucky heat to complete our day's training. All in all, it had been a nice break.

I didn't think about the test again until the following night, other than everyone teasing me about rushing through the test and eating the best of the pastries. I figured it was no big deal. It turned out to be a huge deal. I just didn't realize the implications at the time. I was so pissed at that asshole drill sergeant that I forgot my promise to Drill Sgt. Harper. Keep a low profile, act dumb, and help the other Morons get through basic training. This was not my brightest moment. I was so intent on making Bond look bad that I had blown it.

That evening I received a visit from Sgt. Harper.

"I don't know what the fuck you did, but you really screwed up this time. Come on, Berlin, the command sergeant major and the lieutenant colonel want to talk to you."

Oh shit, none of the trainees had ever been called to talk to the lieutenant colonel. Shit, none of us had ever seen him.

"I tried to warn you, but no, you're too fucking smart to listen to anyone," Sgt. Harper hollered at me. "What did you do that caused the old man to ask for you in person? Is this going to cause me to lose my retirement?"

I had no idea and told him so. The only thing I could think of was the incident in the church, but that was a freaking week ago. Why had it taken her so long to file a complaint? Oh, shit, I thought, I'm dead now. I knew that it had been turned over to the police, and Danny and I were going to be arrested for being perverts. Was there some kind of jail for perverts that the Army was going to send us to?

I bet we were going to be the first guys in history to be arrested for getting a hand job in the church. Even though I wasn't the recipient, they could get me as being an accessory. But my parents didn't raise any stupid children, so I decided to continue to play it dumb.

"Honest, Drill Sergeant, I have absolutely no idea why anyone would want to speak to me."

"Well get moving, shithead, we are going to find out together, and remember if you screw up my retirement, you are dead meat."

Harper muttered, "I should have listened to my dad and raised chickens. At least I could wring their necks if they fucked up."

The walk to the headquarters building was one of the longest walks in my life. I kept looking for the police cars, the MPs, or the dogs, but it was surprisingly quiet. I was sick to my stomach; I knew I was going to go to jail. My own mother would condemn me to hell when she found out what Danny had done, and I was going to be charged as an accomplice.

How am I going to get out of this one?

The only thing I can do is lie my ass off; it's our story against hers, and they can't possibly prove anything. Who the hell do I think I am kidding when they see that sophisticated lady standing in the same room with Private Moron Berlin, and pervert Mussio. We're dead. Then I thought, what if she's some officer's wife? It doesn't matter. I will stick to my story; they have no proof because no one saw. What are they going to do? She was the perpetrator, unless Danny didn't tell the full story.

The problem was that I had bragged to everyone in the platoon about Danny's exploits. Was that considered a confession? Years later, when I watched the Clinton debacle on TV, it reminded me of simpler days before anyone ever heard of DNA. Life's gotten way too complicated. Nowadays, it would have been impossible to get away with. I hope she didn't save that shawl. I wonder what the statute of limitations is for hand jobs.

When we arrived at the battalion headquarters, we were going to meet the sergeant major.

"Berlin, you're going in to see the old man, don't fuck this up," Sgt. Harper had advised. "Walk up to his desk, salute, and say, 'Private Berlin reporting as directed, sir.' Then stand at attention and don't move a muscle until he tells you otherwise, is that clear?"

"Sergeant Harper," I asked, "Do you know what this is all about?"

"I have no fucking idea, but if the colonel's involved, you're in deep shit, trainee."

I knocked on the door and reported to the battalion commander as I had been directed. The lieutenant colonel was sitting behind an old wooden Army desk that was positioned in the center of the room. Directly behind him were two flagpoles. One was adorned with the American flag and the other with the Army flag. There were two crossed swords on the wall and no other furniture or decorations in the room. Standing at one side of the desk was the captain who had given us the West Point test. At the other side of the desk stood two majors in Army dress-green uniforms.

I learned that they were the executive officers from the two other battalions in our training brigade. If being brought in to see one commander was bad news, then three officers from three battalions must mean I was going to be executed. The sergeant major and Sgt. Harper had followed me in, so I was surrounded. I know precisely how Gen. Custer felt at the Battle of the Little Bighorn.

The commander told me to "stand easy." That meant relax, spread your legs a little, but keep your mouth shut. Yeah right, like I would be able to relax with all this brass in the same room as me. I could rest in my prison cell when this was all over. On the desk in front of the commander was the copy of the West Point test I had taken the day before. It had apparently been laid out in a manner which would allow me to see my name in big, bold letters on the top of the page. There was also a long list of what appeared to be test scores and my Army personnel folder.

In a deep baritone voice, the commander asked, "Private Berlin, do you know why you are here today?"

"No, sir," I replied.

"Well, let me explain it to you, son.

"Son, the Army is cautious about how we handle and secure our tests and our test answers, especially the ones for West Point, but every now and then someone obtains the answers and either sells or shares them with other soldiers. Do you understand what I am saying?"

"Yes, sir. You're saying sometimes people cheat on Army tests."

He must be kidding, I thought. When was the last time he went to an Army testing center? Did he have any idea that every test the Army had ever given to me, except for the West Point test, had been set up to provide us the answers in advance. Was he really that naive or just stupid?

"That's right, Private Berlin, sometimes people cheat on our tests."

He was speaking to me as befitted my status as a member of the Moron Corps.

"Private Berlin, the West Point test is a critical test, and we maintain an especially close hold on this test. That's why no sergeants were allowed in the room while you were testing. The only person other than the person taking the test, whoever touches this test, is the captain who is standing here beside my desk.

"Up to now, no one has ever compromised, I mean no one has ever given the answers to the test to anyone. Do you still understand what I am saying, Berlin?"

"Yes, sir," I replied. "You believe that someone gave answers to this test to people taking the test and, because you are having this conversation with me, obviously you believe that I must have been provided the answers in advance."

The colonel looked at me quizzically, probably wondering how my vocabulary had suddenly improved.

"That's right, Private Berlin, we do think someone gave you the answers to this test. Now while this is a grave matter, I want you to know that you're not in trouble. I know you only put down the answers that someone else gave you. We just need to have the names of the people who gave you the answers, and if you still have your copy of the answers, I would like you to give them to me right now or tell me where I can find them."

"Look, sir," I said, "I hate to be the one to burst your bubble, but I really don't know what you're talking about. No one provided me any answers to any test."

The colonel was beginning to lose his temper.

"Goddamn it, Private. You're not in trouble now, but if you insist on sticking to this ridiculous story, I will charge you with hiding information from Army authorities. That's a five-year prison sentence. Do you understand how long five years in an Army prison is? Do you know what they do to eighteen-year-olds in prison? If you continue to lie to me, then prison is exactly where you are going to end up. Are you sure you fully understand what I am saying?"

"Yes, sir, you're contemplating charging me with the crimes of obstruction of justice and conspiracy, and you are threatening me with prosecution if I fail to provide you the information you require. Sir, with all due respect, if you are insinuating that criminal charges will be brought against me, I request that I be made aware of my constitutional rights, and further request that I be provided counsel before any further questioning."

I don't know why I said that. I saw it on a TV show once and it seemed to work. I just wanted to end this stupid line of questioning once and for all, and I was also relieved it didn't involve the church incident. It provided me with a little bit of moxie.

The look on the commander's face was priceless. It was clear I had just totally confused him. Behind me, I heard Sgt. Harper mutter, "Oh fuck, there goes my retirement. Berlin, I'm going to rip that smartass tongue right out of your mouth by its roots."

"Don't interrupt, Sergeant!" yelled the commander. "Private, who taught you to talk like that?"

"No one, sir. If you officers paid attention, you might realize that some of your soldiers are actually more intelligent than you think they are."

"Are you getting smart with me, soldier?"

"No, sir. I just don't like being falsely accused of something I didn't do."

"Sergeant Major," demanded the commander as he slammed his fist into his desk, completely shattering the glass that covered it, "what the fuck is going on here!"

"I don't know, sir, but I'll get to the bottom of this. Berlin, come with me."

"No," said the colonel. "We're going to resolve this here and now."

"Private Berlin, do you realize that as a battalion commander that the Army has given me the authority and the power to lock you up for the rest of your natural life. No fucking lawyers, no fucking rights. This is the United States Army, son. I say what happens and what doesn't happen. If you want to test, go for it, soldier. Now, once and for all, I want to know who gave you the answers to the West Point test. Take your time and think through your answer because I am done playing this game with you. Am I making myself perfectly clear?"

"Sir," I responded, "with all due disrespect, no one gave me the answers to anything. I took those tests myself."

The colonel turned to the test captain, who said, "No way, sir. Not only did he have a perfect score, but he also turned his test in during the first fifteen minutes of each testing period. That's just not possible. It's never happened before."

"Did you say I got all of the answers right?" I asked, my face nearly beaming. I wanted to see Drill Sgt. Bond eat his damn hat. Enough trainees had heard his remark that I bet I could shame him into doing it. Behind me, I heard, "This is a fucking nightmare. No way will they allow me to retire after this."

"Don't fuck with me, Private!" yelled the commander, once again slamming his fist into the already shattered desk. "I have your personnel file right here on my desk. Private, you have the IQ of a fucking carrot. There is no way that someone of your limited mental ability could have scored this high on the test."

"Sir, that's not true. My current IQ is over one forty-five, and I qualified to be a member of Mensa International when I took the test in high school."

The commander looked like someone had just shot his dog. "Someone better start talking," he demanded.

"Sir, how would you have access to my IQ test?" I asked.

"Berlin, I'm looking at your entrance tests scores that you took in Milwaukee, and according to your scores, I have rocks on my unit street that are smarter than you are."

"Sir, I slept through all those tests. I was dead drunk and just never got around to answering any of the questions.

In the tests that I took in high school, I scored at the genius level. My teachers always said I was incredibly smart, but just lazy. As a matter of fact, I aced my SATs."

"You took the SATs?" he asked incredulously. "If you didn't complete any of the tests in Milwaukee, how in the fuck did you get in the Army?"

I explained to him how, at the end of every test, the sergeants entered the room and provided everyone enough answers to get them through the testing. I told him that most of the guys here at Fort Knox couldn't have passed the test had they been required to do it on their own. I further told him that poor Private Luney in our platoon was mildly mentally retarded. The colonel stared at me in shock.

"Captain, could this be true?"

"Sir, I don't know about the tests at the reception station in Milwaukee, but regarding the West Point test, not so, sir. He took the test way too fast, and no one has ever gotten every single answer right before."

The colonel turned to face me and said, "OK, how do we resolve this, because nothing here adds up?"

"Test me," I said. Someone groaned behind me. "Ask me any question on the test."

"Sounds fair," said the commander. "Captain, ask him some questions."

"OK," the captain said haltingly. "Let's see how you do on the advanced math section." As he thumbed through the exam, he said, "How about we go to the advanced calculus question on the test. Only one percent of the personnel who have ever taken this test have gotten that one correct. Frankly, we just put it in there to frighten people a little. We never expected anyone to try and answer it."

"Got it," I said. "Colonel, can I borrow a pen and some paper so I can write down the answer?"

"Aren't you going to wait for the question?" asked the captain.

"That's not necessary. I think I can remember both the question and the answer."

After all these years, I can still remember it like yesterday. After I was given a pen and paper, I wrote down the following information:

# WHAT ARE THE PRECISE LIMITS OF FUNCTIONS AS X APPROACHES A CONSTANT?

## ANSWER/DEFINITION:

The statement **lim f(x) = L** has the following precise definition. Given any real number **e > 0** there exists another real number **8 > 0** so that **lim f(x) = L** has the following precise definition.

In general, the value of **x** will depend on the value of **L**. That is, we will always begin with **E – 0** and then determine an appropriate corresponding value for **x - 8**. There are many values of **L** which work. Once you find a value that works, all smaller values of L also work x will depend on the value of **E - 0**.

"How could you possibly remember a complex question from a test that you took two days ago?" asked the captain.

"Oh, I forget to tell you, I have a photographic memory. Not a real photographic memory where I can remember everything, I have seen but one that for some strange reason allows me to remember everything that I have ever read."

"Sir," the captain replied, "I think he might have a photographic memory. This question and answer are textbook right down to the punctuation marks. I've never seen anything like this before."

"That question really isn't that hard," I boldly intervened. "Let's take it to the next step and have a discussion on the differentiation of inverse trigonometric functions.

"When you are determining the differentiation of inverse trigonometric functions, you have to remember that none of the six basic trigonometry functions is a one-to-one function. However, in the following list, each trigonometry function is listed with an appropriately restricted domain, which makes it one-to-one."

The captain turned white.

"Sir, I'm a math major and teach math at West Point," he said, looking at the commander. "This problem is too complex for me. I don't even know how to check to see if it is correct or not. Taking all of this into consideration, I think we need to reassess the situation. I would like Private Berlin to come in for additional testing."

"Are you out of your fucking mind?" stated the commander. "This shithead is not going anywhere, and he certainly isn't going to take any more tests."

"Sir," interjected the West Point captain. "This is the highest score we have ever recorded for this test. I think that we need to accelerate moving Private Berlin from BCT to the West Point Preparatory School. This is absolutely incredible."

"Are you stupid or mentally retarded!" shouted the commander. "Do you realize how big of a problem that we have on our hands right now? This is a whole lot bigger than another cadet for West Point. We're talking about a big-time political scandal here, and the potential for a monstrous criminal investigation. Didn't you listen to a word Private Numb-nuts has been saying, about the fraud occurring at our reception stations? I guarantee you that if this is happening at Milwaukee, then it is happening all over the country. The irregularities and abuses that took place during his processing are enough to bring down the entire Army. I want no part of this. As far as I'm concerned, this needs to go away and quickly. Do you really think that I am going to allow any of this information ever to see the light of day?"

"But, sir ..."

"Stop!" the commander demanded. "Jesus Christ, I've heard enough. Everyone, stop and think. How do we un-fuck this? Sergeant Major, I want this problem to disappear, today. Is that clear enough guidance for you? The last thing that any of us need in this stage of our careers is the press, or worse yet, Congress, looking into this situation. A lot of people out there do not want the all-volunteer force to succeed and would do anything to stop it from moving forward. If word of this fiasco leaks, we are all finished. This must end and end today. I want everything gone. Do you hear me? This test never happened. This conversation never happened. I never even heard of Private Berlin. If anyone outside of this office ever brings up this subject or his name again, that person will be spending the rest of their career in some ice cave at an Army base in Thule, Greenland. If you think I'm kidding, go ahead and try me.

"Sergeant Major, strike all record of this meeting from all daily logs and files. If anyone has any problems with this, I want to hear it now. After I walk out that door, under no circumstances will I ever hear any mention of this incident again? Is there anyone here that is too stupid to understand these instructions? Sergeant Major, you know what to do."

With that, the commander rose from his desk, the sergeant major called the room to attention, and the three officers left the room and walked out the front door of the headquarters building.

I was getting more than a little nervous at this point. Did make it "go away" mean go away like in the way the Mafia makes someone go away?  Were these drill sergeants actually going to kill me and hide my body somewhere on Fort Knox? No, I reasoned. That only happens in the movies, but deep in the back of my brain, something was saying, don't be too sure, Berlin.

The minute the door slammed shut, the sergeant major began to tear me a new asshole.

"Goddamnit, Berlin, what the fuck were you trying to do? In thirty years with this man's Army, I've never had a situation as messed up like this. Why in the fuck didn't you just stay home and go to college or something? Instead, you have to come here and mess up my life. Do you have it in for the Army, or are you purposely trying to destroy this institution? Drill Sergeant Harper, I want you to figure out how to discharge this asshole as quickly as possible. I want him out of my Army today. Call headquarters and tell them we caught him looking at guys in the shower. That should be enough to get him discharged as a fag. The faster he gets off this post, the better off we will all be. After I leave this office, I never want to see his face or hear his name again."

Sgt. Harper actually came to my rescue. "Sergeant Major, before we make any decisions we might later regret, we need to take our time and think this through. Berlin is not some idiot who is going to go away quietly if we try to railroad him. I know this soldier, and if we fuck him, I guarantee you he will fuck us right back."

He turned to me and said, "That's right, isn't it, Berlin?"

I replied, "Yes, Drill Sergeant. No one is going to discharge me as a fag and get away with it. Besides, if I wanted to go to the press, I could prove how smart I am, and how wrong the Army is. I guarantee you I will tell them a story that will blow their socks off and rock your Army to its core. The Army can't hide things fast enough to stop me from wreaking havoc on your precious all-volunteer force. I guarantee you if you mess with me, you will lose more than I do in this game."

Once again, I had pushed it just a little bit too far. The sergeant major was staring at me like I was a bug that he was getting ready to smash. You know me. Something inside my head just makes me want to keep pushing that envelope. Maybe someday I would learn to keep my mouth shut.

"Shut your fucking mouth, Berlin," shouted Harper. "Be respectful to the Sergeant Major, or I'll rip you to pieces. Stand there, be quiet, and let me discuss this with the sergeant major." He took a deep breath. "Look, Sergeant Major, I can handle Berlin. The safest place for him right now is right here. We can control what he says and what he does. If he gets out of our control, there is no telling what might happen. Besides, I have an idea which I think can help us turn this lemon into lemonade.

"You know how you are always saying how hard it is for our NCOs to get promoted since the Army put the new testing standards in place? All our NCOs must score higher than eighty to get promoted. You and I both know that there is a lot more to being an NCO in this man's Army than the ability to pass a damn test. I don't want a bunch of test-taking sergeants in my Army, do you? Hell, Sergeant Major, most of these guys have had multiple tours in Vietnam. They were good enough to go to hell and fight for this country, but now that the war is winding down, our leaders are going to toss them to the curb like dogs. Same as every war.

"If you are a combat veteran in today's Army, there is no way you could ever be a sergeant major. I know you don't have a high school degree, and that's OK. You can't learn what we do in some damn school. When is the last time that something that you learned in a book saved a life in combat?

Only one thing counts in an Army, and that's combat experience. Are we going to let all of those good men get thrown out to the civilian world, or are we going to take a stand and do what we can to help them out?

"I have a plan that will take care of all of our problems. Berlin here will stay out of trouble because he will be working directly for me on a special mission. He will ensure our deserving NCOs get the promotions that they deserve for their combat experience. More importantly, the colonel will be able to rest easy, knowing that we have saved his precious Army from embarrassment, not to mention his career. We can all come out of this mess looking like heroes instead of zeros.

"Let's use our little Einstein here to help our best NCOs get ahead in the Army. I've known Private Berlin for four weeks now, and I've come to the conclusion that he is good at one thing and one thing only, taking tests. Isn't it our responsibility as NCOs to find the best attributes of our soldiers and capitalize on them? Isn't that what basic training is all about anyway? I have a buddy who works over at the testing station, and he told me that the officers in charge rarely show up to monitor the testing process and that it would be easy to slip in a ringer.

"The testing center is currently running four separate testing sessions a day. The only time the officers ever show up is in the middle of testing, and they do that mostly to make sure that no one is cheating on the examination. Everyone is so paranoid about cheat notes that they are not paying attention to the sign-in procedures. The place is manned by trainees who are waiting for their next assignment, and like typical trainees, they don't know their ass from a hole in the ground and are afraid of anyone with a rank on their arms. It is a two-hour detail. So, at every test, there is a new set of trainees operating the sign-in desk every week. It's like God looked down, saw our dilemma, and provided us an answer to our problems.

"We will run this like a covert operation. If everyone sticks to the plan, we can do this. By the time this is over, Berlin will be able to graduate and leave here as a private first class, another promotion which will be our guarantee that he keeps his mouth shut. I'll be able to retire knowing that I took care of my brother NCOs, and you, Sergeant Major, will probably be selected for division sergeant major because your drill sergeants will be the highest advancing team on Fort Knox. The brass will attribute the promotion rate to your great leadership qualities and ability to train your NCOs." Sgt. Harper was good. By the time he was finished, he had the sergeant major eating out of his hand.

I was standing off to the side while Harper and the sergeant major talked about me like I wasn't even there. Every time I tried to interject, I was told to shut up and listen. I must admit the plan they laid out was simple and seemed to be foolproof. If the information Harper had been provided by his buddy at the testing center was accurate, this could work. It might even be fun.

The sergeant major would move me out of the barracks and into someplace where I would be out of sight and out of mind of the rest of the trainees. He would tell the rest of my platoon and the Wolverines that I was in trouble for back talking drill sergeants and I had been moved to the next brigade down the road. I was going to tell my friends that I was going to have to repeat a week of training and that I would catch up and be back with them on graduation day. The story was that there were too many Morons in our brigade, and one had to move to balance out the units. The rest of the platoon thought I was an idiot. The Wolverines would say that I was getting what I deserved for getting out of work for so long. The sergeant major would move me to an empty trainee barracks behind headquarters. They would give me the room at the end of the bay, the one reserved for drill sergeants.

Harper would arrange for me to be given four brand new ID cards every morning. These ID cards would have my picture on them but would bear the serial number and rank of one of the drill sergeants in the brigade who needed his test score improved, so he could be promoted. Since NCOs could test on their off time, I would wear civilian clothing so I wouldn't have to worry about having the wrong name tags. Harper said it would also prevent me from getting charged with impersonating a sergeant in the unlikely event that I was caught. He did, however, caveat this.

"You know, the only way you can get caught is if you get stupid. If you stick to the plan, it will work, so don't try to get smart on me and change anything or you will blow the whole operation.

"After you complete a test, leave the building and walk back to your barracks and wait for the next test."

Harper knew I was not going to get involved with his plan unless there was something in it for me. He would give me my own room and would ensure that I was provided a TV and a radio. Instead of getting up at four thirty every morning, I could sleep in until seven thirty because the first test didn't start until nine. My day would officially end at five. I would be granted free access to the PX, the commissary, and the clubs on post. I would still have to wear my uniform when not testing, but if I kept my head, I could drink beer whenever I wanted to include keeping some in my room. As long as I stuck to the rules and passed all the tests, this would be our arrangement until graduation. How could I say no to such a sweet deal?

Harper made it clear that he would tolerate no deviations from the plan. One screw up on my part and he would deny everything and kick my ass out of the Army on a dishonorable discharge for being a homosexual. He would allow me to have contact with the Wolverines on Sunday, but under no circumstances was I to divulge any part of the plan or tell anyone about my unique living situation.

At graduation, he would see that I was promoted to private first class. The promotion came with a fifty-dollar-a-month pay raise. Since I would be the highest-ranking Wolverine when we went on to advanced individual training, I would be a platoon leader and have a much easier time of it. I was starting to figure out this Army stuff. The dumber you are, the better you do. The bottom line was that this could be a great deal. I just had to control my mouth and my drinking.

The next day I packed up my gear and told everyone I would be moving to the third training brigade. Sgt. Harper made a big show of yelling at me, telling me to move my ass and get my shit packed.

"Come on, move faster, dumb shit, this is my chance to rid this platoon of one dummy," he said, loud enough for all to hear. "If you're not out of here in the next thirty minutes, the sergeant major will pick some Moron from one of the other platoons to take your place, and that would piss me off because I would be stuck with your stupid ass. Move! Move! Move!"

He was walking around with a big-ass smile on his face. In his mind, he was getting rid of the biggest pain in his ass in the platoon. The entire time I was packing, he kept screaming at me that he had already spoken to the drill sergeants at my new detachment and they were going to kick my ass when I moved over. He said that they had heard what a smartass mouth I had and that they had something to shove in it to shut me up. He was getting a kick out of this. I knew he was full of shit, but nevertheless some of the guys in the platoon were very concerned about me. I told them not to worry.

I should have been given an Academy Award for my farewell performance. I went around to everyone and shook hands and said my goodbyes. The hardest part was lying to the Wolverines, especially Danny. However, I knew that if I told one guy, the story would spread, and my sweet deal would end faster than it started. Despite all the harassment, they were sad to see me depart and tried to raise my spirits by providing me a six-pack of beer they had smuggled into the company area. I let them know I would be fine and that on Sunday afternoon free time, I would work my way over and let them know how things were going.

I overacted just a little and almost blew it when Bob decided that he wasn't going to let this travesty take place.

"Let's just end this, Roger," he suggested. "Tell them that you're not really one of the Morons so you can stay, and they can send someone else. If they make you move, I'm going to have someone from your hometown contact Congressman Smyth. When he finds out that they are moving you away from the rest of the platoon, all hell will break loose. The Army doesn't like it when congressmen get involved in trainee issues. It makes them nervous. We don't have to give up without a fight."

It took almost an hour for me to convince him that it was the right thing to do. I told him that I could handle it and that I didn't want anyone else to get into trouble. After all, I kind of caused this with my dummy game.

"Let's not blow it now," I reasoned. "We're only three weeks away from graduation. I can stand on my head in a bucket of shit for three weeks. Besides, I kind of like being the dummy. No one bothers me, and life's not too bad. In three weeks, we're all going to Fort Benning for infantry training, and we'll be driving there in new cars. I'll even let you drive it if you want."

I promised him that if things got bad, I would let him know, and we could raise hell together. After he calmed down and we said our awkward guy goodbyes, you know, quick hug slap on the back and punch in the chest, I was on my way.

Chapter 20

New Job

After all the farewells, which were a lot harder than I thought they would be, I spent most of the day on Sunday moving into my new digs. I took a short break and went over to the church after services ended. I began in earnest to prepare for my new occupation: Roger Berlin, test-taker extraordinaire.

Drill Sgt. Harper gave me fifty dollars and told me to go to the PX to purchase some civilian clothing, or civvies as they called them in the Army.

After five weeks of basic combat training and the total isolation and restriction from anything associated with the civilian world outside, I was finally free to wander around and see what I was missing. Not that I had much time because Harper had only given me forty-five minutes at the PX and fifteen minutes for travel time. He told me if I got done getting my civvies early, I could grab a beer and a slice of pizza, but my ass was to be back at my new home in less than an hour.

Being a typical guy, it only took me fifteen minutes to buy some clothing, wolf down an entire pizza and a throw down a couple of beers. The most critical items on my shopping list were two baseball hats. I had to find some headgear to disguise the basic training haircut that marked all trainees. No self-respecting sergeant would be caught dead with a trainee haircut.

After outfitting myself with the appropriate gear and finishing the pizza and beer, I headed back to my new hideout. It was time for my training session with Harper. He approached training for the testing center like any other combat mission and wanted to ensure that he covered every possible scenario. I thought he was going a little overboard. His theory was, "train like you fight," and he wasn't going to allow me on this mission until I was ready for every possible contingency.

The testing station on Fort Knox was two blocks from where I was living so getting there and back would be no big deal. I could walk over. Harper gave me a map of the installation and marked out several alternate routes to and from the testing center. To avoid being noticed on my new job, he told me to take a different direction each time I went to the center, and every other day I was to reverse my paths.

To make sure no one was following me, I would delay en route at one of several locations on the installation, such as the bookstore, snack bar, or pizza joint. Harper would provide route coverage assistance with someone monitoring my routes to watch for anyone tailing me, also probably to make sure I went where I was supposed to go.

To be eligible to test for a higher promotion score, the training sergeant at each brigade had to sign NCOs up in advance of the test date. The sergeant major had already prepared and submitted the necessary paperwork. All the sergeants in our unit who needed a higher score were scheduled for testing over the following three weeks. I would get identification that indicated I was the individual scheduled to take the test and had my picture on it. Harper would provide me the credentials of the person I would be posing as about forty-five minutes before each test, so I would never have more than one set of false identifying documents with me at one time. Harper warned me, "If you ever think you are about to get caught, find some way to get rid of the fake ID. I don't care if you have to eat it."

Every NCO who wanted to take the test had to apply through his unit, and the testing center would approve the test and schedule the NCO to come on a specific day and time. The testing center maintained a master copy of NCOs scheduled to test at each session, so the sergeant major had to be careful to schedule only one of his NCOs per session. It would have looked suspicious to show up as two people at the same time.

When the NCOs entered the testing center, the clerk on duty would check the master roster and check off the name on that roster. There was an ID card check to verify names but no requirement to sign in and no signatures required on the test. This was good, according to Harper. He said it would give us plausible deniability in the event "we" were caught. I don't know where all the "we" stuff was coming from because I didn't see how he was risking anything in this venture.

The only other thing I had to watch out for was a rotating lieutenant whose job it was to make sure that no one had any cheat sheets with him. You know how serious the Army was about cheating on tests. We weren't worried about the lieutenant recognizing me coming back for more than one test because there would be a new lieutenant at every session.

Harper estimated that there would be about 150 NCOs at each test. All the sergeants at Fort Knox were trying to get higher scores so that they could get promoted. It was going to be a bustling place. He told me to never be too early or late for testing. I was to arrive when a lot of NCOs were coming in. I had to do my best to ensure I never stood out and did nothing that would draw any attention.

"Don't speak or ask questions," Sgt. Harper advised. "I don't want a sound to pass your lips; don't even make eye contact with anyone. Just identify yourself, take the damn test, and leave. Don't turn in the test early and don't rush through the test and sit at your desk waiting until the end to turn it in, or someone will notice that you're not doing anything. You are going to have to go slowly and time your test taking so that you turn in your test with the bulk of the NCOs so that it won't draw any attention. If for any reason something doesn't go according to plan, keep your mouth shut and let them bring you back to the unit, and I will take care of everything."

Harper would do all the talking for me. This part insulted me. I could talk my way out of anything. I didn't need a mouthpiece to keep me out of trouble. I hated it when they treated me like a dummy.

As far as test scores were concerned, I was supposed to score between an eighty and ninety on each exam. When Harper attempted to tell me how many questions it required me to answer to achieve certain percentages, I had to stop him.

"Come on, Drill Sergeant, I'm not stupid. I guarantee you I will get whatever score you want me to get, so relax. I'm no dummy."

The following morning, I lay in my bunk and listened to the sounds of reveille and the hustle and bustle of all my buddies outside being screamed at while they were doing morning calisthenics. I got up and leisurely prepared myself for the first day of my new job. About thirty minutes before the first test session, Harper stopped by and provided me with the first identification card. He told me to get dressed in my new civilian duds. When I was dressed, he messed me up a little so my clothing wouldn't look so new, then he had me repeat to him over and over who I was supposed to be and the score I was supposed to get on the first test.

I would take four tests a day for the next three weeks. Although I pushed him for all four sets of identification cards and scores, so I wouldn't have to keep coming back to the barracks and having to keep seeing him all day long, he wouldn't bend. He was going to control this operation from beginning to end. He told me he would give me everything I needed, one test at a time, and I damned well better not let anyone follow me back to the unit. When he finished briefing me, I headed over to the test center and prepared for my first performance.

Everything went precisely as Sgt. Harper had explained to me in our briefings. There were a lot of people there to test. I entered with a large group, stood in line, showed my identification card, got my test and took a seat. It was nerve-wracking at first because I thought at any minute someone was going to realize that I was not a sergeant.

Worst case scenario, I thought, was that someone would recognize the name I had signed in under and realize I was not who I was pretending to be. I was sure that everyone in the room was a special agent and that at any moment I was going to be arrested. After my initial panic, I calmed down and got going on my first test. I realized that as long as I kept my head down and didn't talk or pay attention to anyone, no one would know who I was, and anyway, no one seemed to care.

The hardest part of my new gig was the boredom, something I hadn't counted on. After I completed each portion of the test, I would have to remain in my seat and pretend to be still taking the test. By the end of the first day, I had it down to ten minutes per section. My new job left me with way too much time on my hands. I had been forbidden by Drill Sgt. Harper from doodling, writing notes, reading newspapers, or anything else that might draw attention to me. I had to pretend that I was still taking the test and move my pencil or turn a page now and then, as if I were always looking for answers.

I got pretty good at daydreaming and would sometimes catch myself being startled out of a dream when everyone around me started to get up to turn in their tests. When the test ended, I would shuffle up to the front with the other guys in the room. I kept my mouth shut, didn't talk to anyone, and tossed my test on the desk. As soon as I got out the door, I separated myself from the group and headed off on my own, making sure to follow the exact route laid out by Drill Sgt. Harper.

There I was, attending Army basic training and living the life of Riley. I was enjoying basic training more than a trainee had any right to. My friends were killing themselves in training, and I was enjoying pizza, beer, television, my radio, and all the reading material I could handle. I did feel a little bad about lying to my buddies when I told them how tough life was for me at the new unit. However, there was no way I was giving this up. I loved my cozy little hideout. What more could a guy ask for? There were no drill sergeants, no waking up before the crack of dawn, and my TV. This Army life was OK after all.

Everything was going well, better than I expected. I had been testing for almost two weeks, and all was going exactly as planned. I could make a living doing this, then I realized that I *was* making a living doing this. The Army was paying me to be an official test taker. I kept my mouth shut. I followed all the rules and, except for some daydreaming episodes, did everything possible to make sure I didn't draw any attention to myself.

On Friday afternoon of the second week of testing, everything came crashing down. About halfway through the third and final session of the day, a guy in a civilian suit walked up to me. Right away I sensed danger. No one on Fort Knox wore anything except for military uniforms or jeans and a t-shirt, and nobody ever wore a suit. This was trouble for sure. As he approached, I took the identification card I had checked in with and, with a quick sleight of hand, dropped it down a heating and cooling vent that was on the floor near the desk I where I was seated.

When the guy got close to me, he opened his suit jacket, reached into his inner pocket, and removed a small wallet. When he opened the wallet, I realized that it was a badge holder and inside was a shiny silver badge that read, "Special Investigator." On the other side of the holder was some government identification card. He made sure that when he opened his jacket, I saw he was carrying a forty-five-caliber pistol in a shoulder holster.

Feeling like a rabbit facing a fox, I quickly looked around to see how far away the nearest exit was and tried to figure out if I could make it to the door. I wished I had thought about escape routes before I sat down. I had gotten too comfortable and had let my guard down a little. When I took the time to look around, I realized that the Army was taking no chances. MPs were standing in front of all the doors in the room. The guy in front of me identified himself.

"Agent Jackson, Fort Knox Criminal Investigation Command."

Why does this shit keep happening to me?

"Please stand up, spread your legs and put your hands on top of your head."

He then signaled one of the MPs to come over and search me. After a quick frisk, the MP said, "He's clear, no weapons or contraband."

Despite every fiber of my being wanting to say something stupid, I remembered what Sgt. Harper had told me. I bit my lip, shut my mouth, and complied with their instructions.

"Please identify yourself," the special agent said.

"Private Roger Berlin," I replied. Remember, I thought, stay calm, keep your answers short and to the point, and don't provide any additional information. Remember you are a Moron.

"What unit are you assigned to, soldier?"

"I think it's E or five or something like that, but I'm not quite sure," I said, using my best Moron inflections.

He then asked me for my military identification. So, I took out my wallet, removed my ID card, and handed it to him.

"Private, do you have any weapons on you?"

"No, sir," I answered.

He then did a quick search of the area around my desk and looked into my lunch bag, which contained a leftover hamburger and some cold French fries. He asked if I was going to cooperate with him or would he have to handcuff me.

"I don't know what cooperate is," I replied.

He looked at me strangely, took another long look at my face, and asked me if I had any white dots on my hats or boots back at my basic training unit. I informed him that the drill sergeants had put white dots on all my stuff, so they would know that I was one of the smart soldiers. There it was, as apparent as a flashing neon sign: "Private Roger Berlin, Moron Corps."

I could tell that I had rattled him, because all a sudden, he lost his calm demeanor.

He looked at my ID card and seeing the serial number, exclaimed, "What the fuck, Private, is this your real ID card?"

"I don't know if it's real or not, Mr. Special Agent, sir, but it is the one that the drill sergeant gave to me when I got here to Fort Knox."

"Don't call me mister. To you I'm either Special Agent or sir, is that clear?"

"Yes sir, Mr. Special Agent, sir," I replied.

Frustrated, he signaled two of the MPs to come forward and told them to take me outside. As I was removed from my desk area, I grabbed my bag with the leftover hamburger and fries and picked up the test I was taking. On the way past the front desk, I "accidentally" dropped my bag on the front desk, spilling French fries everywhere. I laid my test down on the counter and began cleaning up the mess I had made. Agent Jackson sneered at me with disgust.

"Come on, shithead, let someone else clean up that mess. You have bigger problems than some spilled French fries."

He told the MPs to keep me moving and mentioned to his partner that I was probably one of those boys from the West Virginia hills who ate food they dropped on the ground. For some reason, the sergeants on Fort Knox assumed that the Morons couldn't hear and always talked about us like we weren't there. He told me to keep moving and go out of the building with the MPs. I did as he directed and walked on out of the testing center minus my hamburger and my spilled fries. Also, somewhere on that front counter was a test with someone else's ID on it.

Parked out in front of the test center was a green Army sedan with the back-door open. The MPs put me in the back seat and shut the door. I had been in this situation before. There were no door handles and a wire cage between the front and back seat. There was nothing in the back seat except me. I knew where I was going. The MPs climbed in the front seat, turned on the lights and sirens, and sped down the road to where I suspected the MP station was. When I looked behind us, I realized that the special agent and another guy in a suit were following closely behind in a white unmarked sedan. It had a blue flashing light on in the window, but even without that light, you would have to be an idiot not to realize it was a police vehicle.

I couldn't resist. I stared through the back window until Special Agent Jackson and I made eye contact. Then, giving him my dumbest and biggest smile, I began to wave at him like a kid in the circus waving at the clowns. I could tell by the disgusted look on his face that I had pissed him off.

As soon as the police cars stopped, Agent Jackson came running up to the car I was in and yanked open the door.

Sticking his head in the car, he yelled, "Who in the fuck do you think you're smiling and waving at, dummy?"

"You, Mr. Special Agent, sir," I replied innocently. "I ain't been in a real police car before, and I wanted to thank you for letting me ride in one."

He looked like he wanted to punch me in the face, but there were too many witnesses standing around watching. I realized I was going to have to tone it down just a little or I risked pissing him off so bad he might do something dumb. I was sure my actions would result in me getting my ass whipped inside the military police station. Best to remember what Harper had told me and keep my mouth shut.

I'd been in many police stations before, and this one was no different. Same front desk with the little window, the same cheap furniture, and same interrogation rooms. I suspected the interrogation tactics would be the same also. I had a couple of cards to play here:

They didn't know I had a lot of experience with the police and assumed that I was ignorant of their tactics.

They thought I was a blithering idiot. I was one of the Morons.

Agent Jackson and his partner immediately escorted me to a dark interrogation room with a small metal desk and two old Army chairs. I was left alone. On one wall was a sizeable one-way glass mirror, on the other side of which I assumed was Special Agent Jackson and his team watching me and working up an interrogation technique. On the far wall were two speakers that I thought were listening devices. I knew they were going to leave me in here alone to stew for at least an hour or so before they spoke to me.

I was right. I sat for about an hour and ten minutes. I knew what would happen next; they would leave me alone and hope that I would panic while I got to think about all the things they could do to me and fret about what kind of evidence they had. During my long wait, I was supposed to get anxious and frightened. The goal here was to get me so terrified that I would be talking a mile a minute when they returned. I figured I could last longer than they could.

I wasn't concerned. They had no proof that I was taking the test for someone else. They didn't even have a copy and, unless they found the ID card in the vent, they had no idea what I was doing at the test center. For now, it was all guesswork on their part: no test, no evidence. Most importantly, they had no motive.

I wasn't worried about Drill Sgt. Harper or the sergeant major. If I kept my mouth shut, no one would know to even talk to them. Who was going to believe that a private in basic training would be able to create a conspiracy this complex? Where would I get the information? How would I know when to go to the testing center? How would I be able to get my hands on ID cards? It was just too complicated for a private to concoct. The only thing I worried about was that Harper would be going crazy when he realized I hadn't returned. Word travels fast in the Army, and he might already have known that I had been picked up when I didn't return. I was willing to bet he was a lot more nervous than I was at this point.

It didn't take long for the two agents to start in on the questions when they entered the interrogation room. These guys were so sure that they would be able to break me and solve their big test-taking crime that they were stumbling all over each other to get me to talk.

"Private Berlin, as I said before when we first met, I am Special Agent Jackson, and this is my partner, Special Agent Bufford. Before we waste any more of the Army's time, I'm going to tell you what's going on here. I figure that the more I tell you, the better chance you will realize that I have you dead to rights and that the best thing to do is just tell me the truth. I don't want you lying to us and force us to have to add perjury to the charges that we are going to bring against you."

"What's perjury?" I asked.

"Well, Private Berlin, perjury is when you lie to police officers or special agents. In the Army that is about the biggest law that you can break. We could put you in prison for twenty or thirty years if we wanted to. I'm pretty sure it's thirty years in prison for lying to a police officer. Isn't that right, Agent Bufford?"

"Yes, Special Agent Jackson, perjury is the worst crime in the Army. I hope that this private doesn't lie to us here today."

These guys must think I am stupid, I thought. At least my act was working.

Just then an MP walked in the room.

"Private Berlin, I'd like to introduce you to Sergeant First Class Johnson of the Fort Knox Military Police," Jackson said. "Do you recognize Sergeant Johnson?"

"No, sir," I replied, but something about him did look oddly familiar.

"Well Private, Sergeant Johnson was at the testing center this morning taking a test to improve his scores."

Yup, another idiot who couldn't get promoted because Uncle Sam wanted smarter NCOs to take his place. He was just part of the Army's master plan to make the Army smarter.

"Well, after Sergeant Johnson finished his test this morning, he had to go back to the testing center because he realized that he had left his good-luck keychain on the desk where he was sitting. Do you know what desk he was sitting at, Private?"

"No, sir."

Shit, I remembered him from the morning test session, and I  remembered when he came back in the second session looking for something on the floor around the desk next to me.

"Funny thing, Private. Sergeant Johnson remembers you sitting at the same desk, taking the same test during two different test sessions. He specifically remembered you because he thought you were very young to be an NCO in the Army. What do you have to say about that, Private Berlin?

"Now, Private, before you answer, Sergeant Johnson knew that we were having a problem with people cheating on the Army promotion tests here at Fort Knox, so imagine his surprise when he recognized you taking the same test at two different sessions."

Here we go again, I thought. Can you imagine someone cheating on an Army test? I bet that never happens. Let's get real.

"So, being a good sergeant and military policeman, he came back here to inform me, because I head up the fraud division here on Fort Knox."

I made him answer my stupid questions to keep him a little off guard. I was hoping to break up his train of thought and rhythm. I also needed to blow his motive somehow. He had to take the time to explain everything to me because what choice did he have? What good were his threats if I didn't understand them?

He slowly and carefully explained fraud to me and then continued. "When Sergeant Johnson told me his story, Agent Bufford and I decided to take a military police squad down to the test center to check it out.

"You know what we found when we got to the testing center, Private?"

"No, sir."

"Well, what we found was that not only was someone cheating on the test, but they were so stupid that they were back for the third time on the same day, and you know what's even stupider than that?"

"No, sir," I replied again.

"I'll tell you what's stupider. The guy cheating, and that would be you, Private Berlin, was so stupid that he was even sitting in the same seat and wearing the same clothing."

He had me there. That was stupid on my part. I guess I got so bored that I got a little complacent and wasn't paying attention to what I was doing. I can't believe I sat in the same seat. Drill Sgt. Harper was going to kick my ass.

"Sergeant Johnson, is this the man you saw at the test center at the morning test and when you came back at the afternoon test?"

After Johnson positively identified me, Agent Jackson said, "You can leave now. Thank you for your keen observation. I believe that we have everything we need to put this soldier away for a long, long time." Sergeant Johnson left the room.

"Private Berlin, you and I both know that I have you dead to rights. The only thing left to decide is how many years you are going to get for committing fraud. Speaking of rights, I'm going to read you yours now. When I'm done, you are going to sign this piece of paper saying that you fully understand what I discussed with you."

He read me my rights.

I made a big deal of not understanding and having him explain every one of my rights to me, complaining that they were too hard to figure out. I finally told him that he seemed like a nice guy, and if he said it was Ok for me to sign that I understood my rights, then it was Ok by me. I could tell I was driving him crazy. I knew he was recording the interview, and the last thing he wanted was for someone to think he had tricked me into signing away my rights. Well, that was what he was going to have to do because I wasn't going to back off. I needed a fallback position just in case this all went to hell.

After about ten minutes of mental sparring, he finally gave up and said, "Just sign the damn paperwork, Private."

With the paperwork out of the way, the two agents figured I was ready to spill my guts. "Who put you up to taking the sergeant promotion test, three times that we know of?" Jackson demanded.

"No one, Mr. Special Agent, sir."

"Don't lie to us. You're not even a sergeant. What purpose would a private have to go to the testing center to take multiple promotion tests unless he was cheating?"

I replied, "I didn't take any tests, Mr. Special Agent, sir."

"Of course, you did," Agent Jackson responded. "We have a sworn statement by Sergeant Johnson that he saw you take two tests, and I caught you getting ready to take a third."

"That's not true. I never took a test. I was in the testing center all day. I sat in one of those chairs, but I didn't take any tests. I'm not very good at tests. I don't even like tests, and they scare me."

Jackson slammed his hands down on the desk, "Bullshit, you are guilty, and both you and I know it, so why continue lying? We already proved to you that we know what happened. Who put you up to this? We don't want you to go to jail because of what someone made you do. Tell us the truth, and you can go back to your unit, and we will leave you alone."

"Look, Mr. Special Agents, I can prove I didn't take any tests. Check the records. You will find that my name is not on any list and not on any tests. I'm not afraid for you to check because I know that I never took a test."

This stunned them.

Agent Jackson turned to Agent Bufford. "Did anyone get a copy of the test he had in front of him when we brought him in?"

Agent Bufford left the room and came back about two minutes later. The look on his face said it all. He whispered to Agent Jackson, who slammed his fist into the wall and screamed, "Are you fucking kidding me? Get your ass over to that testing center. I want you to go through every page of every test personally. I need you to find something that ties this shithead to those tests."

He told me to cool my heels and gave me a cup of coffee to drink, then left the interrogation room. He didn't look so sure of himself anymore.

 It was almost three hours before the two agents returned. When they did, guess who was with them? Good ole Drill Sgt. Harper. When they walked into the room, he immediately began to yell at me.

"What the fuck have you got yourself into now, Moron? I can't let you out of my sight for two minutes. When I get you back to the unit, you are going to wish that you never heard of the United States Army. This is the final straw. I'll have your ass discharged from this Army in three days. My goal is to set a new Army record for discharging a Moron. You fuck-up. I'm going to make your life miserable for your last three days."

Special Agent Jackson asked him to be quiet as he needed to ask me a few more questions. I figured that they had brought a drill sergeant along to increase the intimidation factor of the interview. After all, what's more frightening to a new trainee than a drill sergeant? Little did they know that the real criminal was on the wrong side of the interrogation table.

"Private Berlin," began Agent Jackson, "here is what we know. One, you spent the day at the testing center. Two, you are AWOL from your unit. Three, you spent the day in an area restricted to trainees, and four, you broke the rule concerning trainees and civilian clothes. At this point, I have enough to lock you up for five years. However, I spoke to my commander. If you are willing to tell us what you were doing at the testing center, we will allow you to return to your unit. You will probably get kicked out of the Army, and there is nothing I can do about that, but I promise you I won't put you in Army prison. Tell me whom you were taking tests for?"

"Wait a minute," interjected Sgt. Harper. "Are you guys fucking kidding me? Do you understand that this guy is one of my Morons? There is no way he could take an NCO promotion test. Hell, I'm not even sure that he can read. Private Berlin, I want to know right now what you were doing in that testing center."

"Well, Mr. Drill Sergeant, sir, it's like this," I said in my most contrite voice. "When the West Point guys came to test us a couple of weeks ago, they had food and juice with them. I got to get out of the heat for a couple of hours and sit in an air-conditioned room. It was nice. I overheard some of the drill sergeants talking about the test center, and that there was going to be a bunch of tests every day for a month. I remembered about the air-conditioning and snacks. I figured that it was just like the place where we took the West Point test and that it would be a good place to hang out. It's hot outside, and I don't like hot. I was hoping that someone would bring some good snacks there today, just like that last test I went to."

"Are you trying to tell me that you just got some civilian clothing and left basic training to come over here and sit in a test room?" asked Agent Jackson.

"That's right, Mr. Special Agent, sir. I didn't think anyone would mind."

"Why did you wear civilian clothing?" he countered.

"Because I heard the drill sergeant telling the other sergeant that you couldn't wear a uniform to the test. So, I walked over to the PX, bought some clothes, and wore them over to the place where they do all the tests."

"Where did you get the money?" he asked. "Like I said, I just went to the PX store and bought them. The Army gave us some money two days ago."

"Berlin, do you understand what restriction to the company area means?" Sgt. Harper asked. "It means that you are not allowed to go to the PX or any place that is not in the basic training area. I guarantee you that you will be court-martialed for disobeying orders when I get you back to the unit."

He turned to the two Agents. "Ever since they started this Moron crap, this is the kind of shit we have to put up with. It's not hard enough that we have to take all these pussies and make them soldiers. We also have to babysit a bunch of idiots. It's not like when you and I came into the Army. This is bullshit. I can't wait to retire."

"I'm with you, Drill Sergeant. I'm afraid this all-volunteer force is going to be the death of us all," Jackson said.

Agent Jackson looked at me and shook his head. "Berlin, one last time. Are you trying to tell me you just suddenly got up and walked away from your unit, got yourself some civilian clothing, and went to the testing center just to see if you could get something to eat and get out of the heat for a day?"

"Yes, sir, Mr. Special Agent," I answered. "The food was really good the last time and the test buildings are the only ones I've been in that got air-conditioning."

"I've seen everything now," he sighed. "Drill Sergeant, is your sergeant major here yet?"

"Sure is," replied Sgt. Harper. "He's in the lobby talking to your boss. I'll go out and get him."

"Wait," said Agent Jackson. "I don't need to talk to anyone else. Please give him my apologies for dragging him down here for nothing. You can leave now and take this piece of shit with you. I'm sure that you and the sergeant major can figure out how to punish this idiot."

For once in my short Army career, I was extremely thankful that punishment of soldiers was left up to the individual commands. The MPs thought that by sending me to my unit that I was going to get my ass kicked and more than likely be discharged from the Army. I now knew the true meaning of the Br'er Rabbit story to succeed with wits.

Once again, Drill Sgt. Harper's acting skills came into play as he marched me out of the interrogation room to meet the command sergeant major. When we arrived in the police station lobby, they both had a wonderful time screaming at me and demeaning me. As soon as they got me into the unit van parked out front, the sergeant major turned to me.

"Tell me exactly what happened and what you told them."

After my detailed explanation, he visibly relaxed, patted me on the back, and said, "Good work, Private."

We drove back to the unit where they had me change back into a uniform and sent me to my private quarters for the last time. I needed to get my stuff ready to move back into my platoon barracks. Sgt. Harper told me to report back to the unit headquarters as soon as I was back in uniform. "Take your time, Berlin," he said, grinning. "You earned it."

Reporting to the battalion headquarters was getting to be routine for me. I doubted any soldier ever spent as much time in front of the brass as I had during my short time at Fort

Knox. I was rubbing shoulders with the leadership so much that they might as well promote me. I was learning their jobs better than they knew them. Arriving at headquarters, I was ordered by the clerk to report to the sergeant major. After knocking on the door and being told to shut it behind me, the command sergeant major and Sgt. Harper came around the desk and asked me to take a seat. The sergeant major had a bottle of Jim Beam with him and three glasses. Filling the glasses, he said, "Here's to a mission completed."

He looked at me and said, "Drill Sergeant Harper and I just spent all afternoon contacting the sergeants that you took tests for. They will all swear on a stack of Bibles that they were present at the testing center and took the tests in question. You know, Berlin, a lot of good soldiers are going to get the promotions they deserve because of your cool head. You are going to make a damn fine soldier someday. I only wish we had the time to get higher scores. Getting caught was not your fault, and you handled yourself like a seasoned pro. I will stand by my promise. You will get promoted to private first class before you leave Fort Knox, and for your part, I trust that this operation will never be discussed again?"

"Roger, Sergeant Major. This operation never happened. I don't even know what operation you're talking about," I replied with a smile.

Sgt. Harper said he would take care of Drill Sgt. Bond, but that since I was a trainee, I was going to have to act like one, and that meant that I was going to have to accept a certain amount of bullshit and harassment. He then asked me if I was up to take the final tests for graduation.

I replied, "I think I have proven my ability to take tests."

We all laughed, finished our drinks, and then for me it was back to the unit and the Wolverines. They made up a believable explanation, and within a few hours, it was like I had never left. The whole incident never occurred, and there is only one little piece of evidence hanging out there to show otherwise. Somewhere in the bowels of a building at Fort Knox, there is an identification card with some sergeant's name on it, but the picture on the card is of Private Berlin.

All in all, it turned out to be a relaxing week. Too bad it couldn't continue, but, what the hell, only three weeks left, and I was going to get a promotion out of it.

Moron

Chapter 21

## The Range

Getting assimilated back into my platoon and reacquainted with the Wolverines was easier than I thought. The trainees were so drained and beaten down from the constant training, yelling, and harassment that they took my return in stride. It was almost as if I had never left. The only person who gave me a hard time was, of course, Drill Sgt. Bond. Hitler decided the reason I was returned was that I was too stupid to be trained by anyone, so the retraining brigade had given up on me and sent me back. It was hard to hold my tongue as he was laying into me.

It took every fiber of my being to stop myself from screaming out, "Asshole, you owe me. I aced your little West Point test. Now take off that goddamned hat and eat it in front of the entire brigade." I had promised Harper, and he had kept his word with me, so I needed to do the same with him. Besides, we only had a couple of weeks left. I could do anything for a couple of weeks.

The hardest part was that I was once again just a regular trainee. I lost my rock star status. It was time to get back to the grind of basic training. Back to sleeping with fifty sweaty, snoring assholes. I was going to miss my private accommodations the most. At least my first day back would be exciting. It was finally range week. I hadn't missed it. I had been looking forward to firing some of the Army's automatic weapons since the first day we spoke to Big John back home. Despite being woken at three the following morning to get to the rifle range on time, I was thrilled.

For the first time since we had arrived, most of the guys in the platoon were excited as well. What teenager doesn't want to fire military rifles? This was going to be fun and a significant change from the senseless, repetitive training that we had been doing so far. Most of what the Army had done were boring classes on first aid, the law of land warfare. and ethics of war. What the hell, in war, there was no law, and ethics in combat seemed dumb. It just didn't make any sense to me.

Even though I was looking forward to firing weapons on full automatic, I knew the Army was going to find a way to screw it up. The Army didn't want training to be fun, taking the fun out of anything they had us do. If any of the drill sergeants thought you were enjoying yourself, they would go out of their way to make your life as miserable as they could. Basic training was an Army no-fun zone.

When we woke up, it was still pitch dark out, and after a quick three-thirty breakfast, we marched over to the battalion arms room to pick up our weapons. Every soldier in our platoon was bragging about what great shots they were. From all the talk, I figured these guys were direct descendants of Buffalo Bill.

The only problem was that from the way they were talking, it was clear many of the guys in the battalion didn't know the first thing about rifles or shooting. This was going to be the first time they had ever held a weapon, much less fired one. That alone should have set off all my internal alarms. I couldn't imagine most of my fellow trainees being allowed to shoot a weapon, but I figured the Army has been doing this for longer than we've been alive. Surely, they knew what they were doing.

When we arrived at the arms room, the drill Sergeants lined us up in single file and told us we would be required to sign some forms and turn in the weapons card that we had been issued when we got our military ID cards. This card had the type of weapon we were issued and the serial number of the weapon we would be issued typed on it. The Army, true to form, was going to make us fill out a ton of paperwork before we could go to the range. Once all the paperwork was signed, we could walk up to the arms room clerk and request our individual weapon.

The clerk would read the serial number on the rifle, and we were supposed to read the number on our card back to him. If both numbers matched, we were told to sign the third document, and then another clerk would recheck all the numbers on the documents and the weapon one more time. If everything matched, we would be allowed to take our rifle from the arms room and hold it. The clerk reminded us that we had to memorize our serial numbers before the next time we came to check out our rifles.

I hoped that if the Russians ever attacked America, they'd give us a lot of time to get ready because we would have to sign a lot of paperwork before we could fight them. If it took this long to check out a rifle, I wondered how long it would take to check out a tank. I was learning that in the American Army, you were not allowed to start fighting a war without the proper paperwork. At Fort Knox, they required you to fill out paperwork before you could take a shit.

Everything was working like clockwork; that is, if you considered a slow bureaucratic process clockwork. The Army even had a special procedure to ensure that the Morons could sign all the paperwork. Because the rifle serial numbers were considered too complicated for the Morons to remember or even to read them back to the clerks, the Army had designed an alternate form of serial numbers for Morons. The Army covered the existing serial number with a large piece of masking tape and with a black magic marker wrote a two-digit number on each Moron rifle. My rifle was number twelve. How easy was that?

What really bugged me, however, was that the rifles issued to Morons came with a dummy cord. I'm not kidding, there was a white nylon cord attached to the stock of each rifle. The other end of the cord had a metal clip attached to it. This clip was assigned to the Moron's top buttonhole on his uniform. The theory was that even if you dropped your rifle, you wouldn't be able to lose it because it would be dragged behind you wherever you went. Come on, I think I would know if I dropped my rifle.

I didn't care for the cord part. I had been caring for, cleaning, and firing rifles since I was eight-years-old, and to tell the truth, the whole dummy cord thing was more than a little embarrassing. Unfortunately, I had made my Moron bed, and now I had to lie in it. I watched with disgust as the arms room clerk connected the end of the dummy cord to my buttonhole. It was embarrassing to say the least, and my Wolverine buddies made sure I was fully aware of how stupid I looked.

Danny just wouldn't get off my case. "Hey, dummy, do you have mittens with cords to match that pretty white one on your rifle? I know the Army wouldn't want you to get your precious little hands cold." He was laughing his ass off, and the rest of the platoon was enjoying the show like typical teenagers who couldn't wait to join in on the harassment. I probably deserved all he was giving and more. After all, I had pretty much been coasting through basic training while my buddies had been working to the point of exhaustion. I could handle a little grief. At least I was going to be able to do some shooting with a neat rifle. I had never fired an automatic weapon before, and my newly assigned M-16 looked like it could to do some damage.

The rifle they issued us was the latest version of the Colt M-16. In 1967 the M16A1 rifle was the primary hand-held weapon used by the U.S. Army, and it was the Army's standard issue rifle carried by all soldiers. The weapon was chambered for 5.56x45mm NATO caliber, featured a positive forward assist to help close the bolt when dirty, a chromium-plated chamber and bore to resist corrosion, and an improved gas system with a new bolt buffer designed to reduce the rate of fire on full auto. The actual ammunition was larger than a standard civilian .22 rifle round. It was the only rifle issued by the Army, and all trainees were taught to fire it on both semi and fully automatic.

The main complaint about the M-16 from soldiers who had fought in Vietnam was that it was always jamming. They jammed not because they were terrible rifles but because soldiers weren't cleaning them, duh. The Army fixed this problem by teaching soldiers how to better care for their rifles. During the war, they taught guys to shoot but never taught them basic cleaning and maintenance. My grandfather would have rolled over in his grave if he knew there were people out there using rifles they didn't know how to clean. In addition to spending more time on cleaning and maintenance, the Army issued every soldier a weapon cleaning kit they could carry with them into combat. The M-16 that I was issued had space in the back of the rifle to hide the cleaning kit. Now that was a great idea.

The best thing about the M-16 rifle was it could operate in full-automatic mode. An M-16 could empty a thirty-round magazine in just a few seconds. Of course, drill sergeants would do everything they could to try and get us to fire in controlled three-round bursts, but once soldiers started shooting, they were all but uncontrollable. The drill sergeants claimed three-round bursts saved a lot of ammunition and improved accuracy by more than seventy-five percent. This was probably true because on full automatic, guys were spraying ammo all over the place, mostly not in the direction of the targets.

I couldn't wait to fire my rifle and see how accurate it was. The first surprise of the morning was that we would not be riding the cattle cars to the range. Sgt. Harper said that because it was "a mere eight miles" and because we had missed morning PT, we would march to the range. We were going to be humping up and down the hills of Kentucky for several hours before we got to the range to fire our rifles. One of the things I learned my first week there was that Kentucky isn't a flat state. The damn place had more hills than any place I had ever been before.

From the air, it looks relatively benign, but once you are on the ground, you realize how steep the hills are. By the time we graduated from basic training, I am pretty sure we had walked up every hill on Fort Knox and each one we climbed seemed to be higher than the last. You would think that with all the uphill walking we did that there would be an equal amount of downhill coasting, but for some reason I don't remember any downhill stretches on Fort Knox. Those drill-sergeant sons of bitches must have found some way to make us walk uphill the whole time we were there.

Imagine eight miles on the hot dust trails of Fort Knox, carrying a rifle and wearing the full helmet. That damn helmet was designed to prevent you from getting shot in the head, but it also prevented you from getting any air into it. The lack of circulation caused your head to overheat constantly. The worst design feature of the helmet was that it didn't have a brim, so what the sun didn't heat up the metal on your helmet shone directly on your face. We all had sunburnt faces that summer. The helmet must have been designed by a dungeon master as an instrument of torture because it hurt like hell and caused us to sweat like pigs.

Worse than the helmets were the boots the Army issued us. Army boots were pure unadulterated crap. What could be worse for your feet than a pair of black leather, non-breathable boots, especially when they hadn't even been broken in yet? I was taught that you don't go in the woods or attempt to cover ground with boots that you haven't broken in. The Army apparently didn't know that. Two hundred years old and they still hadn't figured out footwear. Army boots had hard, flat leather bottoms that slid on everything. I couldn't understand why they never thought of non-skid soles or rugged soles that would allow the wearer to walk over different types of terrain. If I had worn shoes like this on hunting trips, I would have fallen and killed myself the first time I went into the woods.

Not everyone on the road march was wearing crappy Army boots. Drill sergeants knew the boots were a problem, and none of them wore the Army-issued ones. I had never seen any of them wear any kind of helmet, plastic or otherwise. They wore light cotton baseball-style caps. For boots, the drill sergeants wore green cloth-and-canvas boots they called 'jungle boots.' These boots were designed by combat veterans, specifically made for humping through the jungle, and were great at preventing blisters. They had breathing islets built into the sides and soft, flexible bottoms with tire-like treads to improve traction.

Being a hunter and outdoorsman, I quickly saw the advantages of these jungle boots and asked when and where I could buy a pair. The drill sergeant I spoke to told me that the only boot authorized for wear in the Army was the Army black boot.

"If you want to wear something different in the Army," he said, "then you have to get promoted to sergeant as fast as you can because no one tells a sergeant what he can and can't wear, or you could go to Vietnam. If you're volunteering let me know so I can tell headquarters when we get back."

With that, he laughed and walked away. The Army cut a lot of slack for war veterans because they let the soldiers with combat experience wear whatever equipment they wanted. Most of the drill sergeants had all kinds of civilian equipment. The only concession to the Army was that they made sure the equipment was painted either green or black.

The Army, like the rest of the federal government, insisted on buying items from the lowest bidder. If you want proper outdoor gear, you have to be willing to pay a decent price, or you will get crap. The Army bought a lot of crap. It didn't matter if the equipment caused heat stroke or put soldiers in danger; the only important thing was that the price was the lowest the Army could get.

By the time we got to the range that morning, a mere eight miles, the shoddy equipment had taken a significant toll on the battalion. Five guys had been evacuated for heat injuries, and half of the battalion was limping from the damage caused by the boots they had issued us. I didn't know how this ragtag group of limping soldiers could return this same eight miles at the end of the day.

The only person who didn't seem to be having any problems with his boots was Private Luney. Everyone who met Homer knew instantly that he wasn't the sharpest tack in the box, and anyone with any common sense would realize that he was probably mildly mentally retarded. Despite all this, you just couldn't help liking the guy. I think this had a lot to do with his childlike mannerisms and complete trust in everyone and everything he met. He got talked into a lot of dumb things because of his absolute faith in his fellow human beings and his complete inability to understand nuance.

To Luney there was only black and white, right and wrong. During his first day in basic training, someone convinced him that his new job in the Army was to be the official greeter for all the trainees arriving at Fort Knox. He spent all his free time that first night standing on the side of the road, yelling out to all who passed, "Welcome to Fort Knox, y'all."

If we hadn't heard the guys in the other platoons laughing hysterically, we would have never found out, and he would have stayed out there all night long.

The guys in the platoon teased him, but it was mostly harmless—although Drill Sgt. Bond and one or two sadistic assholes sometimes pushed him to the point of personal danger and humiliation. To Private Luney there was nothing too embarrassing to say or do. He said exactly what he thought when he felt like saying it. He figured if he did something that someone or God told him to do, then it was OK.

He couldn't conceive of anyone one telling him to do something wrong. You always knew that whatever he told you was the complete and unvarnished truth. The guy was incapable of telling a lie or making something up. Anyone who has small children will understand precisely what I am talking about. You may not always like what you hear, and it may embarrass the hell out of you, but it is still true. He was never vicious or vindictive. Homer was so childlike that he wasn't capable of being mean. Everything was directly from his heart. I only wish his mind was half as big as his heart.

Homer was excited to be going to the range. Like everyone else he wanted to fire his weapon, and unlike everyone else he loved to march and was happy that we would be marching to the range instead of riding in a vehicle. He loved being outside and walking. He had been walking and hiking most of his life. According to Homer, "These Army boots are the nicest shoes I've ever owned." He had gone barefoot for so many years that his naturally toughened-and-callused feet allowed him to wear just about anything. He told me that he had owned a couple of pair of shoes in his life, but he never dreamed that someone would give him a pair of boots this nice for free.

Every night after he meticulously cleaned and polished his boots, he locked his boots in his locker because he was afraid someone would try to steal his most valuable possession. He reminded everyone in the platoon every morning when he woke up that he still couldn't believe that the Army had given him such a great pair of boots for free. The entire way to the range he just loped along, keeping up a constant barrage of chatter. He was driving Sgt. Bond nuts.

After four miles of non-stop babbling, Bond decided it was his personal mission to make Homer miserable and shut him up. Every hundred yards or so, he would make Homer stop and do pushups or sit-ups. Then he would make him run to catch up with the battalion. At one point he even had Homer run circles around the formation with his rifle held over his head and yell, "I wish I was an alligator because mama alligators eat their babies and I wouldn't be here." When this didn't seem to faze Homer, Bond had him lay on the ground and perform the dying cockroach until the formation had crossed the next set of hills. A soon as he could no longer see the last man in the marching unit, Bond would scream at Homer to catch up with the formation. It was no problem for Bond because he had a jeep and a driver to help him catch up. Bond would climb in his vehicle and take a long drink of water from his canteen while Homer ran to catch up with the unit. Homer was going through a living hell. I know this because I made the mistake of attempting to defend him and ended up being invited to join him in his endeavors for a mile or two. I had a hell of a time trying to keep up with the battalion.

No matter what Bond did, Homer just kept smiling and talking. I think he was having the time of his life. Other than being physically exhausted, he couldn't have cared less. There were only two things that ever got to Private Luney. Talking about his mother or his religion. To him, these were the only two perfect things earth. They could never be wrong, everyone had to believe everything they said, and you could never joke about either of them. Everyone knew this, and we took great pains to stay away from these areas. Whenever Homer got off on one of his mother or his church tantrums, it was best just to agree, nod your head, and walk away. No matter how outrageous he got, it wasn't worth it to anger him because he couldn't understand. It just confused him.

Bond realized that he wasn't going to be able to break Luney with heavy exercise and the standard harassment techniques. He decided he had two choices. He could let it go. What harm could a happy and smiling, though continuously talking, soldier cause? Or he could take the low road and escalate the harassment, hoping to eventually break Luney. Guess which course of action the asshole decided to take? True to his nature, he went straight for the jugular.

"Luney, do you know what causes mental retardation in people from Kentucky?"

"No, Drill Sergeant."

"Well, dummy, it is usually caused when a brother and sister have sex with each other."

"I don't understand, Drill Sergeant. My mom says that it's against God's law for a brother and sister to have sex together, so I don't know how that could happen."

"What I'm trying to explain to you, Luney, is that I'm pretty sure your mama and her brother were fucking each other, and that is how you were born."

"My mom doesn't have no brother," replied Luney.

"Well then, if your mama didn't have a brother to fuck, then the only other way that she could have had a kid as dumb as you are is if she was fucking that dumb preacher you keep jabbering about all the time. Everyone knows that when a woman fucks a preacher who is not her husband that some bad things are going to happen to any children born because of their rutting around. God makes sure that the babies come out as fucking dumb as you, Homer. That's God's way of punishing the mama. How long has your mama been fucking the preacher?"

Luney froze in place. Some of the guys from the other platoons thought it was funny and started laughing, even joining in the harassment. No one in the first platoon said a word. Even the jerks kept quiet because they knew Luney, and all of us knew what kind of impact the words were having on him. After all, what we were dealing with here was a five-year-old mind in the body of an eighteen-year-old. It was as if someone had just told him that Santa Claus had been killed and we were going to roast the Easter Bunny for dinner.

Poor Luney was caught entirely off guard. You could tell by the expression on his face that his world had crashed. Sitting in his jeep, Sgt. Bond laughed and encouraged the trainees in the other platoons to join in with him. If any of us had any balls, we would have told them all to shut the hell up. While we were not joining in on the laughing, we didn't try to stop the harassment. We didn't want to be taunted and have to join him in being harassed and punished. Rather than stand up for what was right, we just allowed the torment to continue. By not protesting we were in fact condoning. Peer pressure is a hell of a thing for a young male.

Finally, Homer broke. The smile left his face, and he began to sob out loud. "You shouldn't say that, Drill Sergeant. You know that's not right. God doesn't like talk like that." Bond laughed out loud and once again encouraged all the trainees to laugh while beginning to chant:

"Cry Baby Luney,
His mama fucked the preacher,
Mama had a baby and called him crazy Luney,
Luney joined the Army,
and cried like a baby."

Soon he had most of the trainees chanting along with him. With the chanting in the background, he turned to Luney and said, "Shut your pie hole, dummy, and stop crying like a little girl. Now drop and give me pushups until I get tired of watching you."

As Luney knocked out his pushups, Sgt. Bond counted them off, "One, mama fucked the preacher, two, mama had a baby, three, baby is a retard …"

For the rest of the road march to the range, the harassment of Luney by Bond steadily escalated. The physical punishment stayed the same, but the verbal abuse got worse with every mile that passed. Somewhere along that road things began to change. Even the most hardened and heartless of the trainees realized the impact of the torment on Luney, and their laughing and chanting had stopped. By the time the battalion arrived at the range, an unusual quiet had fallen over the platoon. The only person still laughing or talking was Sgt. Bond. Everyone else, through sheer shame, backed off.

It wasn't just the battalion that had gotten quiet; something had snapped in Luney. For the first time since we met him, he wasn't chattering like a magpie, and the ever-present smile that defined his every waking moment was missing from his face. Up to now the only time Luney was not talking his head off was when he was asleep, and sometimes he even talked in his sleep. More distressing than the missing smile was that the happy-go-lucky young man without a care in the world was being mentally destroyed. In his place stood a stranger we no longer recognized.

We were looking at a mannequin. His eyes were filled with tears and snot was running from his nose down the sides of his face. The only sounds he made were muffled moans. It sounded like a combination of crying and painful, pitiful whimpering. Homer continued to obey the orders of Bond and ran up and down the formation, but he did it without his usual exuberance. It was like watching a three-year-old who had been punished for the first time in his life. The kid was heartbroken, and he didn't know what to do or who to turn to.

When we finally got to the range, the excitement of getting to fire Army weapons pushed thoughts of Luney to the backs of our minds. Everyone seemed ready to do something neat for a change. What we hadn't figured on was that the Army could always find a way to strip the fun out of everything we did, even shooting a gun. The first thing we did was put our rifles on stands, and after looking at pictures of weapon sights, we were briefed on how to shoot, how to hold a weapon, how to aim a weapon, how to load a weapon, and so on.

It took a couple of hours before they allowed us to touch our M-16 rifles. It looked like at long last that we were finally going to get to shoot. But no, not yet. Now we would get to spend an hour or two looking down the sights of our rifles and pulling, I mean squeezing, the triggers at the target. No bullets and no clips. We were just pretending. This was getting ridiculous. I decided we were never going to be allowed to shoot our new rifles. I was beginning to think that the Army would train us how to use our weapons without ammunition. Maybe there was some type of ammunition shortage, or they were trying to save money.

Toward the middle of the afternoon, the drill sergeants moved us forward in groups of fifty to the firing line. When we got there, they gave us each three bullets. That's right, three bullets. These bullets were for us to fire at a target one at a time to sight in our weapons. The M-16s that we were using had controls for windage and elevation. Every soldier was supposed to keep adjusting his rifle until he could put three rounds on the target that could be covered by a quarter and be as close to the center of the target as possible. You could pick out the hunters and the farm boys in the unit. They sighted in their rifles on the first or second try and then sat around and watched while the remainder of the trainees continued to shoot at the targets. We fired three rounds at a time.

Some of the trainees couldn't get three rounds together no matter how long they shot or how many rounds they fired. The ones who were the worst shots were the trainees who had talked the most about being experts on the way to the range. It wasn't really their fault. It was bad sights, faulty weapons, old ammo, too much humidity, or not enough humidity. The drill sergeants kept them at it for what they considered an appropriate amount of time and then merely passed them on to the next stage. There wasn't enough ammunition in the Army to get some of these bozos qualified.

When we had first arrived at the range, I was surprised to see some of the guys in the unit had no clue how to even hold a weapon. Anyone who shoots knows that the way to become better is to keep shooting as often as you could. It was a good thing that the weapons could be fired on full automatic because that was the only way that most of these clowns were ever going to be able to hit anything on this range. I read somewhere that for every round the Viet Cong fired at the U.S. Army in Vietnam, we returned over 50,000 rounds. Based on what I was seeing at Fort Knox, I believed this to be a reasonable statistic.

After a late afternoon break for the traditional soup, coffee, and green Kool-Aid, Drill Sgt. Bond once again started in on Luney. He followed Luney wherever he went on the range and kept up a nonstop harassment campaign, using the words that he knew would hurt Homer the most. Pvt. Luney had just finished firing his second three rounds on the rifle sighting range. He had qualified with the first three rounds, but Bond said it was pure luck and made him do it again.

Unfortunately, no one noticed that he had accidentally loaded four rounds into his rifle. Counting was not one of Homer's stronger points. So many trainees were completely missing the target that no one could keep an accurate account of how many times everyone had fired their rifles, and when the range sergeant saw the three holes in Luney's target, he assumed that Homer had burned all his ammo.

Before a trainee can stand up after firing his rifle, a range sergeant is supposed to check his rifle to make sure it is empty. They do this by sliding a metal rod down the barrel just to ensure that it is completely unloaded and safe. Before the range sergeant got to Luney's position on the range, Drill Sgt. Bond was screaming at Luney to move quicker. "Come on, dummy," he yelled. "As soon as you are cleared and rodded, I want to see your dumb ass moving back to the break area."

As could be expected with Luney, he missed the part about "cleared and rodded," jumped up, grabbed his M-16 by the barrel, and began to run to the break area. We turned to look as the range officer screamed from the control tower, "Stay in your position, soldier. Do not move until your weapon is cleared by one of my range sergeants. Do not run on my range. Someone stop that idiot before he kills someone." Then we heard the crack of a rifle shot. It sounded like thunder because for the past hour or so, we had been used to hearing the steady crackle of fifty rifles being fired almost simultaneously. This one lone shot surprised everyone.

Time stopped, everything froze, and all eyes turned to the direction the shot had come from. Lying on the range was

Pvt. Luney writhing around, holding his hand and screaming at the top of his lungs. Blood was pouring from the hand.

I didn't actually see what had happened, but some of the guys in the platoon told me that when the range sergeant yelled for him to stop running, Luney turned and looked over his shoulder.

No longer paying attention to where he was going, he tripped over a firing point marker, and as he fell to the ground, his rifle fell from his hand and went off when it hit the ground. The round caught him in the hand. The guys closest to him said what remained of his hand looked more like hamburger than a limb.

The drill sergeants on the range sprang into action. The tower NCO was attempting to control the trainees who were still on the range and beginning to panic.

"Everyone freeze, place all of your weapons gently on the ground, and take one step back," he ordered. "Now, everyone raise both of your hands in the air. Do not breathe, do not even think about touching your weapon. I want to see nothing but hands and assholes. Anyone who moves is going to get their ass kicked. Keep your hands up and your mouth shut until a drill sergeant tells you that you can move. The drill sergeants will handle this situation. They do not need or want your assistance. Medic to firing point twelve now."

To no one's surprise, the first drill sergeant to get to Luney's side was Sgt. Harper. Even though he was more than a hundred yards away, he got there before Bond, who was less than twenty feet away when the shot went off. Bond was frozen in place, staring at Luney with his mouth wide open and a dumb, startled look on his face. Harper dove to the ground at Luney's side, grabbed the rifle, cleared it, and threw it out of the way. He then grabbed the wounded hand with both of his and began to squeeze. Luney's screaming got louder, and we heard Harper yell at him.

"Shut the fuck up and listen to me," he commanded.

"You're going to be OK. This is not a big deal. I've seen way worse. Hell, this is just a scratch. If you yell again, I'm going to punch you in the face. Look at me, stop screaming, and listen up."

Luney immediately quieted down while Harper kept up a steady stream of talk and at the same time continued to apply pressure to Luney's wounded hand. When the medics arrived, they seemed confused, so Harper reached out and grabbed the first aid kit off one of the medic's belts. With one hand continuing to hold the wound, he pulled open the zipped compartment and then used his mouth to rip open the field dressing. Slapping the bandage on the wounded hand, Harper yelled at the medic to apply pressure to the wound. He then took another field dressing package, ripped it open the same way, and tied it around Luney's upper arm. Pulling it as tight as he could, he then took a wooden splint out of the first aid bag, stuck it in the bandage, and began to twist, making a tourniquet on the upper arm. While he was doing all this, the other medic just stood there and looked at Harper like he was crazy or something.

The entire time Harper was working on Luney, he kept up his steady stream of reassuring comments.

"Everything is going to be fine. This is no big deal, and we'll have you back on the range and qualifying with your rifle by tomorrow. Don't think that this little cut is going to get you out of any work in my platoon. I'm going to have your ass in KP tomorrow for running on the range, you dumb shit. Your ass will be peeling potatoes for the next two weeks, you hear me, Private?"

All of this happened so fast that none of us could believe what we were seeing. I was impressed. Not bad for a broken down, drunken sergeant.

Every sergeant on the range except for Bond, still frozen in place, had sprung into action to systematically taking control of the situation, herding trainees from the range to the bleacher area, bringing in an ambulance, talking on radios, directing medical teams, and keeping us away from our weapons. Somewhere between the bandaging and getting Luney onto the stretcher the medics had brought, Bond finally snapped out of it. Instead of expressing concern or moving to assist in the medical treatment, he began to yell at Luney.

"You stupid, fucking Moron. Were you trying to kill me? Was that your plan, you fucking dummy, get rid of ole Drill Sergeant Bond? I hope you fucking live. I don't want anything to happen to you because I want to be there when the Army court-martials you and finds you guilty for the attempted murder of a drill sergeant. Do you have any idea of what they are going to do to you, dummy? They will fucking hang you. How do you think your preacher-fucking mama is going to take it when she has to tell all her church friends that her baby is a murderer and that the Army hung him? I bet she is going to be very proud of you, dummy."

Because of strict protocols, it is unheard of for a drill sergeant to correct one of his peers in front of trainees. However, Sgt. Harper had about all he could take. We had never even seen drill sergeants disagree with one another over even the most severe circumstances, and I'm pretty sure Harper shattered that code when he looked Sgt. Bond in the eyes and said:

"At ease, Drill Sergeant. Get your ass over here and help me with this wound."

You would have thought he had slapped Bond across the face and challenged him to a duel. Bond's face turned bright red, and he began to stammer an objection but was immediately cut off by the icy stare he got from Harper. None of us could hear what Harper was telling Bond as they worked on Luney. Whatever it was, Bond's face got redder, and the veins in his neck began to bulge.

What we could hear were the snickering and under-the-breath jokes of the other drill sergeants, who began to whisper taunts about Bond. One of them even called Bond a "PX soldier." This only served to anger Bond, and he kept looking around to see if any of the trainees could hear what was going on. We couldn't understand everything, but we could hear enough, and we had imaginations, so it didn't take a brain surgeon to figure out that none of his peers had any respect for him. Up to this point, we thought that trainees were the only ones who knew he was an asshole.

When the medics finally carried Luney out to the ambulance, Sgt. Harper walked beside the stretcher. He continued to keep pressure on the wound and speak to Luney. Just as they were loading Luney into the back, Bond jumped on board and before anyone could stop him, assisted the medics in locking in the stretcher.

"I'll escort him to the hospital and file a report as soon as I return to the unit area," he said. "I was closest to the incident, and it's my responsibility. I want to make sure this is taken care of properly."

Harper replied, "This is over, Bond. I expect you to act like an NCO and take care of this soldier. Take this opportunity to try and fix this. Do you understand me?"

Bond looked directly at Harper. "I understand completely. Please let me make this right."

There wasn't much Harper could say at this point, so he simply gave Bond one more icy stare and told him to take care of the trainee. We knew the ambulance ride was going to be hell on Luney. None of us for one second believed Bond was going to take care of Homer and lay off the harassment. From what we had seen and heard, it appeared that Bond was worried he was going to get in trouble and the cause was the private in the ambulance. We couldn't see the wound under the bandages, and there was a lot of blood, but we figured it was only a hand shot. How bad could it really be? We had been a little reassured by Sgt. Harper's ongoing dialogue, and some of us thought that Luney might be back on the range or at KP the next day, as predicted by Harper.

One of the things the Army does well is get past incidents and move on with the mission. With the sound of the departing ambulance sirens still ringing in our ears, the range sergeant told the drill sergeants to safety check and rod all the weapons, so we could get back to firing. Thank God, now that Homer was going to be OK, we wanted to continue firing our weapons. We had been standing around for almost thirty minutes. The sergeant on the loudspeaker said, "The party's over, children, now get your asses back onto my range and move to your last firing position. I only want to see elbows and assholes, and don't run on my range. I think we all have had enough of trainees shooting each other to last for the rest of training.

"I want to be firing in ten minutes, so move your asses."

It took more like twenty minutes for the drill sergeants to clear five hundred weapons and have us back in our firing positions, but they got it done. Within an hour we were all back to our firing routine, and it was like nothing had ever happened.

The drill sergeants were back in asshole mode, and we were back in range mode. The only suggestion that something had even gone wrong was the blood that stained the dirt at firing point twelve and the tire marks that the ambulance left on the range.

Sgt. Harper had dried blood all over his uniform and hands but didn't seem to notice or even care. He spent the rest of the day on the range walking from position to position, talking to the trainees and reassuring us.

When he got to my position, he bent down and told me, "You better not fuck up on your qualification rounds or I'll have you running back to post with my boot up your ass." He then added, "I've seen wounds like that a hundred times. He's going to be just fine, and now that he has a war wound to show to the ladies, he just might be able to get a little ass when he goes home on leave after basic training."

It made me feel just a little bit better, and I passed it on the rest of the guys in the platoon. No one said anything for the rest of the day, but we were still worried about Luney.

The final events of the day were a full qualifying round, which would be followed by night firing. The qualifying round is a series of a hundred targets at ranges from twenty-five to 350 meters. In case you're not familiar with the metric system, that's over three full football fields away. It's so far that the target looks smaller than the sights on the rifle. It's tough to hit something you can't even see. What I wouldn't have given for a good hunting scope right now.

When it comes down to it, a rifle is a rifle. You don't forget a lifetime of hunting and shooting just because you joined the Army and are using a fancy new rifle. Also, it's a lot easier to hit an Army aluminum pop-up target than it is to shoot rabbits with a .22 rifle or drop a running deer at a hundred yards. Back home we considered it unsportsmanlike to shoot at rabbits when they were sitting still, so we would yell at them to get them moving and take running shots. We got pretty good at hitting targets of all sizes and shapes.

For the guys from the Wolverine platoon, these pop-up targets were a joke. My little sister could have qualified on this course. However, I have to admit firing on automatic was pretty damn cool. The drill sergeants were impressed by the scores the Wolverines were turning in, and I heard more than one of them say that they would like to have some of us in their units should the Army ever go in combat again. I think it was the first compliment we had ever received from a drill sergeant.

During our entire stay at Fort Knox, the drill sergeants had been wary of the Wolverines. They didn't like dealing with groups, and I guess the fact that we all knew each other and had each other's backs interfered with their ability to get us to adopt the Army as our sole savior. Now, they seemed genuinely impressed with something we did. There was a little bit of ammunition left over at the end of the qualification rounds, so they decided to end the daylight portion of the range with a small competition between the top five Wolverines and the top five drill sergeant marksmen.

It was a tense competition, and everyone in the battalion was surprised when Mussio won the shootout hands down. None of the drill sergeants even came close to his accuracy. What they didn't know was that he had been shooting a rifle since he was four years old. He and his younger brother regularly played a game where they took turns shooting cigarettes out of each other's mouths with a .22 rifle for fun.

They would get one another to put a cigarette in his mouth then turn sideways and try not to flinch while the other brother attempted to shoot it. I'm not talking about a modern rifle with a scope here. These nut jobs were using an old single-shot Henry .22 with iron sights. Even though Mussio was completely nuts, it honed his shooting skills, and I am happy to report that both he and his brother were still alive and neither had any bullet holes in their heads.

Harper told me that every training cycle ended the first day on the range with a shooting contest, and this was the first time any trainee had outscored a drill sergeant, much less taken first place in the competition. Not only had a Wolverine taken first place, but we also took third and fifth. For the Wolverines, this was quite a victory.

The final shots of the competition were at a target placed more than five hundred meters from the firing line. The target was so far away, we had to rely on spotters with binoculars to tell us if they went down or not. While this messed most of the Wolverines up because we were used to shooting with a scope, Mussio was right at home. Mussio always told us that he was part Indian and had eagle blood in him. He claimed he could see for miles. After the shooting demonstration he put on that day, some of us were inclined to believe him.

When the Wolverines and the drill sergeants in the competition were lying in foxholes and balancing their rifles on sandbags to get the steadiest shot possible, Mussio was standing up and firing free hand. He looked like a kid shooting at tin cans and didn't seem to have a care in the world. When the range control officer announced that the next target was up and that we had 60 seconds to engage, Mussio's weapon went off almost immediately, and his target dropped every time.

The rest of the shooters, including me, were concentrating on the targets, trying to control our breathing and taking every second of the allotted time to sight in and fire. Frankly, it was disheartening because every time he shot, a large roar arose from the watching crowd, trainees and drill sergeants alike. The rest of us knew we couldn't miss because the Indian had already scored ahead of us. Not once did any of us ever get off a shot before he fired. Everyone present that day knew he was being treated to a magnificent display of shooting accuracy.

The drill sergeants kept us so busy that we soon forgot about the Luney incident, as we referred to it. After our evening meal, we got to go to the night fire range to fire our weapons in the dark. The sergeants told us that most firefights occurred in darkness. No American enemy was stupid enough to attack American soldiers in broad daylight. They explained that it was essential for us to learn how to aim and fire in complete darkness.

Night fire was the best part of the whole range experience. We got to fire our rifles on full automatic, and they issued us tracer rounds. A tracer round is a bullet with a fluorescent tip on it that causes your bullet to leave a green- or red-light trail behind it as it heads down range. The tracer rounds showed you where the bullets were hitting so that you could adjust your aim, according to where the light was exploding on the ground. I wondered why we couldn't use them in the daylight; it would certainly help a lot of these guys to get closer to what they were aiming at. Instead of wasting all that time sighting in, we could have let them walk in their rounds with tracers.

Harper told me that it would not be a good idea to use tracers too often because tracers were a marvel and a menace. They were a marvel because you could walk your fire into an enemy position and keep the bullets hitting exactly where you wanted them to without ever looking through your sights.

They were a menace because they gave whoever you were shooting at the perfect aiming point for return fire. They created a perfectly straight line of light pointing directly back to your position. While the guy you were shooting at may be dead or keeping his head down, his buddies would have a perfect aiming point to take you out of the fight.

Something to think about later, but for now, it was a blast firing the tracers down range. Well, for the most part down range; it was surprising where some of the tracers were going. No wonder some many of these guys had a hard time qualifying. While most of the tracers were going down range in relatively straight lines, some of the light lines were all over the place, and do I mean *all* over the place.

Some were going straight up in the air, some were four to six feet above the targets, and a lot were going so far to the left and right of the range that they apparently were not in the designated safe firing area. I swear I even saw a couple of rounds going backward on the range. The drill sergeants must have been brave or stupid to be out there in the dark with this crew. The last thing I thought about as we left the range for the night was that I didn't want to go to war with any of these bozos. Automatic weapons or not, they simply couldn't hit the broad side of a barn. I hoped that the guys who fired the tanks and artillery for the Army were better at their job. If not, our country was in for a world of hurt in the next war. I was going to do everything I could to stick with the Wolverines.

It was well past midnight when the sergeants got all of us through the firing orders, turned in the excess ammo (and who ever heard of going out to shoot and bringing any ammo back with you, this was nuts) and got everyone loaded into the cattle cars. I hated cattle cars, but I was looking forward to the ride back because I didn't want to march the eight miles back to the battalion area.

**** 

When we arrived back at the unit area, we were dead on our feet and completely worn out from the day's activities. I was looking forward to hitting the sack and getting some sleep, but this was the Army, and it wasn't going to be that easy. In the Army, every weapon has to be cleaned three times before it can be turned into the arms room.

The Amy had a strange preoccupation with the number three. We were told that we were going to have to get our M-16s cleaned and inspected by the arms room clerks three times before we could call it quits for the evening, and since everything you do in the Army is a group activity, we would not be done until the last man was done. It was going to be a long night.

Now, I've cleaned a lot of rifles in my time, and I always thought I did a good job, but I have never cleaned a weapon to Army standards. This was a whole new experience for me. You've heard of white glove inspection; well, this was one of them. White gloves and Q-tips. The armorer would not accept any of our rifles back if he could get any black off them anywhere, and I mean anywhere. I never realized that a rifle had so many nooks and crannies. We were probably damaging the metal on the rifles we were cleaning them so hard. No one should be scrubbing weapons with steel brushes with the force that we were applying. We rubbed the bluing right off our rifles.

I was one of the first guys to get through the cleaning gauntlet, not bad for a Moron, so I decided to help some of the other guys who were not as familiar with weapons as I was. After about two hours of cleaning, several of us decided to sneak down to our barracks where we had hidden a stash of beer under the building. It was warm and covered with dust, but a beer is a beer, and for some reason, beer always tastes better when you're not supposed to have it.

We figured a beer, warm or not, would help our morale and get the weapon cleaning done a little bit faster. This was a little more dangerous than our typical stunts because to get the beer we had to leave our weapons with someone to guard. If we got caught going away from the arms room with a weapon, there would be hell to pay, and it's hard to hide a rifle. The only thing worse than leaving the area with a weapon would be to leave your weapon someplace, but when young men get the idea of beer in their heads, all reason goes straight out the window.

Life is nothing but a series of chances, so what the hell. In our minds, we really needed the beer, and we were willing to take the risk. This should be a simple operation. There were five of us on the mission and once we raided our stash, we each had fifteen or more cans of beer stuck down our shirts to smuggle back to the other guys. Not the best way to transport beer, but what are you going to do? Not being able to resist, we had all popped one open and were drinking as we attempted to navigate the shadows back to the platoon to share our booty with the guys.

No matter how well executed, plans never go exactly as you want. When we came around the corner of the last building, we ran smack into Drill Sgt. Harper. And we really ran into him, almost knocking him down. The five of us shoved the open beers we were carrying inside our shirts with the other cans. We snapped to attention and waited for the explosion that we knew was coming. There was no way he could miss the bulges in our shirts; and we didn't have our rifles with us, a dead giveaway. We were so screwed.

Harper stared at us for a few seconds and then said, "You're supposed to be over at the arms room cleaning your weapons. Now drop down and give me ten pushups and then get your asses back to where you're supposed to be."

I don't know who we thought we were kidding as we dropped into the pushup position. A blind man could see that we were all packing cans of something under our shirts. We began to do our pushups. That's when the beer from the open cans we had each hastily stuffed down our shirts began to empty into our clothing and drip onto the road.

Harper saw the beer beginning to puddle beneath us, squatted down on his haunches, put his finger in the puddle, looked at his finger, and then placed the finger in his mouth, saying, "Berlin, I hope to God this is piss."

I was dead, caught dead to rights. There was nothing any of us could say or do. We were never going to get out of this one. But never say never. No yelling, no screaming or spitting. Just, "OK, guys, hand over every can of beer you have."

We quickly deposited the beer in front of him, and he said:

"Now get the fuck back to the arms room, clean your goddamn rifles, and don't ever leave your weapon with someone else again. If I hear one word about this from anyone, you'll all live to regret it. Now move!"

It must have been Christmas, none of us could believe our luck. As we turned to leave, I watched Sgt. Harper as he sat down to put his head in his hands then leaned back against the building. I was tempted to go back and talk to him, but my brain kicked in, and I realized I would be pushing my luck. It was time to get the hell out of Dodge. Harper looked up at me and smiled as he popped a can and put his head back to let the beer run down his throat. At least someone would get a beer tonight. Hopefully, he would be able to make it back to the barracks when he was done because I had a funny feeling he was going to drink them all. For whatever reason, we had broken two of the biggest rules in basic training, and it appeared we were going to survive to tell our tale, escaping what had moments before seemed like a sure death penalty with ten pushups. My shirt was wet, and I had lost my beer, but it was a great night.

The hardest part was explaining to all the guys at the arms room that we had lost the beer, and, of course, no one believed the story. Even our wet shirts and the beer stains down our pants didn't convince them. They just assumed that we had drunk the beer without them and hadn't bothered to carry any back with us. I couldn't blame them; I wouldn't have believed the story we told either. A drill sergeant couldn't possibly let such grave infractions pass without issue. We spent the next hour finishing up the weapons and talking about the Luney incident on the range. We wondered when

Luney would be back in the barracks and hoped that he was going to be Ok. Pvt. Luney was a pain in the ass, but to the members of the first platoon, he was our pain in the ass.

Because it was so late when we finally finished up everything and got all the rifles turned in and accounted for, they informed us that they were going to let us sleep in until six the following morning. I couldn't believe that the Army had messed up our sense of what was right and wrong so bad that getting up at six had become such a luxury in our lives. When we got back to the barracks, we discovered Harper passed out on the first bunk with a pile of beer cans on the floor around him.

This should have at least convinced the guys we hadn't been lying about the beer. Bob and I hauled Harper to his room and deposited him in his cot. None of us knew nor cared where Bond was. We were so tired that most of us laid on our bunks and fell asleep in our dirty, sweaty uniforms, crappy boots and all.

The next morning, we woke up to the sound of the other platoons being roused from their sleep. We were surprised that we didn't get our standard trash-can alarm clock wake-up. There was no snoring coming from Harper's room. We spent the rest of the morning going to PT, eating chow, and cleaning our rifles two more times. At the time, I thought that I never wanted to fire a weapon again. It wasn't worth all the extra work that came with it, but I knew I would soon get over it. Hunting and shooting were just too much fun to let the Army ruin it for me. I would figure out some way to make this fun even if it killed me. Cleaning weapons wasn't all bad because it did allow us to sit down, and there was a lot of bullshitting going on. The number one topic was Pvt. Luney.

After we got back from noon chow, Sgt. Harper came walking into the barracks and yelled for us all to fall out in formation in front of the barracks. He had a bizarre expression on his face and was not moving with the usual spring in his step.

When the entire platoon was formed and standing at attention, he took off his "Smokey Bear" drill sergeant hat, rubbed his head, and lit a cigarette. None of us had ever seen him without his hat before. It was even fixed to his head when he was passed out cold from drinking and when we carried him to his room. We thought that he glued it in place, and no one had ever been brave enough to try and remove it.

Harper told us to stand at ease and to go ahead and smoke if we wanted.

He then said, "Gentlemen, it is with great sorrow that I have to inform you of the death of Private Homer Luney."

The world stopped, and you could hear the members of the platoon breathing.

Then from somewhere in the back of the formation, I heard, "Bullshit, you don't die from shooting your hand."

The guys began talking at once.

"At ease," yelled Harper. "Shut your fucking mouth. No one told you that you could speak. Private Luney didn't die from the gunshot wound. Sometime early this morning, he hung himself in the bathroom of the hospital. He committed suicide."

Now I knew the saying, "you could hear a pin drop," was true. You could hear everything with crystal clarity.

Sgt. Harper continued, "There will be a memorial service at the main post chapel at 1700. A bus will be here to transport the entire platoon over to the ceremony. This event is mandatory. You will wear your dress uniforms, and everyone will be there. That's it. Get your weapons turned in, get your uniforms ready, and make sure you are on time or I will be kicking some asses."

I wish I could tell you how the memorial service went, but I can't seem to remember anything that went on. The entire service was fuzzy to me.

But I do remember sitting through it while in my head I kept thinking over and over, "Bond, you motherfucker. You will pay for this, somehow, somewhere, someday."

Everyone in the unit knew that Bond was responsible for Homer's death. Homer was not the kind of guy who was capable of suicide. He must have been pushed hard. After the service, we went back to the barracks, and I guess we got cleaned up and went to bed. I don't remember anyone going to the chow hall. We were just too upset to eat. No one was talking, no one was bullshitting, everyone was just numb. I don't think that anyone slept that night. I know I didn't, and no matter how hard I strained, for the first time since we had arrived at Fort Knox, I couldn't hear any snoring.

# Chapter 22
# The 100

After Sgt. Harper told us the news about Private Luney, the platoon went into a state of shock, both mental and physical. Guys were wandering around with blank looks on their faces or sitting soundlessly on their footlockers and doing their best impression of someone with the weight of the world on his shoulders. I don't think anyone knew what to do with himself, and we were basically numb to the world. For many of us, this was the first time in our lives that anyone our age had died. In the Army, there was no such thing as grief counseling or stress relief. The Army expected soldiers to suck it up and soldier on. To show any sign of weakness was a disgrace and would cause you to be looked down upon by your peers and superiors.

The Army didn't want to hear your problems, so there was no one to complain to, especially to a drill sergeant. The Army expected sergeants to keep the troops from showing any signs of mental weakness. It was their job to snap us out of our doldrums and get us back into full training mode.

That night ended up being one of the quietest nights on record in the platoon. No snoring was heard because I think everyone in the unit was awake. Everyone was in his bunk hours before lights out, trying to sleep, thinking individual thoughts.

The next morning came much too quickly, and we were all a little tired. We were still in a state of shock and moping around, but the drill sergeants acted as if nothing had happened. They came roaring through the platoon at the usual time, banging the trash-can alarm clocks.

"Drop your cocks and grab your socks."

The drill sergeants were right back on schedule, but we were still stuck in limbo. Instead of leaping from our bunks and rushing to get into our physical training clothing, everyone seemed to be just a step off. We were moving slow. Guys had the wrong shirts on, and some of them were still lying in their bunks. This was an unforgivable sin in basic training. It was a weird morning. Both drill sergeants seemed eager to get us moving and continued to hustle us outside to get ready for PT. I couldn't figure out why Homer's suicide hadn't affected them the same way it had us.

Sgt. Harper appeared unaffected, but I knew that even he had his limits. I figured he was going to back off us for a day or two to give us time to adjust. Boy, was I wrong. When we returned to the barracks from PT, our world was turned upside down. Harper, as was his normal routine, walked up and down the rows of bunks, yelling at us to get our asses moving and hustle to the showers and then to chow. All a sudden, he stopped dead in his tracks, pointed to the center of no man's land, and hysterically screamed, "Who in the fuck violated my shrine?"

We turned to look where he was pointing. There in the center of no man's land in the middle of our highly polished floor, there was a candy bar. To be perfectly clear, it was a Clark Bar with a bright red wrapper and giant, blue-block lettering outlined in yellow. It stood out on that floor like a black guy in Utah. It wasn't just any ole candy bar. The wrapper on this candy bar was perfect. The candy bar had no creases and was as bright and shiny as if it had just come off the assembly line that very morning. I don't know if there is such a thing as a perfect candy bar, but if there is, we were looking at one. The image of that candy bar is forever burned into my memory. How in the hell did it get in the middle of the floor?

We held our collective breaths; we could hear the guys in the other barracks yelling, joking, and screaming as they got ready for morning chow. The silence in our barracks was finally broken by Harper.

"Get all the trainees from the fucking first floor up here now. I want every swinging dick in the building standing tall in front of me in thirty seconds."

I'd never seen anyone in the first platoon move so fast. I don't know what the messengers who ran downstairs said, but it had an immediate impact. The rest of the plan had run upstairs as if escaping a fire. The entire platoon was soon standing on the line outside of no man's land staring at the "perfect" Clark Bar.

For the first time since our arrival at Fort Knox, there were no jokes and none of the usual crude comments. Half of us had been holding our breath for three or four minutes. No one said a word, and no one moved a muscle. It was Drill Sgt. Harper's show.

With all trainees reporting, Harper was standing at rigid attention, and he was so mad that his entire body was shaking. The veins were popping on his forehead and drool was coming out of the corner of his mouth. This was something none of us had ever seen. Harper was the calm and cool drill sergeant. This time he was losing that cool. Several of the trainees were so frightened that they looked like they were going to pass out. His very demeanor shouted, obey me or die. No one wanted to be caught in his target area.

After the most extended pregnant pause in history, Harper finally broke the silence.

"Drill Sergeant Bond, in my office, we need to discuss this situation."

Harper and Bond walked down the floor and disappeared into Harper's office at the end of the building. The only sound in the barracks as they walked away was the sound of their boots hitting the floor, and the door slamming shut, so hard that even the windows in the building rattled. They must have been in there for ten or fifteen minutes. A short time on the clock but a lifetime for the platoon.

This was too much for us to handle. We were still recovering from the shock of the previous day's events. I thought, what else could possibly go wrong in this platoon? The two most heinous events possible had just occurred in less than twenty-four hours; a member of the platoon had committed suicide, and someone had violated no man's land and left evidence to the fact.

It may sound strange, especially to those of you never serving in the military, that my brain was comparing suicide to a candy bar being left on the floor, but that's how it was in basic training. Everything you thought was important before you joined the Army seemed inconsequential, and little things now took on new importance. The drill sergeants and the Army spent so much time indoctrinating and brainwashing us that they convinced us their petty rules and regulations were as important as the loss of human life. Looking back, I find it hard to believe that I was brainwashed to the point that I didn't know which event was more serious. The Army had done its job well.

The door to Harper's room slammed open just as hard as it had been slammed shut. Harper and Bond exited the room and slowly walked toward us, staring down at the floor with a look of utter disgust on their faces. They had their arms locked behind their backs as if to say, *I can't control myself, and I better keep my arms behind me, or I will hit someone.* Harper looked up at us and said in a voice that was way too calm for the situation:

"Gentlemen, I can barely control my emotions. I am extremely upset concerning the disrespect that was shown to me and my platoon this morning. I am so fucking furious that I'm not sure how I am going to handle this situation. While I'm thinking I want you all to get your asses back outside and redo your physical training session, I need some more time to think. While you are at PT, Drill Sergeant Bond and I will decide how we are going to deal with this grievous situation. Private

Simpson, you are in charge of PT. I'm too upset to lead this platoon in my current mental condition. Get the fuck out of my sight, you disgust me."

This was totally out of the norm for us. We were getting ready to conduct physical training without a drill sergeant. No one had ever imagined a situation where a drill sergeant allowed a trainee to lead any type of training, especially physical training. By this time, PT should have already been done and we were supposed to be at the chow hall with the rest of the battalion, but no one was going to contradict Drill Sgt. Harper, so we went outside and formed up for PT.

To say that the other platoons were surprised was an understatement. Everything in basic training goes by a strict schedule, and our platoon had destroyed that schedule. You could tell by the looks on their faces that they knew something was going on but they, like us, had been conditioned just to accept whatever got thrown at them. Everyone in the battalion knew about the suicide the day before, and they assumed that this change of schedule had something to do with Homer's death.

Funny thing about being in charge of yourself. You would think that because one of your own was in charge of PT, he would take it easy and cut us some slack. Well, you would be dead wrong. Pvt. Simpson took his responsibility as our leader very seriously. That and the authority went to his head.

The rest of the battalion continued going about the usual morning activities. They rotated to chow and got ready for the training day. The only thing indicating everything was not right were the constant stares and sideways glances we were getting from people. We were still doing PT when we should have been at chow, and they wanted to know what was going on, but no one had the guts to ask.

The only soldiers in the battalion area who seemed entirely oblivious to what was happening were the drill sergeants. Whenever they caught one of the other trainees paying too much attention to us, they would drop the offender for pushups and yell at them to keep moving, or they would be joining us. By the end of our one-hour PT session, we were all beat. We had just about had it with Simpson, and a lot of us wanted to tell him to go to hell, but no one was willing to rock the boat. We just sucked it up and trudged on.

When we were finished and completely exhausted, we returned to our barracks, dead tired and hungry. We were used to a routine, and now our routine had been destroyed. Both drill sergeants were waiting for us in front of the building when we got back. It was judgment time. Harper called us to attention and then pulled the Clark Bar that he had somehow retrieved from No Man's Land from inside his shirt. Holding it high over his head, he declared:

"I removed Mr. Clark from his resting place in the center of no man's land. It's apparent to me that a member of this platoon killed him and disposed of his body in what was up to now considered sacred territory. It was not poor Mr. Clark's fault that he was murdered, and his body was carelessly discarded. Whoever did this wanted the body to be discovered. Some uncaring trainee disgracefully left his body where it could be discovered by the rest of us.

"One of you shitheads took it upon yourself to throw him in unconsecrated ground. Trainees, I don't care who did it and, frankly, I don't want to know. The only thing I want is to make sure that Mr. Clark is provided the honor and dignity in death that he was denied in life. Gentlemen, we are going to see that this disgrace is erased. Mr. Clark will receive a full military funeral and be properly interned in hallowed ground." Thinking back on this entire speech, I find it hard to believe that none of us broke out laughing, but I can assure you it was not a laughing matter at the time. We were taking it very seriously.

Harper continued with his orders. "To pay proper tribute to Mr. Clark, one of the bravest Americans I know, I have decided that, before his funeral, in the finest traditions of the South, we will conduct an automobile race in his honor. Since none of you have cars with you here in basic training, you will be my cars. Everyone grab a quick drink of water; this will be your fuel for the upcoming race. We are going to skip chow this morning because I don't want any puke on my race track. Gentlemen, the Clark Memorial One Hundred starts in exactly ten minutes. Get your vehicles fueled up and your engines ready to go. You have ten minutes to get your uniforms on and fall out in front of my barracks."

This was no joke. None of us were laughing. There was going to be nothing amusing about this day.

Other than to hide beer and dope, none of us had ever been under the building before. It was one of the many off-limits areas. It wasn't a very hospitable place. The barracks were built on brick pylons. There was about three feet of head-space under the barracks. I don't know why the barracks were raised off the ground, because the opening made for some nasty drafts. The space was empty except for dirt and rocks. Because there was no sunlight, it was bare of all vegetation except the hardiest of weeds. This barren place was to be the location of the first Clark Memorial 100 road race.

Harper had four trainees crawl under the building and tie white engineer tape around the middle pylons. Engineer tape is a white cloth tape that the Army used to mark everything from wires to minefields. When they were done, we had a loop of engineer tape under the building. The loop consisted of two thirty-foot straightaways and two fifteen-foot curves. The actual path was about five feet wide, just wide enough for four or five guys to pass side to side. This was our racetrack.

"Here's how this race is going to work," Harper explained. "Every swinging dick in this platoon is going to participate in this event. You are each going to go around the track one hundred times. The winner of the race gets to have his name engraved on the wood above the racetrack. This will ensure for all time, or at least until they tear down these damn buildings, that everyone who crawls under them will know who won the first Memorial One Hundred. I know that it is not possible for you all to complete all the circuits of the track without stopping, so I will allow a ten-minute rest or pit stop after the end of every five laps. Anyone resting in between better be dead, because when I get finished with you, you are going to wish that you were dead. To make sure there is no cheating, every time you complete a lap, you will place a pebble in a cup with your name on it. These cups will be located at the start/finish line on the wooden ledge above the track.

"Make sure you get your pebble in the right cup and don't knock anyone else's cup off the shelf. If I catch anyone cheating, we will start the entire race all over again. The competition ends when all of you have completed your one hundred laps. Your squad is a team. Any team who loses a man starts the race over. Any team who has a car going at a speed that I think is too slow will have to start the race over. I can assure you that none of you will want to restart this race. Are you getting the picture?

"OK, everyone under the barracks. Move. Move. Move. Gentlemen, start your engines. There will be fuel, water, for you at the end of every five-lap circuit. You are not allowed to take fuel unless you are on your five-lap break."

With the entire platoon crammed under the barracks, we heard, "Gentlemen, ready, race!"

Imagine fifty guys trying to crawl under a building that is three feet off the ground with hard gravel and sand as your racetrack. You couldn't stand up. The best you could do was get up on your hands and feet. You could only do that for a lap or two before you became so exhausted that you had to drop back down to your knees. It was going to take us a lot longer than any of us thought to finish the Clark Memorial 100. Every lap took about ten minutes, and by the sixth or seventh lap, we had wrapped our shirts and other clothing around our hands and knees to protect them as best we could.

As we were finishing our first five laps, we were already exhausted. It was going to be a long, hot day. I would have bet any amount of money anyone was willing to wager that there was no way that any of us, much less all of us, would be able to complete the one hundred laps. To add insult to injury, when we were on approximately our sixth lap, Harper decided that the cars were running too slow and directed a restart of the entire race.

Everyone made sure that all of the cars kept up a decent speed from that point on. Whenever anyone would try to slow down, his partners would make sure that he sped up enough to keep the drill sergeants off of our backs, although Bond wasn't saying a word. We assumed that Harper had told him to shut up and let him run the show.

The Clark Memorial 100 dragged on all day long. We were going through hell. I take it back, hell would have been a break compared to what we were going through that day. We started the race at about six in the morning, and it was dark when a winner was finally declared.

I can't tell you who came in first. The only thing I remember is that everyone miraculously made it. I never realized how much torture and punishment the human body could go through and keep on going until I was forced to do something like this. Our pants were ripped. Our hands and knees were sore and bleeding. I was covered with so much dust and sweat that you couldn't recognize me anymore. You couldn't even tell which guys were black and which were white.

In the early stages of the race, some of the guys from the other platoons would stop by, point and make cruel jokes, and just be guys. After about six hours, even the hardiest of them gave up the harassment. No one could believe what we were going through. During rest periods, I saw a lot of the other trainees continuing to sneak looks out the windows to see how we were doing, but I never heard another comment after the initial harassment died down.

For most of the day, the only sounds in the entire unit area were the sounds of soldiers dragging themselves through the sand, punctuated by the occasional sobs of someone who had given up followed by the encouragement of his squad members to keep on going.

Exhausted and beaten, we were ready to give up both physically and mentally. Several times during the event, senior leaders of the unit would stop by to observe. As the day dragged on, they would occasionally call Harper over to talk to them. You could tell from the tone and volume that some heated discussions were going on. Every conversation ended with Harper coming back and yelling at us some more.

"Do not be disrespectful to the memory of Mr. Clark by slacking off on his memorial race," he told us. "Get your asses in gear and make me proud to be observing this great event."

When we finished, some of the guys were shaking so bad they could no longer stand without assistance. Sgt. Harper had arranged to have water, Kool-Aid, coffee, hot soup, and sandwiches for us at the end of the race. After a quick wash-up inside the latrine, we were allowed a ninety-minute break to get rehydrated and get some food in our stomachs. Vomiting on his track was no longer a concern. Harper told us to relax, sleep, eat, take a shit, do whatever we wanted, but to do it in the street because in an hour he had another mission for us.

He told Bond to keep an eye on us while he went to complete an important task. I don't know what he thought we would do. No one was going anywhere. As soon as we got some nourishment, we collapsed precisely where we were and fell asleep. It was probably more like two hours before he returned. To the members of the sleep deprived, exhausted first platoon, it seemed like only a minute or two had passed.

The next conscious thought I had was waking to Sgt. Harper's voice. "Rise and shine, my little race cars. Your day is just getting started.

"You trainees now have the privilege of participating in one of the Army's most ancient and honored traditions. Today you get to participate in a funeral with full military honors. We are going to bury Mr. Clark in the center of the memorial racetrack. I can't think of a more fitting tribute."

Incredibly, in the short time that Harper was gone, he had showered, shaved, donned a freshly pressed uniform, and put on a new pair of jet-black glossy boots. He looked like he had woken from a nice relaxing evening at home. He had picked up some supplies. In his arms was a large cardboard box that contained fifty large spoons from the chow hall along with the Army's manual on funeral ceremonies, a bright yellow yardstick, and an American flag.

Harper told us that while the ceremony we were going to take part in was a simple ceremony, it must be conducted with all the dignity and respect that we could muster; after all, we were talking about a burying a hero here, Mr. Clark.

"The gravesite must be properly and meticulously prepared to receive the remains of the deceased," he declared. "The Army doesn't bury its fallen in just any old hole."

Laying the box and the yardstick on the ground, he picked up the manual and began to read.

"To properly intern the remains on the battlefield, it is important to ensure that precautions are taken to prevent the spread of disease. The remains of the deceased should be tightly wrapped in a poncho and secured with rope to prevent disturbance by wild animals." He sent Pvt. Wykoff into the barracks to secure a poncho and shoelaces from a pair of boots. Harper then continued. "The remains should be placed in a grave that is seven feet long, three feet wide, and exactly six feet deep."

At this point, he picked up the yardstick and held it over his head.

"I want you to use this official Army measuring device to ensure that you meet the proper specifications of a battlefield grave." He continued to read. "Soldiers should use their issued entrenching tools to prepare the gravesite." Then he stopped. "We don't have any entrenching tools," so he went on reading. "In the event there are no enriching tools available, soldiers will use alternative means at their disposal."

Reaching into the cardboard box, he held up a handful of the mess hall spoons.

"Gentlemen, may I present alternate means."

He then wrote down the dimensions on the outside of the box saying, "Here's your directions and tools. Someone take charge and let's get Mr. Clark's final resting place prepared." Harper looked at his watch and said, "I'm going to get some chow and some hot coffee. I will be back in about three hours. I expect to find a proper grave ready to receive Mr. Clark's remains when I return."

With that, he and Sgt. Bond walked away.

By the time the other platoons in the battalion were up and moving for physical training the next morning, we had already been outside our barracks and working for hours. They were shocked to see that we were still outside and still attempting to complete our strange mission. None of them understood what we were doing, and no one had the guts to ask. My platoon mates and I looked like death warmed over at this point. We could have easily been used as extras in a zombie movie. We felt tired but too tired to notice how bad we looked. My friends later told me they thought that Harper had finally gone too far and some of us might die before we were done.

It was starting to get light out again. We had been at it for over twenty-four hours, non-stop, with only our five-minute fuel stops and a short two-hour break. It was astounding that any of us had anything left. At this point, we were operating on sheer willpower alone.

As soon as Harper and Bond gave us our instructions and walked away, Bob took charge of the platoon and said, "Let's go. We have less than three hours to get this grave dug. I'm tired, worn out, and I need some real food in my stomach. The faster we get this fucker dug, the faster we can get the hell out of here."

You've never seen anything until you've watched a platoon of exhausted trainees trying to dig a grave under a barracks—with spoons. We were getting more dirt on ourselves than we were getting out of Mr. Clark's grave. Bob finally got us organized and into teams. Each team would dig as hard and as fast as they could and when they could no longer dig, they were replaced by the next group.

In this manner, we were able to get a huge hole dug under the barracks in what seemed like record time. As we got closer to where we thought we should be, Bob and I climbed into the hole to take the necessary measurements. Some of the guys were nervous about a Moron taking the critical measurements, but Bob just told them to shut the fuck up.

Amazingly, when the drill sergeants returned from chow, we were ninety-percent complete. For the last ten minutes or so, the drills screamed at us to hurry up because Mr. Clark was beginning to decompose, and his body was starting to smell. As soon as I finished the final measurements and announced to Bob that I thought we had it right, he ordered everyone out from under the barracks, and we formed up in front of Sgt. Harper. Bob reported that the mission was complete and the grave met all the proper requirements for a full military funeral.

Harper saluted Bob, grabbed the measuring stick from me, and crawled under the barracks to check the grave. After several minutes of measuring the dimensions of Mr. Clark's final resting spot, he crawled back out.

"Mr. Clark and his family would be proud. Good job, trainees," he announced to our relief. "Now, everyone back inside, get out of those dirty clothes, get over to the latrine to clean up, and fall back out here in your dress uniforms. Be prepared for full uniform inspection. We have a funeral to perform." He looked at his watch, "You have one hour to get changed and get back out here for a formal inspection before the funeral. Move out."

Are you kidding me? For the next thirty seconds, we stood there too stunned to move. We thought that it would be over once we had dug the grave. None of us thought we would be required to perform a funeral. I didn't know about anyone else, but I had nothing left. I couldn't imagine a man among us being able to make it for another minute, much less an hour of preparing for a formal funeral.

Once again, the guys in the platoon surprised me. Less than an hour later, we were cleaned in our dress uniforms and standing in front of the barracks for a formal inspection. When we first arrived at Fort Knox, I never would have dreamed we'd be able to accomplish what we had just accomplished.

Right on time, Bond and Harper turned up for the inspection. We were so drained that we had all made a lot of mistakes on our uniforms and we were far from being ready for a formal inspection. We weren't perfect, but Harper let little things go, and he told us that the platoon looked better than he had ever seen us. Once he was done with the inspection, he handed the funeral manual to Bob and told him that he had one hour to prepare the platoon to present formal military honors to Mr. Clark.

When the hour was up, and we were as prepared as we could be, we once again formed up. Harper directed Bob to carry Mr. Clark under the building and with the utmost care place him in his final resting place. When Bob came back out, we staged the formal military funeral. We performed the entire funeral to include a twenty-one-gun salute and the folding of the American flag. We presented the flag to Sgt. Harper during the playing of taps.

Because we had neither weapons nor musical instruments, the twenty-one-gun salute was simulated with loud "bang bangs" from the platoon, and taps was hummed.

After the formal presentation of the colors, Harper ordered us back into the barracks and out of our dress uniforms, back into our dirty PT uniforms from the day before. By now our uniforms smelled so bad that trainees in other platoons would be complaining. I didn't think that mine was ever going to come clean again, and even if it did, it had too many rips and tears to make it worthwhile to repair.

When we were back outside, Harper told us to take our digging instruments, climb back under the barracks, and fill in the hole for Mr. Clark. I didn't know where all the dirt we dug out of the hole went, but we ended up having to scrape dirt from all under the barracks to find enough to fill the void. Once the hole was filled, we placed the headstone, a large white rock with black marker writing that read:

"Here lies Mr. Clark, a real American Hero."

We outlined the grave with the traditional Fort Knox white rocks. It wasn't a work of art, but we were, in a strange way, proud of what we had accomplished.

When we finally crawled back out from underneath the barracks, we were once again met by Sgt. Harper, holding a small piece of paper in his hand. Looking very concerned, he asked Bob, "Private, can you now assure me that Mr. Clark is safe and comfortable in his final resting place?"

Bob replied, "Yes, Drill Sergeant, we have followed all of the instructions to the letter."

"Well," said Sgt. Harper, "I guess we are all done here."

We all relaxed, the ordeal finally at an end. But, once again everything in the Army is not as it seems. As we began to stumble back to our barracks, Harper suddenly asked, "Private Berlin, when you buried Mr. Clark, which direction was his head facing, east or west?"

Everyone froze. We had been in the Army long enough to realize that there was no correct answer to this question. We were fucked. The only thing we could do was hope against hope that we were going to get a break. We really were at the breaking point this time. I for one had nothing left to give. I gulped and replied, "West, Drill Sergeant."

"I was afraid you were going to say that. I just looked at my note card here, and it says to ensure that the deceased soldiers head should always point to the north. There is only one thing we can do. We are going to have to dig him up, reposition the body, and rebury him in his grave. I don't have the heart to tell Mr. Clark's children that their daddy was buried incorrectly."

We had to go through the entire damn thing all over again.

The hardest thing the second time around wasn't digging the grave; it was finding the body of the deceased. None of us could believe how hard it was to find that stupid candy bar. No matter how hard we looked, Mr. Clark was elusive. After what seemed like hours, we finally found the damn thing, repositioned the body, and held a new burial ceremony. When we finished, some of the guys had passed out and were lying in the grass. Exhausted entirely, they had given it everything they had. The longer we worked, the fewer of us remained to do the work. When we finally got the job finished, there were only twelve of us left standing. When we were done, everything we had left in us was under that building in the dirt buried in the grave alongside Mr. Clark.

Sgt. Harper once again brought what was left of the platoon back together. He repeated his thank-you speech and this time asked Bob, "Was Mr. Clark face up or face down?"

I thought I was going to scream. *You must be kidding*! I am not one to give up, but this time I had reached my breaking point.

Bob looked like he was getting ready to panic. He knew he would be wrong again and didn't want to be responsible for any more of this torture.

Knowing I couldn't go on anymore, I stood up as straight and tall as I could manage, and asked, "Drill Sergeant, request permission to ask a question."

Harper answered, "Go ahead, Private."

"Which way is he supposed to be facing, Drill Sergeant?"

Sgt. Harper responded, "Why, face up, of course."

Bob looked at me, smiled, and replied, "That's exactly how we buried him, face up."

Harper smiled and said, "Great job, team, hit the showers, get some clean clothes on, and get back out here." Praise be to God!

"I need to talk to you before I release you for the evening," he added. "Throw your PT uniforms and the uniforms you were digging in into the garbage. I'll get you some new ones. I don't think even the Army laundry will touch those things. Make sure that everyone is accounted for and that they all get to the showers. I don't want to find any members of the platoon left behind. Don't mess up, because I am ready to do this all over again if necessary."

At precisely eight in the evening, thirty-eight hours after the Clark bar eruption began, we were right back where we started, standing in formation in front of the barracks. At that moment, I think that I hated Drill Sgt. Harper with a passion. I hated him more than any individual I had ever hated in my life. We were in the exact same place we started, but we were not the same platoon that had been out there the day before. We were battered, bruised, bone tired, hungry, and thirsty. Guys were swaying and trying to hold one another up. We still had several hours before lights out and didn't know if we could make it.

The rest of the battalion was watching from various vantage points to see if it was over or not. They were probably astounded by how much we had been through and yet were still alive. Sgt. Harper cleared his throat and shouted, "At ease, men."

He had never called us men before. Shithead, dummy, or trainee, but never men.

"Chow is on tables behind the barracks. We have burgers, hot dogs, and pizza. There are also two, and I repeat two, cold beers for each of you. If I catch anyone with more than two, I will rip your hearts out, and we just might have another memorial race. Is that clear?"

"Yes, Drill Sergeant," we responded.

He concluded, "When I say 'fall out,' you will grab a plate, eat up, drink up, and hit the sack. No fire guard tonight, and no details. First call is at 0800 in the morning. Get some sleep, men, and don't make me regret this. Fall out."

No food, beer, or night's sleep had ever felt or tasted so good. That would be the best meal and the best night's sleep I would ever experience. We slept the sleep of the dead that night. The next morning or should I say afternoon—after all, it was 0800 hours and not four in the morning—the attitude and mood of the platoon had changed. We were sore as hell, but everyone was laughing and joking. Mostly we were talking about how tough we were and that we could have kept it up for another twenty-four hours if we had to. We had become a special unit because we had been through something that none of the others had experienced.

"None of them are as tough as we are."

I even heard one guy, who incidentally had passed out, say, "Hell, that asshole Harper wasn't even close to breaking me. I would have dropped dead before I quit."

I love revisionist history.

The events of the previous two days guaranteed us bragging rights that no one else in the battalion could match. Yeah, basic combat training was tough, and a lot of the drill sergeants were assholes, but they couldn't say they had survived anything like the death of a fellow trainee and the Clark Memorial 100.

Oddly, while there was a lot of talk about Harper, I noticed a hint of pride whenever his name was mentioned in the same sentence as our platoon. It was a strange lesson in human dynamics; we had gained respect for the man who had almost killed us.

The biggest revelation for me was that the despair and loss we all felt for Pvt. Luney became tolerable. I'm not saying we didn't talk about him and complain about Sgt. Bond's role in his death, but we had gotten past our pain and depression. I knew that a lot of us still had problems but nothing like the two days prior. I realized it wasn't Mr. Clark that the platoon had buried under that barracks. It was Pvt. Luney.

Drill Sgt. Harper, a veteran of four tours in Vietnam, two of which were cut short by wounds, had a unique method of dealing with grief and making sure his platoon could move forward. At the time, I didn't understand what was going on or why Harper was being such an asshole. It wasn't until many years later when I experienced similar heart-wrenching losses and numbing experiences that I realized Harper was way ahead of his time and had a pretty good system for working through grief.

Time and experience helped me to connect the dots and discover that there was, in fact, a method to his madness. However, at the time, like the rest of the platoon, I just wanted to kill him. I admit I've used his technique several times over the years, at least until everything got so politically correct that it became a crime to treat soldiers like soldiers. Now they call it harassment, but whatever you want to call it, it worked.

Moron

# Chapter 23
## Last Night

It was finally our last night at Fort Knox, and we were scheduled to graduate from basic training the following afternoon. Training was done, and we were ready to get the hell out of Kentucky. Everyone passed, even all of us Morons. No one failed unless they got arrested, were too sick to continue, or had died during basic training. The Army was in desperate need of new soldiers to fill the rapidly depleting ranks of former all-draftee units. People who could get out of the Army were leaving, and Uncle Sam was having a tough time finding replacements. If I were in charge of basic training, fully half of this crew would not have been allowed to move on.

I had learned during my eight weeks of training that many of my fellow trainees didn't have the mental capacity to serve without hurting themselves or someone else. There was also our criminal element. Many of them would end up being arrested for some serious crimes later in their Army careers. For most of them, it was just a matter of time. The only hope the Army had was that they got caught before their crimes escalated to the level that they became a serious threat to other soldiers or soldiers' families.

The mentally deficient trainees were an entirely different story. While they were usually not bad guys by nature, it just wasn't possible for them to comprehend what was going on; most of them would never be able to use the weaponry or the equipment that all soldiers are supposed to be able to use. These poor guys were destined to serve as cooks, garbage haulers, or permanent guards for as long as they remained in the Army. The entire time they stayed in the Army, they were going to be a drain on resources because everything they did took more people, more time, and more effort. Hopefully, none of them would be deployed to a combat zone. If they were, there's a good chance many of them and their fellow soldiers would end up dead. They didn't get it.

The Army had put out the word to all basic training commands to graduate everyone possible. No matter how bad we were at training, or how horrible we did on individual testing, the drill sergeants found a way to move us on to the next stage of our training and to ensure that we all graduated. After our eight weeks of Army hell, we couldn't wait to get a taste of healthy society and ordinary people once again. All the guys were spending a lot of time getting themselves and their uniforms ready for the big graduation ceremony. We wanted to look good.

No matter how badly we hated the Army and the training, and no matter how much we had screwed up during training, most of us were macho enough to be looking forward to being dressed up in our fancy Army dress uniforms and marching across the field in front of our families and friends. One of the things the drill sergeants did well was instill in us a sense of pride about being a soldier and a feeling that we were better than the average civilian. For the Wolverines, there was the added excitement of being able to finally take control of our long-awaited Trans AMs. Of course, everyone else at Fort Knox still thought we were nuts and believed there was no way in hell it was going to happen.

While others busied themselves with final preparations, a select few of us had a more critical mission. It was time to make Drill Sgt. Bond pay up. Operation "Fuck Hitler" was about to be launched.

Ever since the suicide of Pvt. Luney, a group of us had been plotting to avenge his death. As far as we were concerned, Bond might as well have murdered Luney himself. That poor kid never had a chance. What Bond had done was the same thing as a parent fucking with the mind of a seven-year-old. Sgt. Bond mentally destroyed him and then drove him to suicide. He was a criminal and should have to pay for what he had done.

The key to any successful clandestine operation is to keep the number of participants to a minimum. Everyone knows that the more people involved in the process, the better the chance that someone is going to talk or screw up, and the plan will fail. To ensure the success of this operation, we kept our planning and execution team to three members, Danny Mussio, Bob Bradley, and me.

Because Danny was in a different platoon, it made the planning a little harder, but it helped to ensure that there was less of a chance for leaks; besides, I knew him and could trust him not to talk. Bob was the only person in the entire first platoon I considered smart enough and discreet enough for this operation. He was also the best lock picker I knew, and the only lock picker I knew.

It was our last night on Fort Knox, but we hadn't waited until the last minute to prepare for our task. We chose the last night for a good reason, which served our purpose. We knew that Hitler was going to be away from Fort Knox all night. Someone had overheard him telling Sgt. Harper he had permission to head to Louisville where he was supposedly spending time with family before graduation ceremonies. He'd be staying overnight and would arrive back at Fort Knox the next morning. Harper was also heard mentioning it to others but saying he thought Bond had other plans, perhaps of a sexual nature. Whatever the case, it fit our plan perfectly to wait for the last night.

Actual planning and staging work had been taking place ever since Luney's death. The Army had taught us well. For an operation to be successful, it must be meticulously arranged and rehearsed down to the smallest detail. The key to our entire strategy rested on the Army's strange preoccupation with homosexuality and anything that smacked of being gay.

At the time, there seemed to be a major agreement among senior leaders in the Army: gay soldiers had no place in the Army, and they should be aggressively and immediately stamped out when discovered. The Army had been running its little version of the Spanish Inquisition for as long as anyone could remember. If you were gay and in the Army, you had better hide it and hide it well.

An underlying theme to basic training, other than preparing civilians for combat, even focused on the elimination of fags in the Army. Every song we sang, every duty we performed, and every training event we attended, including church services, extolled the evils of homosexuality. The Army training staff at Fort Knox was, for the most part, made up of a bunch of homophobes, and their primary mission in life was to ensure that when we left basic training, we were as homophobic as the rest of them. Imagine what would happen if they thought that one of their own, a drill sergeant, was a flaming faggot.

We decided the best way to pay him back would be to provide the Army all the evidence necessary to convince the dumbest of them that Bond was not only gay but preying on the young trainees, who had been put in his trust by the Army. Some of you may say this was a delicate task, but in our minds, he was dangerous to trainees, so dangerous that he had caused the death of one of his charges, a member of our platoon. To us no punishment was too severe to contemplate.

The same week that Homer killed himself, we held our first clandestine meeting. It wasn't hard to decide what we were going to do to get even with Sgt. Bond. Being a drill sergeant and having complete control over the lives of others was a driving factor in his life. We decided that we wanted to end his drill sergeant days and at the same time prevent him from fucking up the lives of any more trainees. If we could convince his fellow drill sergeants that he was a homosexual, it would be the end for him. Frankly, he'd be lucky if he got off Fort Knox alive.

Danny got stuck collecting the gayest magazines and publications he could get his hands on, and then through the classified sections, establish a pen-pal relationship with the weirdest and most messed-up person he could track down. It was surprisingly easy to obtain gay publications at most of the stores around the post. There were more homosexuals operating in the Army than we had guessed. For all the Army's obsession with homophobia, there was still a big market for this type of stuff, and homosexual activity flourished in an underground environment right outside the front gate of Fort Knox.

While finding gay material was easy, finding the right gay material was tough. There was so much variety to choose from that it made it hard to decide, and we were not experts on gay pornography, at least we took great pains to convince ourselves that we were not. From our extensive research, we determined that we could portray Drill Sgt. Bond in one of two ways. He could be a pitcher or a catcher.

We decided it would be a lot more interesting if we portrayed the tough drill sergeant as a submissive homosexual, so catcher it was. We figured the other drill sergeants would get really pissed off if they believed that one of their own was a little candy ass. Danny, using Hitler's name and address on a typewriter from the library, contacted a guy who said in his ad that he liked to be the aggressor in relationships. He called himself Lenny.

Within the first two weeks, Lenny and Danny, passing himself off as Bond, were the best of gay buddies and began exchanging pictures using a classified ad in the back of one of the magazines. Since every military record has photos of the record holder in them it was easy for Danny to get his hands on Bond's official photos. Lenny was fascinated with the fact that his new gay lover was an Army drill sergeant. Soon we had some tremendous incoming correspondence from Lenny, whose only ambition in life was to pound it to our little Hitler. To amplify the letters, we highlighted the juiciest parts. We figured that when they found our work, whoever found it would believe that Bond had highlighted the best parts for quick reference. I sometimes worried about Danny because he was a little too good at this. He said not to worry about it, that he was a natural born actor and could play any part if he put his mind to it.

My responsibility was to make a series of anonymous phone calls to the chaplain's office and the inspector general's office, complaining about a drill sergeant in my unit who was always hitting on the guys in my platoon. I had to be careful not to give any hints as to which unit I was referring to because early notice would have destroyed the entire plan. If the guys at the chaplain's office thought they could pinpoint a specific unit, they would tear that unit apart looking for the homo drill sergeant.

I used the pay phones at various locations both on and off the post, always ensuring that none were close to our unit, just in case they could trace phone calls. You never know. I would describe how the drill sergeant in question would spend all his time in the platoon bathrooms watching us, especially at shower time, and that he kept approaching trainees with unusual requests, most of which involved some touching. I didn't have to make up most of what I relayed to them. That little shit of a drill sergeant did spend all his time hanging around the bathroom.

Guys in all the platoons had complained about him at one time or another, and he *was* just plain weird. Of course, he said he did this to make sure that there were no fags in the unit; but when I thought about it, maybe he was one of those guys who protested a little too much. I knew that if an investigation ever occurred, it would be easy to confirm that he was, in fact, the weird drill sergeant trainees were complaining about.

There were enough trainees and sergeants who had heard the complaining to support the information in my fake phone calls. The coup de grace of the operation was a series of phone calls to the head chaplain on Fort Knox, Chaplain Jackson. Jackson was an Army colonel of the Baptist persuasion who was famous for his anti-homosexual tirades during Sunday services.

At a typical Sunday service, he would go into screaming raves about how it was against both God's and nature's laws to engage in that type of abnormal activity. According to Chaplain Jackson, those who laid with members of the same sex were destined to eternal damnation, pain and suffering. Whenever he got going on one of his fag speeches, his face would turn bright red, spittle would spray from his mouth, and he would begin to shout at the congregation. While his sermons were a lot of fun and very entertaining, no one wanted to attend, because as a Southern Baptist it was not unusual for one of his tirades to go on for several hours. Give me a ten-minute Irish Catholic priest any Sunday. Chaplain Jackson was a veritable encyclopedia on anti-gay issues and never seemed to run out of opinions or things to say.

Getting him on the phone and into a heated discussion was probably the most natural part of the plan. As soon as the clerk informed him that a trainee complaining of homosexuals was on the phone, you could hear him running to pick up the receiver. While it was highly unusual for a colonel, even a chaplain colonel, in the Army to talk to a trainee on the phone, in the case of Chaplain Jackson, all it took was a little baiting. I would merely contact the chaplain's assistant, a private who worked at the church, and ask to speak to the colonel. As might be expected, the colonel was always too busy to talk to a trainee, but when I explained to the assistant the nature of my problem and added that I religiously attend Chaplain Jackson's Sunday services, I could feel him tugging at the bait. When I said that I agreed that fags were a curse on the earth and would add some fake sobs and tears, the assistant would take a bite of the bait. I would add that I was being forced to perform unnatural acts of a sexual nature and didn't know what to do.

Soon after making my calls, I would find myself speaking directly to the colonel himself. I quickly learned that I needed to spend the first part of the conversation stroking the chaplain and letting him know how important his sermons were to me, and how they were changing my life. I would then go into how the drill sergeant was propositioning me all the time, kept trying to look at me in the shower, and touched me when I was sleeping at night. I told him I knew the drill sergeant was the boss and I was supposed to listen to him, but I thought he was doing some things that were not right by the Army or God's laws. The chaplain always insisted on details. The more graphic, the better.

The whole time I was talking, Chaplain Jackson would attempt to get me to give up my name and location, but I would tell him that I was too embarrassed or too frightened of what the drill sergeant would do to me if he found out I had informed on him. Sometimes I would hang up. Most of our conversations would end with me saying, "I am so ashamed, Chaplain. I feel like the drill sergeant is after me because I have done something to encourage him. I don't want to be evil, and sometimes I think it would be better if I were dead." My actions would drive Chaplain Jackson wild, and he would go into his savior role and give me a speech on how precious life was. The plan was coming together nicely.

Danny had accomplished his portion of the mission with his usual zeal and enthusiasm. Whenever he was out to get someone, his imagination kicked into high gear, and there was no stopping him. When he was in retaliation mode, he was freaking brilliant. If he accomplished everything in life as well as he did his "get-even" plans, the Army would have promoted him to general before the end of basic training. In his evaluation process, he had visited every porno shop in downtown Lexington and had obtained enough gay pornography to make even the most ardent aficionado jealous. His collection included some of the most outrageous stuff that any of us had ever seen or imagined.

His piece de resistance was a three-by-three-foot collage of dicks. I'm not kidding, someone had compiled a poster with nothing but dicks on it. I have never seen so many dicks in one place in my entire life. Every size, every color, and every shape imaginable. It was so gross that it was kind of funny.

Danny had cleverly and mysteriously obtained copies of the official photographs of everyone in the first platoon and all the drill sergeants in the brigade. About a week before each graduating cycle, the Army brings in teams of professional photographers to take pictures of all the new trainees for individual and platoon-level photographs. They are standard military photos, a freshly shorn recruit standing next to an American flag, and the platoons standing on bleachers with their unit colors and their drill sergeants.

I don't know how he managed it, but Danny had been able to get multiple copies of all the pictures. He also had images of all the drill sergeants and brigade leaders, including those of our favorite drill sergeant, Hitler. Today this wouldn't be such a big deal with color copy machines and computers, but in 1973 this was quite an impressive feat. When someone found these photos in Hitler's private room, they would naturally assume that he had obtained them from some official source. Since it would be difficult, almost impossible, for a trainee to have access to these photos only played in our favor. It was just another tribute to Danny's ability to find a way to get things done.

Danny took the photos he had obtained and painstakingly cut the heads off each picture for his special project. He took all the cut-out photo heads and meticulously glued them on a batch of corresponding gay porno photos. All the faces of the first platoon members were placed on gay guys in the pitching position, and the multiple Drill Sgt. Bond heads were glued in the corresponding catcher's position.

If whoever found our artwork was as creeped out by them as we were, and we were the manufacturers of this work of art, then the discovery would raise the alarm, especially in a homophobic Army. Neither Bob nor I liked the idea of seeing our faces and the faces of the other guys in the platoon in the act of sodomizing a fake Drill Sgt. Bond, but Danny said it was essential to get the full creep effect or we would be wasting our time. Bob wanted Danny to remove his picture from the stack, but Danny said that to have one or two people from the platoon missing from the artwork would only raise suspicions as to why. We couldn't risk any evidence pointing back to us, and we didn't want to have to answer any questions.

Danny was concerned about leaving any possible evidence behind and had taken great pains to leave no trails. He had created his artwork at a hotel in downtown Lexington over the weekend while we were on forty-eight-hour passes. He had checked in under a false name and had paid cash for the room. Danny assured us he had worn rubber gloves the entire time he was in the room so there were no fingerprints in the room or on any of the pictures or artwork.

The gloves were stolen from the unit dispensary while he was on sick call one morning. He had taken enough pairs to ensure that we all had a pair to wear when we finished the final phase of our project later that evening. When he completed all his work, he had disposed of all the materials to include glue, paper, and other items by placing them in a large paper bag, which he disposed of in a grocery store incinerator down the street from the hotel.

Before coming into the Army, Danny had worked part-time in a grocery store in Iron City, so he knew that they disposed of all their cardboard and paper stock every evening by placing them in a giant incinerator to be burned. He merely watched the chimney of several stores for the telltale black smoke and went into the store, walked to the back, entered the employee area, and tossed the evidence directly into the incinerator while it was burning at full blast. If someone caught him, his story was that he was looking for a bathroom and got lost. He said he wasn't too worried about getting caught because most employees at grocery stores didn't give a shit. As I knew he would, he had planned everything down to the smallest detail.

Bob's part of the plan was key to the entire operation. He was the important lock picker.

Early in the afternoon of the last day before graduation, the three of us sat down to go over all the supplies and details of the operation one last time:

Two posters of altered gay pornography … check.

Typed letters and envelopes to and from gay lovers and several to a gay magazine … check.

Three weeks of phony phone calls to the inspector general's office and Chaplain Jackson's office … check.

Lock pick for the door … check.

Rubber gloves … check.

Altered photos of every leader in the command and the entire first platoon … check.

Two flashlights with red lens … check.

A case of beer … check.

Two fat joints … check.

It appeared that everything was ready and that the operation was a go.

The only thing we knew for sure was that Bond had to be back at the unit by noon the next day because the graduation ceremony was at one. With an ego as big as his, he wouldn't miss the opportunity to show off to all our parents and girlfriends in his dress uniform. With any luck at all, I was hoping this was one ceremony that he was going to miss.

Bob and I had arranged to be assigned to fire watch from two until four a.m. The three of us agreed to meet outside the barracks at two fifteen. We wanted to make sure that the fireguard going off duty had time to get to sleep and be out of the picture before our rendezvous. Right on schedule Bob and I met Danny outside on the front porch. As planned, the outgoing fire guard was already sound asleep and adding his snores to the choir in the barracks.

At two thirty we made our way into the barracks and crept down the hallway on the first floor to Bond's private room. Trainees in basic training were always so exhausted that we learned to fall into a deep sleep as soon as lights-out was announced. Over the past eight weeks, we had adapted to the point that it would take either an atomic bomb or a drill sergeant's banging on a garbage can lid to wake us up. We had been conditioned to ignore just about everything else. Bottom line, no one even stirred as we tiptoed past their bunks to the room at the end of the barracks.

Thank God for the Army's obsession with uniformity. The padlock on Bond's room was the same as the one on Harper's office. Since Bob and I had so much experience opening Harper's room to deposit him on his cot following his many passing-out episodes, this part would be easy. Bob was a real pro with his lock picking tools, and I didn't think we would have any trouble getting into this room. In less than thirty seconds, with hardly an audible click, the lock was opened and lying in Bob's hands.

The three of us quickly entered the room and closed the door behind us. It was risky having all three of us in the room without a lookout, but we wanted to be as quick as we could, and we needed all of us to get the job done. The key to our operation was to ensure that we set up the room to make it look like a pervert was residing here and hiding his darkest secrets from the world in his room. We knew we couldn't be too obvious or the whole operation would backfire on us. We had to make it look real, but at the same time not too far over the top, if that was possible.

Once again, the Army obsession with everything looking identical played to our advantage. All the drill sergeants' rooms were the same, and I had spent so much time in Harper's room that I knew the layout by heart. Large closet in the back of the room where the sergeants kept their uniforms and personal stuff, small desk, cot, and a footlocker. Drill sergeants worked hard to portray an image of pure military. They didn't want any trainees ever to see them in civilian clothing or appear to own anything that was not military.

They kept their civilian gear secured in their closet, desk, and footlocker. I'm surprised they thought we were stupid enough to believe that all of them were one-hundred-percent military all the time. The drill sergeants carried this little charade so far that none of us had even caught a glimmer of one of them in anything except for military clothing for the entire time we had been there.

Opening the closet door, which thankfully did not have a lock on it, we removed the uniforms and laid them on the cot so we could get unobstructed access to the back wall of the closet. When Bob shone the flashlight on the rear wall, what we saw caused us all to be immediately frozen in shock— there, taped on the closet wall, were all the pictures missing from the mail of the first platoon! The wall was covered with what we assumed were girlfriends and wives, at least all the beautiful ones. I was pissed because my girl's picture was featured prominently in his display.

The photos were taped to pieces of typing paper and printed in neat block letters on each page was a phone number and the name of the girl in the picture. That pervert had been the one making all the calls to our girlfriends. We had been writing them off as coincidence, figuring that guys at home were doing it because they knew we were not around and took it as an opportunity to chase after our women. Hell, if we had known this all along, we could have saved ourselves a whole lot of time setting this son of a bitch up in the first place. Here on the wall in front of us was evidence of multiple crimes, clearly more than enough to get Bond tossed out of the Army. Any doubt or guilt that any of us may have felt about our current operation disappeared as we stared in disgust at the wall in front of us, and it takes a lot to disgust an eighteen-year-old.

Despite our outrage, we tried to be as quiet as possible. Bob was the first to break the silence.

"Hey, Roger, look there are about five pictures of your girl. I recognize her from the pictures you showed me. Look, let's show this to the colonel and the command sergeant major and all our troubles will be over. Even easier, we show this to the guys in the platoon, and they'll kill the son of a bitch. We don't have to do anything to set him up."

I was seething with rage, seeing pictures of my Paula in that pervert's closet.

"Don't be an asshole, Bob," said Danny. "You can't tell anyone what we saw in here tonight."

Bob was having none of this. "Bullshit, let's nail the son of a bitch with this. I'm sure that it's against the law to make obscene phone calls, and I know it's a federal offense to tamper with the mail. He'll go away for ten years for this."

"No, he won't," I replied. "There is no way anyone can prove he made the phone calls. Everything we are looking at right now and everything we know is purely circumstantial."

Danny told Bob to listen to me, as I had experience with the law. "Pay attention, and Roger is an experienced criminal. He knows what he's talking about. Back home he was able to get out of every scrape with the law he ever got into. We can still pull this off."

I added, "How do we say we found this, we just happened to walk by at two o'clock in the morning and the lock fell off the door, and the closet door swung open? If we're stupid enough to tell them that, then we're the ones going to jail, not Bond. The fucking Army will lock us up for the rest of our lives, and he will walk away from this, scot-free. Besides, for all we know, the Army doesn't even care about this kind of shit.

"If I were Bond, I would say that the trainees set him up and planned this shit to get even for him being tough on us. Hell, everything on the wall is something that any trainee in this unit could get his hands on. Who is the Army going to believe, two trainees and a Moron who can't explain how they have this information or an official Army drill sergeant? No matter how bad we want to use this stuff against him, we can't get it set up in time to get him. I say we stick with the original plan."

We all agreed to stay the course, and the three of us took down the pieces of paper and all the pictures on the wall in the closet. Danny went over the rest of the room and the closet with a fine-tooth comb to make sure there wasn't any more evidence. We didn't want to blow our homo setup with pictures of women. It was a good thing he did because he found stuff all over the room.

Drill Sgt. Bond had quite a collection; there must have been pictures here from the last three cycles of trainees that he worked with. We found pictures and phone numbers throughout the room. We began stuffing these materials into the pillowcase that Danny was carrying. We wanted everything cleared out so that we could plant the evidence of the new crime. The pillowcase was so full we had to stuff the additional evidence in and sit on it to get everything shoved inside.

Once all the existing stuff was removed, we replaced them with our stuff, basically replacing one perversion with another. We had the posters and pictures that Danny had prepared. We taped them all over the back wall of the closet, so it looked exactly like the previous display, only this time it was gay-centric. The old tape and pieces of paper stuck to the wall added a nice touch because it gave the impression of past indiscretions. Bond had made our task more manageable because we didn't have to guess where a pervert would hide or place things in his room; we merely put stuff where the pictures of our girls used to be. I realized that Bond had finally taught me something in basic training. It was the first thing that I had learned from him in the eight weeks.

When the wall was wholly and appropriately decorated with our gay motif, Danny put a piece of typing paper in the typewriter on the small wooden desk used by Bond. With his rubber gloves firmly in place, he typed out the address of

Bond's new gay pen pal. Danny then placed letters from the same guy in the top drawer of the desk. He also left a letter Bond supposedly hadn't sent yet. It referred to Bond forcing trainees to perform sex acts while Bond and his gay friends watched. Bond offered to share pictures of trainees with his new pen pal.

At last, we finished. While it seemed like hours, it had only taken less than thirty minutes to complete. We took time to complete one last check of the room to ensure that no incriminating evidence was left behind, and then we slipped back out of the room. Bob removed the receiver from the phone and left it dangling at the side of the desk. This would be used for another part of the plan. He then placed the padlock on the desk, and we closed the door but left it unlocked. We were sure that no one would notice, and even if they did, no one in the platoon dared to enter Bond's room. When we were done, we crept back down the rows of sleeping trainees and exited the barracks.

Outside Danny collected the gloves and all the stuff we had removed from the room. Danny had each of us check off the items we had brought into the room with us to ensure that we had carried it all back out. He made us pull out our pockets and recheck all our gear three times before he declared us clear. After completing his final check, he shook our hands and took off. Bob and I went back inside to finish our fire watch while Danny headed over to the mess hall to throw out all his evidence. Danny tossed the pillowcase and everything we had brought to the incinerator outside the dining hall.

Sticking around only long enough to ensure the incinerator had done its job and all the evidence was now ashes, Danny headed back to his barracks to slip inside and get some sleep before morning wake-up call.

****

When reveille sounded the next morning, we began our last day at Fort Knox just like we started the first day.

Drill Sgt. Harper stormed through the barracks, banging the top of a trash can and screaming at us to drop our cocks and grab our socks.

Waking up for our last breakfast, Danny had one final and critical part of the plan to accomplish. Since this was our last day, the drill sergeants had cut us a little slack and were allowing some of the trainees to make coordination phone calls with family members during breakfast hours. A lot of families were in town for graduation and were staying at local hotels, and this phone opportunity would give many of them one last chance to get everything organized for the day.

Everyone knew that Danny was expecting his girlfriend from Iron City and had been asking all week to be allowed to take advantage of this final opportunity to use the phone. His request was granted.

He began his call, to Chaplain Jackson, by stating he was a private assigned to the first platoon that had been calling for the past several weeks and gave Chaplain Jackson the barracks number to the first platoon. He then told the chaplain that he couldn't take it anymore. He said his drill sergeant was sodomizing him and gave Bond's name. He said he had been warned not to speak but was so ashamed that he couldn't hold it in anymore. He had to tell someone.

"Chaplain, I'm not afraid of him anymore," he said. "I went to your services last Sunday, and I know this is not my fault. I am at peace with myself. Before I leave this earth, I want to make sure that this never happens to another trainee. I know why the other private in my platoon committed suicide, and I think he did the right thing. At least he is resting peacefully now. Drill Sergeant Bond gave me the combination to his room. I'm using his phone right now, and this is where I'm going to end it all. Please send my body to my mother and tell her I'm sorry I sinned and I'm ashamed of what I allowed the drill sergeant to do to me. I wanted to thank you for setting me straight during your sermons at church, and you have given me the courage to end this. Thank you, Chaplain."

When he told this part of the tale, he conjured up tears and was sobbing to make his voice sound more desperate. I would have given anything to hear that phone call. According to Danny, it was an Academy Award performance.

"I realize that I have sinned grievously and offended both you and the Lord. The only way I can make this right is to kill myself."

Chaplain Jackson was in his glory; he had a trainee on the phone who had just informed on a homosexual drill sergeant. He had so much confidence in his abilities as a saver of souls that he was convinced he could talk this young, "anonymous" private down from his suicidal stance and save both a life and a soul.

"Private," he said, "life is too precious to throw away on a whim. I understand that you have sinned and that you are deeply ashamed, but this is no reason to end your life. The Lord forgives you for your sins. You are too young and impressionable to make good decisions. The real sinner here is your drill sergeant. You let me and the Army take care of him. We'll make sure that evil son of a bitch ends up getting exactly what is coming to him."

When he realized the seriousness of the call, the chaplain had his wife on the other line and she was now telling the MPs to dispatch a unit to the barracks as fast as possible to stop the trainee from committing suicide.

Danny was no dummy, and he knew exactly what was going on. He was playing the same game from a slightly different angle. He wanted to keep the chaplain on the phone until the last possible moment, or our plan wouldn't work. The phone that Danny was using provided him with a perfect view of the main street in front of the barracks.

As soon as he saw the military police cars streaming down the road and toward the barracks, he told Chaplain Jackson, "Chaplin, I know what you are trying to do. I see the MPs outside the window. Goodbye."

Jackson began to panic a little.

"Son, relax, they are here to help you, not arrest you, and they will protect you from your drill sergeant. Please remain calm; everything is going to be OK now."

Danny was now raising his voice to sound agitated and frightened. "I don't want to cause any more trouble. Thank you, Chaplain, because of you I can do the right thing."

With that Danny hung up his phone and casually walked over to the mess hall to eat breakfast. As he entered the mess hall, both marked and unmarked police cars came screaming around the corner and slid to a stop in front of the first platoon barracks. Danny sat down to eat his breakfast and observe the action through the mess hall window.

By now everyone in the training battalion was aware that something strange was going on. Sure, there had been lots of police in the area during basic training, but never so many and never with lights flashing and sirens blaring. Chaplain Jackson's wife had put the fear of God in the MPs, and they arrived in our unit area in less than three minutes from the time they were dispatched. Before the first car had even stopped, several MPs jumped out of the vehicle and dashed through the front door of the first platoon barracks.

Bob and I, who were upstairs, heard them run down the center of the first floor. Uh-oh, it sounded like they had run across "no man's land." Harper was going to be pissed. From the sounds we could picture the action below. They ran through the barracks, knocking bunks and lockers out of the way and then kicked down the door to Bond's room. This was entirely unnecessary because if they had checked, they would have discovered that the door had been left open for them. We later learned that the first thing they observed when they entered the room was the phone off the hook and dangling by its cord. It was swinging from the force of their entry, but they believed that it was still moving from being dropped by the unknown private who was trying to kill himself.

The MPs quickly searched the room and opened the closet door, the only possible hiding place in the room, to look for the suicidal trainee.

Outside in the unit street, it was starting to look like a Chinese fire drill gone bad. Cars and people were still streaming into the unit street, including the chaplain's staff car. When the staff car stopped, Chaplain Jackson leaped out of the rear passenger door and bounded into the barracks. Along with him was every senior leader in the unit. It looked like the entire supporting cast was in place.

The MP who had opened the closet door quickly parted the uniforms hanging in the closet to make sure there wasn't a dead trainee suspended in his death throes from the clothes rack. When he saw what was on the back wall, he froze in place. His partner, seeing him freeze, quickly pulled his pistol and moved to cover the closet. When he saw the rear wall, both his gun and his mouth dropped, the gun to his side and his mouth wide open.

We heard that was precisely how Chaplain Jackson and our commander found them. Soon the entire room and the first floor of the barracks were crammed with military officials trying to get a peek at the "queer closet," as they were now calling it.

We heard Chaplain Jackson's booming voice, in true Baptist fashion, drown out the crowd.

"Blasphemy, fornicator, abomination, this is against the laws of nature. How many times have I told everyone what would happen if we didn't drive the curse of homosexuality from the Army? I want that deviant arrested and locked up until we can have him hung for this crime. If we can't hang him, he needs to spend the rest of his natural days in prison."

For the next several hours, we watched as the MPs removed all the evidence from the first platoon barracks and hauled it out to the waiting cars. In their usual inefficient manner, they began to interrogate the platoon members in a feeble attempt to uncover the mysterious, "anonymous" private who had made the phone call. To no one's surprise, they were unable to do so. Most of the guys in the platoon had no idea what was going on and believed that Bond was the deviant that the closet portrayed. A few mentioned how Bond liked staring at them in the showers to support the case, and other sergeants, who didn't like him, had no problem believing it. As for Bob, Danny, and I, we were not talking.

The investigators were unable to locate Bond and were told he would be arriving later. We learned that he had been arrested when he returned to the post later that morning. Completely unaware as to what was going on, he put up a big fight. The MPs were able to add resisting arrest to other charges.

Unfortunately, because of a lack of evidence, and the fact that there was no victim to testify against him, they later had to drop any criminal charges against Bond. However, they were able to get him for homosexual activity and pornography, a severe violation of Army standards.

It worked out for the best because it was enough to get him dishonorably discharged for being a homo. I'm sure that he went through more than one beating before he was thrown out of the Army. A small price to pay for the torture he had been putting trainees through for the past two years.

The biggest homophobe in the Army was getting drummed out of the Army for being a homo. I loved it. He deserved to go to prison for the murder of Homer, but we took what we could get. For the three of us, knowing that he had left in disgrace and would never be able to torment another soldier, made it all worthwhile. If we had failed our mission, we would have left Fort Knox with unfinished business on the table, and we would have regretted it for the rest of our lives. The incident had provided Chaplain Jackson with enough material for several years' worth of sermons, and we heard that he was writing a book on the evils of homosexuality in the Army.

None of us ever heard from or saw Bond again. There were tons of rumors, but nothing you could hang your hat on. The last credible information we heard was that he was pumping gas somewhere down in Mississippi. Probably a better life than he deserved, but I knew it would be killing him not to be able to play the big-shot drill sergeant ever again. The only thing we knew for sure was that he would never be able to show his face anywhere near an Army base again.

Moron

Chapter 24

Graduation

All the police cars, MPs, brass, and chaplains had finally departed the area. There were no more flashing blue and red lights. For the second time since we had arrived at Fort Knox, there was absolute turmoil in the first platoon area. To say the stories were flying would have been an understatement. There were always so many stories going around in basic training that you never knew what was real and what was a rumor. What was real was that Drill Sgt. Bond had been arrested and was done with the Army forever. Now, this was one story that most of us hoped was right. Three of us already knew the truth.

When we fell out in front of the barracks, present for duty and standing tall in our dress uniforms, Drill Sgt. Harper was waiting for us. However, our nemesis, Drill Sgt. Bond, was nowhere to be seen.

This heightened curiosity among the platoon and strengthened the validity of the rumors. We knew he was the one drill sergeant who would never have missed the opportunity to show off to all the civilians who would be attending the afternoon's parade and graduation ceremony. For the past eight weeks, he had been telling us how at every ceremony he literally had to fight the women off.

According to him, the power that he held over us trainees was transmitted through his personality, and it drove women crazy. We knew that if there were any way he could have been present, he would have been here. Hell, it would have taken a volcano erupting in Kentucky to cause him to miss an opportunity to show off. The only thing anyone knew for sure was that every cop in the world seemed to have been in his room earlier in the day, and there were lots of rumors as to his whereabouts.

Like all rumors these bore absolutely no resemblance to the truth and, in a brief time, had grown and taken on a life of their own. All the guys in the platoon were talking about what had happened that morning, and they had inside information because they had either been informed by the investigators, had a friend who knew a friend at division headquarters, or they had sneaked into the room and seen the evidence. I knew that none of them were right, but it was fun to listen to the wild stories.

I heard everything from he had been arrested for distributing child pornography to they had discovered body parts of previous trainees in his room and at his off-base quarters. There were stories that Bond was a sexual predator and serial killer who had sex with young soldiers and then killed them, hiding the bodies and saving the genitals as trophies. The best rumor said that they had discovered more than thirty shriveled-up penises and testicles nailed to his bedroom wall at his house. There were even some guys who swore they had seen Bond bring trainees into his room in the barracks but had never seen them leave.

There was a lot of talk going on about how most of the guys on the first floor had been smelling something that reminded them of decaying flesh the entire time they had been at Fort Knox, but they assumed it was leftover food from the mess hall that they were smelling. It was hard to listen to the stories and not laugh out loud, and even harder not to tell everyone what we had indeed discovered in that room. I think they would have been more pissed about the pictures and letters from their girlfriends. Shriveled-up penises are so abstract, it's hard to imagine them as real, but pictures of your loved ones, now that's a different matter.

The great thing about all the rumors was that none of them said anything about anyone breaking into Bond's room and setting him up. With all the trainees talking to the investigators and making up wild accusations and rumors, they were never going to figure out what really went down. Of course, to the trainees who would talk to the investigators, they weren't rumors but facts. Many of the guys swore under oath that they had personally seen, heard, and smelled things that led them to know what had gone on in Bond's private room. The only reason they hadn't come forward was that they had been convinced no one would believe them.

Every story did seem to have the common theme that they all recounted Hitler hanging around the bathroom and shower all the time, and then there was the smell, everyone remembered the smell. Come to think of it, I did recognize a strange smell on the first floor and informed the investigator of my concerns when it was my turn to be questioned. Surprising how a rumor can spread and convince people that they smelled something that was never there. By the end of the questioning, everyone in the platoon recalled the strange smell. There is no better nor faster rumor machine than a bunch of young soldiers.

Eventually, the Drill Sgt. Bond incident became one of the Fort Knox legends. No one really knew for sure what happened, including the investigators. The one guy who was totally confused and couldn't figure out what had turned his life upside down was Bond. Three individuals will forever remain unnamed who know the truth. Like any good rumor, the story got better every time it was told and over the years, every time a new group of trainees moved into those barracks the legend grew. We were just relieved that Bond was finally and permanently gone from our lives and that he wouldn't be around to screw up the lives of any more trainees.

During that last time standing in formation in front of our barracks, I put aside the talk about Bond as I realized it was finally graduation day. Eight weeks of hell and we were finally going to be able to get out of this place. I don't know how everyone else felt; I for one would be happy if I never saw this shithole ever again, especially the hills.

When it was time to fall out for our final formation, I took a quick glance around and was surprised at how good we all looked in our Army dress uniforms. If I don't say so myself, I think I cut an impressive figure. For the first time since my arrival, I felt like a soldier. What a transformation. Up and down the street and on the adjoining streets for as far as you could see either way was a sea of soldiers in khaki uniforms.

In less than an hour, we would no longer be trainees. We would finally be soldiers. I was looking forward to Drill Sgt. Harper addressing me as soldier instead of trainee. As corny as it sounds, I was proud that I had made it all the way through basic training. There were many times when I almost said to hell with it and just walked away. A lot of us Wolverines talked about it during downtime in the barracks, and while we all swore that we were only staying for the cars, I think it was more of a macho thing that kept us around.

None of us could contemplate going home a failure, and getting kicked out would have been the ultimate failure in our young eyes. It was sorry enough for the guys who never even made it to basic training, I just didn't want to be one of the guys who got sent home and then spent the rest of his life walking around town telling stories of what might have been.

About fifteen minutes before it was time to join the rest of the battalion and march over to the main parade field, Drill Sgt. Harper came out and called us to attention. Once we were all standing tall with our mouths shut and our eyes peeled straight ahead (we had learned something in the last eight weeks), Harper told us to relax and grab a smoke if we wanted one. There would be no mention of Bond, as if he didn't even exist. Hell, Harper might have even been happy about what had just happened to his junior drill sergeant. There wasn't a hint of concern for Bond in his demeanor or voice as he gave us one last speech.

"Soldiers (wow, he called us soldiers), in less time than it takes a monkey to jack off, you are going to join the battalion in your last official exercise here at Fort Knox. First of all, don't fuck it up! I don't want anyone from my platoon passing out like some fag. If you're too big of a pussy to stand in a parade for thirty minutes, tell me now and I will discharge your ass out of my Army so fast, you won't know what happened. I absolutely refuse to get wrinkles in my dress uniform and get all sweaty hauling one of your slimy asses off my parade field. The last eight weeks have been some of the hardest in your life, and while some of you might say the training was a pain in the ass and you really didn't learn much, you would be wrong. What you have accomplished in the last eight weeks is something most of your fellow Americans will never be able to do.

"You have become warriors. Do you realize that in our country, only one out of ten young men your age is even eligible to come into the Army? I know that your recruiters stretched many of the rules to get some of you here, but think back to your high school or street days. Most of your buddies were too strung out on drugs, too fat, too gay, or just too big of a coward to even consider coming into the Army. Like it or not, you are now part of something special, something bigger than you are. Your new family may suck, but after the ceremony this afternoon, it is your family.

"The Sergeant Major is an asshole, and most of what he says is bullshit, but he was right about one thing when he gave you his welcome-to-Fort-Knox speech eight weeks ago. You are now, in fact, brothers. The only people you can count on or trust from this day forward will be your Army brothers. The sheep that make up the population of this country will never know or care what you do and will never fully respect you for doing it. The only thing that they want is someone to do their dirty work for them. They easily forget that they only get to sleep at night because American soldiers, men like you, the members of the first platoon standing here in front of me, are willing to fight to keep them safe. To the sheep of this country, you are like the circus coming to town. Everyone wants to see the high wire act, and they cheer when you perform your act, but when you're done, they want you to get out of town and leave their daughters alone.

"I know it's somewhat of a joke to most of you, but the one thing that makes you different from all other soldiers since the Revolutionary War is that you are all volunteers. I know many of you came into the Army to get away from the police, keep out of jail, or were forced in by parents, teachers or irate fathers of pregnant daughters, but no matter what reason you're here, you had to volunteer, or you wouldn't be here today. More importantly, no matter how easy or how hard you thought your training was, no matter how many times you had to repeat some of the training, you, unlike those who quit or got kicked out, are all finishers. You made it through eight weeks of the worst hell that we could devise for you. That is something very few people will ever be able to say in their lifetime.

"Making it through eight weeks at Fort Knox is more important than any of you realize right now. Men your age don't finish many things that they start. It really doesn't matter why you made it through. Some of you just loved this shit, some of you stuck it out because of peer pressure, and some simply stayed to avoid the shame of failure. What matters is that you did, in fact, make it. I know you don't care, but I'm proud of you, and someday you will all, I promise, look back upon the past eight weeks, and you too will be proud of yourselves and your fellow soldiers with you today. It's probably beyond your comprehension at this point, but someday the past eight weeks will become one of the highlights of your life, and your fellow trainees, whether you like it or not, are now your comrades forever.

"Yeah, yeah, I know you think that ole Drill Sergeant Harper is full of hot air, and you're tired of standing out here in the sun, but tough shit. Someday you'll remember this sappy speech, and you'll say, 'Damn, that ole son of a bitch was right.' Gentlemen, you are now members of the most honorable profession in the world, the profession of arms. This country only came into existence because of brave men willing to bear arms and risk everything in defense of their fellow Americans, and the only way that it will continue to exist will be because of brave men like you.

"I'm just about done, but I want to leave you with one final thought, a free country needs strong soldiers and, to quote George Orwell, 'People sleep peaceably in their beds at night only because rough men stand ready to do violence on their behalf.'

"All right, assholes, I'm done talking. Now let's get our asses over with the rest of the battalion, and, remember, if you fuck up this parade and cause me to lose my retirement, I'll fuck with you for the rest of your Army career, no matter how short it is."

Finally, we were near the end of this nightmare called basic training—me, the Wolverines, and five thousand of my closest friends getting ready to graduate. Risking a little sentimentality here, it was pretty awe-inspiring. Eight short weeks ago we were a mob of teenagers with long hair, a thousand different ways of dressing and talking. No amount of yelling and pushing in the world could have gotten us all moving in the same direction.

I hate to admit it, but it seemed as if we had learned something during our time at Fort Knox. If nothing else, the Army had cleaned us up, and instilled in us the ability to understand and respond to simple commands. As we marched onto the field to take our final positions for the graduation parade, it was wild to see all five thousand trainees moving in the same direction, making the same marching movements and responding to the same commands. You almost would have thought that we were soldiers or something.

To the uninitiated, an Army parade is both impressive and a little bit frightening. There are five thousand guys all snapping to attention at a single command. The air filled with an audible click as we locked our heels together. It made you feel part of something much bigger than yourself. It was impressive because it was like watching five thousand synchronized swimmers and frightening because you realized that in front of you were five thousand young men with rifles, ready to fight, kill, and die if ordered to do so. It would only take a simple command from the man standing at the front of the formation to activate this war machine. Now that is a lot of power.

My parents later told me that you could feel the raw power coming from the field, and my father, ever the philosopher, said that you could easily imagine this power being focused toward an enemy of our country. He said it made him feel proud to be an American and especially proud of me.

Throughout the entire parade, all the Wolverines, especially me, we're looking for some sign of either Big John or the new Trans Am classics. The adjutant whose job it was to start the parade had just given the five-minute warning, and so far, nothing, no cars as far as the eye could see. We were starting to get a little nervous.

From what we had learned about the Army over the past eight weeks, I guess being lied to and screwed over was something that we should have expected. I just hoped that Big John had been true to his word. I was Big John's biggest supporter, and even I was starting to wonder if it had all been a big scam and that we were about to learn the true meaning of getting fucked by the Army. We had to hope that Big John would keep his word and that everything would work out as he had said it would.

It did make us feel halfway comfortable that when we were out-processing from Fort Knox, the unit clerk had informed us that the post headquarters had approved POV (personally owned vehicle) as the source of travel to our next duty station. He told us he had never seen that on a private's orders before because they usually made everyone travel by bus or plane. He didn't know who had approved the forms but assured us that the Army never made a mistake, so everything must be all right. Of course, he was laughing his ass off when he told us that.

As the adjutant yelled for all the units to come to attention, most of us had lost hope of ever seeing those shiny new cars. I was mentally cursing Big John and thinking of all the things that I was going to do to him when I caught him. The adjutant's voice and the Army band were suddenly drowned out by the sound of roaring engines. Every head in the parade stand and most of the ones on the parade field turned to see what was causing all the commotion.

There to the left of the parade field thundering down the main boulevard of Fort Knox were two rows of brand-new, jet-black Trans Ams traveling side by side in a perfect parade formation. What a sight! I swear I had tears in my eyes. The sun reflected off the highly polished paint and chrome, giving each of the cars an unearthly glow that was only surpassed by the gleaming gold screaming chickens on the hoods of the vehicles.

Tied to the top of each radio antenna was a small American flag, flapping in the wind as the cars made the turn to the edge of the parade field. I sneaked a quick glance around, and the few Wolverines that I could pick out were all staring at the cars with big shit-eating grins on their faces. For the first time in eight weeks, it appeared as if we finally had the upper hand. It looked like the Wolverines were going to be traveling to Fort Lewis, Washington, in style, POV style. At this point, I think that we were the envy of every trainee on that parade field. We had all been talking about our new cars and receiving so much trash talk from our fellow troops for being naive, I'm sure they now believed our story.

It was like a dream. It was almost as if it had been meticulously rehearsed in advance. Knowing Big John, I would bet the farm that he had planned everything right down to the final parking places of the cars. At the exact instant that the adjutant signaled for the parade units to move forward to their final parade positions, the double row of Trans Ams formed a V formation and pulled to a halt at the side of the parade field. When all the cars were stopped and in perfect alignment, out from each car jumped a soldier in full dress uniform to include white gloves, gleaming silver helmets, and white Sam Browne leather belts, and get this, they were all wearing bright silver sabers attached to their belts.

The soldiers snapped to attention and, in perfect unison, moved to the front of the vehicle that each was driving and stood as still as statues. When they were all in position, another soldier carrying a cased flag moved to the front of the V formation and unfurled the banner. The flag was Army gold with dark blue trim, and in the center was a giant, white, snarling Wolverine. As soon as he finished uncasing the flag, the soldier positioned himself and the flag in front of the cars as if they were his troops in the graduation parade.

Now this parade was ready to kick off! The reviewing stands were packed with our parents, loved ones, and all the Army brass. The Army band was to our right, and on our left was a double row of gleaming jet-black automobiles with the Wolverine flag at their head. It was hard not to be impressed. For a bunch of kids, now men, fresh out of high school, especially from the UP, it was a little overwhelming. Here we were, getting ready to graduate basic training, and our new cars had been chauffeur driven and personally delivered. Big John had set up such a spectacular, and strictly against protocol, grand entrance that he had everyone in the reviewing stands, and most of the soldiers on the parade field, pointing, staring, and talking about the sudden appearance of the cars. During the parade, I heard, "What the fuck kind of flag is that?" more than once.

Not that Big John was going to let anyone wonder for very long. It would soon be made clear to the entire audience. Over the loudspeakers, we heard:

"Ladies and gentlemen, to your immediate left, you will see the new cars of the Army's Wolverine platoon. The first platoon to enlist in the all-volunteer Army. The members of the platoon all graduating here today are from the Upper Peninsula of Michigan and are all graduates of the Iron City High School. The cars were purchased with the enlistment bonus money that the Army is now offering to any high school graduate who enlists in the Army for four years as a combat arms soldier. Ladies and gentlemen, let's hear it for the patriotic volunteers of the Wolverine platoon."

In addition to his little show, Big John had invited the press and every elected official from our district that he could find to the graduation ceremony. Because Iron City was such a small town in a relatively insignificant part of the country, I think every official who was invited made it a point to travel down to Kentucky and attend the event. It was a big deal.

Once the Army protocol office on Fort Knox found out about all the press and the elected officials, it became a feeding frenzy for the Army. With all the bad news from the war and the bad start of the all-volunteer Army, they needed all the good press they could get. The post commanding general was made available to give the graduation speech, and during the ceremony he recognized both the Wolverine platoon and the new cars.

"For the first time in the history of the Army," the general said, "we have an entire group of young men from one community who had the patriotism and courage to volunteer to

join the Army and serve as a platoon, the         Wolverine
platoon."

Well, I joined for the new car, but maybe some of the
other guys were patriotic. We had suddenly earned both the
envy and jealousy of every other soldier on that parade field.

I thought at this point, nothing could surprise me, but I
was wrong. When the general finished giving his speech, he
asked all the members of the Wolverine platoon to step to the
front of the formation. This even surprised the drill sergeants,
who seemed perplexed about how to handle this change in
their long practiced and strictly rehearsed parade sequence.

As drill sergeants always do, they figured it out. When
we arrived at the front of the formation, they assembled us in a
hasty platoon formation so the general, along with his staff
and selected politicians from our home district, could come out
onto the parade field, shake each of our hands and thank us
for joining the Army. Of course, there were ample photo
opportunities for both the politicians and the Army senior
brass. When they were finished, and the general marched
back to the podium with his entourage, I figured we would be
returned to our units for the parade, but not quite yet.

You could have knocked me over with a feather when the announcer suddenly said, "Private Berlin, please move forward to the podium." The first thing that went through my mind was that once again I was in big trouble. I began to quickly run through all the things I had done over the past eight weeks that could have gotten me into trouble, the problem being there were so many potential issues that I couldn't figure out which one.

Most of what I had done was severe enough to have me court-martialed and thrown in prison. The Bond incident suddenly came back to haunt me. I feared they were going to humiliate me publicly and toss me out of the Army. I was more afraid of the disappointment I was about to cause my father and family than I was of what the Army would do to me. I couldn't believe they had waited to the very last minute to nail me. This must be considered cruel and unusual punishment, but it *is* the Army, and things aren't what they seem.

When I arrived at the front of the podium with my legs shaking and my mind going a thousand miles an hour, the speaker announced that Private Berlin, in recognition of his outstanding performance of duty while assigned to basic training at Fort Knox, Kentucky, was about to be promoted to Private First Class Berlin. In addition to being promoted, the Army was presenting me with the award of the Army Achievement Medal for graduating as the honor graduate, and for duty above and beyond in support of my fellow trainees and the cadre of my basic training brigade.

Holy shit, now I'd heard everything. I was the biggest troublemaker and fuck-up in the Army and I was not only being promoted, but I was also receiving special recognition and my first medal. It looked like I had found a home and an employer who recognized my unique talents and abilities. Truth was stranger than fiction after all.

Reporters and photographers were recording the event. I recognized both the photographer from our hometown newspaper and a television reporter from the only TV station in the Upper Peninsula. Hell, I was a freaking movie star. As the promotion and award ceremony ended and the general shook my hand, I saw the command sergeant major standing behind him with a big smile on his face. He winked and mouthed, "I told you I would take care of you." As I listened to the roar of the crowd cheering my promotion, I could see my father standing and out-clapping, out-yelling the rest.

If you think the proceedings surprised me, you should have seen the looks on the faces of my fellow Wolverines when I rejoined them in the center of the parade field. "Are you fucking kidding me?" whispered Danny. "Who did you blow to get them to do that?"

"At ease, Private," I replied with a big-ass grin on my face. "You are addressing a senior soldier."

Damn, I thought, I now outrank everyone on this field except for the drill sergeants. This was some cool shit. While all the Wolverines were proud and full of ourselves for having been singled out in front of the formation, they were perplexed by the honors I had received, and it was clear from the looks on the faces of our fellow trainees that they were not impressed with these upstarts from Northern Michigan stealing all the attention. Besides, it was hot outside, and every minute that the Wolverines were up front sucking up all the publicity, the others were stuck in the rear, sweating and cussing in the ranks. Once the Wolverine ceremony was completed, we were ordered back to our units so that the graduation ceremony could be achieved.

As we were marching back to our units, I was glad the drill sergeants had allowed us white-dot soldiers to remove the dots from our helmets and boots before the graduation ceremony. I would have had a tough time explaining that to my friends and family.

Arriving back at the unit formation and getting into our positions again, I overheard remarks such as, "How in the fuck did a white dot get promoted? Is this some kind of promote-the-handicapped program?" Sgt. Harper just looked at me with what appeared to be a disgusted look and whispered, "Wipe that smile off your face, dummy, or you'll be busted back to private before this parade is over. I've seen the Army do some stupid things in my life, but this one takes the cake." However, it made me feel halfway decent when I caught him smiling at me most of the time he was giving me a hard time. At least he was harassing a private first class and not a private.

All Army parades and ceremonies end with a troop movement called the pass-in-review. This is the part of the show where all the units, one by one, turn and march around the outside of the parade field and march past the reviewing stand where the general and sergeant major are waiting. When the soldiers reach the front of the reviewing stand, they salute the officer in charge of the parade, then they simply march off the end of the parade field, kind of like marching off into history.

As corny as it all was, I could tell we were proud to be marching as a unit in front of friends and family. We were proud to be soldiers and proud of what we had accomplished. As soon as we crossed that parade field, we were officially soldiers and no longer trainees. Like a bunch of kids who had just learned to do something new, as we got closer to the reviewing stand, we stood a little taller and marched a litter sharper. Naturally, many of us stole a quick glance to the side to make sure everyone was watching us, especially the women in the stands.

Surprising what belonging to a group can do for your self-esteem. For the first time, I realized that none of us were kids anymore. No more high school students, no more bums from the streets. Eight weeks ago, we had been a gaggle of immature young men with no real direction in our lives, and no future to speak of.

We were still immature, but we now knew where we were going and what we were going to be doing, at least for the next several years. We had something that no other young men our age had. We were now part of something bigger than ourselves. We were part of a big family, and we had thousands of brothers. They say you can never go back, and for the first time in my life, I knew what that meant. Nothing was ever going to be like it was. For better or worse, we had changed, and that change was permanent.

The entire parade lasted less than thirty minutes. For the past week, we had been practicing up to eight hours a day to make those thirty minutes perfect. It was a pain in the ass, but that's what the Army does. You train for long hard hours, doing the same thing repeatedly until you can do it in your sleep. The goal is to be able to accomplish your mission when all hell breaks loose, and everything is falling apart all around you. Soldiers rely upon rote training to get them through everything. I guess it makes sense, but at the time, it just seemed stupid.

Once our platoon finally cleared the parade field, Harper halted us and called us to attention one last time. Reaching into his pocket, he pulled out a brand new immaculately wrapped Clark Bar. Ripping open the end of the wrapper, he pushed the candy bar up and took a big bite. With his mouth full of chocolate, he smiled at us, and said, "All your gear is packed and out in front of my barracks. The civilian crap that you brought with you is with your military gear. I want your shit off my street in the next hour, or it gets thrown in the trash. Welcome to the Army, shitheads, don't forget to watch your back and take care of your brothers. Dismissed."

With that, he turned on his heels and walked away, continuing to eat his Clark Bar. That was the last time any of us ever saw Drill Sgt. Harper. Years later, I heard he had finally retired and that no one knew for sure where he had gone. It was rumored he was living somewhere down in Central America. I was betting he had purchased a little place on the beach. He was watching girls and drinking beer and would continue to do so until he was dead from either alcohol poisoning or sunstroke. I hoped that was true; he deserved it after all the shit he had gone through in his life. We should all be so lucky.

As soon as we were dismissed, the guys began slapping one another on the back and making false promises to stay in touch forever. While the other members of our units headed over to see their families, the Wolverines had a big decision to make. We were dying to get over to the cars, but most of us had family and girlfriends who had made the long trip down here to see us graduate. We didn't want to seem crass by ignoring them for the cars. After all, they had traveled almost sixteen hours, most of them driving straight through the night to share the experience with us. It turned out the Army training had an impact on us because eight weeks ago, selfishness would have won out. We now made a good choice.

Paula, my girl, and Laura, Danny's girl, had driven down with my parents. When we turned to walk to the reviewing stand, they both came running at us and nearly knocked us over in their enthusiasm. It would have made a great scene for a movie. I for one was glad that I had chosen girl first, car later. It felt good to have Paula in my arms again; I didn't realize how much I had missed her.

One problem with eight weeks of abstinence during basic training, meeting your girl resulted in an instant hard-on, which was quickly followed by an excruciating set of blue balls. We suffered in silence because it was worth every minute of the pain. Our mini scene was being repeated all over the parade field. Everywhere you turned trainees were strutting around in their brand-new Army uniforms, trying to look cool and dangerous at the same time. We were now all trained killers, weren't we? And we did almost go to war. We felt and acted like conquering heroes as we received well-deserved hugs and kisses, although we had to act a little bit reserved as soldiers.

It turned out that the girls, if possible, were more excited to get to the new cars than we were. Before I could put Paula back on her feet, she was dragging me over to the line of vehicles, which by now were entirely mobbed by people on the parade field. "Which one is ours?" she asked. Watch out, that little voice in my head reminded me. She is talking as if we are married or something, have to be careful here.

Once we were able to fight our way through the crowds, it was a lot easier to figure out whose car was whose than we could have imagined. The front license plate of each of the vehicles was a jet-black triangle, outlined in bright silver chrome, with the first name of the owner printed in gold on them. There at the end of the row was "Roger." As we walked up to the cars, we heard the speaker systems in all the Trans

Ams, perfectly synchronized and in crystal clear booming stereo, the Rolling Stones' song by Keith Richards and Mick Jagger, *Paint it Black*. Big John had done it again, the perfect song.

When we arrived at the cars, the press and the politicians had already arrived. They were mixed in with the trainees, who were asking what the hell the deal was, how come they didn't get new cars, and why did the Wolverines get all the special treatment? Big John had anticipated this reaction and had it all covered. He had brought along with him the Pontiac dealer from Iron City and they quickly set up a small booth at the end of the parade field. He and the dealer were carefully explaining to anyone who wanted a new car that when they received their bonus checks, they could trade the checks for a vehicle. If they didn't have a bonus, Big John would check to see if they could add the additional years to their contract to make them eligible for a bonus.

All they had to do was give their names and addresses to the dealer, who would contact them and make all the necessary arrangements. I don't know how many more guys got talked into signing up for more years or signing over their bonus checks, but the dealer retired the following year and built one of the most significant homes in the city. So, if I had to guess, I would suspect that they had done well.

After fighting my way through the crowd, shaking the obligatory hands, and talking to the press, I finally got to touch my new car. I once heard that in life, our most anticipated achievements and our worst expectations are never realized. Well, in this case, the vehicle was more, way more, than I had anticipated. It was absolutely worth the wait.

There it was, a sleek, shiny marvel of modern automotive engineering. Nothing stock-made in the world could match it for speed or performance. My name on the front plate attested to my ownership of this land rocket.  Hanging from the rearview mirror was a set of dog tags with my name on one tag and a Wolverine on the other. Lying on the front passenger seat was a green folder with a note on top from Big John:

Congratulations, soldier,

I'm proud of you. Inside this envelope, you will find the title to your new car made out in your name and your insurance certificate for thirty days. After thirty days, you are on your own. Enjoy the car and the goodies. Good luck at Fort Lewis.

WOLVERINES!

Inside the envelope was a title, marked paid in full, and made out to Roger Berlin. The insurance, good for thirty days, was also made out to me. In the back seat were two Army baseball-style hats, two Army T-shirts and a green cooler with the Army logo on the side. When I opened the cooler, it was full of ice and cold beer. Not the cheap stuff either. Big John had somehow managed to come up with a case of Coors for each of us. Back in the seventies, Coors could only be purchased in Colorado and was considered a delicacy by young men (beer connoisseurs) all over the country. We had heard about it, but only Danny had ever tasted it. Now we were each owner of a full case of this liquid gold.

In addition to the beer and the clothing, Big John had outfitted each of the cars with the latest in stereo equipment. Installed in the front dash of each of the Trans Ams was the hottest eight-track player on the market. The one with the ten-pack cartridge changer. The stereo systems had eight speakers and a set of controls that allowed the driver to manipulate the sound any way he desired. To go with the eight-track, each car had a leather case with six brand new tapes in it. I don't know how he did it, but for an old guy, Big John had pretty good taste. Next to the stereo system in the dash was a twenty-one-channel citizen band radio so the Wolverines could communicate with each other. Bottom line, these cars were state of the art and ready to go.

For the next several hours, we showed off our cars to anyone who wanted to see them. Most of my buddies were more interested in Paula than my car. Being the center of attention was something I could get used to. Every young man should have a time in his life where everyone is clamoring for him. I laid it on thick. With my promotion and medal, and with a pretty girl on my arm, I was pretty much the hero of the day. At least in my mind.

Of the five thousand trainees on the field that day, Roger Berlin was the only one promoted and the only one to receive a medal.

Those guys would never know the real reason I had been promoted was in exchange for my test-taking skills, and my ability to keep my mouth shut under pressure. I'm pretty good at keeping secrets, especially the ones that will end up getting me in trouble if anyone found out. Even the other members of the Wolverine platoon never knew the full facts. They did, however, know me well and knew there was no way I had been promoted for doing an outstanding job during basic training. To the best of their knowledge, I had scammed my way through basic training doing as little as possible all the while pretending that I was a feeble-minded member of the Moron Corps.

I kept explaining to them that I was sure that the promotion was part of some weird affirmative action program for dummies and that the Army wanted to show that it was working to make the Morons feel needed and accepted. That and the Army's desire to show that young men were willing to enlist as a platoon. I told them the Army just wanted to get as much publicity as they could out of us, and this was all a big marketing ploy. "The reason they selected me," I said, "was because I was the one the Army thought need the most help."

I think for the most part they believed my explanation. That is, everyone except for Danny. He knew me too well and knew my answer was full of shit. He knew there was a rest-of-the-story but just couldn't figure it out. Maybe I would confide in him someday, or not.

After several hours, the parade field had finally emptied of newly appointed soldiers and families taking pictures and exchanging hugs. The crowds had moved on, and a new batch of freshly shorn trainees was dragging through the area, picking up the trash left behind by the masses. The whole scene made me just a little sad. Once again, we were passing through a critical decision point in our lives and, like when we had graduated high school, nothing would be the same after basic training. We were once again moving on and moving forward, and at the time we didn't realize it, but we were leaving family and friends behind forever.

When we finished on the parade field, we headed over to the company area one last time to gather our equipment and gear from the company street and load it into our cars. None of us thought Harper was serious but didn't want to take a chance and have to go digging through the garbage to find our stuff. I took one last look at the company area and said to Danny, "You know what? I'm really going to miss this place." Danny looked at me, burst out laughing, and we both yelled out, "No way!"

Those of us who were lucky enough to have our girlfriends travel to Fort Knox for the ceremony had them sitting in the passenger seat, looking pretty and ready to go. All the Trans Am engines were running and were growling like a pride of lions. We were the kings of the world. All the Wolverines stood together in front of the cars and had one last huddle, and one last beer before we headed out. The final toast from Danny said it all:

"Here's to the Wolverines, one team that takes no shit from anyone. Fuck the Army!"

In the center of that lonely company street, minus all the trainees and drill sergeants, exchanging back slaps and drinking our Coors, the Wolverines permanently cemented the platoon and lifelong friendships. We had earlier decided that we would convoy back to Iron City together and were already looking forward to our next Army adventure. When you're eighteen, even a long car drive is an adventure. We were going to drive straight through because we wanted to get home and we didn't want to waste one minute of our fifteen days of leave.

We figured it was going to take at least two or three days to travel the 2,500 miles from Iron City to Fort Lewis. When we added in the day from Fort Knox to Michigan, we only had about ten days at home. Ten days to show off, brag, tell tall tales, make up some lies, and be the envy of our buddies. We intended to make every second of those ten days count. I was already imagining the entire town turning out to greet the conquering heroes as we returned in triumph.

After shaking each other's hands, a few quick but manly hugs and some final goodbyes, we were set to go. Danny, in the lead vehicle, hit his horn, stuck out his arm, and signaled us to follow him. I felt like a member of the Hells Angels. All of us in brand new cars in a single file, heading out the main gate. Now, this was a military formation. As we filed past the main entrance, Danny once again stuck his arm out the window and gave the finger to the gate guards. Taking a cue from our unofficial leader, we all matched his action. Anyone watching would probably never forget the sight of twenty brand new, black Trans Am classics driving out the front gate with all the drivers flipping off the military police at the entrance. I can't speak for the other guys, but I was feeling pretty powerful and influential.

As I drove out the main gate and watched the post getting smaller in my rearview mirror, I thought over the events of the last eight weeks. Some tragic, some exhilarating, and I smiled as I put my arm around Paula. What a day—my girl in one hand, a cold beer in the other, and a big world out there just waiting for me. I hoped that Fort Lewis was prepared for the onslaught that was about to occur. I don't think they had any idea what was heading their way.

Not the End … Just the Beginning …

Follow the adventures of Roger and the Wolverines as they head out to Fort Lewis in Book 2, *West*.

# Afterword
## Moron

In 1966 at the height of the Vietnam War, Secretary of Defense Robert McNamara implemented a new and novel program to draft into the military 100,000 mental Category IV young men. Mental category IV was a designation by the Department of Defense used to identify potential recruits whose scores on mental qualification and aptitude tests put them in the lowest mental quarter of American society.

These mental Category IV recruits were young men with IQs of 65 or lower. Women in this category were prohibited from enlisting. Leaders in the military referred to these low mental category recruits as McNamara's 100,000. The 100,000 were mostly black and poor whites, from large inner-city ghettos and the remote back roads of America. When McNamara's grand experiment was done, a substantial number of low mental category young men had been recruited.

Conservative estimates put the number at about 354,000. They were primarily recruited for the Army and the Marine Corps. The Air Force and Coast Guard, still popular for high school graduates, refused to participate, and the Navy kept the numbers as low as possible.

These young men were mostly illiterate, and many of them were mildly mentally retarded. Because they couldn't read, the Army developed comic books and implemented oral tests instead of written ones to help train them. Many of them could not dress themselves, were unable to function in typical society, and in some cases didn't even know how to tie the laces on their shoes. Army instructors were informed that they were to work with these recruits and under no circumstances were they to fail these young men. They were literally trained over and over until they either passed or someone got tired of them and moved them forward. The government was concerned that large numbers of failures would prove that the program was not feasible, and they wouldn't allow this unique social experiment to fail.

To add insult to injury, the military created its own special version of the Scarlet Letter. To make sure that everyone in the military would be able to recognize the 100,000 and their lack of abilities, they assigned the Project 100,000 men special serial numbers beginning with the code "US67." When they arrived at Army basic training locations, many Army drill sergeants further identified them with special markings on their equipment and uniforms. The other soldiers in the Army quickly recognized these markings and soon began to refer to them as the "Moron Corps."

On the 30th of June, 1973, the all-volunteer Army was born, and the first volunteers entered an Army filled with 354,000 members of the Moron Corps. To make sure that the Army met all its recruiting goals for the all-volunteer force, the Army not only lowered mental requirements, it also waived criminal offenses. The Army at the time was made up of discouraged soldiers who had faced hostility and indifference from the American public when they returned from Vietnam.

Drug use was rampant, and discipline was almost non-existent. Racial tensions were at an all-time high and all out-race riots were erupting at American bases in Germany, Korea, and in the United States. The Army of 1973 was understaffed and was short of critical pieces of equipment and weapon systems. Its leadership, especially in the NCO ranks was made up of many of McNamara's 100,000. Not surprisingly, most of the good NCOs were getting out of the Army as fast as they could. The recently promoted members of the Moron Corps, on the other hand, remained in the Army because they simply had no place else to go.

Moron

## About the Author

Danny G.I. Pummill is a retired colonel from the U.S. Army. He enlisted in the Army in 1973 in the Wolverine platoon from Northern Michigan and served as both an enlisted soldier and an officer. After retiring from the Army, he served as the Deputy Assistant Secretary of the Army and later in the Veterans Administration as the Acting Undersecretary for the Veterans Benefits Administration. He lives with his wife, Paula, whom he met in high school. They live in Triangle Virginia right outside the front gates of Quantico. If he is not working, you can find him fishing or hunting with his grandchildren.

"Never be first, never be last and never, ever volunteer for anything."

— Murphy